SOOLIE BEETCH
AND THE DYING LIGHT

GYPSIE RALEIGH

BOOK ONE OF THE DEAD SOULS TRILOGY

Copyright © 2016 by Gypsie Raleigh

Published in the United States by User Shoes, LLC.

ISBN-13 978-0-9971983-0-0

Printed in the United States of America

www.sooliebeetch.com

gypsie@sooliebeetch.com

BOOK DESIGN BY ANDREW BERKOWITZ

AUTHOR PHOTO © JACKALDOG PHOTOGRAPHY

for those to whom dreams never come easily
and for the people who dare to love them

Do not go gentle into that good night,
Old age should burn and rave at close of day;
Rage, rage against the dying of the light.

Though wise men at their end know dark is right,
Because their words had forked no lightning they
Do not go gentle into that good night.

— Dylan Thomas

ONE

Punka the Mountain hated the flies. They swarmed, buzzing in her ears and licking at the corners of her eyes, crawling down the wet folds of her neck and chest and squirming along the creases where her garments sawed through soft flesh. She could feel them laying maggot worms in the raw patches she couldn't reach, burrowing into the crusted sores that cracked and curdled yellow milk, flesh sticking to cloth sticking to crawling flesh. In the dark back of the wagon, they were the only motion, the only sound. Black bodies buzzing in her ears: you're already dead and we know it.

"Adrana! Adrana, open this wagon. Your mother needs to breathe!"

Had she been heard?

"Adrana!" Punka choked and coughed. Wetness dribbled out of her mouth, tasting of blood. Adrana didn't care about her any more. Adrana despised her. No matter. Punka had her other child.

"Adrana!"

"I heard you the first time; stop yelling."

The light of the evening sun spilt in as Adrana untied the canvas door flaps and began securing them to the side. More than beautiful, Punka's daughter was devastating. With golden skin burnished bright by the sun, hair that rippled like dark molasses, and kohl-painted amber eyes, it was no wonder her dancing name was 'Rahka,' the lioness. She looked just like her mother did ten years ago. They both knew it, and they hated one another for it.

"I thought you preferred the dark, Punka," Adrana said. "Where you can snore all day and no one has to see you."

"I can't breathe with all this dust. I need air. Clean out this wagon. I need a bath."

"Why would I ever touch you?"

"I'm your mother."

"That's never been reason enough before." Adrana folded her arms, the tips of her long elegant fingers making the slightest dimples in her lean brown forearms. "We will be at Ravus in four days. Maybe we can drop you in the square and wash you off with the elephants."

"At least clean out the wagon. There are flies."

"Flies are attracted to punka mountains. Clean it yourself."

"Then bring your mother something to eat. I am starving!"

Adrana didn't answer. She just turned away and glided off, her brown feet dancing lightly, her skirts brushing the dry grass of the field, the warm evening light casting her shadow out behind her so it lingered at her mother's wagon just a moment before it, too, left Punka alone.

'Punka.' It meant shit. That was what everyone called her: Punka the Mountain. Come see Punka the Mountain! The fattest woman in all the world! The woman so fat that once, when her dinner was fifteen minutes late, she ate her own horse, and when her food came, she ate that too and still howled for more. Don't miss it, ladies and gentleman! Stare in awe! Gawk in horror at Punka the Mountain! Why, our carnival once escaped the cannibals of the HokHok jungle, because they couldn't stop fighting over who got to take her home! I speak truth! The chief said she could feed one family for fifteen seasons! This is a woman so enormous (ladies, cover your children's ears) that only one man ever dared try to make love to her, and he fell into a belly fold and hasn't been seen since! As far as we know, he may still be in there!

"Punka Mountain." Shit Mountain. Just a funny joke the

Midlanders didn't understand.

"Let me sleep now," she whispered.

Not yet, the Child said.

"You see how she treats me. You see what I must live with. Let me dream."

Not yet.

"You're just as bad to me as she is," Punka sulked. But she didn't mean it. The Child was all she had. And she didn't want to anger it. If she made the Child angry, the Child might take the dreams away.

A wisp of violet smoke plumed across the rosy colored sky. Someone had lit a fire. The lilting voice of the vielle reached her ear. There would be dancing tonight. They would all dance, all of them. All the ones who never spoke to her any more. They would dance until the stars came out and the fire burned low. And Adrana would be at the center, whirling in the embers and the smoke, twining her arms and writhing her hips. It was just as well Punka couldn't see any of it from the wagon. She was too tired to move. Even speech exhausted her. Adrana had better remember to bring her some food.

Food. They would be heating stew and crack bread and roasting raw nuts now. Punka licked lips rough with splits and scabs. She was so hungry. Starving. No one understood the hunger. The way it gnawed at her belly every waking moment. She remembered the hunger when she was carrying Adrana. That was nothing compared to this. It was as if she carried all the gutter babies of Ravus in her belly. And they were all, all of them, starving.

A thin boy ran into view and pointed at her.

"Ooooh! Look! It's huge!"

Two others joined the first, some thirteen or fifteen years. In the Southern Lands, they would be considered men, but Punka could tell by the way they gaped, pointed, and jostled each other that these were only boys. Punka hated boys.

"Skagging disgusting!" the second crowed.

Too old, the Child said.

There must be houses nearby, maybe a small village, and these three had snuck out to the carnival caravan to see if they could catch a glimpse of a jungle beast, or maybe one of the freaks. Well, they'd found one. Maybe if she just didn't say anything, they'd go away.

"Are you Punka the Mountain?" This boy had squinty eyes and a fuzzy lip. "I'll bet 'Punka' means 'butt fat.' Are you the Butt Fat Mountain?"

"It's not answering," the short one whined.

"I think it's female!" fuzzy lip said.

"What? Siiiiiick!"

"I dare you to poke it!"

Poke it. Like a curious animal carcass. Punka closed her eyes, trying to block them out. This was all Adrana's fault. She had known there was a village nearby and had left her all alone and vulnerable. Just let me dream now, she begged.

Not yet.

Why? She whined. You don't want them. They're too old for you.

Punka knew this was true. Though lately she had been finding it difficult to remember why it was important.

"Poke it! Poke it! Poke it!"

Something sharp jabbed in the folds of her belly, tearing at her flesh. They had found a stick.

Please. Don't make me take any more of this, she begged.

The Child was silent.

Jab. Jab.

"It's not doing anything!"

"Say something, Butt Fat, say something!"

"Hey! Stop that! Stop that now!"

A different voice, an older voice. For a moment, Punka thought maybe one of the carnival members had noticed and come to defend her, but no, this voice had a Midland dialect.

"Hobby, Kip, Bernad! You need to head home now, or I'm telling your mothers. Get out of here, go on. Go home."

Open your eyes.

Without considering whether or not she wanted to, Punka obeyed. The boys had gone, laughing and mocking as they went. She could still hear the adult scolding after them just out of view from the wagon doorway. Directly before her, where the three boys had been moments before, stood a young girl, perhaps twelve or thirteen, with delicate tawny curls, a sharp face, and intelligent brown eyes that met Punka's gaze unashamed and unafraid. Punka didn't care for girls either.

"I'm sorry the boys were so unkind to you. They're bullies. That's my Papa chasing them off."

HER.

Punka cringed. The Child was shouting, and Punka didn't know why. There was something she was supposed to remember. Something important. Something she had been holding on to for far too long that had been shrouded and buried in dreams. How she needed to dream. To escape this fear, this ugliness. She was never confused in the dreams, never afraid. In the dreams she was always beautiful and the Child always adored her. Let me dream.

"Is Punka the Mountain your real name?"

"Come on, Soolie, leave her alone. It's time to go." A tall bearded man came up and put his arm around the girl's shoulders. "I'm sorry for the trouble, Miss. I hope you have a nice evening."

GET HER FOR ME. The Child's words hurt.

No. She wasn't supposed to. But the thought was more reflex than resolve.

DO YOU WANT TO DREAM?

She did. She needed the dreams.

GET HER FOR ME.

Why? What do you want with her? Punka whined. You have me.

DO NOT DISOBEY ME.

Punka winced. She didn't dare make the Child angry. It would hurt her and take the dreams away. The man and the girl were leaving.

"Wait!"

They paused.

"Do you have food? No one cares about me here," Punka whined. "You see how they abuse me. They just leave me here in the back of this wagon while they eat and sing and dance. And I'm starving."

The man hesitated. She could see him debating: why should he give his food to a woman so large, so diseased? Surely she didn't need it. Most of all, Punka could tell, he wanted to get his daughter away from her. Before he could make his decision, the girl tore away from her father and ran up to the edge of the wagon.

"I have cheese in my pocket from lunch. It's smushed, but still good."

Bring her to me.

Perhaps it would be okay. Perhaps the girl was too old. Too old for what? Punka couldn't remember.

"Come up and give it to me. I can't reach down."

"Soolie," the man objected.

"Just a moment, Papa. It'll only take a moment." The girl grabbed hold of the canvas and nimbly lifted herself up into the mouth of the wagon.

Punka watched the girl's face as she took in the wagon's interior. Heaps of filthy soiled cushions nestled in picked-over rotting prairie hen carcasses and fruit cores. And Punka: an immense mound of sickly pale flesh wrapped in threadbare chartreuse. They had made her robe out of an old carnival tent, one of the few details the barker used to entice gawkers that was actually true.

"You can't clean yourself, can you?"

"Just give me the cheese," Punka muttered. She didn't like this girl. She didn't understand what the Child wanted with her.

"My Mama couldn't clean herself toward the end," the girl said, fishing into her dress pocket and pulling out a lump wrapped in wax paper. "Papa had to wash her like she was a baby. And she smelled too, like death. She said you can always tell when a sick person is nearing death, because they smell different. You smell really bad."

She is young enough. She is strong. She will not be too easily broken.

"Soolie, come on. We have to go."

"I have to go."

The girl held out the lump of cheese to Punka. Punka reached for it. She would take the cheese, and the girl would go away. The girl would go away, and then the Child would let her sleep and give her good dreams, because she had done what it wanted. She had done everything it wanted, and everything was going to be okay.

As Punka's fingers touched the waxed paper, her hand moved swiftly on its own, grabbing the girl harshly by the wrist pulling her close with a strength Punka did not have.

"What are you doing?" Punka squealed.

"What are *you* doing?" The girl's eyes were wide with surprise.

The girl's frail frame was pressed against her body. Punka's arm muscles were burning. The man had leaped up into the wagon and was trying to pull the girl away. What was happening? What had she done wrong? Why was the Child angry with her?

Dark clouds boiled over Punka's vision. Flies. They were hatching. Hundreds. Thousands. Millions of buzzing little bodies filling her throat and mouth, clogging her ears and eyes, wriggling, squirming, burrowing out of her very skin, breaking free from deep down, deeper than her ample flesh, deeper than her heart, spooling out through the very cracks of her being, ripping her apart.

Then the Child was before her, blazing merciless and white.

Punka screamed. *Don't leave me. Don't leave me, please. Adri…*

Now, said her Child, *you rest.*

THE FAT WOMAN's thick squishy fingers clamped around Soolie's wrist, pulling her close with sudden violence. The woman's head wrap slipped sideways, revealing thinning patches of white hair clinging to a scaly gray scalp.

"What are you doing?" the woman screamed, bloody spittle hitting Soolie in the face.

"What are *you* doing?" Soolie gasped.

"Soolie!" It was Papa. She could feel his strong arms wrapping around her waist, pulling at her, but the fat woman was too strong.

The woman began shaking violently, her flesh shuddering and jostling, the wagon shaking beneath her. Papa was pulling at Soolie, calling her name. The woman's mouth frothed, her head snapped back. The foul smell of rot and disease was replaced by the smell of fierce heat like melting iron, and Soolie felt numbness traveling like a shock up her arm from the woman's grip, stopping her heart, stilling her lungs, filling her ears with deafness, her body so suddenly overtaken that it forgot how to feel and she could neither move nor cry out, but only stare into the two great eyes that filled her vision as white, glaring, and cold as clear day snow. Then, it stopped.

Soolie was out of the wagon. Papa had caught her up in his arms and was holding her close to his chest, carrying her quickly away from the carnival camp.

"You should listen to me," Papa was saying. "Don't ever do that again. You could have been hurt."

Looking back over Papa's shoulder, Soolie saw the encampment of carnival wagons and carts clustered around a bright fire and, off by itself, one lone wagon facing away into the setting sun. Its canvas sides were painted in scrolling red and gold script that read, "PUNKA THE MOUNTAIN," and in the back lay a yellowish green heap that didn't move.

TWO

"Silas Beetch, you sit right back down in that chair!"

"I just wanted to…"

"Sit." Ellena pointed sternly with her ladle. "I bring the dinner. I make the rules."

"If I had known there was going to be such a fuss, I would have had us meet at your house," Silas grumbled.

Ellena hadn't just brought dinner. She had also brought matching bowls, utensils and napkins, a tablecloth and a little copper vase of frilly red field flowers. Since the Beetch house didn't have a dining table, she had cleared off Silas' small battered work table, dragged the two rocking chairs up beside his work stool, folded the embroidered tablecloth in half so it didn't pile on the floor, arranged the place settings and flowers, and ordered Silas and Soolie to sit down. Ellena didn't visit; she invaded.

Silas leaned back in the rocker, watching the top of the table get farther and farther away. From her perch on his work stool, Soolie looked down at him and giggled.

"Start eating before it gets cold." Ellena set her soup down and pulled her rocking chair as close to the table as it would go. "And, Silas, you can tell me why your face looks like it was left out in the rain. Don't tell me this is about Soolie going to school tomorrow."

"He's mad because I jumped in a wagon with a fat lady, and she died," Soolie said. She ripped a large hunk off the crisp-crusted bread loaf and began sopping it in her soup.

"Soolie!" Silas chided, "Wait until everyone has been served, don't dunk your bread, don't call that woman fat. And as far as we know, she may be fine."

"She was *SO* fat!" Soolie whispered to Ellena.

"Land's sake, someone died?" Ellena scooted to the edge of the low rocker. "What happened? Silas? Why is this the first I'm hearing about this?"

Silas sighed. Soolie was always highly excitable when her Aunt Ellena was around, and Ellena loved to encourage her. Any other night it would have been a minor inconvenience, but after today's fright, Silas desperately wanted a quiet evening home alone with his daughter. Maybe if he was concise, this would end quickly.

"On our way back from Malswood pond, I saw a caravan camped in a field beside the Eastern Road."

"Not just any caravan, Ellena," Soolie chimed in around a mouthful of soggy bread, "a carnival from the Southern Lands! They had giant carts and wagons. Huge covered cages. Can you imagine what might be under there? Maybe serpents. Or talking birds. Or hound cats!" She paused to swallow. "Ellena, this soup is the best!"

"Soolie. Slow down and don't speak with your mouth full."

"I'm sorry, I'm just so hungry. I'm starving!"

"You're not starving."

"I feel like I'm starving."

"For land's sake!" Ellena cut in. "What happened at the caravan?"

Silas didn't want to think about what happened. He didn't want to remember the woman lying in the back of the wagon, so grotesque and alone. There had been something about her. Something beyond her scaly scalp and swollen sickly flesh. More than a sight, more than a smell, there had been a sense he didn't understand. All together, it had frightened him badly. Tell truth, it still frightened him.

Soolie, on the other hand, seemed obnoxiously fine. She was

perched on his work stool cramming her mouth like a squirrel moving its larder.

"Well?" Ellena prodded.

"I saw Hobby, Kip, and Bernad heading towards the caravan, and when I got closer, they were tormenting a sideshow performer."

"She was so fat, Ellena!" Soolie interjected. "She was 'ate-all-the-elephants-and-didn't-chew fat.'" Soolie puffed out her cheeks and crossed her eyes to illustrate.

"Did you want to finish telling the story, Soolie?" Silas asked wearily.

"No, that's okay. You go ahead."

Silas took one calming breath in and fully out before continuing. "So. After I sent the boys home, Soolie jumped up in the wagon, even though I told her not to, and the woman grabbed her by the arm and started shaking violently. And I had to get up in the wagon to pull them apart. That was the end. That's all that happened."

"It was very exciting," Soolie added, scraping the bottom of her bowl with her spoon.

"That sounds awful," Ellena said. "Is she okay?"

"She certainly seems okay," Silas gestured. "Her appetite hasn't suffered any."

"Not Soolie. The woman. You said she had spasms. Is she okay?"

"I ... don't know," Silas admitted.

"You didn't tell anyone?"

"I was so concerned for Soolie."

"Silas, what if she needed help?"

Silas sat back in the rocker slowly. "I hadn't thought of that."

Soolie gasped, "Should we go back?"

"The time to have done something was when it happened," Ellena said. "We can only hope she's all right."

Silas studied the edge of the table, and Soolie slowed her voracious chewing, looking back and forth between them.

At last, Ellena shot Silas a look to let him know this certainly wasn't over, then winked at Soolie. "You just want to go back to try and see a monster from the Southern Lands, don't you?"

Soolie immediately brightened, "Man-eating goats, flying serpents, whole forests that spring up in the night and are gone by dawn!"

"The animals from the Southern Lands aren't monsters," Silas objected, "they're just animals."

Ellena leaned forward conspiratorially, her voice low. "I heard there is a tower in the Southern Lands where a dark mirror is kept that captures the souls of all who look upon themselves in its depths."

"Ooooh," Soolie's eyes glittered. "Please say we have time for a story tonight, Ellena, please!"

"Well," Ellena glanced over at Silas.

"Maybe some other night," he said. "When there isn't school in the morning."

"I could start my education early!" Soolie clasped her hands. "I'll wash all the dishes?"

"We've had enough excitement for one day," Silas said firmly. He knew he'd had.

Soolie scowled. "You never like the stories."

"Silas," Ellena winked playfully at Soolie, "can schoolgirls have dessert on a school night? I brought blackberry tarts."

Soolie leaped from her chair and threw her arms around Ellena. "Aunt Ellena's the best!"

AFTER DESSERT, THEY WASHED THE BOWLS and utensils. There were no leftovers. (Soolie would have licked the dishes clean if Silas had let her.) The two rocking chairs were moved back by the fireplace. The tablecloth was carefully shaken out, folded up, and placed back in Ellena's basket with the other dinner things. Soon Ellena's makeshift dining room had disappeared, and the little house was back to normal.

Most of the room was devoted to Silas' shoe making: wood and leather, dyes, paints, trays of hooks, buttons, and spools of thread.

The tools of his trade hung high on the walls where he had strapped them years ago, safe out of little Soolie's reach. Silas' bed was tucked behind the ladder that led up to the small loft where Soolie slept. The only visible feminine touches were the patchwork bedspread, the rag rug by the fireplace, and the blue ruffled curtains Tara had fashioned from the dress she had worn on their wedding day. Anything Ellena brought when she visited, she took with her when she left.

Soolie washed up and said goodnight. Ellena made her promise to stop by the bakery after school to tell her about her first day and take some rolls home, which Silas insisted they would pay for. When at last the excited girl had hugged them both goodnight and scurried up the ladder into her loft, Silas took the kettle off the fire and poured Ellena and himself a cup of tea. They sat across from one another gazing into the low flames, sharing a moment before Ellena headed back home to her room above the bakery.

"I'm sorry," Silas offered, speaking in a low voice so as not to wake Soolie in the open loft just above their heads. "I don't know what had her tonight."

"She was fine," Ellena said softly. "I'm more concerned about you."

Of course she was. Ever since Tara had died, Ellena had been there for the husband and daughter her adopted sister had left behind. Sometimes Silas wished Ellena would be just a little less involved, a little less opinionated. But he could see how much she cared for Soolie, and Soolie absolutely adored her Aunt Ellena. If he had to put up with a few lectures, it was worth it.

Ellena studied him for a moment, the only sound between them the soft hiss of the logs and occasional snap pop of the fire. The tight bun that she had twisted her hair into that morning had grown frizzy and disheveled throughout the day. Now, in the evening firelight, her hair settled about her face in a soft golden halo. Silas just wished that when she lectured him she wasn't always right.

"How are you doing?"

"Well," he started deliberately, "business is decent. I'm receiving a growing number of orders from Ravus. Soolie and I are helping the Cornells build a tiered garden out behind their home. In exchange, they're giving us use of one of the levels to grow our own vegetables. I'm looking forward to butter squash. How are you?"

Ellena wasn't so easily deterred. "You were frightened today. Are you okay?"

"I'm fine."

"You ran away from a woman who was having a spasm."

"She grabbed Soolie. She grabbed my daughter. You didn't see it."

"She might have been dying, Silas."

Silas looked away. "Soolie has seen enough death already."

Ellena closed her eyes the way she did when she was about to say something difficult. "Tara taught Soolie to face her fears. Don't take that away from her."

Silas bristled. "You have no right to criticize me for how I raise my daughter."

"Oh, Silas, that's not what I meant."

"She's only a child."

"Yes," Ellena murmured. "Which is all the more reason for her to be fearless. You do enough worrying for all of us. Just…" she searched for the right words. "She's a strong, beautiful girl with a father who loves her very much. You don't have to be afraid for her all the time."

"Hmm." Silas took a sip of tea. He heard the words. He had heard them before. Maybe one day he'd be able to let them sink in.

After that, they talked of little things. Ellena was helping organize the harvest festival. Silas was worried it was going to be a long winter. Rod Cornell's wife Milin was looking very pregnant, and Mrs. Svenson had told Ellena that Mergo Pelig, the mayor's wife, was having an affair, which both Silas and Ellena agreed was an ugly rumor and probably true. After a while, they ran out of things to say and sat in silence for some time, listening to the hiss pop of the fire and letting time roll languid. When Ellena finally stood, the fire had burned down to red black embers, and the tea at the bottom of their mugs was cold. She placed her mug on his work table, pulled on her boots, boots he had made, and laced them up. She wrapped a woolen shawl around her shoulders and hefted her basket of dinner things.

Ellena walked over to where he sat, still holding his tea mug and staring into the flickering embers. She placed one hand to his bearded cheek, gently turned his head, and kissed him softly on the forehead.

"Good night, Silas."

"Good night, Ellena."

Then she opened the front door, stepped out onto the dark, and closed it carefully behind her.

IN THE LOFT, Soolie listened to Ellena leave. She lay awake, thinking about the strange woman in the carnival caravan. Wondering if it had been just a spasm, if she had imagined the invading numbness and fierce glowing eyes. Wondering, too, what it would be like to go to school in the morning, to be around other young people her own age. She lay in the dark playing conversations in her mind. "The buttons? They're turquoise." "You like to embroider? I paint! We should make something together." "Sure, let's have a picnic. I'll show you my favorite climbing tree by Malswood Pond."

When Soolie finally did drift off to sleep, a dark shadow was cast over her dreams. She dreamt of going to school, not in the little schoolhouse at Hob Glen, but to a school at a carnival in the center of Ravus full of colorful acrobats, dancing monkeys, and beautiful singing fish with wings. She dreamt her mother was there, and Ellena was there, sometimes one, sometimes the other, and sometimes it seemed they were one and the same. She dreamt she danced and her father was happy. That he lifted her over his head like when she was small and swung her around and around until they were breathless laughing. That he whispered in her ear, *"There is no time. The Dead Man is rising."*

When she awoke the next morning, the dream was gone. The shadow was all she remembered.

THREE

Soolie got up plenty early. She unwrapped the rope securing the roof hatch, pushed it up with both hands, and peered out over the shingles. Sometimes she would stand on her tiptoes and imagine she could just make out the tips of the buildings of Ravus poking up from the horizon like new grass, and sometimes in the evening, when the sun was setting splendidly, she would sneak Papa's stool up to the loft and strain as if she might catch a glimpse of the sun being pierced by the Regent's tower, bleeding out, drenching the sky in amethyst and coral light. But no matter how tall she stretched, the city was always just out of sight, and right now it was too dark to see much of anything.

Of course Papa was already up, but the lantern light from downstairs barely reached into the loft. Soolie had set out her favorite dress the night before, the bright cranberry wool with turquoise buttons, and her newest pair of stockings. As she fumbled in the dimness, she noticed the skin on her right wrist where the woman had grabbed her felt strange, thin and papery like an old burn. She pinched it and felt nothing. It didn't matter. She wasn't going to let anything stop her today. Still, it was probably for the best that the dress had long sleeves. No sense worrying Papa.

"Slowly," Papa cautioned as she swung over the edge of the loft and hurried down the ladder.

THE SCHOOLHOUSE WAS NO MORE than a single room shack on the other side of Hob Glen. The walls were woefully thin, but painted a fresh light blue with white trim and kept in good repair. The students sat on long narrow benches in front of long narrow tables facing Miss Felice Pont's desk and blackboard, younger children towards the front, older children towards the back. There was a little coal stove in the corner, but once the winter chill set in, even with the stove glowing so hot the students closest found their faces flush and sensitive, the ones farthest away still shivered in the draft.

School days were only four hours, and homework depended greatly on whether or not the child's parents could afford books. Everyone under sixteen years in Hob Glen, whose parents could spare them, went to Miss Pont's little school fall through spring. Everyone, that is, except Soolie, who had been removed from the school by her father when she was nine and been taught at home ever since until today.

In the gray morning light, Soolie skipped lightly down Main Street eating the lunch Papa had packed for her, past Ellena's Bakery, through the central square with the old oak tree, past the Pelig's house, which was the largest in Hob Glen with two full stories and an attic, and finally out near the edge of the town. There, at the end of a side road, sat the little blue and white schoolhouse, and there, just now turning the key in the front door, was Miss Felice Pont.

"Good morning, Miss Pont!" Soolie shouted from up the road, waving her free arm wildly.

Miss Pont turned and raised her thin eyebrows, "Miss Beetch. Will you be joining us today? Is your father ill?"

"Not at all!" Soolie scurried forward, clutching her books and an empty lunch satchel to her chest. "Papa is letting me attend school now that I am thirteen years." Soolie curtsied brightly.

"I see," said Miss Pont. "I'm glad he has decided my teaching is good enough to allow his daughter to sit in on class."

"Oh, I don't think your teaching has anything to do with it," Soolie assured, following close on the older woman's heels as she entered the schoolroom.

Miss Pont turned and pursed her lips, causing Soolie to step back, bumping into the door frame. "I see you brought books, Miss Beetch."

"Yes!" Soolie held them up. "Papa says many books make a sound mind. I brought three: 'The Complete History of Ravus City,' by Mikus Orlin. 'Horticulture of the...'"

"Put them under your seat," the teacher said, hanging her cloak by the door. "You shouldn't flaunt having books over the other children. You may sit in the back, Miss Beetch."

Soolie was disappointed. She had wanted to like Miss Pont, and it looked like she wasn't going to like her at all. Nevertheless, Mama had taught her to embrace new experiences, and school was a new experience. Who knew what might happen? Perhaps she might even make a friend.

The other students arrived. Some of them were siblings; a little girl and boy, possibly twins, held on to their older sister's hands. A shapely girl with bright straw-colored curls bounced and flounced through the door, giggling ferociously and swishing thick petticoats that were the latest style from the city. Soolie recognized her as Winny Baldrick. Winny considered herself the most popular girl in school, but this was Hob Glen, and there wasn't much competition.

There weren't many children older than Soolie this year. Winny and two other girls sat a couple of benches up whispering, giggling, and glancing back at her. It was nearly time for school to start, and still no one had joined Soolie in the back two rows. She was beginning to consider this might be Miss Pont's way of punishing her for not having been around for the last four years. Just when she concluded this must indeed be the case, Hobby, Kip, and Bernad arrived and headed straight for the back. Hobby plopped himself right next to Soolie, pinched her arm hard and grinned wickedly, showing off uneven teeth. Soolie realized she had underestimated Miss Pont.

"Now that we're all here," Miss Pont announced, "let us begin."

Today, Miss Pont was teaching letters, drawing them one by one on the blackboard and having everyone say them out loud. Soolie already knew her letters, but she understood the young children needed to learn them as well. What made the lesson truly dismal was that every time Miss Pont turned her back on the classroom to write on the blackboard, Hobby's thick, vicious hands would dart in to torment her. He poked her ribs, pinched her arm, and pulled her hair: anything to elicit a yelp or a squeal. Soolie, however, was still and silent as stone. Hobby could poke, prod, and pinch all he wanted: she wouldn't even flinch. Mama never flinched. Mama made peace with pain. Soolie wasn't always good at making peace, but she was very good at not flinching.

Then Hobby wiggled a wet slobbery finger in her ear, and Kip let out a snort.

Miss Pont turned. "Is everything all right, Miss Beetch?"

"Quite all right, Miss Pont," Soolie said evenly.

Hobby tucked his hands under the table. Kip was still choking back snorting giggles.

"Perhaps letters are boring you, Miss Beetch. Perhaps you would rather be reading those books you brought?"

I am quite certain now, Soolie thought, I do not like you at all.

The fact that the boys sat in the back row was no coincidence. Neither was the empty row in front of them; this was an arrangement. Well, if Soolie was going to be punished, it was about time she did something to deserve it.

Everyone in the classroom was turned around in their benches looking at her, waiting to hear what she would say. Soolie smiled demurely.

"Actually, Miss Pont, you have no idea what a relief it is to have escaped my father's attentive instruction and finally have the benefit of receiving my lessons from such a lovely blackboard."

Silence. The students looked back at Miss Pont, waiting to see if this had been received as an insult.

"Since you are our guest, Miss Beetch," said Miss Pont, "what would you *prefer* to be learning today?"

"I'm sure," said Soolie calmly, "I would be delighted to learn whatever you might know, Miss Pont."

"The Southern Lands!" one of the twins piped up from the front.

"Not now, Luka," Miss Pont said, not taking her eyes off Soolie.

"No, that's quite all right." Soolie waved her hand graciously. "I think that's a lovely idea. You asked me what I would like to learn. Let us learn about the Southern Lands."

"Very well," said the teacher. "Miss Beetch, you will assist me with the lesson."

Of course I will, Soolie thought to herself as she slid out from the bench and began walking to the front of the classroom. What did she know about the Southern Lands? Nothing more than Ellena's stories and fantasy tales. At least she didn't have to deal anymore with the back bench trolls.

"Miss Beetch, you will clean the blackboard. Since you are so fond of it." Miss Pont turned her back on Soolie and began addressing the class. "Now, the Southern Lands are the primitive uncivilized lands of the known world. We are privileged to live in the Midlands only a few days travel from the largest city in all of the known world. Can anyone in the front row tell me the name of that city?"

Soolie found the dust cloth and began wiping the letters off the board, reducing the hard lines to a thin chalky haze.

"That's right, Ravus," Miss Pont was saying. "Ravus is a civilized city with civilized people, full of commerce and laws, great businesses and universities. It is the center of art, fashion, and modern thought throughout the known world."

She hasn't said much about the Southern Lands, Soolie thought.

"I said *clean* the chalkboard, Miss Beetch, not 'smudge it around.'" Soolie looked back. Miss Pont had her hands on her hips. "I expect you to clean the chalk off, not redistribute it."

Someone giggled. It sounded like Winny Baldrick. Miss Pont

turned back to the class again.

Soolie went back to wiping at the chalkboard. Show no weakness. Win.

"Does anyone have any questions? Yes, Luka."

"Are there monsters in the Southern Lands?"

"No, Luka. Only untamed animals and savages. Any other questions?"

"I have a question," Soolie said.

Miss Pont turned, "You can ask questions, Miss Beetch, when you learn how to properly clean a chalkboard."

Soolie smiled. "I'm afraid my father was too busy instructing me in philosophy and arithmetic to show me how to use a chalkboard. Perhaps you could show me, as it appears to be the one thing you know that I do not."

"Miss Beetch!" Soolie had struck the right nerve. "You will bend yourself over that desk now, and I will whip you until you learn respect!"

Soolie didn't move. "Are you sure you wouldn't rather have Hobby do your hitting for you?"

Miss Pont slapped Soolie hard across the face. Soolie did not flinch. It stung, but it didn't matter. Miss Pont could hit Soolie as often as she wanted; Soolie had already won.

"Get out of my schoolhouse! Get out!"

Soolie had forgotten for a moment that Miss Pont could do that. Miss Pont could kick her out of school. Even though Soolie hadn't even attended a full day, hadn't made a single friend, hadn't even spoken a single word to someone her own age ... Miss Pont could make sure she never got the chance. Well, so be it.

Miss Pont was glaring, shaking, her face blotchy and ugly with fury. Soolie lifted her chin proudly and prepared herself for the slow march out of the schoolhouse, but a faraway voice stopped her.

"Lak nunn masli ko pan daruka."

It was a sorbile tongue, strange syllables, beautiful foreign words that lilted like verse. Soolie wished she knew what they meant.

Miss Pont's face had gone white.

"What did you just say?"

Soolie realized the voice was hers.

"It's a saying in the Southern Lands," she heard herself say. "It means, 'The Northern man uses violence when he should use manners.'"

"Out!" Miss Pont screeched. "Everyone out! Class is dismissed, and, Miss Beetch?"

Soolie heard something creep into the teacher's voice. Something not unlike fear.

"Don't *ever* come back."

THE STUDENTS FILED OUT around the schoolhouse, chattering and whispering, glancing sideways at Soolie. They were still an hour early to head home. Soolie kept her eyes forward and her head high.

Where had she heard those strange words before? Perhaps she had read them in a book. She had spoken them awfully clearly for something she had only seen with her eyes and never heard with her ears. Not that it mattered. She had bested her opponent, and that was what mattered most.

Wasn't it?

Soolie bit her lip, blinking back bitter disappointment. Four years of waiting to go back to school, and it had only taken her one day to ruin it.

It wasn't that she didn't love Papa. And Ellena was so wonderful, it didn't even matter that she was an adult … but Soolie'd only had one chance to prove to the other students she was someone worth spending time with, or even getting to know. Instead they'd laughed at her, and she'd shown herself to be a complete freak. What for? To humiliate a teacher who meant nothing. Yes, she'd won, all right.

Oh, what did she care. It didn't matter. Not really.

Papa was going to be furious.

"Wow, you really messed her."

Soolie spun, startled. It was Bernad, the Pelig boy. He had followed her.

"What do you want?"

He grinned. He was a few years older than Soolie, with dark hair, pink cheeks, and funny round ears that reminded Soolie of dried apricots.

"I mean, I've seen her messed before, but never that messed. What did you say to her at the end? You were so quiet, none of us could make it out."

By 'none of us' he meant Hobby and Kip. Soolie shrugged and kept walking. "I told her she wasn't a very nice person."

"Is that all?" He fell in step beside her, "She acted like you cursed her grave. You're kind of rot bones."

"Rot bones?" He said it like it was a good thing. "Is that a good thing?"

"Yeah." He hooked his thumbs in his pockets. "It's good."

Apparently he was walking with her. Soolie held on to her books more tightly and tried to walk at a casual pace. Though she wasn't entirely sure what a casual pace was. She tried not to think about it. She didn't trust him. But he was being nice, and she was just a little bit flattered.

"I saw you yesterday. When your dad started yelling at us."

"You mongrels," she tossed her head scornfully, "tormenting that poor woman."

"Hardly a woman."

"Just like you were tormenting me in the schoolhouse."

"I had nothing to do with that! Though I am sorry about it." He tousled his hair and grinned. He didn't seem very sorry. "Hobby and Kip are sucks. Total rot. You were right ballard, though, not letting them get to you."

"They didn't get to me."

"Do I get to you?"

Soolie wasn't sure if he was threatening or flirting, and thought those two things shouldn't be so easily confused. They were almost at Main Street. When they reached Main Street, she would have to turn left towards the square, out of sight of the other kids still lingering around the schoolhouse. Out of sight of Hobby and Kip. Would he keep walking with her or would he turn back?

Soolie realized he had asked a question that she hadn't answered and kept it that way.

"You know," he jogged up so he was just a little in front of her, trying to get her to look at him, "I'm not really like those two. I just hang with them because there's no one else."

"No one else?" Soolie could think of plenty of other people in Hob Glen besides Hobby and Kip.

"No other guys my age," Bernad shrugged, "in this small suck town."

"That's a skagged up reason," Soolie cussed bluntly.

Bernad threw back his head and howled. "I guess it is! A skagged up reason." They had reached Main Street, and Soolie hesitated for a moment to see what he would do.

"See you around, Beetch. You're not half skagging bad."

Bernad turned and jogged back towards the schoolhouse where Hobby and Kip were taking turns knuckling one another in the arm. It looked like Hobby was winning.

Soolie turned down Main Street. 'Not half skagging bad.'

FOUR

Soolie stepped into Ellena's Bakery, the little brass doorbell jingling and clanking. A stray leaf of mottled green and yellow snuck in on her skirt hem, and she picked it up and tucked it in her hair. Soolie breathed deeply, inhaling the smells of warm vanilla, sweet cinnamon and cloves, roasted onion and toasted nuts, shiny dark egg braids and soft feathery sourdoughs encased in crunchy rustic crusts thick like tree bark.

The windows were open wide to let in the cool autumn air, but the oven heat prevailed, and soon she wished she was wearing a linen dress instead of a wool one with long sleeves. Soolie ducked around the counter and stashed her books and satchel under the corner stool. Ellena had to be around somewhere or she would have locked up.

A tray of sugared hazelnut twists were cooling on a nearby rack, and Soolie snagged one, stuffing the soft sticky morsel into her mouth, chewing with her mouth open to try and cool it off for swallowing.

The bakery was a second home for Soolie. She loved it from the weathered floorboards to the racks of loaves with pale slash marks and wheat patterns in the crust. Most of all, she loved the paintings on the wall.

The first painting had been done by Ellena. Stripes of green, slashes of purple, zig-zags of gold. Papa said it didn't look like much of anything, but Soolie said it made her think of some far-off exotic land. Which made Papa say it was better to appreciate home and that you had one, but Papa was always saying things like that.

The second picture had been painted by Soolie. Ellena had mixed the paint base with boiling water, clay, and flour and colored it with cherries, beets, carrot, spinach leaves, and iris root that she had ordered special so Soolie could have black. Soolie had used the iris root to paint a swirling black and purple sky above a field of red large-petaled flowers. Ellena said she showed immense talent, and even Papa said it was nice to look at.

The third painting was Soolie's favorite. Papa had made the wood frames and stretched the canvas, but hadn't wanted any part in the actual artwork, so Ellena and Soolie had decided to paint the last one together. It was the smallest, shaped long and thin. There were three vaguely human figures standing on a tall green hill staring up at a large, wobbly lavender moon. (Soolie'd had trouble getting it entirely round.) Down near the bottom of the painting was a small flock of white birds circling the top of a tree. The painting reminded Soolie of Mama, because it seemed like it meant something very deep, but she couldn't quite grasp what it was. When she thought of Mama, she often felt that way. The only thing about the painting that bothered Soolie was that there were only three people on the hill. Sometimes she would study the painting, trying to figure out if the three people were her, Papa, and Mama, or her, Papa, and Ellena, but it was a mystery she wasn't going to solve today.

"Soolie!" Ellena was coming down the stairs carrying her shawl and a shopping sack. "You're early. I was just about to run to the grocer's for cinnamon sticks. School doesn't let out for another hour or so. Did something happen?"

Soolie hastily wiped her mouth with the back of her sleeve and rubbed her sugary fingers on her skirts. "Oh, nothing much. I just got kicked out of school."

"Well, that sounds like a story." Ellena set the shawl and sack down. "First things first. Come give me a hug."

Soolie ran across the bakery and wrapped her arms tight around her aunt. As far as Soolie was concerned, Ellena was the most wonderful person in the whole world. She smelled of baked wheat and sugar, and she had eyes that said, 'You can trust me. I know how to keep secrets,' and she lived up to them.

"Now," Ellena held Soolie's face in her hands and kissed her on the forehead. "Have a seat. Kettle's already on the stove, and I just made cardamom hazelnut twists. Start telling me what happened."

Soolie took a perch on the stool in the corner and kicked her feet against the bottom rung. "I don't think Miss Pont cares for me very much."

"Not surprising. Miss Pont has always taken it personally when a parent thinks they know how to raise their own children better than she does."

Soolie smiled. Ellena was always on her side.

"So," Ellena paused to pour hot water into Soolie's favorite blue clay mug. She placed the kettle back on the stove, walked over and handed the mug to Soolie. "I know you, Soolie Beetch. You did something. What was it?"

She sipped her tea: not too cold, not too hot. It tasted like raspberry leaf and orange peel.

"Miss Pont said that the residents of the Southern Lands are savages. I said that maybe Southerners think that *we* are the savages."

"That's a very intelligent perspective." Ellena slipped a twist on a plate and set it on the counter next to Soolie. "Is that exactly how you phrased it?"

"Pretty close." Soolie grinned and took a large bite of the sweet roll. It was just as delicious as the first.

The shop bell rang. Instinctively, Soolie ducked quickly below the counter before she could be seen.

Mrs. Svenson bustled through the door in a plum colored dress stretched so tightly at the seams you could almost hear the individual threads creaking under the strain. Papa had once said that it was almost as difficult for Mrs. Svenson's clothes to contain Mrs. Svenson as it was for Mrs. Svenson to contain a delicious piece of gossip.

"Whooo!" Mrs. Svenson hooted like a tea kettle, "Elly, it's warm in here! You should leave the door open! Lands alive! Did you hear about the schoolhouse?"

Ellena disliked Mrs. Svenson as much as Papa did, but Mrs. Svenson bought two loaves a day for her and Mr. Svenson, so Ellena put up with it.

"Mrs. Svenson, how are you today?"

"Did you hear that little Beetch girl went to the schoolhouse today? Mrs. Baldrick told me. I know you're partial to that family, Elly, you have to be, but lands-all knows that child is a strange young thing—two of my regular, Elly dear, the freshest ones you have—now, Winny told her mother, who told me, that niece of yours marched right into that classroom, bold as you please, and called poor Felice a string of naughty words, bold as you please! Just like that! Now I don't abide language, Elly, you know me. Children need to be taught to keep civil tongues in their heads—are those fresh? Well, I trust you—now, I'm telling you poor Felice was shocked right out of her wits! Of course, dear thing had to call the whole day to a close and send those children home. Told that wild child never to show her face there again and rightly so. I tell you, it isn't right the way that man has isolated that child these last four years. She's turned into a little wild thing. No manners, no respect…"

Soolie stayed crouched on the floor, munching the last of her twist and licking her fingers. Ellena hadn't said a word. Not that Mrs. Svenson would have heard her if she had. Soolie heard the crinkle of brown paper as Ellena wrapped up the two loaves. If it wasn't for those two loaves, Soolie would have been glad to stand up and give Mrs. Svenson a sassing, but she didn't want to harm her aunt's business. It was a small town, and Mrs. Svenson had a big mouth.

"Soolie is a lovely young woman," Soolie heard Ellena say. "I'm sure there is more to the story than we know."

"Children are fragile, Elly," Mrs. Svenson said with the surety of a woman who had heard the voice of truth and it was her own. "Especially frail ones like that. Frail body, frail mind. And what with her mother's death. Not good for a child's mental health. And then cooped up with that man all these years. You know what they say." Mrs. Svenson trailed off as if implying something too dreadful to clarify.

"Why, no, I do not, Mrs. Svenson," said Ellena coldly. "What do they say?"

Mrs. Svenson leaned in, her voice a low hiss, "That sister of yours, praise lands she wasn't your blood, always wrapped in bandages, hiding her face. Surely you know, Elly: they say she was a dark one, one of the devil's wives."

Soolie couldn't help it. It was the most ridiculous thing she had ever heard. She laughed. And once she had started laughing, she couldn't stop. She sat back on the wood flooring, threw her head back and cackled.

"Soolie." It was Ellena looking down at her.

Soolie covered her mouth with both hands to stifle her merriment.

"Would you like to come up and say hello to Mrs. Svenson?"

There was nothing for it now. Soolie popped up to her feet and tried to look serious. Mrs. Svenson was gaping at her like she had sprung up bare naked with all the wrong parts.

"Mrs. Svenson. So good to see you this afternoon. If you see Miss Pont, please tell her for me that I do hope I didn't agitate her nerves with my savage speech. I am, after all, fragile minded and poorly educated. I just don't know any better."

Mrs. Svenson clutched her bread loaves to her ample bosom like a pair of infants she wasn't sure whether to protect or suffocate. "Well! I am certainly appalled, Elly, that you have taken to harboring delinquents beneath your counters to mock and assault innocent patrons!"

"Of course, Mrs. Svenson. Thank you for stopping by," Ellena said dryly. "Do say hello to Mr. Svenson for me, won't you?"

"If he is in a humor to hear me, after all, his rheumatism is doing quite poorly. Good day!" With a bustle and a jingle of the front door, Mrs. Svenson was gone.

"Soolie!" Ellena scolded, "Did you really call Miss Pont a bad name?"

"No," Soolie protested, "I just quoted something."

"Well, what was it?"

"I…" Soolie paused. She had absolutely no idea. "I don't remember."

"You don't remember?" Ellena folded her arms, eyebrows raised.

"Honestly, I really don't."

"Are you *quite* certain?"

"Absolutely."

"Hmmm," Ellena said, unconvinced.

Soolie shrugged. She didn't know what else to tell Ellena. Whatever words she had said to Miss Pont were gone.

"Well, whether or not you do remember," Ellena said, "if you ever want to make friends in this town, upsetting people like Mrs. Svenson and Miss Pont won't help you."

"Maybe I don't want friends like them." Soolie thought about how gleeful Bernad had been at the way she had upset Miss Pont. "Maybe I want friends who like me for who I am, like you do."

Ellena sighed. "That's very sweet of you to say, Soolie, but you may feel differently some day."

Soolie doubted it.

"Well," Ellena said, "since your father isn't expecting you for another hour, how about you come with me to the grocer's to get that cinnamon, and then we can come back and pick out a few rolls for you to take home to your father for dinner. And you can tell him I wouldn't let you give me a single coin."

In answer, Soolie dashed over, scooped up the shopping sack, and handed Ellena her shawl.

"So," Ellena said, wrapping her shawl around her shoulders, "other than terrorizing poor Miss Pont, how was your first day of school?"

"Unremarkable. A boy talked to me."

"And you lead with 'I got kicked out of school?' Come on. Spill."

As Ellena locked up the shop door, a light breeze lifted a leaf from Soolie's hair. It was brown and fragile, and when Soolie stepped and turned it beneath her boot, it crumbled to dust.

SOOLIE TOOK HER TIME getting home. When she arrived, Papa was furious. Mrs. Svenson had traveled straight up the street from Ellena's bakery to tell him how his daughter had shut down the school, been kicked out on the first day, and guffawed in her face when she so much as suggested Soolie behave like a young lady. Papa was embarrassed and he was angry. It didn't matter if the teacher had been unfair; a student must show her teacher respect. It didn't matter if Mrs. Svenson hadn't told the whole truth; the fact that it was even a part truth was enough. He didn't want to hear any excuses, and he talked for a long time.

Tomorrow, Papa told her, Soolie would go back to school, and he would go with her. She would apologize to Miss Pont, she would promise to only speak when addressed, she would be polite and respectful, and maybe Miss Pont would be kind enough to allow her back into the classroom. Tonight, Soolie would go to bed with no supper.

Soolie didn't cry. She'd had all the time with Ellena to prepare herself. If Papa had been there in the classroom and heard Miss Pont, if he had been in the bakery and heard Miss Svenson, then, perhaps, he might have taken Soolie's side. But he hadn't been there. It had been her responsibility to handle on her own, to represent their family, and she had shamed him.

In the morning things would be better. He might even apologize for being harsh with her, though he would still take her to school to ask forgiveness of Felice Pont. Soolie didn't mind. She had seen the look on Miss Pont's face. No apology was going to take that away.

In the loft, Soolie finished the last of the rolls—she had eaten half of them on the way home—and changed into her nightgown. Her fingers traced the strange papery skin on her wrist. It felt sunken and squishy. No matter. It didn't hurt, and it wasn't wet or oozing. When she sniffed at it, it didn't smell like much of anything. Maybe she'd tell Papa about it tomorrow.

Soolie quietly stacked the three books on the floor, stepped up on them on tip toe, and carefully lifted the roof hatch to look out in the direction of Ravus. The sun was setting pale blue and gold with only a few clouds resting in the sky like thick dollops of gray icing. The idea of that distant city seemed so full of wonder and promise after a day like today. Full of vibrant and strange people, people with opinions and thoughts, people who weren't afraid to question and be. So many people that a boy—no, young man, she told herself—like Bernad would never have to be friends with idiot rots like Hobby and Kip in a city like that.

Soolie quietly lowered the hatch and curled up on top of her bed in the dark.

It didn't seem right. Papa loved her. Ellena loved her. Why did she feel so alone? And she wasn't the only one. Everyone was alone. That was what was so wrong about it. Papa downstairs, worrying, fretting. Ellena too, all by herself in her room above the bakery getting ready for bed like she did every night. And Soolie. Soolie imagined she was the most alone of all. How could people all love each other and still somehow, at the end of the day, end up in their own dark little rooms with their dark little thoughts, and no one to hold them and say 'I understand.' It didn't seem right.

You're not alone.

Soolie's eyes flew open. A voice. A distinct voice. A voice she knew.

A tiny white star appeared in the center of the loft. It began to grow and spread, fiery tendrils shooting out and licking the rafters, ripples and splashes swirling the shadows out of the corners. Soolie expected Papa to come running up the ladder, but the downstairs was silent, and still the light grew. It grew until it engulfed the little room, eating away the defining edges in unbearable brightness, and just when Soolie thought she might go blind, it softened to an ethereal glow, and Soolie saw her.

Long golden chestnut hair settling in delicate ringlets around her sharp pale face, thin but elegant arms reaching out, large enigmatic hazel eyes, the serene smile that turned up just a little bit more at one corner than the other. There was no doubt.

"Mama?"

Hello, Soolie. I've missed you.

FIVE

Mama's dress was soft and flowing, her hair as silky as lambskin, her scent fresh and sweet like honeysuckle. While the mother Soolie remembered had been swathed in bandages and marked with a lifetime of scrapes and scars, the woman standing before her was flawless, not a bandage in sight, not a single scratch, scar or bruise. She was more beautiful and perfect than she ever had been. Soolie ran to her and hugged her tight, afraid to let go, afraid to speak, afraid even one word, like warm breath on an ice crystal, might make her mother melt and disappear again forever.

Mama stroked Soolie's hair and kissed the top of her head.

It's all right. Everything is going to be all right.

It was Mama's voice. Soolie looked up, tears in her eyes.

"You said you were never coming back."

Mama smiled. *Look around. What do you see?*

They had left the darkness of the loft and were standing in the middle of a cobblestone street that bustled with all manner of people. Soolie saw elegant women wearing tiny pin hats and layered ruffled dresses that rustled as they swept by. Young men in tightly tailored waistcoats and tall platform boots of the latest style strutted, swinging shiny-handled canes. There were other people too: men in threadbare jackets and cropped pants that showed their bare ankles, women with ragpile skirts towing children who carried trays of colorful silk flower buttons and twisted sticky sweets in wax paper for sale. There were people the color of milk and people the color of toffee. People with hair frizzed up on top of their heads like piles of wool, and men and women with their hair shaved close to their scalp to show off the dark blue geometric tattoos of the islands.

Directly in front of Soolie stood a familiar building. It was larger than any building in Hob Glen, stretching up five whole stories and easily four times as wide as it was high. The sides were a rough mottled gray and tan, riddled with a hundred evenly spaced little windows with white criss-cross bars. A rank of stairs led up from the street to a set of wide double doors, and painted next to the doors was the image of a violet crane.

It was the hospital in Ravus, and Soolie had only been here once before in her life, with her mother.

"Why are we here?" Soolie asked. And silently added, 'Why are you here?' But she didn't want to interrupt. Mama always did things at her own speed and in her own time. She used to say, 'Life is not a skin that it will stretch if you stuff it with twice the things.' Mama would want her to be patient. Whatever the reason, it must be a very important one.

Mama took her hand just like she used to when Soolie was little and smiled at her. Her smile was so blissful. So at peace.

This is one of your preferred memories, Mama said. *I thought you would like to see it.*

As they walked up the step, the large doors opened in greeting. People flowed around them. Two women in lavender coats pushed up the step, hauling a stretcher. As they passed, Soolie saw a young man swathed in a white sheet damp with sweat and body fluids. His eyes were rolled back in his head, and where his teeth should have been were powdery yellow stumps: signs of topaz addiction. Soolie knew that now. She hadn't known that back then.

She had been eight years old then, the year before Mama died, the year Mama told Papa she wanted to take Soolie to see the city. Papa hadn't wanted to go. Papa hated Ravus. He said a city was nothing but a bunch of people who didn't have the sense to spread out, but Mama had insisted. Mama rarely asked for anything, which was why, when she did, she always got it. "That's one of the best things about dying," Mama had whispered, winking at Soolie. "The words you have left carry the weight of all the words you will never get the chance to say."

It was too quiet. As soon as Soolie thought it, all the sounds came rushing in: the percussion of hundreds of feet. The squeak clatter of cart wheels, voices, orders being called, a baby crying. And the smells … as soon as she thought to miss them, they were there: the fetor of humanity, a dull sickliness, the sharp stench of waste from the man who had just been carried by, lemons, soap, and hot linen.

Do you know what that is? Mama asked.

It was a familiar question. They stood in the doorway to the hospital now. Mama was nodding at the painted crane beside them.

"The hospital in Ravus," Soolie said. "We came here when I was eight."

It's a crane, Mama said. *There is a story that once the people in the world were very very sick from a disease that was carried by the frogs. They killed hundreds of frogs and burned them in massive stinking piles.*

Soolie had heard these words before. They were what Mama had told her when she was little. "Do you know what that is?" Mama had asked. "A bird," Soolie had said. "It's a crane," Mama had said. "There is a story…"

They were replaying her memory, word for word.

Everything was exactly as she remembered it. The people sitting on the bench, waiting for someone to help them. The ladies in lavender uniforms with tassel-topped hats entering the room with tablets and chalk to write down ailments and usher people to other rooms. The little boy sitting next to his ashen-faced mother. In a moment, he would look up at her, and eight year-old Soolie would stick her tongue out at him, and he would stick his tongue out right back, and Soolie would complain to Mama. Any moment now.

Mama was still talking.

…But they could never get rid of the frogs, and the people just kept getting sick and dying. Then one man had an idea to save his people. He went to the crane, which was the wisest of the animals, and he asked the crane for help. The crane listened to the man, swept down and ate up all the frogs! Not only that, the crane taught the people medicine, so that when they were sick, they could fight the sickness, and when they were dying, they could lessen the pain. Wasn't that nice of the crane?

Mama was looking down at her expectantly, waiting for her to speak.

"Very nice," Soolie murmured obediently.

Mama was still waiting. Five years ago, Soolie had told her mother that she wanted a crane of her own, but she didn't want to say that now. She wanted to know why Mama had brought her here. She was trying to be patient, but something felt wrong.

"Why are we here?"

Mama smiled kindly, *Not all beautiful things are better for having. This building has a crane on the side of it, can you guess what happens here?*

Why wasn't Mama talking to her? *"I thought you would like to see it,"* she had said. Was something watching them? Could Mama be trying to send her a message? Mama had told Soolie she was going away and never coming back, but here she was. She had come back. And Soolie couldn't shake the feeling that something was horribly wrong. Soolie tried to play along.

"Are there cranes?"

No, no cranes.

"Frogs."

No, no frogs.

"I don't know."

This is a hospital, Soolie. This is where people fight death.

"Do they get better?" Soolie asked, rattling off the words from her memory while her eyes darted around the room, trying to find something out of place that might indicate what they were doing there.

Sometimes, Mama said. *For a little while. Would you like to go inside?*

They stepped in through the doorway. The little boy stuck his tongue out at her. Soolie ignored him.

She knew that next, one of the lavender ladies, the one with the tight black curls tucked under her hat, would come forward with her slate tablet and ask Mama for her ailment. Then Mama would explain she had no ailment, and the lavender lady would see Mama's many bandages and would ask many questions until Mama explained she was just teaching her daughter about death.

"This is not an exhibit," the nurse had snapped. "This is a hospital. And if you have no business here, I must ask you to leave."

On the steps outside, eight-year old Soolie had asked, "Why did you lie to the nurse?"

"Did I?" Mama had replied.

"You said you weren't sick."

"I'm not the kind of sick hospitals can help. I have to fight on my own, but that's okay. Do you know why?"

"Because Papa and I give you something to fight for?"

"That's right, and I will always fight for you, Soolie."

That was the memory, and it was special, because Soolie had known Mama was sharing something important with Soolie, because she knew Soolie was strong enough to handle it even if she didn't understand it. Mama was strong, and Mama expected Soolie to be strong, and the trip to the hospital had been a secret between the two of them that Soolie had never shared with anyone, not Papa, not even Ellena.

And here they were again. Except this time, Mama had no bandages, and Soolie was not eight years old. They were just repeating lines of something that had happened five years ago, only they weren't really repeating the past, they were repeating a memory. Every time Soolie thought to look for something, it was there. She was starting to think there was nothing new to see, nothing to discover. It was all perfect, but it was so perfect that it was all wrong. It was all fake. They were just acting.

Could that be the only reason they were here? *I thought you would like to see it.* Soolie had been sad and lonely, and so she was in a memory with her mother?

They were both just acting.

Soolie let go of her mother's hand. Mama's head turned towards her sharply, her eyes glinting hard like polished glass.

"You said you were never coming back," Soolie whispered.

You aren't enjoying this. It was a statement. Flat and emotionless. Mama tilted her head to the side. *Why aren't you enjoying this? Everything is the way you remember it.*

Soolie felt sickening horror knot her stomach. This wasn't her mother. Something was playing with her. It had tricked her. And Soolie had no idea what it was, what it was doing, or what it wanted with her.

She teetered between terror and rage. It was as if a moment in time had been launched into the air and hung, suspended at the apex of its arc. She looked into the glazed eyes of the thing that resembled her mother, and as the moment fell, Soolie chose rage.

She launched herself away, grabbed the slate from the nurse's hand, spun around and hurled it straight at her mother's face with all her force. In mid-flight, the slate blinked out of existence, the hospital with it, and Soolie found herself in an expanse of blankness, featureless but for the image of her mother just out of reach. Soolie screamed.

And screamed, and screamed, and screamed. Her confusion, her lack of control, her fury.

She struck out with her arms and legs, trying to get at it, trying to reach it, but no matter how she kicked and struggled, the image of her mother stayed the same distance away, watching like a bird eyeing a wasp flailing on its back on the surface of a pond. Which only made Soolie scream more.

She screamed until her throat should have been bloody, and still the figure stood passive. Soolie spat at it and nothing happened.

Why did you not appreciate the dream?

Soolie bared her teeth and snarled.

The hospital was a time when you felt happy, loved, and valuable, but now you respond with different emotions. Why?

Cucking skag, Soolie thought.

I can give you whatever you want. You can dream that your father is happy. Or your mother alive. You can spend time with the one called Bernad. We can help each other.

Soolie wanted to rip the face of her mother off its skull. It wasn't even moving its mouth anymore when it talked. It just stared, unblinking, giving Soolie the unnerving feeling it wanted to eat her.

Her mother's mouth pulled up in a smile. *It is not my goal to harm you.*

Soolie realized: it could hear her thoughts.

We can help each other, it said again. *How can I calm you?*

Calm her? Soolie sneered. It could tell her how to reach it so she could scratch out its cucking eyes.

Your hostility lacks insight. Why do you wish me harm?

Because it was *her* memory. Her memory, with her mother. It was not this cuck's to give or take or skagging share.

My last vessel found pleasant dreams gave her peace in difficult times. This may be a difficult time for you. I only wish to ease your trouble.

If only Soolie could figure out what the skag it was.

I am your mother.

Liar.

Your guest.

It was telling her nothing.

Ask better questions.

Soolie clenched her hands into fists. "Whatever the skag you are, I WILL END YOU!"

It tilted its head as if its neck was on a hinge. *Your struggle will only cause harm. You are being willful, and I do not have time to subdue you.*

"LEAVE ME ALONE!"

"Soolie! Soolie, wake up!"

It was dark. Someone was holding her down, a heavy weight on her chest, her arms pinned to her sides, and she hurt. All of her hurt. Her head was roaring, her hands and legs burned and surged with pain. She bucked and kicked, trying to break free. Papa's voice saying her name over and over again.

She was back on the floor of her loft. Papa was here. It was Papa kneeling over her, holding her down. Soolie stopped fighting.

"Soolie? Soolie?" His voice cracked with desperation. She couldn't see his face in the dark. The weight shifted, his voice again, close to her face. "Soolie, honey, are you awake?"

Soolie tried to speak, but managed nothing more than a painful squeak.

"Oh, Soolie."

Papa wrapped her in his arms, holding her close, and Soolie gasped in pain.

"I'm sorry, baby girl. I'm sorry. I'm going to pick you up and carry you downstairs right now, okay? This might hurt, but hold on. You're going to be okay."

It did hurt. Soolie felt tears streaming down her cheeks, dripping down her neck. She squeezed her eyes tight and put her face against Papa's shoulder as he carefully held her with one big strong arm and began descending the ladder.

It was the middle of the night. The fire was out, no lamps were lit. The only light was the dim gleam of moonlight that snuck in below the ruffled window curtain. Papa was setting her in the rocking chair. He was placing the quilt over her, getting a lamp, lighting a fire. Soolie just huddled, trying not to cry, trying not to move.

The flames in the hearth crackled and began to lick the new dry logs that Papa had arranged for the morning fire. The room filled with long dark shadows, and Papa knelt by her side.

Soolie turned slowly toward him, squinting at the bright light. She caught a glimpse of something dark on her hands where they rested on the blanket. She was bleeding on Mama's quilt. She whimpered, trying to push the blanket off without staining it further, but Papa shushed her, wrapping the blanket back up around her with strong calming hands.

"No, it's okay. It's okay." Papa said. "Your Mama never saw anything wrong with a little blood. Can you speak?"

Papa's face was frightened and concerned, but his voice was calming and reassuring. Soolie tried to, but only managed to a hissing croak. She mouthed: 'a little.'

"Okay," Papa said. "Can you tell me where it hurts?"

Soolie nodded and winced.

"Just mouth the words. I think you cracked your head against your bedpost."

'Yes.'

"Can you move all your fingers and toes?"

Soolie wiggled her fingers. Her toes. Pain shot up from her right foot. Papa lifted up the blanket and examined her foot and ankle. Unwelcome tears traced Soolie's face as he gently probed her ankle and heel with his fingers, but she didn't cry out.

"I don't think you've broken anything, baby girl. But you have some very deep bruises, and you've bashed yourself up pretty badly. I'm going to wash your wounds."

Soolie nodded. Papa had brought the basket out, Mama's basket, full of rolls of linen strips, ointment, salves, and clean folded cloths. He removed a pot of water from where he had set it heating on the fire, dipped in a cloth, and wrung it out steaming in the firelight. Then he knelt before her, took her foot gently into his lap and began to wash her wounds just the way he used to for Mama when she was too weak to do it for herself.

"I couldn't wake you." He didn't look up. His deep voice trembled at the edges. "I heard you screaming, and I ran up the ladder. And I tried to wake you, but I couldn't wake you."

Papa submerged the cloth in the hot water again, stirring it back and forth. When he wrung it out, the water from the cloth was tinged copper with blood. Soolie's head, back, and limbs throbbed. The hot cloth stung, but Papa's practiced gentle touch soothed her.

"And you were on the floor thrashing and kicking and hurting yourself, and still I couldn't wake you. When you went still…"

Papa paused. He set down the wet cloth, picked up a dry one, and carefully dabbed Soolie's foot dry. Then he salved the wound so the linen wouldn't stick to the raw flesh and wrapped the foot carefully in clean bandages, keeping them loose in case of swelling.

When Papa spoke again, his voice was hoarse, "I thought. For a moment … I thought I had lost you." He looked up, and she saw his eyes were soppy with tears. "I thought I had lost you, baby girl."

Soolie wished she could say words to comfort him. She mouthed his name: 'Papa.'

"Just tell me if you can," he whispered, taking her battered little hand into his big strong Papa's hands. "Why were you screaming? Was it a bad dream?"

She nodded gingerly. 'Yes.'

It hadn't been just a bad dream. Soolie remembered every detail. The tilted head, the emotionless eyes, Mama's face, but not Mama… But she was in too much shock and pain, too exhausted right now to be terrified. And Papa looked so worried.

"What did you dream, baby girl? Can you tell me in a few words?"

'The fat woman.' She mouthed the lie.

"You had a dream about the woman in the wagon?"

'Yes.'

"Oh, baby girl. I didn't realize how much that must have frightened you." Papa squeezed her hand gently, rubbing his thumb reassuringly against her wrist. "You know you can always talk to me. You never have to be brave for me. I'm your Papa. That's my job."

Soolie smiled for him, but Papa had stopped looking at her. His eyes were cast down to where his thumb had traveled up her wrist, now lingering slowly across strange skin. He turned her wrist toward the firelight, and there it was, the papery wound.

It was wrinkly, yellow purple-gray, sunken and shriveled. It wasn't a fresh wound, a scrape or a bruise. It wasn't just a bad dream. It was a thumb and four fingers, the grip of the carnival woman, still not letting go.

Soolie saw the fear in Papa's eyes. Fear she couldn't explain away.

Papa set her hand down on the quilt. "We can talk more about it later," he said reaching for the cleaning cloth. "Once your voice is better. Right now, we'll clean and bandage you up. I'll get you some licorice tea for your throat. You can sleep downstairs tonight. Everything is all right now. Everything is all right."

He wasn't just talking to her.

Papa was washing her left foot. It didn't hurt as much as the right. Soolie wondered if either of them were going to get any sleep tonight. She wondered how long it would take Papa to forget. He shouldn't have seen the skin on her wrist. She should have kept it hidden. She shouldn't have lost her temper. She should have won.

She wondered if it was still there, listening to her thoughts even now. The thing that looked like her mother.

Papa was wrong. Everything was not all right.

Are you listening? Soolie thought. *Are you listening, you skagging harpy? I hope you're paying attention. Because I'm going to cucking destroy you.*

SIX

Dog existed to serve the Master.

The Master told him when to kill and when to cause pain, when to sleep and when to feed, and Dog obeyed. Dog existed to obey. The Master had created Dog, and without obedience, without the Master, Dog was nothing.

Dog was the Master's closest and most trusted, the most loyal and the most obedient. The Master gave him alone the ability to walk in the sun, the strength and speed to out-match any other member of the pack, and the frame of a boy so, if he needed to, he could pull a hood over his head to hide his black eyes, predator's teeth, and gray skin, and pass among the city people unnoticed. Since the day of his creation, Dog had been the only one at the Master's side, though he had not been the first.

When Dog first opened his eyes, there had been an older, weaker dog serving in his place, and Dog had understood immediately that the Master was the most powerful, and so the Master deserved the strongest. The old dog was no longer worthy.

So the young and the old had fought. The old had never once considered running. He had defended his right to serve at the

Master's side with every bit of his aging strength, loyal to his purpose to the very end. And when Dog ripped the head off his predecessor's shoulders, it had snarled defiantly in his hands.

That had been many decades ago, centuries perhaps, it had never occurred to Dog to count. For all that time, he had served at the Master's side, guarding the Master and the Master's rooms, always watching, moving only on command, until today. Today, for the first time, Dog was no longer the strongest.

As Dog looked into the dead cold blue eyes of the Master's newest creation, he knew his time had ended. Just like the dog before him, and the dog before that, and the dog before that, he knew this was a fight he would lose. He knew he was weak. He knew he was unworthy. But unlike his predecessors, he knew he would not stay to fight.

Dog ran.

SILAS AND ROD CORNELL had done a beautiful job on the gardens. From up by the Cornell's house, Ellena could see the six box tiers staggered down the hill in pairs of two. There were tall corn stalks, sprawling pumpkin vines, shriveling herb plants, and bramble berry bushes just settling down with the new autumn frost, all boxed in by heavy trimmed logs like abstract paintings in rustic wooden frames.

"Silas!"

Silas looked up from the zucchini plant he was inspecting to see Ellena carefully making her way towards him around the gardens through the soft hill mud and slick wet grass.

"Forgive me if I do not greet you," he said, holding up his wet muddy hands for her to see. "My hands are all covered with earth."

"The garden looks wonderful!" Ellena stopped to admire a fat green and yellow gourd that hung off the side of one of the tiers, resting lazily on the log that shored up the rich growing soil. "This one's worth presenting at the harvest festival."

"Rod and Milin's gardens are doing well," Silas said, brushing his hands off on his pants. "Ours hasn't fared quite as well, I'm afraid."

As she got close, Ellena could see that Silas spoke the truth. Where the Cornell's boxes were verdant, overgrown, and abundant, the Beetch's garden box was stunted and gray.

"Look at the leaves." Silas lifted up a limp brown rag that clung sadly to a withered zucchini vine. "Soolie and I have been perfectly attentive. I don't think we've done anything different from the Cornells, but our plants all withered up and died."

"Oh," Ellena fretted, kneeling by the vine. "It's so sad. Poor thing." She lifted a leaf to get a look at its base, and it broke off in her hand. "Worms?"

"None." Silas shook his head. "Some sort of blight, I suppose. Rod says he's never seen anything like it. We should just be grateful it hasn't spread to their plots as well."

"Has anything survived?"

"Nothing worth eating. I was really counting on this garden to help get us through the winter."

"I'm sorry, Silas."

"No matter."

The farmers were saying it was looking to be a hard winter. The birds had already gone south, and the husks were thick on the corn. Once the snow and ice made the roads hard to travel, Silas would stop receiving specialty orders from Ravus until the thaw. His shoes and boots were the best crafted in all the villages east of the city. They lasted for years. Ellena didn't think he charged enough for them, but he charged what the country people could afford, and what the city shops bought and resold at higher prices. Ellena had tried to convince Silas he could make the shoes a little faster: fewer stitches, a little more glue, a lower finish on the wood. Add a little paint, colorful buttons, and they would sell just as fast in the city with half the effort. She said the wealthier people never even wore their shoes long enough to appreciate the quality and craftsmanship. But to Silas, that wasn't the point. He took pride in his work, and he made the best shoes east of the city. He may not be a skilled tradesman, but he was an excellent craftsman.

"Silas." He flinched and turned away. "Let me help you and Soolie out a little this year."

"No. Absolutely not." He began walking back up the hill.

"I make more than I need with the bakery. You two are all the family I have, please." He felt her hand on his arm. "Please let me help you."

Silas turned and looked down at her. She did make more with her loaves and rolls than he did with his boots and heels, and that hurt him to admit. But it was his job to provide for his family. His job to care for Soolie, to watch over her and keep her safe, to make sure she was warm, fed, and clothed. That was his job, and he could not fail at it.

"Please," she repeated.

"You know I cannot accept your charity." He gently placed his hand on hers and removed it from his arm.

He didn't want to hurt her, but she didn't understand how it wounded him to see himself in those pitying eyes as if he were weak, failing. He knew what he must look like: dull puce bags hanging under eyes strained with worry and sleepless nights, cheeks gaunt beneath his poorly trimmed beard. He had hardly slept or eaten since the night of Soolie's nightmare. Her bruises and bashed skin had healed, the lump on her head had gone down, she barely limped when she walked, and the nights had been peaceful. But the strange marks he had found on her wrist: sallow like the belly of a dead eel, wrinkled and sunken, wrapping around his daughter's wrist, the imprint of a grotesque stranger's dying grip. Those marks had not gone away and neither had his fear. It gnawed at his skull like cadaver beetles. Had the carnival woman been poisoned? Was it a sickness? A contagion? Was it really just a nightmare that had shaken Soolie so violently, screaming in the night? Was his daughter truly safe? And every night he tucked his daughter into the downstairs bed, pulled the covers up near her small beautiful face, kissed her goodnight, and took his place in the rocker by the fireplace. Keeping watch.

"There must be something I can do."

"There is one favor."

"Anything."

"I do have a few orders left that I won't be able to finish in time for the coach to Ravus. I will need to take them to the city myself. I was hoping Soolie might stay with you while I'm gone."

"You could always take Soolie with you. I'm sure she would be very excited to see the city again with her Papa."

"No."

"Silas…"

"You know how I feel about Ravus. I wouldn't be going myself if I had a choice."

"I know." And she did. "Of course Soolie is welcome to stay with me."

"Thank you," Silas said solemnly. "I will, of course, repay you."

Ellena lifted her cloak to keep it out of the mud and walked past him. "Don't insult me."

Silas nodded once and continued up the hill with her. They were agreed.

Ellena smiled, turning back to him as they walked past the Cornell's house. "Will you both be at the harvest festival?"

"I don't know," Silas said. "I was hoping to have those shoes finished by then and be halfway to Ravus."

"Oh, you have to come!" She fell in beside him. "Working on it is such a nightmare. Mrs. Svenson turns every little decision into a crisis, and Mergo Pelig isn't even on the festival committee, but *of course* she's still there, putting herself in charge of everything, bossing everyone about like she's the Opal Priestess. Silas, if I wasn't such a lady, I'd punch her in her pretty pink little face and soil her horrid white gloves in her own nose blood!"

Silas raised an eyebrow. "You've thought much about this?"

"Every land-awful day," Ellena muttered. "Silas, that woman asked me to watch my drinking during the festival because 'people are relying on me.' As if she's letting me work on the committee out of charity. As if, because grandad liked his wine, I have some kind of problem."

"I told you."

"You did. And you were right."

They stepped into the cobbles of Main Street and began walking to the Beetch house just up the road.

"So, will you come?"

"Well…" Silas spoke slowly. "It isn't that I don't want to…"

"Oh, you have to, Silas! You have to. You're coming." She clasped her hands. "Please come. Please? They put me in charge of the pie judging. I'll be eaten alive."

Silas couldn't resist. "Not unless you're placed with the mince meats. If you're with the fruit pies, Mrs. Svenson won't allow it."

Ellena clapped her hands. "Ooh, you're coming!"

"I didn't say…"

"You made a joke. You're coming."

"Hmmm."

Silas tucked his hands in his pockets and hid a smile beneath his beard. Of course he was coming. As far as he was concerned, from the moment she asked, he never really had a choice. After all, he had asked a favor, and if this was Ellena's request, this was how he would repay her.

"You should wear your blue dress."

"I was thinking the red and black."

"The blue is better."

"You just say that because blue is your favorite color."

"The blue is better."

Master's new creation was a new kind of monster, a Wolf. Sharper, faster, and more obedient, with a presence that made Dog's ears prick and skin crawl as if in sense of a silent keening just beyond the reach of sound. When Dog turned and ran, it hadn't followed. Because the Wolf stayed by Master's side and the Wolf didn't abandon its duty. Wolf was better than Dog.

So the pack had turned on Dog and chased him up from the

under tunnels into the streets of Ravus. They wouldn't kill him. He couldn't die, not the way the living died: their souls severed from their bodies. But he could be crushed. The pack would shred him flesh from flesh, sinew from sinew, they would shatter his bones and scatter the pulpy shards in the street. It was no worse a fate then he would have met at the claws of the Wolf, only, at the hands of the Wolf, he might have died with honor.

Individually, Dog was stronger than every one of the pack, but together … the pack was large in numbers, larger than it had ever been before. Master had been forging more, enlarging the pack, and now there were scores, all of whom knew the city better than Dog did. They had been running the Master's errands, doing the Master's bidding and finding their own feed, while he had stayed at home playing pet. But Dog was faster.

He careened through the slop-slick streets, wrecking carts and knocking down awning poles, dashed through the Crimson District, shredding cloth doorways, slashing through incense-soaked rooms and tangled bare bodies, not even stopping for a taste. Dog skittered across the loose shale rooftops, throwing himself through the air, catching corroded gutters that crumbled beneath his long claws, holding just long enough to vault himself up and leap again. Every step of the way, the pack was close behind him, whooping, howling, and cackling in his wake, and every step of the way, he stayed just one pace ahead. He didn't stop, he didn't look behind him, he never grew weary. He only had to hold out until dawn. Then he hit the open square.

It was sudden. One moment he was leaping through a narrow alleyway, and the next he was pelting across a wide open space of paved stone, empty but for a gathering of tents and wagons on the other side.

Dog snapped around, looking back the way he had come, dragging his long nails shrieking on the stone, skidding to a stop. He hadn't been paying attention. The pack had let him grow cocky, let him think he could outrun them forever, all while they had been splitting up, flanking him on either side, and driving him into the open.

It wasn't the whole pack; his instincts told him it was only a few over forty. Still, Dog couldn't take them all, and the rest of the pack would arrive soon.

They stepped out of the darkness of the buildings on all sides, cautiously, knowing they had him cornered, shoulders crouched, snarling, yapping, spittle dripping from quivering lips, flashing yellow fangs, their pack leader Horse at their head. Dog should have known it was Horse as soon as he recognized the trap.

The pack leader leered at Dog and cackled, his long thick teeth gleaming in the moonlight like bleached pine, the massive iron-head sledgehammer hanging down from an oversized corpse-gray hand. Horse's hammer had ended more members of the pack than any tooth or claw, more than the Master himself.

"Finally!" The leader hefted the hammer, bellowing loud so the whole pack could hear. "I will pulp your bones, puppy, until I have to eat them with a spoon!"

The pack howled a jubilant bloodthirsty chorus and charged.

Dog turned and dashed towards the carnival tents and wagons on the other side of the square as the pack closed in around him. In one great leap, he landed on the roof of a wagon and spun around. One of the young pups sprung after him, teeth bared, claws extended. With his fingers flat like a shovel blade, Dog rammed his hand straight through the pup's neck, shattering the windpipe, severing the spinal column. With his other hand, palm open, Dog punched the pup in the chest, propelling the body straight outward so it collided with an oncoming mutt at the same time the head flew loose from the shoulders in a shower of cold blood.

Dog dove from the cart to the top of a red and blue tent, slicing through the canvas with his nails like tearing through a frail membrane. He fell through the air and landed crouched in a dirt ring. Dog snarled. The inside was bare, useless, nothing to use as a weapon and nowhere to hide.

A mutt dropped through the hole in the roof, and others were pouring in through the main door.

"PUPPY!" Horse's voice bellowed from outside. "YOU CANNOT ESCAPE THE PACK!"

Dog sprinted out the side door and into a pup ripping out the throat of a large bald man, dropping a long blade from his fat, quivering fingers. Dog ducked, spun low, sweeping his foot to knock the pup's legs out from under him, grabbing the blade, and bringing it up to sever the pup's head from his shoulders as he fell.

The fat man gargled and toppled over, blood spraying out from his neck. There was blood in the air and humans in the wagons. That was good. The pups' attention would be divided.

Dog dropped the blade, rolled under the canvas of another tent and up into a crouch as a shocked bloody-faced head flew past him, hit the bottom of the tent, and rolled out the way he had come in.

This tent was purple, hung with silk and azurite crystals, with tasseled pillows and a mirror bowl on a low pedestal in the center. Beside it, a young woman was kicking a newly headless corpse in the chest. It toppled backwards, falling beside the body of a quivering young man, naked but for his own guts spilling out from the gash in his belly.

The young woman caught sight of him and spun, her swords at the ready. She had long black hair, large amber eyes, and burnished skin that had been brushed with gold dust so it would shimmer in the lantern light. Her short cropped top and long flowing skirts were spattered in gore, and she wielded the two slender curved blades with deadly grace. Dog recognized her stance. A sword dancer. Most likely from the Southern Lands. Not that her skill was enough to protect her from the pack. If the monster at her feet hadn't gone for her partner first, she might already be dead.

This tent was also useless. He needed an escape, an advantage, he needed fire.

"Come near me, and I'll kill you just as I killed him!" The woman shrieked, her voice shrill with adrenaline and thick with Southern dialect, her blades a twisting blur like hummingbird's wings. Dog was smaller than the mutt she had just dispatched. Perhaps she really thought she should could take him.

Dog bared his fangs. He darted behind her spinning blades and seized both her slender wrists in his large taloned grasp, squeezing viciously tight so her swords loosed from her hands and fell to the tent floor. She cried out as he wrenched her arms, pulling her against him, his sharp yellow teeth grazing the tender edge of her ear.

"Want to live?"

"Myrta gahaghi," she hissed. "I knew worse monsters than you before I was born."

She was rigid and shaking in his hands. She smelled of myrrh, fear, and the musk of wild animals. Her life surged through her blood, begging him to taste it.

"Where is fire?"

"The wagons."

"Show me."

He released her arms, and she pulled them in, cradling her bruised wrists and glancing toward her swords where they lay near the headless monster and the young man gurgling his last breath.

Dog snarled, "Leave them."

Without another glance back, she darted for the tent door, Dog at her side. Three of the pack appeared in the doorway. Dog grabbed the nearest one by the skull with both hands, bringing his knee up and slamming the head down so hard the skull cracked between the two like a green chestnut. The other two charged. He punched one, knuckles forward at the bridge of its nose, crushing the nasal bone and rupturing the eyes, ducked the slash of the other, grabbing its arm and pulling its momentum through, throwing the monster onto its back, then driving his heel down into its skull with a wet crunch.

Dog turned back to the woman and saw the flicker of her skirts disappearing around the corner of the tent. No time to chase her down. She'd said there was fire in the wagons. Out past the tents, Dog saw a promising glow.

"Puppy dog!" Dog glanced back to see Horse advancing on him, flanked by a score of weathered hounds. Horse hissed, flicking a gray tongue across his plank-like teeth. The hammer was dripping blood. "You're MINE."

Dog sprinted for the glow, vaulting over a mutt feeding on an old woman, pushing off the top of a wagon with both hands, carrying himself over to stone below. Horse and the hounds howled behind him. Dog rolled under another wagon, leaped up, ripped through the side canvas, and pulled himself up and through.

Inside the wagon, a lit lantern had been tipped over, abandoned, its flame spilling out and licking at the fibers of a wool blanket. It was a good start, but Dog needed more. He glanced about and saw there, tucked into an alcove in the corner, a little copper oil can.

Dog lunged for the oil can, grabbed it, and ripped off the top.

Horse's voice called from outside the wagon. "You're surrounded, puppy dog! Are you coming out, or do we need to haul you out by the scruff of your neck?"

Dog swung the open can, slinging oil around the wagon, across the floorboards and the canvas overhead, across the flaming blanket, the fire splashing up eagerly at the easy fuel, flaring to the roof, and crawling across the floor and ceiling, engulfing the wagon in flames. Dog dropped the empty can and waited as the air filled with fire.

The pack would not come to get him. The Master had given them an aversion to the light of day, and they could not look into the heat of the blaze. He waited, eyes closed, until his clothes caught, his hair shriveling off his scalp, his skin blistering and splitting in the heat. Only when the wagon was fully alight did Dog run forward, drop out the back of the wagon, turn, and shove, running with it, propelling the burning wagon, a blazing torch, into the side of a nearby tent. The oiled canvas caught quickly, flame rippling up green and silver cloth, the fire spreading.

Animals screamed. The pack shrieked and averted their eyes. In the center of the furnace, Dog burned. But he would last until the sun. He would heal, and he would survive.

SEVEN

"Please, Papa? Please?"

"Soolie, you need to stay home and get better. How is your ankle feeling this morning?"

"It feels fine. See?"

"What about your head? Does anything hurt?"

"No pain! I feel great. Papa, please let me come?"

"I don't think you should be traveling right now."

"I'm all better, I promise! I haven't had any more nightmares."

"Soolie, stop asking. Now brush your hair and wash up before breakfast."

"I'm going to miss you."

"You always love staying with your Aunt Ellena."

"But I'd rather go with you."

"I'll only be gone six or seven days."

"That's such a loooong time. Take me with you?"

"Soolie."

"Mama would let me come."

"You know that isn't going to work."

"Papa! I could help. I could hold the horses while you make deliveries!"

"That's enough. You're staying with Ellena, and that's final. One more word, and you aren't going to the harvest festival either. Now go wash up."

THE HARVEST FESTIVAL was held at a large empty barn that now functioned as the meeting place for Hob Glen and the surrounding area. Farmers and artisans from all around the village arrived with their families in carts piled with produce, crafts, and baked goods. Inside the Barn, rows of hay bales serving as makeshift tables were quickly covered with quilts and sheets and loaded with wares and home goods for bartering and selling. Knitted blankets, beaded bangles, carved walking staves, rag petticoats. There were jars of canned prunes and peaches, bramble berry preserves, wild honey, applesauce, tomatoes, and assortments of pickles. Bags of candied fruit and nuts piled next to kegs of smoked and dried meats while wheels of white cheese studded with nuts and herbs lay near shiny bottled cordials beneath racks of hanging sugar candies that clustered on strings like brightly colored gems.

But the real celebration was outside.

Behind the Barn, pigs, chickens, and cobs of corn were roasting over fire pits that hid baking squash and potatoes in their coals. There were crocks of fresh cream butter, barrels of sweet cider, and heaps of apples and raw nuts for roasting after dark.

There were also games. Pumpkin tossing, the carving contest, apple bobbing, bean bag for the little children, and in the nearby corn field, the hay ride circled a meandering continuous loop.

Soolie licked at the butter that dripped off the corn cob and down her fingers, sweet hot and delicious. This was her third one. She'd been eating a lot lately. Ellena had congratulated her, saying it looked like she'd finally started to put on a little weight, but Soolie knew if she gained too much more weight, she'd outgrow her dresses, and she wouldn't be able to get a new one until next year. Fortunately, her green dress was loose and flowy, with long sleeves that covered the funny wrinkly skin on her wrist and pockets big enough to stuff apples in.

Soolie took a big bite of the hot sweet corn, the kernels popping against her teeth, buttery juices running down her chin. She dabbed her face with a rag napkin before they could drip on her dress.

It was a rare moment where she was entirely free to occupy herself as she saw fit. Right now, Papa was in the Barn bartering for canned goods, lamp oil, and soap, and Ellena, who had helped to organize the celebration, was rushing about refilling cider barrels, assigning judges for the canned goods contest and mitigating display disputes. Any other year, Soolie would be seizing the chance to run about the festival sniffing soaps and oils, bobbing for apples, dancing in the firelight, and finding errands to run for Ellena. But tonight she didn't feel like it. Papa was leaving for Ravus in the morning, and she still hadn't figured out how to get him to take her along.

It was so frustrating. Soolie scowled and picked at the corn stuck between her teeth.

She *had* to go. Ravus was where the carnival from the Southern Lands had gone, and she had to ask them about the fat woman and the thing in her dreams. But the more she pressed, the more adamant Papa became that she *wasn't* going. But she *had* to. But she couldn't. But she had to.

Soolie spat a piece of corn hull into the dirt and sighed. Being a daughter was impossible. Especially with a father like Papa.

Beside the Barn, a man was sawing briskly at the strings of a fiddle while young people danced. A little girl up on her father's shoulders waved her hands about and giggled while her father's legs pranced a jig.

Of course she couldn't tell Papa about the nightmare creature. He would never believe her, and if he did... Soolie thought of the dark circles under Papa's eyes, eyes that watched from the rocker by the fire as she tried to fall asleep. Besides, Soolie didn't even know for sure the creature was still here. There hadn't been any sign of it since it had invaded her memories a moon ago. Maybe it had decided she wasn't what it wanted. Whatever it wanted. Maybe it had moved on. Maybe Soolie could forget about dream creatures and just enjoy the evening.

More people young and old were joining the dance. On the other side of the fire, Soolie could see Winny Baldrick dragging someone into the revelry. Winny was wearing the tight petticoat dress that she had been wearing the last time Soolie saw her, but the neckline seemed even lower cut than before, pushing up her breasts so they mounded, well-shadowed in the firelight. Soolie heard Winny's caustic giggle and scrunched her nose. Winny had a horrible laugh, like someone was squeezing her by the chest and forcing it out too fast, too loud and shrill. Soolie rolled her eyes and was about to look away, but then she saw the subject of Winny's attentions. It was Bernad.

Winny dragged on his arm, then let go to spin, giggling, her skirts flaring, her flaxen curls bouncing around her chest. Bernad didn't seem much for dancing, but he grinned and watched her, basking in the attention.

Of course Winny would like Bernad. They were the obvious match. The Peligs and the Baldricks, both well established members of Hob Glen, both families with money and connections back in Ravus. It was a good thing Soolie didn't care for either of them.

"Soolie!" Ellena ran up from the direction of the Barn entry. She was wearing a red and black gingham dress under her gray wool cloak and had let her hair down, pulling it back at the temples with a white ribbon that nestled in her soft frizzy curls. Soolie thought she looked absolutely beautiful.

"Soolie!" Ellena held out her hand. "What are you doing sitting here all alone? Come, let's dance, you and me!"

"Elly dear!" It was Mrs. Svenson.

Ellena called over her shoulder, "Just a moment!"

"Elly!" Mrs. Svenson hollered, "Mrs. Dowright put quince in her pumpkin pie, and Miss Pegru says quince in a pumpkin pie makes it a fruit pie that belongs in the fruit pie competition, and Mrs. Dowright says it's still fundamentally a pumpkin pie despite the quince, and of course I told them that quince does not belong in a pumpkin pie, it has never belonged in a pumpkin pie, and that that pie doesn't belong in any competition! To which they said…"

"Ugh!" Ellena rolled her eyes, ran forward and kissed Soolie on the forehead. "I have to go."

"Okay."

Ellena rushed off toward Mrs. Svenson, then turned to call back to Soolie. "Enter the pumpkin carving contest!"

"I don't know…!" Soolie shouted back.

"It starts in a minute!" Ellena was pointing towards the corner of the Barn where a long row of pumpkins sat on hay bales beneath the watchful gaze of a scarecrow.

Soolie looked down at her half-eaten corn, then up at where Winny was still giggling, swishing, and spinning around Bernad. Didn't she ever get dizzy? Well, if Ellena thought Soolie should enter the pumpkin carving, Soolie would. She wasn't accomplishing anything by sulking. Just as long as no one told Papa. He was nervous letting her go to sleep, much less carving something up with a knife. But since it was Ellena's idea…

Soolie tossed her corn into the grass and walked over to the pumpkins to find the perfect one. Several young people had already taken their places, standing guard over their chosen gourd. Soolie didn't even know what she wanted to carve. She approached a small unassuming pumpkin and studied the blank orange surface, searching for inspiration.

"Hey," a voice spoke in her ear.

Soolie spun and almost punched someone in the nose.

"Whoa! Tight wired much? Can't a bloke give 's greets?"

Bernad. The older boy grinned that lopsided grin and ruffled his hair. He must really like the feel of his own hair, Soolie thought.

"I thought you were dancing with Winny Baldrick," Soolie said, turning back to study the pumpkin.

"Oh?" He hopped up on the hay bale and looked down at her. "Were you watching us?"

He was too close. Soolie stubbornly refused to back off, turning her pumpkin to get a good look at it from every angle. It looked pretty much the same from every angle.

"Hard not to notice," Soolie said. "Winny was spinning so much, I almost hurled just watching."

He rested his chin on his hand and smirked at her. "She thinks it shows off her hair."

"And what do you think?" Soolie asked primly.

"Oh, I weren't watching her hair." He flashed his teeth wickedly.

Soolie decided she'd carve a tree into the pumpkin. Like the oak tree in the town square.

"I haven't seen you in a while," he said.

"Hmm," Soolie responded. An oak tree with a single leaf, the last leaf, falling toward the ground. Mama had always loved the falling of the leaves. They used to collect them and then drop them one by one into the fireplace.

"Do you really not like me?"

He was leaning in towards her, his face only a foot away from hers. His mouth was set in a serious line, but his eyes were mocking.

"Where are your friends?" She responded.

"Who, Hobby and Kip?" he rocked back. "Oh, rot, I never mind. I think Hobby's tossing pumpkins, burly skag. Wherever Hobby is, Kip ain't far, you know. Right skew, those two. And you? You gonna carve a pumpkin?"

"Yes, are you?"

"Naw," he scoffed, hopping off the hay. "Pumpkin carving's for crawlers. Later, Beetch."

Soolie stiffened as he walked away. She heard a squealing aggressive giggle behind her and didn't turn to look.

Nine young people entered the carving contest. It turned out the prize was a set of water paints, and Soolie saw why Ellena wanted her to enter. Soolie would love to have a set of water paints. Soolie took off her cloak, folded it up, and laid it out of the way against the Barn. She was ready.

"Contestants, begin your carving!"

The carving started really well. Soolie cut off the top of her pumpkin with the saw tooth knife and scooped out the slimy stringy innards with a spoon.

"Go, Soolie!" Ellena was watching.

"Soolie, be careful!" And so was Papa.

Soolie glanced up to see both of them, back-lit by firelight, Ellena clapping her hands, eagerly cheering her on. Papa looking stern, his brow dark and heavy.

Soolie tried to focus. There was only so much time for the contest, and she wanted her pumpkin to be perfect. First she drew her oak tree on the pumpkin in chalk, licking her thumb and rubbing out the branches until she'd drawn them just right. Then she carved out the trunk of the tree in one big piece, reaching inside the pumpkin and pushing the long thin rectangle out with her fingers. Next she started carving the branches, and that's when the knife slipped.

She was grasping the knife blade with both hands, sawing smoothly through the firm pumpkin flesh, when suddenly the knife hit a soft spot, cutting a deep gash through the pumpkin, the knife slipping quickly through and sticking straight into the hay bale. It was just an accident. She was okay. But the pumpkin was ruined.

"Soolie!" Papa ran up to her. Soolie let go of the knife, and Papa grabbed her hands, examining them. "Are you okay? Are you hurt?"

"I'm fine!" Soolie tried to pull away. Everyone was watching.

"What happened?"

"The knife just slipped, I'm fine."

"Well, no wonder the knife slipped," Papa exclaimed angrily. "This pumpkin is rotten. It isn't safe. Who picked these out? You could have been hurt."

"I did," Ellena spoke up, stepping forward. "I picked out the pumpkins for the contest. It's my fault. I didn't notice any soft spots, I'm sorry."

"She could have been hurt," Papa snapped.

No one was carving anymore. Soolie wished she could crawl into her pumpkin and hide.

"Papa, I looked at the pumpkin, and I didn't see any soft spots either."

Papa put his hand on her shoulder. "Come on, Soolie. We should go home. Go get your things."

Ellena pleaded with him, "Please, Silas, stay."

"Soolie, put on your cloak."

"Papa, I don't want to go."

"Now, Soolie."

I'm never going be one of these people, Soolie thought. Who dance and laugh, play games and go to school. I'm just going to dwindle away. No one will come looking for me. No one will miss me. One day, Papa's going to lock me up in a cellar and never let me out.

"Now, Soolie."

With all the people looking at them, and Ellena standing bleary-eyed, Soolie turned and picked up her cloak.

"Silas, please," Ellena tried again.

"I'm sorry, Ellena," he said, not looking at her. "We need to go home."

From off by the fire, the fiddler picked up a reeling tune. Around them, the carving recommenced, and those that still watched them looked askance and feigned indifference.

"At least let Soolie stay," Ellena offered. "She hasn't even been on the hay ride yet. I can bring her back before it gets too late."

"You let her carve a pumpkin, Ellena." Silas looked at her now, accusing. "You didn't even ask me."

"It's pumpkin carving, Silas, I didn't think I had to."

"You should have," he said. "Come on, Soolie, let's go home."

He turned to his daughter, but Soolie was gone.

EIGHT

Soolie pelted through the tall corn, arms up around her head to protect her face from the whipping leaves. It had grown dark, and the field was tall, but it was also the most likely place for her to have run to. Her ankle throbbed, but was holding strong. She knew they were going to come looking for her. Well, Papa and Ellena. She doubted anyone else would care. And she just needed to get far enough that they wouldn't find her right away. She needed to be alone.

She broke through the corn and stumbled on the change of earth, pitching forward and landing hard on her hands and knees in the middle of the hay ride path. Something rustled in the stalks behind her. Papa had found her already. She scrambled back to her feet and pushed through the corn on the other side of the path.

"Hey! Wait!"

Faster. She had to run faster. To get away just for a little bit. Dear lands, just let her get away for a little bit. Away from all the pain and the fear, everyone looking so worried. Papa staying up by the fire watching her every night as she tried to sleep, Papa examining the marks on her wrist every morning, Papa asking, 'How did you sleep? How do you feel? Are you sure you're all right? Is there anything you want to tell me?' Right now, the people were worse than the monsters.

"Stop!"

Faster.

Someone grabbed her by the back of the cloak and pulled. Soolie tried to break free, but they hung on, dragging at her neck. She reached up, fumbling at the hook clasp, struggling with the choking weight as a hand grabbed her shoulder. The clasp split beneath her fingers, the cloak tearing away from her neck, but an arm came around the other side, wrapping around her chest. She wrenched away, her footing giving beneath her again, and she tumbled to the ground, taking the person heavily down on top of her.

Soolie tried to twist off her belly and onto her back, but her loose cloak was tangled about her feet.

"Sock it, Beetch! Stop!"

Hands helped her, turning her over, and she was on her back looking up at Bernad straddling on top of her.

"Get off of me," she hissed.

"Yeah, sure." He lifted a leg over to sit on the earth beside her.

"Leave me alone." Soolie untangled her cloak from her feet; it was covered in grime and muck.

"I just thought, when your Pap comes looking for you, you might not want to be found."

She stopped. He had her attention.

"I got a place you can hide." He stood to his feet and offered her his hand. "Come on."

Soolie considered it, then accepted it, letting him help her to her feet.

"Follow me."

"You smother her!"

"I'm helping her!"

"What, by not sleeping and eating? You think she doesn't see what it does to you?"

"She's my daughter! I'll do whatever I have to!"

They hadn't fought like this in a long time. No one had followed them to look for Soolie, and Silas hadn't asked. Now they were thrashing through the corn yelling at each other. Soolie would be able to hear them coming a mile off.

"This is not the time for this!" Silas roared.

"Then when is?" she snapped back.

"How about when my daughter's not missing?"

"Your daughter's not missing, she's hiding! From you!"

Silas stopped. Ellena stopped. They faced each other in the corn stalks, breathing hard, anger flashing between them like static. No one was speaking carefully now.

Silas jabbed a finger at her, "You have no idea! You have not seen the things I've seen. You were not there, Ellena, you were never there!"

"Because you won't let me!"

It was a truth both of them already knew, and neither was ready to have said.

They panted at each other. The sounds of the harvest festival were far off, and the silence was loud.

Silas turned away first and started rustling again through the corn. "We have to find Soolie."

"Silas!" Once again, Ellena found herself running after him. "Silas, you're right. I haven't been there. And maybe something is up with Soolie, I don't know. But I do know, if Soolie feels like you can't handle whatever she's going through, she's going to start keeping it from you!"

"Soolie!" Silas called. "Soolie! Where are you, Soolie!"

He knew she already was.

BERNAD LED HER A LONG WAYS. Out of the corn, then down through the grass fields, running. Every once in a while he would glance back over his shoulder with a grin, his teeth white in the moonlight, to see if she was managing to keep up.

It wasn't fair. He was in a tunic, jacket, and britches. She was in a dress and heavy cloak. Her lungs burned, her chest ached, her legs and ankle felt wobbly, but she didn't stop. She thought they were circling Hob Glen, but she wasn't sure. Papa never let her out of the house after dark, much less out to the fields. She didn't recognize anything.

When she saw the long stretch of trees, she knew she was right: they had circled Hob Glen. Papa would never find her now. She tried not to think about Papa. She growled with her breath, trying to tap into her frustration, anger, and betrayal to give her feet speed. She wasn't a runner, and her stubborn streak alone wasn't going to be able to carry her much farther.

They entered the trees, branches blocking out the moonlight, dark shadows obscuring the uneven ground. Just a little bit farther, she told herself, though she didn't really know.

"We're here."

Bernad stood, his arms spread out like a king welcoming her to the great hall, but all she saw beyond him was a small clearing and a tree.

"This is it?" Soolie tried to sound casual while desperately gulping at the burning night air. "All that running for a suckin' tree?"

"Not just any tree!" Bernad said indignantly. "MY tree."

It was a big tree, a grandfather evergreen with bulging roots that split out from the trunk and burrowed into the earth.

"Come on." Bernad offered her his hand and, with less hesitation this time, she took it.

He helped her around the tree, over a twist of roots here, then ducking a low branch, around to the other side. Two large roots heaved parallel out from the trunk at shoulder height, and someone had pegged a large piece of oil cloth over the top to make a structure that was half tent, half tree.

"Wait here."

He dropped her hand at the entrance and ducked into the dark mouth of the oil cloth. Soolie was still trying to catch her breath. Her muscles had started shaking from the run. When she looked straight up, she could see a little window of spangley stars like white sand sprinkled on a piece of black slate. The trees at the edge of the clearing were a black foreboding wall.

A warm yellow light bloomed from the opening of the tent and Bernad's face reappeared next to his hand holding up a glass lantern.

"Well, come on."

He disappeared back inside, and Soolie lifted up her skirts and cloak, ducked down, and followed.

It was larger than she had expected, smaller than her loft at home, but not horribly so. Instead of ending at the base of the tree, the opening recessed beneath the trunk like a small cave. Someone— Bernad, she assumed—had dug out the dirt and packed the floor with sawdust. A sailor's chest was tucked in the corner and, along the opposite side, canvas bedding and a wool blanket were rolled out on a box frame to keep them off the sawdust. Bernad hung the lantern from a nail sunk in the tree root and sat cross-legged on the bed. Soolie saw he had taken his boots off and set them against the wall near the doorway.

"What do ya think?"

"Where did you get all this stuff?"

He shrugged. "My pap owns the general store. I can get anything."

"You stole it."

He grinned. "Stop standing in the door like a thick skull. Take off your shoes."

Soolie bent over awkwardly, undoing her laces and loosening her boots. Papa made these boots. She pulled them off and put them at the door. Bernad patted the blanket beside him, and Soolie came closer and sat down on the far edge of the bedding, putting as much space between them as she could.

Bernad sighed contentedly, tilting his head back.

"Isn't it ballard? Right ballard."

"Do Hobby and Kip know about this place?"

Bernad made a face. "Those sucks? You think I'd let them near a glorious thing like this? Not like. This place is too beaut for jits like them."

"You let me in."

"Yeah, well," he winked at her. "Don't mess it."

He was watching her now, a bemused confidence on his face, taking his time. She studied the oil cloth ceiling. She wondered how dry this place stayed in the rain. He was still watching her.

"You wrinkle your nose when you're nervous."

"No I don't," she shot back.

He grinned at her. "Naw. You don't."

Soolie could feel the blood flushing her neck and face. That happened when you had been running.

He inched a little closer on the blanket. She should have given herself some room to move. The only place to go now was onto the sawdust.

This was all very confusing. Soolie wasn't used to anyone wanting to talk to her, much less show her secret forts, and he made her feel all anxious. She had finally slowed her breathing, but her heart was still catching up. He had freckles on his nose. She hadn't noticed that before.

"So, I guess your Pap likes to yell."

Soolie blinked and looked down at her hands in her lap. "Sometimes. He's just worried's all."

"Why's he so worried?"

Soolie twisted her dress around her fingers. "I dunno. Isn't that what parents do?"

He shrugged. "Mine don't."

"No?"

"Naw. Pap's always at the store tryin' to avoid Mam. And Mam's always trying to tell him how he should be more like her sister's blo' who's some spak-eating councilman in Ravus or other. Pap pretty much leaves me alone. And Mam. Well, she's no bother if she can't find me."

"Ah." It was all she could think to say.

"Gotcha somethin'." He fished into his jacket pocket and pulled out something long and rectangular wrapped in brown paper.

"What is it?"

He tossed it in her lap. "Open it, goose."

As soon as Soolie held the thin rectangular box in her hand, she guessed. He hadn't. She slipped her finger under a fold of the paper, popping loose the glue that held down the corners. Pop. Rip. Pop. She unfolded the paper from around the box and swept the paper off her lap and onto the floor. In her hands she held a little case of water paints.

"You stole them."

He shrugged. "You get hung up on that, don't you? They're yours now."

"I didn't win them." She pushed the stolen paints towards him, and he grabbed her hand, holding it tightly around the little case, his fingers gripping ever so close to the marks on her wrist.

He leaned in, studying her eyes. "Hey, I'm not taking them. Paint's for crawlers. You deserve them."

She tried to jerk her hand back, but he held it tight. He was going to pull her in. Pull her towards him. Her heart pulsed in her ears.

"No," she said, "I really don't."

"Yes," he said, leaning in. "You do."

His face was coming too close and it kept coming; he wasn't going to stop. Soolie ducked. She felt his lips brush her ear, and she pushed off away from him hard. In a moment she was on the floor in the sawdust crouched against the tree root of the opposite wall.

The paints had fallen out of their case and lay scattered in the sawdust. Bernad wasn't looking at her. He was bent over where she had just been, his hand clenching the blanket in a fist. His jaw set, his brow low over his eyes.

Soolie wasn't sure what he had just tried to do. She didn't know these things. Had she said or done something? He hung out with girls like Winny Baldrick, and maybe there were rules and ways that people interacted that she wasn't used to, but it certainly felt like he had been about to do something. Something that she didn't quite feel like she wanted him to have done. She could still feel the soft sweep of his lips against her ear, and she wanted to take her nails and scratch the feeling away.

"I'm…" She didn't want to say it. She was in a tent in the woods in the middle of the night, and she wasn't sure she knew her way home. "I'm sorry."

"No matter," he said dully. He didn't mean it either.

He got off the bedding and reached toward her. She flinched away, but he was only grabbing his shoes. He began slipping them on.

"Where are you going?"

"Just need to clear my head," he said, and he grabbed the lantern and ducked out of the tent into the night.

Soolie waited, not knowing whether or not she wanted him to come back. It was cold, and the ground was hard, but she refused to touch the bedding. She wrapped her cloak around her shoulders and huddled in the dark.

No one knew where she was. Papa was going to be so worried. He was never going to let her out of the house again. She was so unearthly miserable. She hated herself.

The night was long.

Once Soolie felt nearly certain Bernad wasn't coming back, she passed into a fitful doze, too uneasy to lay down, hunching against the curved tree root wall. Time and time again, she woke up to darkness. By the time she opened her eyes to gray dawn leaking in through the tent opening, she was sore, grimy, and exhausted.

Soolie stood painfully. She pulled on her boots, laced them up, and stepped out into the sharp morning air.

In the early light, the clearing looked less formidable. The trees were just trees, and the grass beneath her boots was stiff with a light frost. She shivered and longed for a hot cup of tea. Perhaps she should go to Ellena's first. If she was lucky, Ellena might give her a hot cup and something to eat before Papa arrived. If Ellena wasn't with Papa still looking for her right now. If Soolie could find her way back to town.

Soolie walked around to the other side of the clearing. She checked that the sun was indeed rising in what she thought to be the east and began walking in a roughly northerly direction, what she hoped was the direction back to town. She walked for long enough that it made her nervous, but once in while she would notice a broken branch or a torn bit of moss, and she felt relatively certain she wasn't the first person to have come this way, and that gave her hope.

At last the trees thinned, and Soolie stepped out into a wide open field that stretched to the distant back ends of houses facing away toward Main Street. Just ahead sat the familiar blue and white structure of the schoolhouse, and waiting outside to file through its doors were the children of Ravus.

Now that she knew where she was, she was almost home. She could walk back along the tree line, cut up past old Mr. Hobbin's place to avoid being seen by the Svensons, and run across the street to the bakery. She was almost there. She was so cold, tired, and sore, she wouldn't even mind if Papa yelled and cried as long as he let her sit down with a blanket first. Soolie untangled her cloak and ankles from a patch of bramble runners and turned to duck back into the tree cover before she was seen.

Across the field, someone hooted. It was followed by a hawk-call and a shout, "Hey! There she is!"

It was too late. Soolie wasn't in the mood to deal with Winny or Bernad and their friends, but she'd be cucked if she let them watch her skulk away. Soolie squared her shoulders, lifted her chin, and set her feet straight for the schoolhouse.

She imagined what a picture she must make: hair mussed and disheveled, her dress and cloak crumpled and smeared with dirt, her face gritty and puffy. Soolie thought of Mama. Mama always held her head high, no matter how people stared at her bandages or the way she wore her cloak in the middle of the summer sun. Mama never seemed to care what other people thought. Mama was impervious.

The students gathered on the edge of the field, watching as she marched through the grass toward them. They were all there now. The girl with her twin siblings. Winny and her friends. And there were Hobby, Kip, and Bernad.

As Soolie drew closer, so did her feeling of unease. Everyone was watching her. Winny's friends whispered behind their hands, and Kip hooted and punched Bernad in the arm while Bernad grinned smugly like the kid who just snagged the last candied plum on Solar day.

"So it's true," Winny sniffed, her arms folded primly beneath her tightly bodiced breasts.

Soolie told her feet to ignore them, to keep walking, but their judgmental gazes snared her like spider threads. She stopped. The students half circled her. Why was everyone looking at her that way? Like any moment they might declare her a blood sorceress, beat her with white willow switches, and light her on fire.

Keep walking, Soolie thought.

She stepped forward, but Winny was in her way.

Winny face contorted in an ugly sneer. "Skag." She spat in Soolie's face.

Soolie didn't wipe away the spittle. Anger flashed white hot behind her eyes. Acceptance and detachment never were her strengths. Sorry, Mama.

"Get away from me."

Winny flinched. "Your little trick might scare off Miss Pont, but you don't frighten me," she sneered, but she backed away.

Soolie was exhausted, she was hurting, she was angry. Everything was getting skagging hellish, and she had quite enough to deal with without these malicious petty children's games. She didn't know whether she was going to cry or scream.

Show no weakness. Win. Her own thoughts came back to her like a voice in her head.

Fine, she thought. If this was what had to happen, this was what was going to happen.

Another wad of spit hit her upside the face, and she heard Skip and Hobby hoot and slap hands.

Gain control.

"What is going on here?" she asked.

A fire burned inside of her, and as she grabbed a hold of it, she was not weak. She was electric.

"You're a skag, that's what," Winny sniped from a safe distance. "Bernad told us all about how you lured him back into the woods."

"And?"

"Let him cuck sack you!" Kip crowed, excited to have a part.

Hobby grabbed his own crotch crassly. "I got a better piece for ya."

"Ha ha!" Kip yelped.

Soolie didn't look at them. She looked at Bernad. Standing on the outside of the circle at a safe distance, as if he was too good for all of them. Arms crossed, smirking, not saying a word.

She walked towards him, and Kip automatically dodged out of the way. She stepped close enough that she could count every freckle on his nose and look into his smug mocking eyes.

"Is this true?"

Bernad smirked his well-practiced smirk, his eyes darting sideways toward Hobby, Kip, Winny, all watching, waiting.

He looked back at her. "Go home to your Pap, little skag. I only wanted you once."

That was all she needed to hear. The fire in Soolie blazed sharp and white and hot. Bernad had just a moment where he saw the flash of white in her eyes, the white light that had terrified Miss Pont those several weeks ago, the white light that made Winny flinch and back away. The light that was just a tiny flash, a flicker of a window into a blazing sun.

Soolie smiled.

Now, win.

Soolie punched Bernad in the face with every bit of strength she had, and he smushed beneath her fist like a rotten pumpkin.

NINE

Felice heard the children outside, shrieking and shouting. It was probably just Hobby or Kip at their wicked antics again, pulling up the girls' skirts or shoving a younger boy's face into a cow pudding. Felice sat behind her desk, pursed her lips and thumbed through the faded text book for today's numbers lesson. Inside the schoolhouse was her domain, but outside her classroom, students had a dreadful tendency to turn into children.

They were still screaming. Felice checked her pocket watch. They had six minutes before they would be late for class. She would wait another six minutes.

"Miss Pont!" Misy Swin was in the doorway, tears streaming down her cheeks. "Oh, Miss Pont! Winny has fainted, and Bernad! He's been horribly hurt!"

This wasn't the first time Winny Baldrick had fainted. That girl laced her bodice so tightly, she was like to faint if she caught the hiccups. But the Pelig boy. Felice stood up quickly. If something happened to him, Mergo Pelig would make sure Felice never taught in Hob Glen again.

Felice pushed her chair back, taking the time to neatly tuck the brown paper cover of the book into the pages to mark her place at today's lesson.

"Hurry, Miss Pont!" Misy cried.

"Please, Misy," Felice set the book down with both hands. "Compose yourself."

Misy nodded, made a desperate squeaking sound and hurried out of the way so her teacher could walk around her desk and step through the schoolhouse doorway.

Children were wailing, milling and scattering. Something really had happened. Lands preserve them the Pelig boy hadn't died. Felice lifted her skirts and hurried around to the side of the schoolhouse. There was Winny Baldrick, collapsed on the ground, her head resting in the lap of her other friend, Clarel. Misy ran past to throw her arms around Clarel and fuss over Winny.

Beyond them, Felice could see the troublesome Skip and Hobby. When they were the responsible party, they either stood by cackling and congratulating one another, or they ran off to duck responsibility. Instead, Skip was squealing like a piglet and hiding behind Hobby, who was shaking and cussing up a vile cloud.

Off to the side, Felice saw her. The Beetch girl. Felice hesitated, not wanting to come any closer. There was something terrifyingly wrong with the Beetch girl. Felice had heard it in her voice, seen it flashing in her eyes, and had never wanted to see the child again. Now, filthy and disheveled, Soolie Beetch was here, standing dispassionate and silent as a grave phantom. And at her feet was Bernad Pelig, writhing in the dirt, squalling as if in horrible agony, his voice distorted, his hands to his face.

"What happened here?" Felice demanded, keeping her distance.

The Beetch girl didn't move.

"Get." Felice made vague shooing motions, trying to get her to back away from the older boy. "Go. Get out of here."

The Beetch girl looked up, and her eyes were distant, her expression vacant. She stepped back and drifted toward the schoolhouse. Keeping a wary eye, Felice advanced, placing the body of the Pelig boy between them. She knelt down next to him. He wouldn't stop struggling.

"Stop," she snapped. "Stop moving about. I can't see."

With a distorted howling cry, he took his hand away from his face just long enough to push her away, and she saw it. Where the one side of his face was still flush and pink and young, the other side of his face was shrunken like old rawhide, dry and plastered to his skull, the bloodless lips pulled tight across his teeth, the eyelid shriveled and retreating into the bone, baring a gaping socket where a withered raisin-like polyp stuck to the base of the crater. They both screamed.

Soolie sat beside the schoolhouse. She didn't answer any questions. She didn't speak. She didn't move. After she'd punched Bernad, everything had happened so fast. She had felt so raw inside, and when she'd touched him, it had been a horrible rush like the shock of cold, the rage of heat, a much needed drink of water, a desperate breath that rippled through her belly. And he had dropped to the ground screaming, and then the teacher was there, and Soolie had walked over to the school in a daze and let the noisy troubled people carousel around her.

She was aware when Doc Wilkins arrived and Mr. and Mrs. Pelig arrived, and other people arrived, some to stare, some to take their children home. She was aware when they loaded Bernad up on a stretcher, though from all his thrashing, it seemed he was capable of moving just fine. Then Papa and Ellena were running towards her, and Soolie closed her eyes and let everything drift away.

She was suspended in blankness. It was easier to think of it as white, but it wasn't white. It wasn't anything but void and the feeling that a thousand invisible eyes were peering in under her skin.

"Show yourself! I know you're here!"

The blankness before her began to ripple and crackle thin, fragile skin oozing light like an infection that burst apart, erupting into a violent blaze that seared and assaulted her eyes. Soolie gritted her teeth, glaring into the nova. There, in the center of the blaze hung an amorphous form that shifted like the reflection of a man upon troubled water, and where its heart should have been, dwelt a deep and hungry darkness that seethed and pulsed as if threatening to devour her whole.

As quickly as it began, the ripples resolved and the fire pulled in. Light solidified into human form and extinguished, stepping forward to face her; not Mama, not a monster, but a child.

It was a small child, a girl of about nine years dressed in a pale yellow tunic. Long wavy hair like dark bramble berry juice tumbled over smooth bronze shoulders, and startlingly large honey-amber eyes looked up through feathery black lashes. It was the most beautiful child Soolie had ever seen, but the expression was the same: cold, predatory, and still. A demon. Was this the image of a daughter someone had loved and lost? How many faces of dead loved ones had this thing stolen to get what it wanted?

Soolie held its frozen gaze and took a deep breath to still her shaking chest.

What would Mama do? Mama was always strong and quiet. She waged her battles without struggle: fighting for the possible, but accepting the inevitable with serenity and grace. Then again, as far as Soolie knew, Mama had never been infested by a demon that shrunk people's faces, and Soolie had never been good at being passive. She was not serene and she was not her mother. Somewhere beyond the mask of a little girl's face, a black-hearted figure still burned, and Soolie had to face it alone. Well then. She would just have to be better at being Soolie.

"You hurt someone."

The one you call Bernad? I did not. The child's voice intoned flat, stilted and wrong.

"I think he would disagree."

He is meaningless. You are the one who wished him harm.

"I did not!" Soolie snapped.

You did.

Soolie swallowed back anger that rose in her throat like bile. She couldn't let it shake her.

"What *are* you?"

You are the wrong vessel. It tilted its head, the soft hair shifting, hanging heavy and glossy. *The time has come for me to take flesh, and you are unfitting.*

Soolie stiffened at the abrupt turn. 'Take flesh?' What did it mean, 'take flesh?'

You wish to be rid of me. I also wish to be rid of you. We are not at odds. There is no need for anyone else to come to harm. Bring me to a better vessel, and I will leave you.

It said it as if it were simple. And it was horribly simple.

Soolie felt a sick rot turning in the pit of her stomach. What had she been expecting? A battle of wits? A series of riddles? A jape's trick? But this wasn't one of Ellena's stories. Instead it was making her an offer. A way out of the nightmare. Not a trick. A price.

Younger than you, but physically capable. It looked at her expectantly. *The soul must be malleable and the body able to be of use to me.*

"You want me to get you a crawler."

A walker, it corrected.

It wanted her to find a child to take her place. Soolie was pleased to find she could hate it even more. She smiled.

"You underestimate me."

This is in your best interest.

Soolie nodded slowly, feeling her determination grow hard and bitter. She *would* track down the Southern Lands Carnival. She would find a way. And if they couldn't tell her how to destroy it, she would find someone who could. And once she knew what black pit of underworld this creature came from, she would break it apart and throw those pieces back into that darkness one by one.

"Then I suppose," she said smoothly, "we should keep an open dialogue."

It blinked slowly, long lashes sweeping its cheeks, the movement too large on its tiny face. *The one called 'Punka' was strong once. She resisted my will and brought corruption upon herself. My need for a final vessel is great. I do not experience regret the way you do, and I will do whatever is necessary.*

The little girl held her gaze and morphed like wet clay. Ellena stood before her, eyes wide and afraid. *Soolie?* Then Papa looked down accusing, cheeks gaunt, raw-rimmed eyes wet with tears. *Get me what I need, baby girl. There is no time. The Dead Man is rising.*

Dead man? What dead man?

It didn't answer. She was alone, but for the emptiness that surrounded her, watching.

TEN

Silas looked down at his little girl. She looked so small with her head on the pillow, the quilt pulled up to her chin. She also looked so much like her mother. He had felt the same feeling of hopelessness when Tara was slipping away, like he was watching a glass tip off a tall table, spinning through the air, too far away to stop it from hitting the floor and shattering into a thousand pieces. The difference was that, with Tara, he had known tragedy was coming from the moment he fell in love with her. Even so, he sometimes doubted he would have survived if it hadn't been for Soolie.

Was it really only fifteen years ago that he had come to Hob Glen? A sack on his back, old shoes on his feet, a young man running to a different future, just passing through. He hadn't intended to stay, but the elderly couple who ran the local bakery had let him split wood for a loaf of bread, and he had met their granddaughter, a loud-mouthed energetic girl with frizzy dark hair, and her sister: thin, pale, with brilliant hazel eyes and a beautiful rose bud mouth that curved up in a deliciously secretive smile.

The sisters had told him they weren't blood. That Tara was an orphan whose mother had died of an illness that Tara had inherited at birth. The illness meant that when Tara got hurt, she didn't heal, or if she did, it was so slowly that a scratch or cut could last for years. It was the reason for her long sleeves, boot-length skirts, many bandages, and cowled hoods to protect her from the burning sun. Her mother had lived long enough to give birth, but only just. So baby Tara had been taken in by a kind elderly couple in Hob Glen and raised with their granddaughter, Ellena.

The two girls were as different as the snow and ice. Ellena talked incessantly, always flitting about, laughing, speaking her mind, and pestering him for stories from his years as a ship's hand. Tara let him be, never asked who he was, rarely spoke, but when she did, it always seemed to be important. Ellena was emotional and passionate; she wanted to run, and climb, and dive into Malswood Pond. Tara's will and emotion ran deep and strong; they were not easily stirred and not easily dissuaded.

Ellena had liked him. Everyone had been able see it. She wasn't the sort of girl who hid an infatuation. But he had fallen for Tara, the quiet girl, the one who never healed, the one who let him keep his secrets and never expected to be loved the way he had loved her: hopelessly, completely, no reservations, no defenses. He had given her all his heart, knowing that it would be broken, and she had redeemed him.

He had not wanted a child. He had begged her. "I don't want to lose you." "That is why you are wrong," she had said, and she had given him a daughter. A beautiful, perfect little girl born with her mother's hair, but mercifully without her mother's sickness. And Silas had fallen in love all over again. For nine years he had been at the mercy of the two girls he loved. Together, Tara and Soolie were unstoppable. Anything Tara wanted, he could not deny her. She would look at him with those deep hazel eyes, "Please, Silas." "Please, Papa!" Every moment was sweet heartbreak and gone too fast.

Then it was as if one morning Tara woke up and realized she had done everything she had needed to do. As if she had been holding her body together by sheer force of will and could finally close her eyes and loosen her grip on the world. So she laid herself down in this bed and never got out of it again. Two weeks later, she was gone.

He hadn't known how to raise a little girl, much less without her mother. He had been terrified. But he had promised himself he would give his daughter everything he and Tara'd never had. She would grow up knowing both her parents had loved her very much. She would have the food, shelter, clothing, and education she needed to be everything she ever wanted to be. And she would be safe. No harm would come to her as long as he lived.

Now, Silas looked down at his daughter, her eyes closed, her hair fanned out on the pillow around her, resting quietly in the bed where her mother had died. It was as if that glass were falling again, only it wasn't a glass, it was his whole world.

He could hear Ellena's soft snoring in the loft above. She had stayed up all night helping him search, roaming the fields, coming back to the house, checking the bakery, then back out to wander the hills and roads. He could never repay her, but he was grateful. They were just coming back from the pond to check the house again when Rod Cornell had come running up the road shouting; they had found Soolie, and the Pelig boy was injured.

He didn't know what had happened. No one seemed to. But Silas knew Bernad was trouble, and he was certain no matter what had transpired between Bernad and his daughter, Bernad had been at fault. He'd only hoped the Pelig boy hadn't harmed Soolie in any way. Because, if he had, even having a mother like Mergo Pelig wouldn't be able to save him.

In that moment when Silas saw Soolie sitting lost and alone by the side of the schoolhouse, all the night's panic and the anger had dissolved into exhaustion and relief. He had gone to her, picked her up, and carried her home. Ellena had helped him wash her hair and change her clothes. Soolie hadn't even objected. She hardly opened her eyes. She was in his arms, but still so far away, and Silas had been so relieved, so concerned, he almost hadn't noticed the strange wrinkly marks on Soolie's wrist were gone. Her skin was as smooth and pink and young as if they'd never been there.

"Silas! Silas, wake up! Silas, it's me, Rod!"

Silas shook his head, trying to clear the fog of half-wakefulness from his throbbing skull. All was dark in the house except the yellow glow of lantern light creeping in though the window curtains and the spectral white of a nightgown descending the loft ladder. He wondered for a moment where Soolie had come by such a nightgown before remembering it was Ellena, not Soolie, who had been sleeping above.

"Silas!"

Someone was shouting and pounding on the front door.

"Silas, answer the door," Ellena hissed. "I'll light a lantern."

He unbent his body from the rocker, wincing as he forced his neck and spine straight, and hobbled stiffly across the floor.

"What's going on?" Soolie's voice came from the dark corner of the room.

"Silas, open up!" Pound, pound, pound, pound...

Silas turned the lock and opened the door, squinting against the acid burn of light upon his night-raw eyes.

"Rod," he croaked, "it's the middle of the night."

Ellena came up behind him, holding her own lantern high. "Rod? What's happened?"

The neighbor glanced nervously down the street toward Hob Glen. Rod was a short man with thinning mousy brown hair and a softly shaped face hiding behind a small beard. He was the sort of man who made a decent neighbor and the closest thing Silas had ever had to a friend. His eyes darted back to them.

"Mergo Pelig happened," he said. "Can I come in?"

Silas and Ellena stepped aside to let him enter. Soolie stood by the work table rubbing her eyes, her hair loose around her shoulders, barefoot in her cotton sleep tunic.

"Papa?"

Rod edged nervously into the home, keeping an eye on Soolie, trying to not be obvious about it and failing.

Silas nodded to his daughter, "Go back to bed, Soolie."

"I'll just hear you anyways."

"Go back to bed, baby girl."

Soolie sulked halfheartedly and dragged her feet back to the dark corner behind the ladder.

Ellena closed the front door and secured the lock. "Won't you have a seat, Rod?"

"I'll just stand, thank you. I can't stay long."

Silas waited while Ellena set the lantern on his work table and came to stand at his shoulder, her arms folded, shoulders hunched against the chill. "Well, Rod?"

Rod licked his lips and leaned in. "You have to leave Hob Glen tonight. Now. The town is all gathered at the Barn, and Mergo Pelig is riling them up like an eastern priest. You know that woman is a force."

"She should be home with her son," Silas said.

"Well, she's not, and she has all the town believing," Rod looked again to the dark corner of the room and hissed out the side of his mouth, "your daughter's some sort of devil child."

Ellena cut in sharply, "That's horse shit!"

"Maybe." Rod sounded unconvinced. "Maybe it is. She won't let anyone see the boy, but those that have all say his face is half eaten away. That your daughter..." Rod hesitated.

"Spit it out, Rod, before I slap some sense into you," Ellena snapped.

"Removed it with a touch," Rod finished quickly.

"What nonsense!" Ellena was livid. "She's a little girl! You and Milin have known her all of her life, for land's sake. Don't tell me Milin believes..."

"Milin is at nine moons," Rod protested, finding new courage in defense of his wife. "We're about to have a baby. A baby, Ellena. And no one's children are sleeping tonight. They're all up crying. And, Silas, you know this, every seed Soolie planted refused to sprout, everything she touches dies."

"Rod," Silas' voice was low. "Go home to your wife."

Rod swallowed and nodded. He was a short man, easily intimidated, and Silas had a full head's height on him, but it was toward the dark back corner of the room that Rod glanced as he moved toward the door. He placed a hand on the latch.

"Silas, we've known each other many years. You've always been a good neighbor to Milin and me." Rod looked at his friend. "Go now. Take Soolie and get out of town. You can borrow our cart. You know where it is. Just leave. At least for a few days until everyone calms down. It isn't safe for you here tonight."

Rod opened the door quickly, nodded to the two of them, and with a shiver of relief, stepped out into the night.

"I can't believe him!" Ellena gripped her arms angrily over her nightgown. "Did you see how he was acting? I mean, Mergo is a vicious shrew viper, we all know that, but Rod and Milin? They should know better."

Silas was moving quickly. He grabbed his coat and broad-brimmed hat from where they hung by the door.

"Silas..." Ellena softened, unfolding her arms.

"Soolie, were you listening?"

"Yes, Papa." Soolie stepped into the lantern light. "They think I hurt the Pelig boy."

"Get dressed. We're going on a trip."

"But surely Rod's overreacting." Ellena objected. "Everyone knows us. Silas, they know us."

"Ellena," Silas said quietly. "If Rod thinks we should leave tonight, we leave tonight."

Ellena paused. "Well, then," she nodded brusquely, heading for the ladder, "I'm coming with you."

"It would probably be better if you..."

Ellena cut him off with a raised finger. "Silas. Don't you dare pretend I am not part of this family. You get the Cornell's cart. We'll pack."

"Papa." Soolie edged nearer, looking up at him as he shrugged on his coat. "Are we ... are we going to Ravus?"

"Yes, baby girl. Now go get dressed."

"All my dresses are dirty."

"Then put on the warmest one and pack an extra. Ellena, you know where everything is. I won't be long."

He opened the door.

"Papa?" Soolie twisted the front of her night tunic around her fingers.

He stood in the doorway and looked back. "Make it quick, Soolie. What is it?"

"I didn't hurt him."

"I know, baby girl." He reached out, pulled her small body close with one arm, and stroked her silky hair. "I know." Still, he was glad to hear her say it.

He kissed her on the head. "Now get dressed and help your aunt. We leave as soon as I get back."

⁂

A THICK COLD FOG smothered Hob Glen like dank sodden wool. Ellena heard the slow jangle, clatter, clip-clop of the cart and horses, but couldn't make out Silas' face until he was no more than a few arms lengths away guiding the horses through the gloom, his lantern unlit.

"Come on!" Silas whispered loudly, standing up in the driver's seat and stepping back into the bed of the cart. "Start bringing me things. Let's go."

Ellena handed up a package of dried goods: tea, crackers, cheese, and dried fish. "Are you sure this is going to be enough food?"

"It will have to be."

Ellena leaned over the cart wall. "Prices are higher in the city. Let me go back to the bakery. I can grab some food, money, a change of clothes. All I have now is what I brought with me to the harvest fest."

Silas tucked the package down beside a crate of eggs and half a loaf of bread, then went to the back of the cart to accept several linen bags of boots that were too heavy for Soolie to lift up over the side. "Too dangerous. We leave now."

"Fine," Ellena hissed, "but I'm paying for my share of the trip when we get back."

Silas didn't argue. He had just gone to his neighbors' home and taken their cart, horses, and a large tarpaulin to secure the goods and sleep under. He was already accepting far too much charity, and now wasn't the time for disagreements. Tonight he needed to do everything necessary to keep his daughter safe.

It didn't take long to load up the cart. Ellena climbed up into the driver's seat beside Silas, and Soolie crawled in the back, hiding under the tarpaulin like he told her to. The horses shifted their hooves and flicked their ears. Silas made a soft clicking sound and lightly touched the reins to get the cart moving at a smooth trot. The black fog was heavy, and Silas wasn't willing to light a lantern. He had no choice but to trust the horses to stay on the familiar path and find their way.

"Maybe everyone has gone to bed," Ellena whispered.

In the thick dark, the creak clatter of the cart and clop of the horses' hooves rang severe and strident. He should have wrapped the horses hooves to deaden the sound. But that would have only slowed them down. Dear lands, they just needed to get out of Hob Glen. In a few days, everyone would calm down. In a few days, he would sit down with the parents, they would have a reasoned discussion, and everything would return to normal.

In the meantime, he could find out what really happened from Soolie. She was a good girl, and he could trust her to tell him the truth. Besides, he already knew who was really to blame: Bernad, Kip, and Hobby. He gritted his teeth. It was just like those plague-frogs to blame someone else for their own mistakes. When he got back, they would be lucky if he didn't talk sense into them with his fists.

Poor Soolie, she was just a little girl. A world that should have adored her and laid a perfect life at her feet had taken her mother and was now driving her from her home in the middle of the night. He resisted the urge to stop the horses and run to the back to check on her, to hold her close and never let her go. It was too dark to tell where they were in the village. They just had to get out of Hob Glen and onto the open road.

Hang on, baby girl. I'll take care of you. Everything is going to be okay.

SOOLIE LAY CURLED on her side on a blanket, her back pressed against linen bags of shoes, her feet tucked against a hatchet and bundle of kindling. She closed her eyes and opened them, closed them and opened them again, but it made no difference. The cart was as black as the backs of her eyelids. She listened to the creak of boards and tackle, the percussion of shod hooves and wheels on stone, feeling every bump and jostle in her bones.

She was going to Ravus. It wasn't the best of circumstances, but she was going to the city. Where the hospital was. Where the learned men were. Where people came from all over the known world. Most importantly, where the Southern Lands Carnival had gone. She was one step closer to answers. Answers that would lead her to victory.

You must not go to the city. A little girl voice interrupted her thoughts.

Cuckin' skag. Soolie cussed. It was talking to her while she was awake. Well, she must be doing something right.

It is dangerous. You are not the right vessel.

Dangerous for me or just dangerous for you? Soolie thought back bitterly.

It is dangerous for all. You must get me to a young soul. I must not go to Ravus.

Why, because of this 'dead man?'

Get me to a young soul.

What's in the city?

Get me to a young soul.

The voice was getting sharp. It stung like spatters of grease from a frying pan.

Skag you, Soolie thought, pulling the edge of the blanket over her, wrapping herself up as if a layer of cotton and wool could keep herself safe.

GET ME TO A YOUNG SOUL.

Soolie dug her fingernails into the side of her hand to distract herself.

GET ME...

'To a young soul,' Soolie snapped silently. I heard you.

It seethed.

Let me tell you what's happened, Soolie thought. You cucked up. You infested me, invaded my mind, threatened my family, and the fact that you really don't want to go to Ravus is the first good news I've heard. So please, go ahead. Scream.

There is a world you do not know, Soolie Beetch, the voice menaced. *If it finds us, the world you know will be destroyed.*

The pain ebbed into stillness.

Soolie waited, but there was nothing. She could almost imagine she was alone in the darkness. She hugged the blanket tightly and listened to the rattle of the cart carrying her away from home.

SILAS RELEASED A BREATH as the cobble stones of Main Street ended, and the sharp clattering of cart wheels gave way to a dull thumping and creaking of the Eastern Road. They had escaped Main Street without trouble, but they couldn't breathe freely yet. The Eastern Road wound inland to the plains and stretched westward to Ravus and the sea. It was the only road out of Hob Glen, and it passed within a mere half a mile of Hob Glen's gathering place, the Barn.

The dim glow of a lantern wavered in the fog before them. Ellena nudged Silas, but he had already seen it. He didn't want to stop. He wanted to urge the horses on, past the lantern before they could be identified, but it was in the direct path of the cart, and he still couldn't see the edges of the road well enough to swerve around. Hating himself, Silas pulled back on the reins, slowing the horses to a stop.

"Eyyh, rampagers! Hooligans! Whatcha be hurtling about in this dark without a light for! Like ta run a body over! Almost killed me, you blasted…"

It was the unmistakable wavery nasal voice of elderly Mr. Svenson. Silas ducked his head, hiding beneath his hat brim as the lantern bobbed slowly towards them.

"Ruffians!"

"Mr. Svenson?"

Ellena was calling out to him. What was she doing? Off in the direction of the Barn, Silas could make out a broad glow, fuzzy and distant as if obscured through a thick pane of acid-etched glass. The townsfolk had certainly not gone to bed. In fact, from the breadth of the glow in the dark, it looked like the whole town was still awake. He didn't want to be spotted. They should go.

"Mr. Svenson, is that you? It's me, Ellena."

"Ellena? Oooh my." The lantern bobbed up to the side of the cart, Mr. Svenson holding it high with a scrawny hand. "Sorry I yelled at you, dear. Startled me. Startled me. Where is your light?"

"I'm so sorry." Ellena leaned toward the old man. "I'm with Rod, and his lantern just burnt out. We hoped to get to the Barn to relight it. It's been such a horrible day."

Under his hat brim, Silas squinted into the darkness. Were the lights moving? It was hard to tell in this fog. Yes, they were. Slowly but truly. The townsfolk were coming back from the Barn. He elbowed Ellena. They needed to get going.

"Rod Cornell, that you? I thought you were going home to your wife."

"He was," Ellena explained hastily. "He met me on my way back home and said there was something I needed to see."

"Ooh," the old man shook his head. "Bad business, Ellena. It's a bad business. People all riled. Frightened, scared. Of course my Pawla is right in the middle of it having herself a Solar Day! I had to go. I need my rest. Rheumatism's acting up, and rabble rousing isn't for me." Mr. Svenson leaned in, holding his lantern high.

Silas' heart throbbed against his ribs. The people were headed their way. In a few minutes that 'rabble' would reach the Eastern Road and be between him and escape. They would be trapped. It was time to move. He elbowed Ellena again. They needed to go. They needed to go, now. It was time to strike the horses, make a dash for it. He felt her hand squeezing his knee.

"They've been arguing back and forth a long time," Svenson continued, "and most everyone is set on running that little blood witch and her pappy outta town. You be careful. Hearts be high." He patted her on the arm. "Rod! Take care of this lady. She makes the only apple bran muffins I can stomach."

"Good night, Mr. Svenson!" Ellena called as the man turned to go. "Light your lantern!"

Silas touched the reins and the horses started moving forward. He had been holding his breath, and he shakily let it out, slowly breathing back in. They just had to get past where the path to the Barn met the Eastern Road without being noticed. He touched the reins again, urging the horses into a canter. He would have to risk the extra noise. Ellena clutched his arm, and he prayed for the horses' steps to stay sure on the dark dirt road.

"Come on," he whispered.

The cart jostled and protested. The rest of the world was grim silence. No angry chants, no shouts or cries from the moving lights.

"We're going to make it!" Ellena said in his ear.

They passed by so close, he could make out the individual lanterns bobbing through the fog, separating one from the other and drifting toward them as if on an inevitable tide, and he was sure they would be found out. But he kept the pace, clenching the reins, and slowly, despite the betrayal of the horses' pounding hooves and the louder pounding in his chest, they passed the lights and began to leave them behind.

He glanced back once, and then again. Were they being followed? The horses continued, and the lights began to fade into dark obscurity. Still he didn't say anything. What if the townsfolk were following without lanterns? What if they were tracking them with dogs?

"Silas, we made it," Ellena said. "We're out of town."

At last, he slowed the horses to a walk and finally to a stop.

"I need to check on Soolie."

There was a flare of sparks beside him as Ellena struck her lighting sticks. She touched one to the lantern wick and shook them out. Silas took the lantern, jumped out of the cart, circled around to the back, and lifted the heavy tarred edge of the tarpaulin. Soolie lay curled up in a blanket in the back of the cart, safe.

She groaned. "Papa?"

"It's okay, baby girl." Silas patted her quilted feet. "Go back to sleep."

"Okay."

He lowered the tarpaulin, went back to the front of the cart, set the lantern beside Ellena, and hoisted himself back into the driver's seat.

"We keep going until dawn."

Ellena nodded, he flicked the reins, and the cart continued toward Ravus.

ELEVEN

Dog hadn't left the city. It wasn't that he couldn't escape. It wasn't that he couldn't stay out of reach of the Master's pack, at least for a time. It was that he had nowhere to go. Dog had been created to serve the Master, and when his service came to an end, so he also should have ended. But instead he had run. He was alone and shamed, with no Master, no home. He had rebelled against his purpose, and he was lost. So he stayed and hid.

He'd considered hiding in the Dark Districts. Lost among the throngs of humanity crawling over one another through narrow filthy alleyways and rag-windowed houses, his scent would have been masked by the foul tannery street run off and overflow of human filth. Unfortunately, not only did the pack hunt and conduct business for the Master at night in the Dark Districts, taking advantage of the easy access to the tunnels and the throngs of the poor and forgotten, but the streets were thick with the ghosts of the dead, refuse from the pack's many kills. Dog didn't usually pay attention to the lost souls, but they would be sure to see him and know him for what he was, and one of them would be sure to betray his location to the pack.

Next, there was the Sun District, home of the aristocracy and the Regent's tower. But even if Dog got past the wall undetected, the

Sun District was too open and clean for hiding. He needed a place bustling with movement, heavy with smells, and choked with people who would not be missed. So Dog ended up in the market streets.

Near the great Iron Gate, the market streets were a continuous inundation of people and wares from all across the known world. Crowded stalls and tightly wedged storefronts traded crocks of suet, barrels of dried fish and animal gizzards, bags of corn meal and rye flour, racks of hanging spices, and skins of mead, wine, and vinegar. At night, when the pack came up from the tunnels to run and feed, Dog hid near butcher shops, his scent at home among the dead blood and meat. In the light of the day, while the pack was exiled to the shadows of the underground, fleeing the sun that scorched their flesh, Dog was free to hunt the streets.

He ducked through the throngs of people, hunching over, hiding his sharp teeth, black eyes, and sallow skin in the deep hood of a stolen guard's cloak. No one challenged him. The streets were full of many strange and dangerous people, and the Regent's men had long stopped coming to the aid of those who cried out in distress. Every person fended for themselves, and none of the common folk sought out trouble. They knew it was too easy to find.

Dog wasn't picky about his meals. Young or old, sick or able didn't matter. None of the human throng were strong enough to resist him. He looked for someone alone, preferably near an alleyway or side street. Someone he could sweep away into the shadows unseen. He only needed a moment.

People jostled against him, swirling through the narrow cobblestone corridors like water over a pebbled stream bed. Vendors and hagglers shouted above the throng, a bladder pipe and drum were playing on the street corner. Dog drew near to the musicians, keeping his head low. No one stopped to listen to the music, no one even turned to look at the two ragged street youth: both boys in baggy drawn-up trousers, oversized undershirts, and many-patched jackets, and both just barely too old to be sweeps or taken for the Master's use. The sour intonation of the pipe and faltering cadence of the drum betrayed their newness to the instruments. Dog wasn't interested in them. They were being entirely too visible. He stood in the shadow of the building, sensing the milling crowd, finding the person who moved, but never moved on. He found her.

A girl of roughly the same age, a gray cap pulled low over her face, threading her way deftly between the people, her slender fingers darting in and out of pockets, lifting a coin here, a purse there, undetected and unseen: the real reason for the corner minstrels. She came and went unnoticed, and it made her the perfect target.

Dog waited. One more lift. The girl cut the strings on a fat man's purse with a pen knife, tucked it into her large trouser pockets, and without looking around, wove swiftly through the crowd. Her companions would finish this one song and meet her just a few streets over where they would divide their stolen earnings. She slipped into a narrow connecting alleyway, and Dog was waiting for her.

The girl caught a flash of blood-misted eyes, sharp yellow teeth, and a nearly human face. Then her pen knife dropped from her fingers and clattered on the street.

IN THE EARLY MORNING, they stopped for breakfast. Silas took care of the horses while Ellena and Soolie scavenged enough wood for a small fire. Once the fire was coaxed to life and the horses were free to graze on their tethers, the three of them huddled around the little roadside blaze sharing the loaf of bread, eggs, and tea, and Soolie finally had the chance to tell Silas and Ellena what had happened the night of the harvest festival.

Upset by their arguing, Soolie had run into the trees, gotten lost, and decided to stay put until she could find her way back in the daylight. In the morning, she had just begun making her way home when she heard an explosion followed by the sound of yelling. Running toward the sound, Soolie had discovered Hobby and Kip dragging a wounded Bernad away from a clearing and the haze of smoke. Hobby and Kip made her promise not to tell anyone what she had seen and, wanting to get Bernad to Doc Wilkins, Soolie had agreed. Once they reached the schoolhouse, there had been a lot of running and screaming, Winny fainting, and more screaming. Weak and exhausted from her night in the woods, Soolie had sat down by the side of the schoolhouse where she had been when they found her.

The truth was, she didn't know how Bernad had been hurt. She hadn't even touched him. She'd just been at the wrong place at the wrong time, an easy and available stand-target.

By the time Soolie finished her story, both Silas and Ellena were livid. Hobby, Kip, and Bernad had been allowed to run wild through Hob Glen for years. An accident like this had been bound to happen sooner or later, and it was just luck no one else had gotten hurt. Or even killed. Ellena brought up how all three had gotten horribly drunk one Solar Day from liquor Bernad stole from his papa's store and broken the Crewgar's chicken coup roof by climbing on it. Papa pointed out this wouldn't be their first experience with explosives, since it was only last summer they'd been caught lighting cow puddings on fire and flinging them at the side of the Barn.

The worst thing, both of them agreed, was that the boys never learned, because no matter what they did, they never faced any real consequences, because Mergo Pelig was Bernad's mother. Now, once again, the boys were trying to duck responsibility, only this time someone had finally come to serious harm.

Well, something needed to be done. Would be done. As soon as Silas, Ellena, and Soolie got back to Hob Glen, they would set the record straight, and those boys would finally have to take responsibility. For the first time in their lives.

Soolie ate the last egg.

THE FIRST FULL DAY'S TRAVEL passed uneventfully. They drove all day, Papa at the reins, Ellena at his side, Soolie in the back. They played games, told stories, sang songs, and sat in silence watching the rolling hills and patches of tall bushy trees unfurl past. Soolie thought the rock formations looked like lonely giants waiting to ambush unwary travelers. Papa pointed out a herd of horses let out to pasture on the distant hills, and Ellena spotted a gray fox with a mouse in its teeth heading back to its cubs.

There was cold sausage and crackers for dinner, and they rolled out their bedding underneath the shelter of the cart, huddled under the blankets and went to sleep.

That night, Soolie had nightmares.

Papa and Ellena, skinless, bloody, lidless eyes wide, never closing, mouths gaping, screaming, always screaming. And the white merciless eyes of the demon.

BRING ME A YOUNG SOUL. THE DEAD MAN RISES.

She woke up many times, and every time she fell back asleep, the nightmares were waiting. She tried not to stir or show how poorly she slept, and Papa didn't seem to notice. He would have said something if he had.

The next day was much like the first. Papa and Ellena fell to talking and gossiping about the people of Hob Glen, wondering if Milin Cornell had had her baby yet, if it was a boy or a girl, and what it might take for Mergo Pelig to finally leave her husband.

Soolie listened for a while before her mind began to drift and she started drumming her fingers on the boards of the cart, twisting her blanket up in her fingers, and thinking about all the things she could not say out loud.

That night, they camped again on the side of the road and rolled out their blankets under the cart. There was tinned fish and canned tomatoes for dinner, and raw flesh, blood, pain, and screaming for dreams.

TWELVE

Early the next morning, it began to rain. When Ellena woke, it was still dark outside and water was pooling beneath the cart, soaking into their blankets and clothes, numbing fingers and toes.

It was too wet for a fire, so Silas rolled up the blankets loosely, stuffed them in the back of the cart, and hoisted Soolie in under the tarpaulin after them. He offered a hand to Ellena, but she shook her head, pulling her wool cloak around her. She had ridden beside him this far, and she intended to keep it that way. So he lent her a hand and helped her up onto the driver's bench next to him instead, and they continued toward the city.

It was a wretched day. The sun never fully showed its face, and the rain fell constant and permeating. It obscured the sky, covered the road in troubled muddy little lakes, and collected on the bench between them, spreading until it soaked the seats of their clothes. Ellena's wool cloak grew sodden, heavy, and cold. Water trickled down her face, her back, and between her breasts. The cold sunk through her wet clammy skin and into her belly, and no matter how she hugged herself beneath her cloak, she could not hold herself tightly enough to still her shivering.

Eventually, Ellena reached the point where she didn't think she could take it any more. Then she reached the point where she couldn't believe that every dreadful moment could be followed by another, and then another, each just as dreadful as the last. Then she reached the point where she truly thought she was going to begin crying from pure misery. But every few minutes, she would look over at Silas, water streaming off the brim of his hat, his white wet hands grasping the reins, his eyes set forward beneath the tortured heaviness of his brow, and she smiled at him just in case he saw her out of the corner of his eye, and told herself to be strong.

The horses plodded heavily in the mud, and time plodded even more slowly, the road and the hours all looking the same through a veil of rain and cold. Ellena took to waiting out the hours huddling, staring down at her lap, no longer watching the mud pass below the cart. It had to end eventually. The day couldn't last forever.

EVENING CAME SLOWLY. Silas drove the horses long and hard without stopping, continuing even after dark, wanting to be close enough to reach the city early the next day.

When he finally turned the cart off the road and under a dark dripping stand of trees, Ellena was too cold and tired to offer help tying up the horses. Silas squeezed her wrist and climbed down from the bench. She huddled hopelessly, unable to bring herself any warmth. She could hear the creak and jangle of the harnesses and Silas' reassuring murmur as he led the horses free of the traces and tied them to a nearby slender trunk.

He came up on her side of the cart and offered her a hand. "Are you okay?"

Ellena reached out stiffly, shakily unfolding herself like a new colt. "Jus' c … c … cold."

He placed his other hand steadying on her back. "It's all right. I've got you."

She half stepped, half fell from the seat, her painfully numb feet providing poor purchase on the soggy uneven ground, but he held her, one arm wrapping around and supporting her against his chest.

"I never should have let you ride up front," he muttered, hoisting her at his side, supporting her as she tottered shivering beside him toward the back of the cart.

There wasn't much room, but Soolie had cleared space for them the best that she could. Bags of shoes were stacked up on top of the food and supplies, and Soolie curled up to the side, hugging the wall, for all appearances fast asleep.

Silas placed his hands around Ellena's waist, lifting her up into the cart, her wet cloak pooling water on the floorboards below her. Silas climbed in after, pulling his boots up into the cart, laying the tarpaulin back over the edge. He lit the lantern and set it on the floor. Soolie groaned a little but didn't stir.

The tarp was much too low for moving about, and they would have to curl up on their sides to fit. Silas' feet would probably still hang off the back.

Ellena tried not to whimper with exhaustion and cold. Her cloak felt like it had soaked up several stone worth of water weight, and she peeled it off, dropping it in a heavy dull pile in the corner. She tried to undo her boots, but the tight laces eluded her numb fingers. Ellena pawed at the strings, her fingers fumbling over the wet knots, then held her hands around the lantern in an effort to warm them.

Silas knelt before her and took her wet boot into his lap. He had already undone his own, and his strong craftsman's hands navigated the ties of her laces with ease. He loosened them all the way down to her ankle and then carefully pulled the boot off her foot. It made a dull sucking sound, and a tablespoon of gray water piddled out the boot and onto the floorboards. Silas removed both her boots and set them at the door by his own as she began to roll the sodden stockings off her feet. Her dress was also soaked, and all she had with her was the frilly cotton nightgown that was her grandmother's: warm enough in bed at home, but a frail barrier against tonight's unforgiving cold and wet.

She tossed her second sock on top of her cloak. Silas reached across in the lantern light and handed her his own flannel shirt and pair of woolen socks.

"I'm sorry I don't have anything else to give you," he whispered.

Ellena accepted the clothes with a weak but grateful smile and put them where she wouldn't drip on them.

"You change first," he said and turned away, facing the back of the cart.

Ellena tried to unbutton her dress, but the buttons were too small and tight. Her fingers weren't close to being warm enough. She was too exhausted.

"Silas?"

"Yes?"

"Help me?" she whispered. "Please?"

He turned hesitantly, and a look of relief passed over his face when he saw she was still fully dressed.

Ellena flopped her hands in her lap. She felt an exhausted tear trickle down her face, followed by another and another. She was so cold and so tired. Hungry, tired, and so cold. And she couldn't even change clothes.

Silas didn't know what to do. He just looked at her sitting there silently crying, frozen, uncertain.

"I…" Ellena sniveled, her voice spasming. "C … c … can't unbu …utton my d … d … dress."

Silas's eyebrows peaked in conflicted concern. Still he didn't move.

"Help me?"

The words came out in a pitiful squeak. It was, perhaps, the first time she had ever truly asked. She had demanded, she had been kind and caring, she had insisted, she had pried. She was always the one helping him, the single father, always insinuating herself into his life. But she sat before him now shivering and crying. All because he had insisted on keeping long hours, driving all day and long into the night, even in the heavy autumn rain, and she had insisted on staying up on the driver's bench by his side. And now she needed him to help her.

Each round cloth-covered button was no bigger than a fingernail. They went straight down from her neck all the way to the hem of the dress. He fumbled with the top button, trying not to touch the soft hollow of her throat that pulsed as she sniffed and swallowed back tears. Second button, third. He focused on the buttons, trying to ignore the soft swell of her breasts beneath his hands. Five buttons, six, seven, he counted to himself. She was shivering badly. He should have paid more attention. She had gotten too cold. If he didn't warm her up soon, she might catch cold sickness. Nine buttons, ten. His hands at the base of her ribcage now, and he realized she wasn't wearing her corset. His hands inched their way down towards her navel. There were too many buttons. No dress should have this many buttons. She breathed in, and her abdomen swelled just enough that he felt the soft touch of her bare skin against his fingers. Silas dropped his hands and turned away from her.

"Th … thank you."

He nodded, not speaking. Even with his back turned, he could feel her closeness in the cramped quarters of the cart as she stripped off the wet gingham dress.

"Ok," she whispered.

He shot a tentative glance over his shoulder. Ellena had put on his flannel shirt over the top of her grandmother's nightgown, and his thick woolen socks on her feet. She was shivering, pulling a blanket over herself and tucking it around her legs. She lay down on her side facing Soolie and curled up.

"I won't look."

He undressed as quickly as he could, his head lifting and disturbing the clammy cold tarpaulin above. He tossed his wet pants, jacket, and shirt with Ellena's sopping things. He had given her his last dry shirt and socks, but he had a mostly dry pair of pants that he slipped on and buttoned. Ellena had seen him shirtless innumerable times back when she and Tara used to go down to Malswood pond with him in the summer, but now he felt overly aware and self-conscious. He mopped up the water on the floor of the wagon with a rag, quickly blew out the lantern, then covered himself with the third blanket and lay down, pressing his back against the opposite wall of the cart, his feet hanging over the back and lifting up the tarp.

It was still cold. He was cold. He was glad Soolie had managed to fall asleep. Nothing strange had happened with her over their trip. Every day he'd asked her how she felt and if she'd had any dreams, and every day she'd laughed and told Ellena to tell him he fussed too much, then clapped her hands and exclaimed how excited she was to be going to the city. He was glad to see her so carefree, so resilient, his vibrant little girl. It was fortunate that the incident with Hobby, Kip, and Bernad hadn't caused her any more nightmares. He thought of those boys and felt rage. He never should have let her go back to school when there were boys like that in town. He should have protected her. He would deal with them when he got home. He would make sure they never dared speak to his daughter ever again.

He could hear Ellena shivering. He wished there was a way he could help. She had come all this way with them. After all, she *was* family. His wife's sister. Adopted sister. What if she became ill? Soolie would never forgive him.

She was still shivering. Silas pulled his blanket over and, kneeling next to Ellena, draped it over her. He made sure the second blanket was over her feet, then turned to crawl back and lie down on the bare boards of the cart. Ellena grabbed his ankle. Her hand groped around and found his hand in the dark.

"Ellena," he whispered.

She didn't speak, she just pulled him in towards her. He relented, laying down beside her and pulling the blankets over the two of them. She was shaking. He let her curl up, her back to his chest. He kept his hands on her arms. He stayed awake until she stopped shuddering and started breathing evenly. He heard a soft snore and considered tucking her in, now that she was asleep, and crawling back onto the bare boards of the cart, but he was so tired. Weariness was a sharp ache in his bones, and Ellena was soft and warm. He stayed under the blankets, holding Ellena, thinking of Tara and their daughter Soolie until he drifted off into a restless sleep.

SOOLIE WAS PREPARED for the bloody violent dreams, but the dreams never came. She was hanging in a familiar blankness. Skag it. This again. If the demon was going to ruin sleep for her, it could at least be bothered to create a decent environment.

You think I am evil.

It was behind her. A petty move and not exactly clever. Well, this time Soolie was ready for its games. This time, she was the one in control. She turned to face it. The pretty little girl in the sunny egg yolk shift looked back, poised like a soulless little statue.

"Got tired of giving me nightmares?"

You think I am a demon.

Soolie rolled her eyes. "Can we go back to the nightmares? I think I prefer the nightmares."

They are not nightmares. They are shadows of what will come.

"Maybe you should save your threats for when they mean something."

I am not your enemy. You desire me gone. I have told you how.

Soolie shrugged. "I'm considering other options."

All things are at stake, it insisted. *The Dead Man is rising.*

"The dead man, the dead man," Soolie scoffed. "The dead man is a bunch of cucktwad."

It blinked, long black lashes disrupting the stillness of its delicate face. *Your disregard is unsound. The Dead Man binds souls to flesh and tears holes in the world. He has stolen my strength and will use it to bring an end to all things.*

Soolie smirked. Sometimes goading worked better than questions. "Then maybe *he* has a young soul you can borrow."

You attempt to manipulate me as you did the school teacher.

Skagging mind reader. "I only want answers."

Not that she could make much sense of the one answer it had given her: 'Binds souls to flesh and tears holes in the world.' So this dead man could forge life and destroy realms like the Ancient Ones?

Either the demon was making things up, or it actually wanted to fight a god. Either it was delusional or it was insane.

I have given you answers, it said. *I have told you to bring me a young soul, but you choose to risk yourself in attempt to cause me harm. You resent me because I violate your sense of control.*

"Or maybe," Soolie snapped, "I'm just not the child-sacrificing type." She was letting it upset her. She needed to focus.

Your concern is not for the young soul, it stated flatly, *but for your own self-perception. You were not angry that the Bernad boy was injured. You were angry that you were the one that wielded that injury.*

Soolie's temper flared, burning off the last of her false civility. "I know what you are," she sneered. "You're a helpless, creepy parasite with the personality of a plate of boil worms. You're nothing. And when I destroy you, the world and all its souls," she spread her arms wide, "will go on as they were. Completely, absolutely fine, and with one less piece of skagging trash around to harm anyone."

It observed her outburst, wide eyes unmoving, fixed like a night owl's hunting gaze. As Soolie glared back, that watching gaze seemed to expand beyond the golden globes and into the vacant space, and she had the sudden horrid unease that facing it was only an illusion. That even now it was still behind her, always behind her, just out of sight. Not always visible, but always there. She gritted her teeth, refusing to look away.

The child's voice sounded again in her head. *I do not have my own strength. If you force my hand, it is you I must draw upon. It is you who will come to harm.*

"Can I get back to sleeping now? I have a big day of traveling tomorrow."

Do not get caught in the city after dark. Stay out of the dark.

"Yeah? Well, skag off."

THIRTEEN

.

Ellena woke up. Her ankles and feet were still cold, but her chest was wrapped in warmth that pulled her in and tucked her close. Something tickled her ear. Then stopped. Then again. It smelled stale and boggy with sleep. Breath.

She cracked the gritty seal on her eyelids. Silas' large loosely curled hand lay by her face. He was holding her, and he was still asleep.

Something snorted. Ellena looked up and saw Soolie sitting cross-legged, smirking down at her. Soolie grinned.

Ellena moved a stealthy finger to her lips in a silent shush and ever so carefully lifted that wonderfully strong heavy arm, untucked the blanket from underneath herself, and slid out.

"Are you wearing Papa's shirt?"

"Yes," Ellena whispered, hugging the shirt around herself. "He offered it to me like a gentleman."

"Looks like that's not all he offered." Soolie waggled her eyebrows.

Ellena poked her sharply in the ribs. "Shush, you!

"Aha!" Soolie squealed, trying to protect herself with her hands. "So *that's* what you two get up to after I go to bed."

Ellena pressed her attack with sharp pinching fingers darting around Soolie's flailing arms. "Not another word out of you!"

"What in land's name?" Silas pushed up on his elbow and scowled groggily.

Ellena and Soolie froze, then glanced at each other.

"We're hungry," Ellena said.

Soolie snorted. "Yup."

"Then stop scrapping near my head," Papa groused, pulling the blanket up to cover his woolly bare chest. "And go gather wood for a fire. We need to dry Ellena's clothes. The sooner we get to Ravus, the sooner we can be headed home."

"You heard the man." Ellena pushed a giggling Soolie towards the door. "Come on, let's go."

THE MORNING SKY was gray and cottony. With Ellena finally dressed again in her own clothes, mostly dry and smelling of wood smoke, and with Soolie hidden safely under the tarp with strict instructions from her father to not show her face under any circumstances, the cart continued towards Ravus.

As the gray of dawn began to spread behind them, Ellena spied the city before them, curled on the hazy horizon like a black sea dragon's back breaking the surface of the brine, looming larger and larger as they rode closer, spreading out in all directions and, jutting up, the sharp white monolith of the Regent's tower stabbing the sky like an undergod's poniard. Ellena had heard it said that the surface of the tower was slick as ice and smooth as a mirror, that the edges were sharp enough to split skin at the touch, and that the very alabaster from which it was carved had a taste for human blood. Looking upon the tower for the first time, Ellena found such rumors easy to believe.

Soon they were close enough that Ellena could make out the twin pillars of the Sun Gate, one on either side of the road, marking the eastern entrance to the city. The pillars used to stand tall, carved in intricate spirals, painted with gold paint, each supporting a large copper shield engraved with radiating lines so the morning sun's rays would catch in their polished curves and reflect shining out on the hopeful upturned faces of the weary pilgrim. Now, the shields were gone, fallen, lost or stolen long ago, the paint scraped or worn away, the pillars crumbled with age like salt licks in the rain.

Then there was the smell.

Ellena grimaced, wishing she had a handkerchief to cover her nose. There was a reason the locals coarsely referred to the Sun Gate as the 'Mud Pucker' of Ravus. Not only was the Sun Gate the entrance to the Dark Districts and the Crimson District, it was also the gate by the tannery street, and without an above ground water source, the tanneries had taken to dumping their slurries and sloughs outside the city limits, forming a putrid lake of toxic rot. It was that stench mixed with the overflow of undealt human waste and black coal smoke that defiled the air, burning in Ellena's nose and throat, the smell so strong that it didn't even register as a smell any more as much as a violent assault like breathing toxic ammonia vapors. It was so much worse than she remembered. She found herself holding her breath, her head beginning to ache.

Silas directed the horses to turn left, away from the gate to circle around Ravus' outer wall. They were better off going a circuitous rout than attempting navigation of the Dark Districts where the streets tangled like unspooled thread and were often too narrow and cluttered for a two-horse cart.

Silas guided the horses past the smaller Stone Gate marked by a simple granite archway barely large enough for two wagons to pass beneath side by side. As they rode, Ellena saw more and more people heading toward or leaving the city, a cart here, a wagon there, men and women on horseback, and inside the city limits, the unsettled milling of early morning life. Finally, the cart rounded the southwestern corner of the city, and came upon a crowd of people lining up to enter. They had reached the Iron Gate.

The Iron Gate was the largest of Ravus, named for the great double gates of thick spike-topped iron bars that loomed seven men high like insensate sentries to the masses that passed below. Facing toward the ocean, the Iron Gate was the entrance to the Craftsman District, the Artisan District, and the market streets. It was said all the known world came through the Iron Gate. Farmers brought grain, sugar, produce, and cattle. Merchants brought wood and cloth, exotic spices, oils, and ivory from the Southern countries, fish, eels, shells, and sea plants from the fishing villages. And, from the rich kingdoms of the isles, rare dyes, medicines, silks, and of course, the illegal topaz trade.

Even this early in the morning, a line of carts, wagons, pedestrians, and caravans laden with goods for bartering and selling waited to enter the city gates, while on the far side of the road, the carts and wagons left the city with lighter wheels and, hopefully, heavier pockets.

Silas guided the horses past heaps of tarped goods, stacks of rope-bound barrels. Every face, local and foreign, looked forward to the Iron Gate. No one turned to acknowledge them or raise a hand in greeting as he pulled the cart in behind a wagon stacked high with a small mountain of barrels roped down, draped in oil cloth, and reeking of fish.

The procession moved slowly. Up ahead, men dressed in the long black cloaks and gray tunics of the city guard stopped each cart and wagon. They didn't appear to be checking under tarps or prying open barrel lids for contraband.

"What are they stopping people for?" Ellena asked.

"I don't know," Silas answered.

Ellena squinted. Were the guards questioning people? Perhaps delivering a warning? Then Ellena saw the glint of silver passing hands.

"Silas!" She grabbed his knee.

"I see," Silas said grimly.

The guards were charging entry into the city.

"We still have time to go back to the Stone Gate?"

"We've lost too much of the day already. We can't risk trying to find our way through the upper slums and factories."

"But, Silas," Ellena hissed, "this is the Regent's guard. If you don't have enough to enter the city, they might just take what you have and turn you away with nothing."

"And if we turn out of the line now, they may stop us and take what money I have anyway," Silas responded. "Worse, they might search the back of the cart."

Ellena could understand why Silas didn't want the guards going anywhere near Soolie. The Ravus city guard had a reputation for being bad company for pretty young girls.

The wagon before them rolled onward, passing through the city gates. Silas touched the reins, and the cart pulled slowly parallel to the black-cloaked figure who approached, sweeping aside his cloak, revealing a wood-handled pistol strapped low across his chest.

The guardsman was a young man, perhaps nineteen or twenty in years, with pewter gray eyes, a ruddy face, and a flaxen-stubbled chin. He looked past Silas at Ellena and lifted his upper lip, showing teeth corroding like yellow pollen in the crevices. A topaz user.

"Gate tax," the young guard said.

"How much?" Silas asked.

The guard grinned again, still watching Ellena, and reached up to stroke the handle of his pistol. "How much you got?"

Silas pulled out his purse. Before he could count the coins, the guard snatched it from his hands, turning it upside down and dumping the remaining coppers into his palm. He looked at them for barely a moment, then tossed the empty purse to the mud, and tucked the coins under his cloak where they made the light clinking sound of company.

The guard spat through his front teeth. "Not 'nough. Turn around."

"It is all I have." Silas kept his eyes down, his hands in his lap, trying to appear submissive and non-confrontational.

"Well, you'ad sot, and now you got not. So get," the guard leered, touching his gun. "'Fore I find something else o' yours I want for myself."

"I have some money," Ellena said, reaching under her cloak and pulling out a white deerskin purse.

"Give it." The guard held up his hand, and Ellena tossed the purse past Silas, who clenched the reins painfully tight and didn't look up.

The guard tipped two silver coins and a handful of coppers into his hand, closed his fist around them and grinned at Ellena. "If the skag wants to earn her coins back, I'd be glad to arrange a way to," he sucked at his teeth, "fill her purse."

"May we enter the city?" Ellena asked levelly.

"Your wish." The guard stepped back and motioned them forward. "Welcome to the greatest city of the known world, cuckers!"

DOG CLUNG TO THE UNDERSIDE of the butcher shop awning. This was how he spent his nights. Hands and feet hooked over the iron trusses where they sunk into the brick and mortar, arms curled tight, cloak wrapped up about his waist, body straight and tense, tucked up into the shadows out of sight.

He hadn't slept in weeks. The Master always said the pack should sleep; it made the mind last longer. But Dog had to stay alert and hidden through the dark hours where neither pack nor living could find him. All habitable spaces were inhabited, and all uninhabitable spaces were possessed by the dead and the monsters. So Dog clung in the shadows and stayed awake, waiting for the dawn.

For the most part, the market streets closed down at night. The shops pulled their shutters, the inns bolted their doors, only the occasional tavern stayed awake to pour mead and spirits for the travel-weary merchants and life-weary locals. Even most of the factories and tanneries of Ravus shut down to preserve lamp oil. Few slept with any peace in the Dark Districts, but only the Crimson District came alive at night, opening eyes, doors, and legs to the traffic of the dark.

The worst part of waiting through the night was the hunger. Dog could smell the people all around him, stacked up, one on another in the close quartered dwellings, mixing with the savory smells of the shop wares. The butcher shop below him smelled of meat, salt, spices, of offal in waste bins waiting to be carted out of the city, of sawdust and blood on the floors. And living above the shop: eleven. Three sleeping small ones, four adults, two old, and the young mother, awake in the early hours of the morning, letting down warm fresh milk from her breast into the wet toothless mouth of an infant. Both so soft, so warm, so vulnerable, so close. It would take the action of a moment to tear through the heavy canvas of the awning, climb through the upper window, and sink his teeth into that soft flesh.

But he couldn't let himself feed on those in the houses. It left traces, caused a stir. It was better to wait for the light of day and hunt the streets while the pack slept underground. Still, the waiting was agony.

As soon as the darkness began to turn ashen with the coming dawn, Dog unhooked his toes from the trusses and swung down, released his grip and dropped to the cobbles. Soon the rest of the humans would be stirring, the man and his son would come down into the shop to unpack the salted smoked meats and hang them on iron hooks for carving, to reset the rat traps and pull open the shutters to the street, and by then he needed to be gone.

Dog untucked his cloak from about his waist, letting the fabric hang loose from his shoulders, and glanced across the street. The ghost of a small coal-skinned boy startled and darted away through a plastered wall. Dog took the edges of his hood with both hands and pulled it over his face. They were everywhere now: the refuse of his kills. That boy had been an easy feed. The son of a merchant. Dog often targeted visiting foreigners: people out of their element, easily misplaced. He had consumed the entire family, crushed their bodies, and thrown the pieces in among the waste and offal of the butcher shops. Their bodies would never be missed, but their spirits were conspicuous. Too many spirits in the market streets would draw attention from the pack. This was not sustainable. He needed a new plan.

Dog moved through the streets smoothly, silently as the city came awake around him. Vendors setting up stalls, shops pulling up or folding out the shutters. Servants to the Sun District, primly pressed in their gray and white uniforms, were already scouting the meats and produce for the freshest ingredients to tuck in their wicker baskets for their masters' meals. Dog moved. There was no hurry. No rush. The merchants were only just beginning to crowd through the Iron Gate. He would know his next meal when he saw it: someone vulnerable. Someone who wouldn't be missed. Yes, he needed a new plan. But first, he needed to feed.

STAY HIDDEN.

The city is full of dangers. If they find me, they will tear you apart.

GET OUT BEFORE THE DARK, SOOLIE BEETCH. DO NOT SHOW YOUR FACE.

Soolie rolled her eyes. It was amazing that a voice in her head could shout so loud. 'Stay put.' 'Don't show your face.' 'Don't let anyone see you.' 'Death, destruction, dismemberment.' As if Papa hadn't said enough of the same thing that morning, the night before, and the night before that. With the way Papa acted, you'd think they were entering an enemy fortress instead of a city.

It wasn't going to be easy to convince Papa to take her to the carnival. She hadn't brought it up yet. She needed to find a moment where it would be easy for him to say yes, or, more accurately, difficult for him to say no. When she could look up at him with excitement in her eyes, 'Oh, please, Papa! Can we?' Perhaps she could win Ellena first, and once she had Ellena on her side, find a way to convince Papa. She would find the right moment, she had to.

Of course, right now nothing was happening, because she was stuck in the back of a cramped, musty, dark cart with a bunch of shoes, unable to see anything. Soolie desperately wanted to peek out the back, but they were moving slowly, stopping and starting, and the sounds outside were muted and quiet. Clopping, rolling, the snort of an animal, clink of a harness, distant muttering of words. It was much too quiet for a city street. For some reason, the cart must still be outside the city gate.

Soolie heard the familiar low notes of Papa speaking with someone, and pressed her ear to the canvas to try and make out what they were saying, but the sound was too muffled. Her left bum cheek was achy and numb from her sitting position. She tried to shift quietly, holding her breath.

Then the cart was moving again. New sounds began to fill the dark space of the cart: the clatter of wheels on stone, splashing of water, clopping hooves, the clamor of voices in languages familiar and foreign, haggling, hawking, and hollering.

They were inside the city. Unable to stand the wait any longer, Soolie dragged the canvas over the side of the cart, over her head, and let it drop behind her. She knelt blinking in the sudden daylight.

"Hey, it's our burrow woman surfacing!" Ellena called, waving back at her from the driver's seat. "Welcome to Ravus, Soolie!"

Soolie squealed and clapped her hands.

"She should really stay hidden."

"Oh, Silas. You can't ask her to go through the city with a tarp over her head."

There was so much to see. Holding on to the side of the cart, Soolie strained her neck like a fruit picking pole.

Even in the gray morning, the wide street was milling with people who walked and darted around the slow moving cart, careless of the rolling wheels and sharp horses' hooves. Some of them looked just as she remembered from when she was little: women in ragpile skirts, lace-up bodices, knit snoods and caps, the men in jackets, loose shirts, and pants that bared their ankles. It was the people in the brighter colors who were wearing new and exciting things.

Tiny hats had been replaced by tall chimney pipes festooned in flourishes of feathers, sprays of colorful wire mesh, and ripples of taffeta ribbon. The men wore intricately carved knee-high boots, and the women's skirts were thick with ruffles like sea foam gathered and drawn up on one side, sometimes two, like curtains. And the colors! They bustled through the browns, stones, and grays of other people like the brightest of flowers opening to the first of muddy spring in fabrics of carnelian, emerald, amethyst, and sapphire.

Soolie looked around, trying to see everything at once. Now the cart was passing two of the Regent's guard in long black cloaks questioning a man behind a street stand. An island slave with sharp-angled tattoos netted across his bare skull strode by balancing a barrel on his shoulder, large enough to pack a horse in. A half-dozen Emerist votaresses glided past in gray robes. Something flickered in an alleyway. Soolie squinted after it, but the alley was empty. She scowled. She had been sure she had seen something. An image lingered in her mind of a little black boy and a pregnant woman in a gray and white pinafore, standing staring at her ... but the alley was empty. Her overloaded brain was teasing her. Perhaps it had been nothing more than an oversized rat.

She needed to focus. She wasn't the same giddy little girl who had visited the city five years ago, much as that was what Papa needed to see. This was her one chance to find answers, to destroy the demon. She had to smile and bounce, she had to be enraptured. If Papa was going to take her to the carnival, Soolie was going to have to be flawless. And able to find it. She hadn't seen any signs or posters yet. No roaming bands of acrobats and zanies handing out fliers. How were people supposed to *find* the carnival? Well, she could always ask someone.

"Pretty girl! Pretty girl!"

A man hung onto the side of the cart. His face was old and weathered, spotted with sun, and sprouting with patchy long gray hairs. Soolie saw he was missing most of his front teeth. He stretched out a hand, palm up.

"Pretty girl! Coppers? Got any coppers for an old man with no home? I used to be a sea captain. Thirty years, pretty girl. I'm lame. Half blind. Help an old man, pretty girl. Coppers, pretty girl?"

Soolie leaned in toward him, "Do you know which way to the Southern Lands Carnival?"

The old man massaged his slack neck skin with one hand. "Ahhh," he rasped. His breath was sour. "Information for a copper."

"Papa!" Soolie hollered.

Papa glanced back tensely. "Soolie, I have to direct the horses!"

"But this man needs help!"

The man pulled himself toward Papa and Ellena, clinging to the side of the cart with one hand, reaching with the other. "Please, good mister! Pretty lady! Got any coppers? Any coin would help…"

Ellena smiled kindly. "I'm sorry, we don't have any money."

Papa barely looked back and snapped, "We have nothing for you. Leave us alone!"

The man sneered. "May yer whelp skag's milk curdle in her nubs! Tikan's spear cuck yer crawlers in their puckers bloody!"

Soolie giggled at the sudden bile, and the man turned on her wild-eyed. "What you chacking at, filthy little skag?" He shook a crude gesture in her face, then pushed off into the crowd.

Soolie clapped her hands gleefully.

"Soolie!" Papa shouted back, "Don't speak to anyone else!"

"Yes, Papa!" The next person would know. She was sure of it.

Papa directed the horses over to the side of the street and handed the reins to Ellena. He hopped down to the cobbles and began scanning the crowds.

Soolie leaned over the top of the tarp toward her aunt. "What's Papa doing? Are we at the first stop?"

Ellena nodded. "He's looking for a boy to hold the horses."

Soolie stood on tiptoe searching over the tops of the people. There! Something flickered against the stone of the building across the street. It had only been a moment. A filament of an image. Something staring at her. A boy, perhaps a girl, wearing a little gray cap. Soolie glared stubbornly across the street, but the mirage was gone.

"What is it, Soolie?" Papa called. "Do you see someone?"

"No!" Soolie shouted back. "Nothing!"

"Keep looking!"

It was several minutes before Papa spotted two boys a couple years younger than Soolie and waved them over to the cart.

"I don't want to pay for both of you. I only need one."

"Shine both us or find some' else," the taller of the boys said.

The other nodded and added, "But y'on't find no solone. No alley tyke goin' solone now. Solone is ganked 'n gone."

Soolie had never heard anyone talk like these boys did before. It was kind of like the way Bernad slung words, only even more so. Maybe they knew something about the carnival.

Papa frowned with his hands on his hips. "Fine. I'll pay both of you. But not until we get back."

"Shine for one now. Shine the other when ya get back."

"I gave all my money to the guard at the gate. You have my word you'll be paid. After or nothing."

"After, then. Don't trim us."

Ellena handed the reins down to Papa who passed them to the boys. "Don't give me reason to."

Soolie ducked under the tarpaulin to grab the linen bags for the first drop-off. Six bags of shoes, each bag with a little black pin stuck near the top. Black pins for the first drop-off. Silver for the second. Brass for the last. Soolie grabbed all six bags and wiggled her way back into the sunlight where Papa and Ellena were already waiting. Soolie handed the shoes off to Ellena's ready hands, scooted off the end of the cart, and hopped down to the street.

"Now," Papa pulled them in close. "We stay together at all times. Pay attention." He pointed at Soolie seriously. "Don't wander off. Don't touch anything. Don't talk to anyone. We're here to do business. I want to be well out of this city by dusk. Got it?"

Ellena winked at Soolie. "Understood."

Soolie nodded. "Got it!"

The cobbler's shop was a narrow building with plaster white lion's heads and curling fern molding around an expensively smooth glass window. The shoes on display were unlike any of the shoes in Hob Glen. Tall lace-up boots the color of blue wren's eggs, black high latticed platforms, and sharp-toed flats with the points dipped in crimson. All were arrayed on white fur platforms of varying heights, and from silver chains, a single pair of glistening green boots with scalloped carving up the sides hung suspended in the middle of the window.

Soolie squealed and ran forward, resisting the urge to touch the smooth surface of the glass lest she smudge it, but standing close enough that the window began to fog up below her nose.

"Soolie! Stay close!"

Papa was holding the door as Ellena entered with the shoes, and he waved Soolie to follow. Soolie bounced away from the window and into the shop.

It was smaller than she expected. Shoes of all shapes and colors lined the walls on smooth wood shelves. Several customers examined the wares, but only the shopkeeper looked their way as they entered. Ellena delivered the shoes to the counter, and soon the shopkeeper was examining each pair and haggling prices with Papa.

Soolie spun back and forth to see all the people. Surely one of these knew where to find the carnival. An elderly man with half-moon glasses stood by while a woman with silver hair tried on crumpled velvet slippers. He caught Soolie looking at him and winked at her. Soolie started to wave back, but the woman spoke to him, and he turned away.

"Well?" Ellena stood at her side, self-consciously trying to smooth out her travel-frizzy hair. "What do you think of the city?"

"Oh, Ellena!" Soolie grabbed her aunt's sleeve. "There's so much to see! Did you see the shoes in the window? Papa never made shoes like that!"

"No," Ellena said. "And I don't think he ever will."

Maybe this was her chance. "Ellena?"

"Yes?" Ellena glanced back to check on Papa, then leaned in with a somber face. "What is it?"

Soolie hesitated. She was being too hasty. She remembered Papa's knotted brow and many commands, the way he had yelled at the toothless man. Papa was even more anxious and afraid in the city than she had anticipated, and Ellena was watching him. Ellena might be Soolie's favorite person, but she was still an adult, and one who had feelings for Papa. Soolie had a sudden misgiving that she wouldn't be able to convince Ellena of anything.

"Nothing."

"Are you sure?" Ellena raised an eyebrow. "I think I recognize 'nothing' when I hear it."

Soolie shook her head and smiled. "I'm just glad you're here."

"Oh, sweetie!" Ellena pulled her in for a hug. "I'm really glad I'm here too."

Soolie was going to have to get clever or lucky or both.

Papa was walking towards them, the shoe sacks in his hand, all empty but for one weighted low with coins. "All right, ladies! Let's make quick steps!"

Soolie squeezed Ellena one last time and turned to follow Papa for the door, but then she stopped. Something caught her eye. It was her own reflection in the shop window. The blurry slanted image of a girl in a green dress, and behind her, just over her shoulder, a strange pale face in a gray cap meeting her gaze in the window and glaring back. Soolie spun around, but there was no one. Only Ellena looking at her quizzically in the middle of a shop of people minding their own business.

"What is it, Soolie?"

"Soolie!"

Soolie shook her head quickly and grinned, "Isn't this the best day ever?"

Dog saw ghosts everywhere. He shouldn't have been hunting where he slept. He realized that now. He shouldn't be hunting now, but the hunger was demanding.

He lingered for a moment, watching two street boys holding the reins to a set of cart horses outside a shoe shop. Not long ago, it would have only been one boy, easily swept into the dark corner of an alley, but now the boys stood together keeping watch. Dog could dispose of them easily enough, but could he do it silently and unseen?

He snarled and moved on. More and more, the living were taking precautions. Even the street sweepers were working in pairs. This was trouble. If he didn't find a solution soon, the pack would find him. Unless he left the city. Were there even enough people for feeding outside of the city? Dog wouldn't know his way. Where would he go? Dog had never been outside of the city. Especially not alone. Dog had never been alone. Dog felt very alone. Dog deserved to be alone.

The street widened out to accommodate a covered market of small stalls selling hot street food, baubles, necklaces, rugs, and scarves. It was much too busy and crowded for a killing, but ... Dog saw her. The lone street performer.

In the bustle and pack of the street, men, women, and children made room, backing up, forming a tight-walled circle. Within the circle, the dancer danced. Gold and teal skirts flaring, flashing, arcing into perfect fans with an elegant high kick and swirling out like a whirled parasol with every spin. The dance coursed like ocean waves through powerful bronze limbs and an elegant arched neck that whipped a full head of shiny black hair. The only music was the bells about her ankles, the ripple and snap of silver ribbons pulled through the air by deft fingers, tying the audience and holding them captive with her every move.

Dog watched from a distance, tucked against the side of a building, unable to see anything through the press of people but the occasional flair of teal and gold. He didn't need to see. He remembered her smell. The warm dark spices of the Southern Lands, the fear and adrenaline on her neck. That smooth, warm, pulsing neck so close. "I knew worse monsters than you before I was born." His fangs hurt just remembering it.

The dancer. The lone living survivor from the night of his shame. The carnival massacre. She was alone. Like him, alone. Perhaps that was why he hadn't killed her yet. Perhaps it was because she was a fighter, a survivor, and Dog respected her struggle enough to prolong it.

It wasn't that he didn't have ample opportunity to taste her. She came here every day to dance in the streets, leaving just before dark.

He'd even followed her once before, intending to take his kill as soon as she was alone, but a violent suitor, one of the Regent's Guard, had devised a similar plan and attacked her in an alleyway. The dancer had pulled a dagger from beneath her skirts, and the man had suffered a stabbed hand for his trouble. He hadn't needed to suffer long. As soon as the dancer had moved on, Dog had fed, kept the cloak, and stuffed the dessicated corpse down a chimney.

There was applause from the crowd and the ringing of coins on stones to reward the dancer's skill. The tightly pressed crowd shifted, people displacing others flooding in to fill the gaps.

It was a fitting final meal. A goodbye to the city, a goodbye to all he had known. He would take only his failure with him.

It would be several hours before the dancer left her post for the night. He had time. Dog moved through the throng, head down, face hidden in the hood of the dead guard's cloak. When the dancer took her last bow, he would be waiting for her behind the curtain.

THE LAST OF THE SHOES had been delivered. Soolie hadn't been able to talk to anyone with Ellena and Papa always nearby, and Papa hadn't let up for a moment. He shuttled them through the chaotic many-colored maelstrom with the drive and focus of a herding hound, while the city pulled Soolie's attention this way and that and offered no direction. It was difficult to believe that after all the traveling, the planning, the nightmares, time in Ravus could go by so quickly. That it was almost gone.

Reassured by the knowledge that they would be leaving soon, Papa had suggested a hot lunch from the street markets as a reward for their hard work before hitting the Eastern Road home. It was her last chance. One last stop before Ravus was gone forever, and the demon was here to stay.

Soolie squealed general words of excitement while Papa guided the horses to the side of the street, pulling in beside several other carts, wagons, and small carriages that had travelled from outside the city and gathered here in a waiting huddle. The street beneath the hooves and wheels was mounded with layers of mashed horse pies that, mercifully moist now, would reduce to a thick choking dust when the summer heat returned.

"Silas," Ellena leaned over Soolie, who was crammed up front between them. "I'll hold the reins while you two get the food."

Papa shook his head. "We need to stick together."

"And we need someone to watch the horses, which has been near impossible all day." Ellena reached across and took the reins. "Plus, I'm starving. Something hot and meaty please. Preferably not rodent."

"We'll be quick." Papa stepped off the cart. Soolie scooted across the seat after, and his big strong hands reached up, caught her at the waist, and lowered her to the street beside him. He took her firmly by the hand. "Stay close, Soolie. Don't let go."

The street market was a milling corral of people hemmed in by buildings and vending stalls beneath a large wood and stone pavilion that kept the elements off through the seasons. The rich salty smell of roasted sausages, sweet bread puddings, and savory meat pies floated over the city stench and made Soolie's stomach growl.

Papa wove through the people with Soolie tucked in close at his side scanning the crowd. She saw a man with corded orange hair that hung to his knees. Two identical young girls in gray and white pinafores hurried by carrying paper-wrapped loaves of fried fish. An island woman as tall as Papa stood bare to the waist even in the autumn cold, heavy drapings of gold and brass chains laden with raw jade and black glass hanging over her breasts, her forehead shaved high to show sharp-cornered tattoos that grew up from the ridges of her eyebrows. Really, Soolie thought, any of these people could be part of a carnival. The market was its own show.

Papa stepped into line before a wooden stall. A man with a sweat-drenched gray cloth tied around his head took coppers and handed back blackened lumps of meat on long skewers like sticky meat abacuses.

A small man with a face like a wrinkly brown walnut stepped in behind them. Soolie glanced up at Papa, still holding tight to her hand, glaring forward through tense eyes.

"Excuse me," Soolie hissed to the walnut man.

The man's eyes glanced up at her warily, but his head stayed down.

"Do you know where the Southern Lands Carnival is?"

The man shook his head. "*Nah balo. Nah balo.*"

Of course, some of these people wouldn't speak Midland. Soolie stood up on her tiptoes, weaving back and forth to see through the crowd. For a moment, she thought she saw someone in a gray cap. There were probably hundreds of people wearing gray caps in Ravus. Somewhere nearby, little bells began a rhythmic jangle as a street performer started up their routine. Papa moved a step forward in the line, dragging Soolie with him.

Soolie jumped, trying to see above the people to the sound of the bells.

"Soolie." Papa tugged her arm to keep her down. "What are you doing?"

"I wanted to see where the bells are coming from."

"Don't draw notice." Papa let go of her hand and squeezed her shoulder. "Stay close."

Papa reached into his coat, pulled out a few coppers, and stepped up to the stall to exchange words and coins with the sweaty man.

Soolie bit her lip, looking around for someone, one last person to ask.

Something flittered right beside her like a gray flame. Soolie almost yelped. It had only been a moment and out of the corner of her eye, but this time she was certain she had seen it: a girl, sharp-featured with short shorn hair and a gray cap.

The little old walnut man scowled at the street stones. Soolie looked this way and that. Where had she gone? The gray-capped girl was here. She had been following them.

"Hello?" Soolie hissed to the air. "I saw you."

There she was. A girl with a gray cap standing in the crowd. She motioned for Soolie to follow, then turned and folded away into empty air. Gone.

Soolie gaped, then glanced back at Papa who was reaching up to take the first meat skewer, then looked back to where the girl had disappeared. A ghost? A spirit? A demon? There was no good reason for her to be surprised. She was possessed by one. Perhaps help from a spirit was exactly what she needed. She had to decide now.

Before Soolie knew what she intended, she broke away from Papa and ducked into the crowd.

There were people all around her. Soolie pushed blindly forward, keeping low, worming her way through. The ghost girl had to be here somewhere, directing her toward something.

Behind her, Soolie thought she heard a panicked cry, Papa calling her name. There was nothing for it now. This was the second time she had run away from Papa, and he would most certainly make sure it was the last. This was her only chance.

Soolie saw a flicker of movement that might have been a small person weaving through the throng. She pushed forward, the jangle of bells growing louder. Here, all the people stood wedged together facing one way, looking on. Soolie turned sideways to squeeze through, pressing doggedly between the stalwart bodies. There was a swash of turquoise and gold, the flash of silver cloth, the rhythmic stomping chime of bells. Soolie broke through to the front of the people. And saw the dancer.

The woman leapt high, kicking out her bare feet, silver ribbons trailing through the air like arcs of water. She lighted on the ground with feline grace, spinning, her skirts flaring, every movement a seamless continuation of the last. Soolie stared in sun-struck awe. The dancer whirled full circle, facing the crowd, golden eyes glancing across Soolie, and halted abruptly.

It was sudden, startling. Silver ribbons rippled to the stones. Her skirts wrapped up around her legs, and the golden eyes stared at Soolie, piercing, intense. Familiar.

"*Mirna sutja.*"

The words hissed out from the woman's white teeth like a curse. A restless murmur moved through the crowd. Soolie heard Papa's voice calling her name, pushing towards her.

The woman's face, elegant nose, high cheek bones, and full mouth were contorted in a vehement look not unlike hatred. "Why are you here?" Her accent was Southern.

Soolie clenched her fingers into knots and swallowed. "I need to find the Southern Lands Carnival."

Seeing that the dancing had ended, people around them began to turn away, grumbling to one another.

"Soolie! Soolie!"

Papa...

The dancer unhooked bells from her ankles and began to wrap then up in the ribbons, folding them up into little silver bundles. "I can't help you."

"Please!" Soolie begged, stepping toward the woman. "You have to."

The dancer's eyes snapped to her, her body tense.

Soolie stepped back again. She was begging now. "Please."

The dancer pursed her lips, then set her jaw.

"Wasya nakra," she muttered, then tossed her head toward a side alley. "Follow me."

The dancer moved swiftly toward the alley, bare feet nimbly darting around street filth, sliding between people.

Desperately, Soolie reached out and snagged a gruff looking woman in a servant's pinafore by the sleeve.

"Hey, unhold, gutter spak!"

The woman moved to shake her loose, but Soolie held on fiercely, "Tell the shouting man Soolie went to the carnival!"

"I be no gutter's courie!"

"Tell him!" Soolie let go to run after the flickering skirts of the dancer disappearing between a pair of stalls. "Soolie's at the carnival!"

FOURTEEN

Silas couldn't breathe. His vision shuddered and shook before his eyes, frenetic, rabid, drunken. He was ready to punch through a stone wall, to crumple to the ground, to kill a man, to kill himself. He had lost her.

"Soolie! Soolie!"

He moved frantically, now one way, now another. Afraid to push too far through the people lest any move take him in the wrong direction. Afraid to stay still lest she was getting farther away.

Had she been taken? Kidnapped? He had dropped her hand for a second. A second. A second was all it took. The worst things happened to girls in the city. The worst things. The world screamed, and he screamed with it.

"SOOLIE!"

"Silas! What happened?" Ellena was at his side, clutching his arm. He shook her off.

"She's gone!" His voice was loud and high. People moved past, hardly glancing their way. The crowd kept moving as if nothing mattered. As if everyone had something else to be doing while his little girl was missing.

"SOOLIE!" This wasn't happening. What did he do? Where did

she go? He grabbed Ellena by the shoulders too tightly. He was grabbing her too tightly. But he couldn't stop himself. "I let her go for a moment, Ellena! A moment! Oh, gods, Ellena!"

He was crying. Not sobbing. Tears fled from his eyes like melting ice.

Ellena didn't flinch, didn't wince at his strong hands crushing her arms. She grabbed his wrists. "We'll find her! You go that way; I'll go this way. Circle the market and meet back at the cart. Got it?"

He nodded.

"Go!"

"SOOLIE!"

They parted ways. Silas divided the people forcefully, pushing them one way and the other, heedless and blind to anything and anyone but her.

"SOOLIE! SOOLIE!"

Behind him, he could hear Ellena calling. If Soolie was here, she had to hear them. She wouldn't just hide from them. She wouldn't run away. Not in Ravus. She wouldn't do that.

"SOOLIE!"

"Ho!" A servant woman with a cook's face waved a bundle of herbs at him.

Silas pushed the people aside, coming up on the woman, hulking close and shaking over her. "I'm looking for my daughter! Have you seen my daughter?"

The woman grimaced like he was spitting in her face. "Small snipe. Your manners."

"Where is she?"

The woman shrugged and tucked her herbs into her basket of produce. "Said she be going to carnival."

"Carnival?" Silas shook his head. "What carnival? Why the carnival?"

"Tha's all is," the woman said and started to turn away.

Silas grabbed her shoulder, forcefully turning her back. "Was she with anyone?"

The woman pushed his arm off angrily. "I told what I know. The rest is no matter o' mine! Now, off me!"

The woman cast off into the crowd that swept around him like a river eddy.

The carnival? The woman must have heard wrong. Why would Soolie need to find a carnival? Why would Soolie leave him to find a carnival?

The Southern Lands Carnival. The carnival woman. The marks on Soolie's arm. The bad dreams. The pestering to come to Ravus. Perhaps even the Pelig boy.

Soolie had been lying to him.

He needed to find her now.

Silas forged back to the cart. Left unattended, sitting by the side of the street, thank lands it looked unharmed.

Ellena was running from behind to catch up to him. "Anything? Did you find anything?"

Silas vaulted up into the driver's seat and took the reins as Ellena ran around the other side and scrambled up beside him.

"Silas, what is it?"

"She went to the Southern Lands Carnival."

He turned the horses into the street, people clamoring and dodging out of the way. Someone shouted obscenities, and a horse pie hit the side of the cart.

"The carnival? Why?"

"I don't know."

"How do we find it?"

"It'll be in the great square just north of the Dark Districts."

"But where…?"

"I know where it is."

Ellena didn't even ask how he knew.

IT WASN'T NEAR DARK, and the dancer was gone. Dog scowled and scuffed at the stones where she'd been with his dirty sharp-nailed toes. He paced the market, eyes darting, ears keen, pulling the air in through his nostrils and over his tongue, straining the broth of people and animals for the taste of her. There, trailing off into the shadows, the myrrh and musk of Southern spices. His upper lip curled, and he swallowed the saliva that pooled behind his teeth. He would find her. Tonight he wouldn't wait until dark to feed.

THE DANCER MOVED EFFORTLESSLY. She skimmed from one alley to another, across streets and through crowds while Soolie labored to keep up.

Soolie had no idea where she was. She had lost track of turns and corners. The streets had grown dimmer and grayer, and with them the people. They were headed deeper into the heart of Ravus.

She dodged between pedestrians, around carts and beggars sitting under the eaves with their dogs. Her feet splashed still water up under her cloak, her hood fell back from her face.

What, no words of doom and gloom now? Soolie thought, dashing down the muck-slick stones of a narrow alley and leaping over a ragged form on the ground that might have been a pile of discarded clothes and might have been a body.

The demon was silent.

Ahead, the aqua teal skirts rippled and whisked like the billowy tail of an elusive island fish. What would Mama do? Not this. Mama would never abandon the people she loved, who loved her. Mama would never go racing through dangerous streets after a complete stranger. Mama would never hurt Papa. Unless she didn't have a choice.

Don't think. It was too late for thinking.

The dancer ducked under sagging clotheslines and hopped over broken pottery shards. Her nimble feet were nearly silent while Soolie's leather-soled boots pounded the stones like sledges. Shadows danced on the sides of buildings and flickered in the windows. Eyes watched just out of sight. Soolie glanced over her shoulder, trying to pin the unease she felt, and seeing nothing.

A woman carrying a basket stepped out from a doorway and screamed as Soolie almost collided into her. The basket hit the stones, spilling linens into the muddy water. Soolie didn't pause, darting on as the woman yelled curses at her back. The dancer was too far ahead. She was going to lose her if she didn't run faster. Why were they running? Why hadn't the dancer just given her directions?

Don't think. Run.

Soolie gulped and shook her head, trying to push herself to new speed.

Still no words of anger? Soolie prodded. You don't want to chastise me before it's too late?

There was no response.

Soolie couldn't see the dancer. She had lost sight of the fluttering skirts. Panic fueled her heavy feet, and she pelted forward trying to catch up.

The open space was sudden. Soolie flung herself from the narrow alley like a bug from a straw. The dancer was nowhere to be seen.

Soolie cantered to a panting stop, feeling the blood flush up into her cheeks. In the woods, this wide-open city space would have been a clearing, a meadow where the buildings didn't grow. In the city it was a cobbled square, like the town square of Hob Glen, but ten times the size.

There were no people here, though there should have been. Instead, laid out in the middle of the square like food on a gray platter was a scramble of black wreckage. Soolie approached cautiously, trying to step softly on the ball of her foot, grit grinding loudly underfoot between leather and stone.

Something had been here in the center of the square. Something great. She toed up to a mound of rain-weighted ash. Broken shafts of charred wood trailed black scabby remnants of canvas. Soolie stepped carefully around the rubble. She saw the few frail spokes of a wheel, sad wooden fingers reaching out to touch the tarnished metal rim that remained. Something shiny caught her eye, and she knelt to pick up a single metal button, half melted, its brass surface crusted in black. She tipped it off her fingers and reached out to pick up a broken chunk of something rough-edged and slightly curved, half sunken in the ash. She rubbed at it with her thumb and turned it over. It was a piece of bone. There were more of them. Soolie set that piece down and picked up another. A skull, and it had been crushed. Though it was difficult to tell if it was human.

Someone was watching her. She felt it again. Soolie looked up and saw a flicker between the buildings. Uncertain shapes and dark eyes. She glanced the other way in time to see shadows melting back into shadows.

Soolie stood hurriedly, clutching her skirts, turning this way, then that. The square was deserted and she was alone, but all around her, the unseen billowed like smoke.

"They see you." Soolie started, spinning about to see the dancer walking across the square toward her. "As do I."

The dancer was like a merspirit gliding over dark waves of ash and rubble, her head held high, the silks of her skirt playing in the breeze, every step an unfinished dance. She made Soolie feel clunky and heavy. Soolie could spend a lifetime learning to walk like that. And those golden eyes. She knew them.

"I know you."

"No." The dancer stopped a stride away and crossed her arms, one eyebrow arched coldly. "If you knew me, you never would have left the safety of your mum and da."

"There is no safety." Soolie faced the dancer, feet apart, hands at her sides. "Bad things happen to parents too."

The dancer's eyes sized Soolie up and down.

Soolie swallowed, but kept her head high. "Who is watching us?"

"You." The dancer corrected. "The *bahuta* are watching you."

'*Bahuta.*' A Southern word. Ellena had used it in her stories. It meant 'spirits.'

"Why?" Soolie whispered, her eyes darting to the side, to the shadows, then back again, afraid to part too long from the dancer.

The dancer sneered, her teeth looking clean and sharp beneath her soft lips. "Don't ask jit questions."

Even sneering, she was beautiful. Soolie didn't think there were ever women this beautiful in the Midlands. Everything about the dancer was familiar, like a memory, full to the brim, waiting to be shaken to spill over.

Soolie clenched her fists tight in her cloak to keep from shaking. "This," she already sounded uncertain, "is the carnival?"

The woman didn't contradict her.

"What?" Soolie gulped. She mustn't feel frightened. Being frightened wouldn't help. "What happened?"

The dancer tossed her thick black hair. "Do you really have nothing to say to me?"

Soolie stammered. "I … I don't know what you would want…"

"I'm not talking to you, *choti lirna.*"

The shadows roiled. The dancer unfolded her arms and shifted her stance, one foot in front of the other, poised for music, or attack. Soolie felt fear begin to churn like a current in her belly, turning the solid earth of her resolve into an impending sinkhole.

She had to gain some kind of control. There was no one here to help her. She was on her own.

"Hana," the dancer's head lowered like a bull, golden predatory eyes looking up through a soft black curtain of hair. *"Enle maje bacita mem eha vhasa apa sajhana."*

The words were foreign, but like a memory, Soolie heard their meaning: 'Well, let me speak in a language you understand.' The dancer wasn't talking to her; the dancer was talking to the demon, and in that moment Soolie knew where she had seen those golden eyes. In her dreams. The little girl in the yellow tunic. It had to be.

"You're Punka's daughter!"

"No." The dancer's teeth were bared in rage. "You were Punka's daughter."

Soolie didn't see the dancer pull out the knife.

The dancer's arm was a deft blur, the blade's flight a streak of silver aimed for her heart. Soolie saw it and knew with the surreal surety of a dream that the throw was true, knew that she didn't have time to move out of the way, knew that she was about to die.

A blaze erupted behind her eyes like a violent crack to the skull, and the voice of the demon hissed in her mind.

I WILL NOT BE BOUND TO YOU, SOOLIE BEETCH.

The silver blade cut through the cloth of her cloak under her arm, missing her side by a lick.

The dancer pulled her arm in from the throw, gathering herself up like a snake.

"There you are."

The demon's presence hummed under Soolie's skin, bleaching out her sight.

YOU EXPOSE ME IN THE PLACE OF MY ENEMIES.

"My fault," the dancer said, shifting her weight over her feet. "I meant to kill you."

The dancer and the demon were speaking to one another.

"Wait!" Soolie spread her arms wide to try and show no harm. The force of the demon pulsed under her skin. "You have to help me, please! I don't even know what it is. I'm sorry about what it did to your mother. I just want to destroy it."

The dancer looked irritated that Soolie was there. "That *fagga* skag was no mother to me."

"Please," Soolie begged. "There has to be a way to destroy it. Please help me."

"Some call it a death spirit. Others, *Ikma na Sitari*. The Soul Hunter. You cannot be helped."

The dancer sprang forward in a powerful sprint, feet skimming around ash and debris. Soolie raised her arms to protect herself. Her heart felt like a hot coal in the furnace of her ribs.

The demon's voice. *HURT HER.*

The image of Bernad Pelig, his face leathern and dead, flickered behind her eyes.

I don't want to.

HURT HER.

She could feel the urge, the ability, that aching demand, that thirst, waiting for her to lash out, to defend herself.

No!

The dancer struck, a sharp kick landing right below Soolie's raised arms, driving in where her ribs met her belly. Soolie doubled in pain.

HURT HER!

Images of Bernad's face spun with the explosions in her head. Something hit her in the chest and drove her to the cobblestones, her spine and skull snapping with pain.

The dancer knelt, one knee on Soolie's chest, the compression boiling with agony, the other pinning her right arm. In one hand, the dancer held a second bright silver blade like a slender leaf, poised over Soolie's heart.

HURT HER.

The demon's voice caused her no pain. Everything was pain. And the hot demanding hunger asking her to lash out, to strike the dancer. All it would take was a touch.

I. Will. Not.

"It thinks you can hurt me?" The dancer sneered. She was still hearing the demon's words.

Soolie tried to speak, but the pressure on her chest crushed her words into a painful gasp. The dancer shifted, relieving the weight, but the pain was still there.

"Yes," Soolie gasped.

The woman leaned in, her hair draping down and brushing the side of Soolie's face. "Then why don't you?"

"Because," Soolie whispered painfully, "it wants me to."

The dancer leaned up, shifting her full weight back onto her knee, crushing Soolie's injured ribs, the knife blade now held sharp-edged to her throat.

"I see why it doesn't want you," the dancer said, her lilting words beautiful and callous. "I have to kill you. But, trust me, I'm doing you a kindness. Your mam and da will be safer with you gone."

THEN I MUST HURT YOU BOTH.

Soolie screamed. The furnace within her grew talons that ripped in, threatening to pull her out of herself like a raw egg blown out through a pin hole in its shell. The dancer twisted away as a flash of white slammed up into her body, throwing her away from Soolie, the knife skittering into the ash. The dancer cried out in pain.

And just as suddenly, it was done, and Soolie found that she was still alive. But barely. She felt as if her heart, lungs, and bowels had been squeezed out like fruit. It felt as if she had aged forty years by force. As if she was half dead. Perhaps she was. She hadn't been willing to hurt the dancer. So the demon had hurt her.

Soolie lay on the hard ground, too weak to move. She could hear the dancer whimpering and gasping with pain, but couldn't turn to see if she was moving or if she was badly hurt. Soolie was in a heavy haze. The rubble was uneven and jagged beneath her. There was ash in her mouth.

The demon spoke.

You would have made an excellent vessel, Adrana Rahka. Your mother should not have stopped me. It was not good for her to hold me for so long. In the end, I made sure her soul was not lost.

"*Lirna,*" the dancer's voice was quiet. "If you live, there is one thing you can do."

Soolie was too weak to ask. She was almost too weak to hear.

"What my mother failed to. Kill yourself."

FIFTEEN

Silas ricocheted through the streets of Ravus as if he was born to them. The cart careened around corners, dodging down wide streets and narrow alleyways. He steered clear of clogged corners and street fairs, never once stopping to ask for directions. With Soolie in trouble, it was as if her father had been granted a seer's sense.

Ellena clung to the seat boards as if her fingers had been screwed down, bracing her feet and leaning against every corner. She didn't understand where Soolie was or why she had gone there, but Silas seemed to know where he was going, and dear lands, she prayed Soolie was there when they got there. If she wasn't, Ellena didn't know what they would do. She had no idea how she would help him.

The horses tossed their heads, nervously contending with the reins as they galloped between a pair of naked iron flag poles and into the old great square of Ravus.

"SOOLIE!" Silas screamed.

Ellena strained to see what he could see, not daring to loosen her vise grip on the seat. Silas swung the cart up beside a mass of burned wreckage, what may have once been a number of tents and wagons. Silas tossed the reins to Ellena, jumping out of the cart before it stopped rolling, running towards a small figure collapsed in the midst of the ashy ruins.

"SOOLIE!"

The horses rolled their eyes, their hooves hopping like water on an overheated pan. Ellena fumbled her grip on the reins, gathering them and pulling the horses up. They did not like this place.

"Silas! How is she?"

Silas was bent over the little form. She could hear him sobbing.

"Silas? Silas, is it Soolie? Is she all right?"

Something was moving in the rubble behind Silas. A young woman pulling herself painfully up. She looked hurt.

"Silas! Behind you!" He wasn't listening to her. "Silas! Someone else is hurt!"

Ellena desperately wanted to drop the reins, but the horses tossed their heads, wanting to run. Silas was lifting the head of a small form, supporting it carefully. It was Soolie.

The young woman was walking now, stiffly, staggering, but she wasn't heading for Silas and Soolie, she was heading towards Ellena.

Ellena gripped the reins tightly, leaning out toward her. "Miss, are you okay?

She was hurt. As she came closer, Ellena could see what must have once been long flowing skirts, crinkled and melted with heat, her hair, full and black on one side, burned short and frizzed on the other, and her side, bloody, caked in chunky black ash. And she was cradling her right arm in her left. She looked like she had fallen into a live fire.

"Oh, lands!" Ellena forced back impulsive tears. If this woman was hurt, what might have happened to Soolie? Ellena cringed, tensing as the young woman came closer, not sure whether to help or feel threatened.

The young woman looked up with eyes of hot amber. "Hey, *mahla.*"

The woman stopped a stride away from the cart. Ellena couldn't tell if she was panting or sneering, from pain or malice.

"Is that cucking *lirna* yours?"

Ellena shook her head, confused. "I'm sorry? Do you need help? Can we get you help?"

"Is that your girl!?" The young woman snarled savagely. Ellena saw now that there was a black hunk of broken spar lodged deep in the base of the young woman's right hand.

"Oh, lands," Ellena gasped. "Silas?"

"Who are you! Stay away from her!" Silas was headed towards them, Soolie small in his arms.

Instead of looking back toward Silas, the young woman lifted her injured hand to her mouth, took the butt of the hunk of wood between her front teeth, bit down and pulled. The piece of spar was longer than Ellena had thought it was, easily a full third finger's length lodged deep up the young woman's wrist. Ellena cringed as the woman yanked the bloody splintery piece of wood free and spat it out, her mouth ringed in blood and ash.

"I said, back away!" Silas shouted at the woman, his voice erratic and shaky, his eyes red from an impossible number of tears.

The woman finally looked over at him, then up at Ellena. Her body was stiff from the raw ash-caked burn on her back, but her voice and eyes were bilious with contempt.

"Don't let her near young ones. And she will use your love against you." The woman turned her back on them and began to walk carefully, stiffly away. "She is not your little *lirna* any more."

As soon as it was clear the woman was walking away, Silas lost interest in her.

"Soolie's been hurt."

"Oh, lands, what's wrong?" Ellena leaned towards them, trying to see. Soolie lay curled in his arms half covered with his coat. Ellena didn't see any blood. All she could see was that Soolie looked weary and tired. Perhaps sickly. Almost old.

"I don't know." Silas petted his daughter's hair hastily and kissed her head. "I don't know. I need you to sit with her in the back while I drive us out of this city."

"Perhaps we should take her to a doctor?"

"She needs to go home."

"Silas, the best hospitals are in the city."

"I never should have brought her here. We get out of Ravus." Silas said harshly. "Now."

The horses skittered again, their ears flattened, eyes glancing back. Ellena wrestled with the reins. "Lay her in the back!"

Silas was already headed toward the back with Soolie in his arms.

Ghosts piled in the alleys like wet leaves in the gutters. Pressing, whispering, pointing, their bodies sliding through the building walls as they tried to see over one another, trying to catch a glimpse of the girl whose soul was on fire. They were in every shadow, every alley and street entry to the square. Every entry, that was, except one.

Dog had been tracking the dancer from the market when he had caught the scent of something new, something separate from the cloying musk of the dancer, something exciting. This scent tingled in his mouth; it was ancient and tantalizing, powerful and acrid like the smell of coming dawn, burning metal, impending death. There was a presence too. Something beyond hearing like the way the Wolf had made the hair on his arms want to run for the shadows. Something that called to him. Something that reminded him of the Master.

He had answered, galloping thirstily after it, pulling heavily at the air, dragging it through his waxen nostrils and deep into his lungs, saliva pooling behind his lips and trickling out the sides of his mouth towards his ears as he sprinted down the streets, black cloak rippling behind him, the claws of his feet scraping at the dirty street stones.

As he had reached the square, gathered spirits had scattered before him like frightened gulls. He had run up to the edge of the buildings and halted, staying in the shadows, and he had seen her.

Standing, facing the dancer, she didn't look like much. A girl a little smaller than he was. He was surprised to note she seemed alive, outwardly unremarkable. But there was something about her.

Something within her.

Suddenly, the dancer threw a knife, and the girl blazed forth with a glare of light. Ghosts gasped and shielded their eyes, bending away from the searing flash that was blindingly there in a moment and then gone. The knife cut through the girl's cloak, flitting harmlessly into a pile of debris. Dog held perfectly still, clenching his hands, his nails cutting cold bloody sickles into his palms.

The girl and the dancer were shouting, but he couldn't make out the words.

The dancer charged, landing a sharp spinning kick to the cowering girl's belly, then coming around, swinging her down onto the ground and pinning her to the stones. Dog was disappointed. Had he been wrong? Had the dancer won? He didn't know what he had been hoping for. Perhaps what he deserved least: hope itself.

The dancer produced another blade from high on her thigh and held it poised to the girl's throat. This was it. The end of the strange being whose very presence called to him so deeply.

Then the dancer cried out, twisting to get away as a violent blast of light erupted from the girl's body, throwing the dancer into the debris where she landed with a tortured scream.

Dog was enraptured.

What was this being that wielded life itself as a weapon? That could inhabit the bodies of the living, the one thing the Master had never managed nor dared to do. This was a being of strange power. This was a being with no one to serve her.

He snarled at himself for even thinking it. The only one who had ever owned him was the Master, but he had failed the Master. Shame and self-loathing battered him, and he covered his face with a grimy hand, the tips of his gunky nails snagging on the inside of his hood. That he, Dog, could ever hope to be of use. Could ever hope to serve, to have another master. After his betrayal. His failure. He could never redeem himself. He could never serve a purpose again. He was useless.

Yet still he watched.

A cart came cannoning into the square, ghosts and spirits

scattering, frightening and spooking the horses who rolled their eyes and hopped their hooves, sensing the death that clung around them. A man jumped from the cart, running to the fallen girl while a woman held the reins. The dancer was alive, but injured. Dog could smell her raw charred flesh and fresh oozing blood, but he was uninterested. The dancer was less tantalizing damaged, and now there was the girl.

The dancer dragged herself away while the man placed the girl in the back of the cart, appearing a moment later to run up and switch places with the woman. As soon as she was in the back with the girl, the cart began to move again, turning, rattling back the way it came, the horses cantering, tossing at the reins, anxious to be free of the haunt-heavy square.

Dog whined. She was leaving. The strange girl was leaving. He couldn't let her. He didn't know what she was, what she held, what she might be to him. He had to follow. He couldn't let her go. If she was leaving the city, he would follow.

Dog hooked his claws on the cloak around his neck and ripped, tearing the thick black wool and tossing it to the ground. He crouched forward, a crossbow bolt sliding into position, and launched himself into a run, his powerful back legs propelling him toward the cart nearing the edge of the square. Dog dove, flipping onto his back, sliding on the knobby hard stones and skidding between the back wheels. His hands caught the front wheel shaft, his feet hooked over the back shaft, and he hauled himself up, gripping strong, tensing his body rod-straight close to the bottom of the cart, the street stones passing rhythmically below him. It was almost like hiding up beneath the butcher shop awning.

Dog gaped his mouth, holding it close to the underside of the cart, breathing in the smell of wood, tar, resin, and the two women above. One warm and wholesome, untainted by the acrid tang of topaz in the blood that always burned his throat. The other young, tender, but full of old power, promise, and mystery.

A new Master was too much to hope for. He didn't deserve a new Master. A chance for belonging, for redemption? He had failed too greatly, fallen too far, to ever earn the right to such service again.

But he needed it anyway.

THE IRON GATE WAITED opened towards Silas like the giant covers of a forbidding book. And through those covers, the free road, the rolling hills, home.

Silas gripped the reins so tightly that his hands began to cramp. He never should have brought Soolie to the city. Ravus was a rotting wound festering with necrotic disease that infected every poor soul that stumbled through its gates. Ravus destroyed children, turned families into death dungeons. Silas hated Ravus. He had spent fifteen years trying to scrub himself clean of that diseased touch, to forget his debt, and now the city had come back to take his daughter away from him.

Pray lands she was okay. He still didn't know how she might have been harmed.

And she had been lying to him,

To the left, horses, wagons, carts, mules, crates, cages, and barrels continued their slow pilgrimage into the city. Silas could see the black-cloaked guards stopping every entering merchant and traveler, one hand on their pistols, the other palm up. There were fewer people leaving, and no one seemed to be staying them. Silas kept his eyes straight ahead, his head tilted down. Just go straight, don't attract attention.

The horses stepped past the edges of the open gates, spiked iron bars rising high above them like limbless winter trees. The cobbled road lay out before them, curving with the slow waiting line. He would drive out straight, then cut behind the line, driving back south around the city to finally get back on the Eastern Road home.

"Hey! I 'member you!" A straw-haired, black-cloaked figure was headed toward the cart, arm raised. It was the same guard from the morning.

Silas froze, eyes ahead, panic rising in his chest. Should he make a run for it? No, the guards had pistols, and others might intervene. It wasn't safe.

"'Ey." The guard smacked the side of the cart and spat into the mud. "Where's yer skag?"

Silas kept his eyes on the rumps of the horses. "We paid our tax."

"Not what I asked." The guard stood close, looking up at Silas, one hand stroking the handle of his pistol. "I 'member there was a skag. Where's the skag? I wanna give my regards."

Cold sweat stung Silas' eyes. The muscles in his forearms were twitching from tension. "She stayed behind."

"Did she." There was the sharp click of a cocking gun and a hard clunk as the guard rested his pistol on the foot-board of the cart. "Didn't seem a city skag."

"She has a sister."

The guard nodded and scratched his stubbly cheek with his free hand. "Good fer her." He pointed the gun at Silas' face with one hand and reached up with the other, taking the reins from Silas' reluctant grasp.

"'Course," the guard grinned with his upper lip and tossed the reins down between the horses' traces, "if you're split tonguin' me, I'll cuck the both 'a you."

Silas sat on the driver's bench, his hands cramped, sweaty, and empty, the horses' reins tossed out of reach. The guard waved the mouth of the pistol at him.

"Don' scramble bush-boy."

The guard moved toward the back of the cart. He was going to check the cargo. Soolie and Ellena were under there. Silas should have gotten a weapon. A knife. A skillet. Anything. Across the way, several other black-cloaked figures worked the wagons. He should have taken a different gate. He had driven them right into a trap. The guard would be raising the tarpaulin now. Silas had to do something before it was too late.

Something clunked into the bottom of the cart with a muffled crack. There was no shout, no scuffle. There was nothing.

Silas was shaking.

"Silas?" Ellena's voice hissed from under the tarp behind him.

She shouldn't be speaking up. She should keep silent.

"Silas! Are you okay?"

Silas didn't move. He spoke low. "Are you both all right?"

"Yes! What's going on?"

Silas was too afraid to look back. He crawled forward over the traces, balancing, his face down near the horses' haunches, reaching out until his finger snagged the edge of the reins. The horses snorted, and he sat up carefully, quickly, pulling in the reins; they didn't snag. He snapped them sharply, holding his breath, and the cart wheels rolled forward, leaving behind a pistol and a small black patch of blood soaking into the cobble stones.

SIXTEEN

The night was still and dark. High clouds cloaked the moon and stars, and when Silas lifted the tarpaulin, yellow lantern light spilled out like hot butter onto burnt toast.

"How is she?"

Silas climbed up into the cart, not bothering to remove his muddy boots. Soolie lay propped up by blankets and luggage, a quilt tucked up under her arms, looking awake, but barely. Beside her, Ellena knelt, her hair down wild about her shoulders.

"I don't know." Ellena welcomed him with a hand on his shoulder as he crawled up to his daughter's makeshift bed and kneeled, his head bent low under the tarp.

"Hi, Papa." Soolie looked up weak, solemn, sorry.

He had hoped his eyes had played him false in the Ravus sun, but they hadn't. Soolie didn't look right. There were little wrinkles at the corners of her eyes and mouth, creases in her small neck. Her hair had gone bleached and pale at the temples, and her eyes ... she had always had his chestnut eyes with her mother's sparkle. Her mother's eyes never looked so old.

Ellena reached across Soolie's quilt-wrapped chest and touched his hand. "She seems all right. She says nothing hurts or feels broken."

Silas felt under Soolie's jaw for her pulse. Her skin felt loose, soft, and warm. "Did you examine her? Did you check for wounds?"

"Yes." Ellena was watching him closely. "She appears to be fine."

Silas found the little heartbeat and counted. It seemed a little fast, but steady.

Soolie smiled at him. "I'm fine, Papa, really."

"But you're not," his voice was harsh and forced, "are you, Soolie?"

"Silas." Ellena's hand was on his forearm.

He closed his eyes, breathing shakily. The cart was too small. The tarp was too low. There wasn't enough room, and there wasn't enough air.

He squeezed Ellena's hand back. "I'm all right. But it's time Soolie started telling us the truth."

Ellena's eyebrows bunched. She pursed her lips and nodded.

Silas looked down at his baby girl looking up at him with weary tremulous eyes. He sat on the thick heels of his boots and let go of Ellena's hand to take up his daughter's little one in his. It was so frail, so white, veins crawling along her wrists like blue cobwebs.

"Soolie." He tried to hide his fear, his terror. He needed to be strong for his baby girl. "You ran away in the city."

"I'm sorry, Papa."

"Why, baby girl?" He encased her little hand in both of his, safely sealed away in his strong grasp. "Why did you run away?"

"I…" Her eyes glanced over at Ellena, then back to him, then down at the quilt. At last she whispered. "I don't know."

A lie. It stabbed him. Why didn't she trust him?

The doubts climbed like a dustplains tunnel. He beat at himself. This wasn't about him and his insecurities. It was about Soolie. Stop thinking about yourself, and think about Soolie. Soolie was all that mattered.

He could feel Ellena's eyes on him, ready to step in the moment he faltered. It wasn't her job. He was Soolie's father. It was his job to protect Soolie, to take care of her, no matter what.

He was failing. He couldn't fail.

He looked down at his baby girl looking so small, vulnerable, and frail. His tongue was old clay. He breathed in through his nose, out through his mouth.

"Silas," Ellena sounded worried.

"Ellena." Her name came out more harshly than he intended. "I am in control."

She nodded.

"Soolie." He squeezed his littler girl's hand again, reassuring, not too hard, looking into her aged eyes, trying not to flinch. "A lot has happened in the last two moons."

Soolie nodded slightly, trying to look serious but receptive. He knew that look. She always looked that way when she expected him to yell at her. When she stopped listening.

"You had a strange run-in with that woman in the wagon."

Soolie nodded.

"You had a really, really bad dream."

Soolie nodded.

"And," Silas said, earnestly watching her, "you ran away from me at the harvest festival…"

"I'm sorry," she said in a small voice.

"And at some point," Silas continued, "the Pelig boy was badly injured."

She blinked and swallowed, but her facial expression didn't change.

"You need to tell me exactly what is going on." He looked at her sternly. "You can't keep anything from me any more."

Her eyes evaded his, sliding sideways, then studying her lap, her free hand fidgeting with the fringe along the edge of the quilt.

"Soolie." His chest was pinching him. Like his ribs were curling into his lungs. He leaned in, willing her to look back to him. She glanced up and met his eyes again.

"You need to talk to me."

Soolie bit her lip and whispered. "I don't know."

"What *do* you know?"

Soolie twisted at the blanket fringe. "I don't remember."

He needed to be patient. Perhaps she was scared. Perhaps she was confused.

"Soolie," his voice betrayed him, taut and quavering. "I only want to help you. To protect you."

"I know, Papa."

He reached across the quilt, carefully, controlled, and loosened her fingers' twisting grip on the blanket fringe, taking both of her little hands in his. "Whatever it is," he said, trying not to choke, willing her to hear him, to believe him, "you can tell me. I will protect you."

"I don't remember, Papa."

He wanted to scream. His pulse was rushing. It was difficult to think. The lantern was making it so hot in the cart, and there was no air.

"What *do* you remember?"

Soolie looked at the lap of her nightgown. "I don't know."

She was shutting him out.

"SOOLIE!"

He was shouting at her. He could hear himself shouting at her. It wasn't helpful. He shouldn't yell. He couldn't stop.

"I don't know."

"Don't lie to me!" Silas snapped. He needed to stand. He needed to pace. The tarp was smothering him. He heard Ellena gasp, and it angered him. "Tell me the *truth*, Soolie."

Soolie lifted her fragile little chin and looked him in the eyes, "I don't know."

"You're lying!" Fear, anger, and panic pressed on his eyes. How could she expect him to protect her if he didn't know what was happening to her?

"Silas!" Ellena exclaimed.

"Not now, Ellena!"

"You're shouting."

"I am not shouting!"

He was shouting. He couldn't stop. He couldn't breathe.

Soolie didn't flinch or look away. She stared him boldly in the face, her jaw set, her eyes hard and stubborn, as if daring him to hurt her. The look in her eyes: *Go on. Hit me. You're just like him.*

The air was blinding.

Silas' face was gray under his beard and slick with sweat. His breath was ragged, choking.

"Silas." She tried to calm him down. "You're shouting."

"I AM NOT SHOUTING!"

He glanced back at Soolie and, abruptly, pushed away and dove back out of the cart into the dark.

Ellena patted Soolie on the arm. "I'm going to go check on him. Are you okay?"

Soolie nodded.

Ellena crawled for the back of the cart. She didn't bother with shoes, instead pulling off the over-large woolen socks Silas had lent her, lifting up the tarp, and lowering her bare foot gingerly to the cold rough ground.

It was dark and silent but for a distant cheeping sound of a night sparrow. Ellena dropped the tarpaulin behind her and shivered, hugging herself. She should have grabbed her cloak.

A soft sound came from around the side of the cart, and she moved towards it, keeping one hand on the edge of the cart and carefully tiptoeing around heavily shadowed sticks, twigs, pebbles, and potential brambles. There he was.

Silas leaned against the side of the cart, his head tipped back, the scarce light falling in the hollows of his eyes. She could hear him breathing fast, choking breaths that crowded over one another, each gagging gasp cut off by another spasming failure at intake, his chest heaving.

She ran to him, careless of the rough ground, and threw her arms around him. Standing up on tiptoe, she wrapped one arm up over his shoulders and held him close.

"It's okay," she murmured. "Just breathe. Everything is okay."

His chest heaved against hers, lurching, gagging. "No. I ... I..."

He tried to push her away, shaking his head. She grabbed him by the shoulders.

"Silas Beetch," she hissed, "there's a little girl in there who needs us. And I'm terrified, do you understand? Now shut up and hold me." She squeezed him tight. "I need you to hold me."

One strong arm wrapped around her lower back, and the other behind her shoulders. He was shaking now, sobbing. One big hand buried in the snarled tangled mess of her hair, her face held close to his chest, her lips brushing his collarbone. She felt his tears trickling into her hair, and she said nothing more.

As soon as the man crawled up into the cart, Dog dropped the guard's body quietly to the ground and lowered himself beside it. He hadn't wanted to leave the corpse on the road anywhere close to the city where it might be found and lead to him. It had been a long ride, clutching to the underside of the cart, the heavy flesh of the guard laying on top of him, residual blood drizzling from the guard's neck and across Dog's face. He had been forced to press hard up against the guard's body to keep it firmly pinned between himself and the cart above so it wouldn't come loose from the jostling and rocking of the road. Even still, every once in a while, a leg or an arm would sling loose, dragging down and bouncing against the muddy road, forcing Dog to jockey position, holding on with one arm while rearranging his burden.

By evening, Dog was sore and in pain. But he had been created without an aversion to discomfort. He would gouge out his own eyes if the Master asked him to.

He just hadn't been willing to face destruction.

The man was shouting in the cart above. Dog listened. He considered entering the cart, but uncertainty held him. The girl might be everything, or she might be nothing. Perhaps this girl being would be weak, and he would kill her. Perhaps she would be strong, and he would anger her. Dog wasn't even sure how to introduce himself. Had he ever introduced himself to anyone? He bared his teeth instinctively in a submissive grimace. Perhaps if he had a gift. If he could find something to leave at this being's doorstep as an offering...

Dog crawled over the guard's body and slunk for the hills, scampered out of the trees and up an incline matted with dead brown grass and mud. He stood tall on his legs, stretching his shoulders back, panning the fresh damp night air with his nostrils as a dreamer pans for gold.

There was so much open space, uncluttered by tunnels, walls, structures, and living flesh. A giddy excitement welled up in his bones, and he danced a little on the hill top, scampering one way and then the other to drink thirstily of the newly washed air. He had never known such an expanse before. Master had always kept him close by, in the Master's home, in the city tunnels. Rarely had he ever been alone, and when he had been sent out, it had only been because the Master had a specific task for him: something that needed his speed, his skill, his reliability, and then he was back by the Master's side and rewarded with a tender sweet-blooded soul. Never had he experienced such ... space.

Perhaps. He could explore it. Just a little bit.

With an excited yelp, Dog hurtled himself off the hill, his leathery bare feet tearing at the soft mud and sod, spewing earth in his wake. He ran. For the sake of running, for the sheer jubilation of it. He tossed back his head and loosed an unbridled curdling shriek of wild ecstasy. The fields fell away beneath his flying feet like the falling of water. He could run forever. A pungent new scent tickled his senses, and he arced his path towards it. It was wild, it was powerful, it was alive. But not as wild and powerful as he was.

Dog bounded over a rise and saw the herd. Horses. Dog had met horses. Not very many, and never horses like these. These were free in the night like he, some two dozen of them, sleek-bodied and powerful, huddled up in a stand of trees. He could smell their fear as they sensed him.

A wild gaping grin exposed Dog's sharp teeth, and he picked up pace even faster than he had been running before, bearing down on the warm-blooded earthy creatures. As he came down upon them, they startled, milling and turning about, then rallying and breaking into a full panicked gallop, their ears flat, nostrils wide, eyes rolling wild. The air was thick with their adrenaline, and Dog was pelting in the midst of them, whooping and howling with glee.

He leaped up onto the back of one of the creatures, his sharply nailed feet slicing its back to the bone so it screamed a bloody terror scream. Dog reached forward with both hands and dove his fingers into the animal's eyes, blinding it and yanking back its head hard so it faltered, its long neck arched painfully back. In one swift motion, he loosed his grip on the eye sockets, reached around, dug his nails into its neck and, slicing through the soft warm hide and heavily corded muscle, shattered the windpipe, blood bursting out through his fingers, the horse buckling beneath him. Dog leaped free. The horses were screaming, and he joined them exultantly, drunk with the power of the kill, shrieking to the night.

THE WEEK BEFORE Mama died, Papa stopped eating. Soolie remembered laying awake in her loft listening to the irregular gasping breath of her father sitting below in the dark softly sobbing. In the morning, she would come downstairs to find him already sitting at Mama's side, holding her hand, looking more weary, his eyes more sunken. "Trying to make me look good," Mama had said. Mama didn't eat anything either.

It was a drudging seven days. Every morning, Papa would call Doc Wilkens over to take Mama's pulse and thump on her back, to prescribe willow tea for the pain, and lots of rest. Then the doc would tip his hat to Mama, nod to Soolie, and Papa would take up pacing from the work bench to the fireplace to Mama's bed and back. He tried many things to make Mama better. He poured soak baths with gray mineral salts, mixed bee pollen poultices for Mama's wounds, and wrapped her feet in leek leaves. Then every evening, he would call Doc Wilkins back to the house to ask if Mama's symptoms had changed.

"Doesn't he bother you?" Soolie had asked. "Doesn't he keep you awake?"

"He is doing what he must," Mama said.

Soolie scowled, unsatisfied. "You're dying, and he's making it miserable."

"Soolie, I've been fighting all my life. For him, for you. What your father doesn't understand is that I won." Mama reached out, smiling softly. Soolie took her mother's hand and lifted it to her own cheek. "I'm going away, and I'm never coming back," her mother murmured. "You were born strong, Soolie. You always will be. Your father was born gentle and made weak. When I am gone, he will need you. Be kind to him."

"I promise," Soolie had said.

The night Mama died, Papa yelled and cried for a long time. Then he had gone very quiet. Then Papa got up and walked out into the night without saying a word. After several hours, Ellena had sent Soolie to bed while she sat up with Mama's body to wait for him. Soolie had fallen asleep wondering if Papa was going to make it back. Wondering if she had lost both parents in one night.

Soolie couldn't tell Papa about the demon.

The demon might be able to hurt him, but more importantly, the demon wasn't an enemy Papa could face, it wasn't an enemy he could defeat, and he would destroy himself trying, trying to protect her, trying to keep her out of harm's way. Papa wasn't strong enough to understand that this was her enemy, her fight. And for once in her life, she had to make her own decisions. He couldn't make them for her. She had to decide what she was willing to risk, what she was willing to sacrifice. She didn't know the answer yet, and Papa's shouting and tears only made it worse.

Mama had taught her to accept the inevitable. "The tree that fights the wind will break. It is the tree that bends with the wind that can survive the storm." But this was too horrible to be accepted. Too dreadful to be inevitable. She didn't know how to fight, and she couldn't accept. She was a tree in a hurricane.

"Do what my mother failed to. Kill yourself." Those were the dancer's words.

She couldn't kill herself. Killing herself would be giving up, and she would never give up, and there was no guarantee her death would even harm the demon. She would never consider it. It was cowardly. She was afraid. It would hurt Papa, and she had already hurt him so much.

You should be afraid.

Soolie bristled. She wasn't afraid.

The demon stood before her in the empty expanse, gazing at her with those familiar golden eyes, the dancer's eyes, set in a little child's face.

Human souls have such a peculiar predisposition to self-destruction. I have tried to spare you, Soolie Beetch.

"Is *that* how I ended up half-dead," Soolie sneered.

She didn't want to talk to it. The demon always said the same things: 'get me a young soul,' 'the dead man is rising.' Hounding her with that relentless emotionless script before further invading her life and violating her will. Unless it had grown terminal, she didn't want to hear it.

It nodded. *You are not the first to resist me. You will not be the last. You have heard the one called Punka attempted once to end her life.*

"Yeah, and how did that turn out for her?"

I agreed to let go of the one in her womb.

Soolie laughed bitterly. It was such a shockingly heavy statement to be delivered so blankly. "You evil skag."

I am not evil, Soolie Beetch. It blinked at her like a perplexed doll. *Under my influence, the one called Adrana would have grown into the perfect final vessel. Young of soul, able-bodied, obedient.*

"So, strategically evil." More importantly, Soolie thought, Punka had tried to stop the demon from getting a hold on her unborn daughter by killing herself, and it had worked.

The golden eyes glistered. *I tell you this so you will understand. Her resistance cost me seventeen years and cost her everything. You saw her in her final state: rotten, diseased in body and mind, and alone. You cannot stop me, Soolie Beetch. You can only harm yourself. I am* Ikma na Sitari, *The Soul Hunter. I must face the Dead Man and take back the strength he stole from me. I must stop the dead from draining the life from the living world. I will not now allow a human soul to cast me off. There is no escape through death, Soolie Beetch. If you come to harm, I will hold your soul for always.*

"I don't believe you."

I speak truth.

"I still don't," Soolie shrugged maliciously. "'Death Spirit.' 'Soul Hunter.' Fancy words for a skagging parasite that harms unborn children."

Your attempt to anger me is without point. I do not feel as you do.

"I know," Soolie said. "Creatures who feel know better than to impersonate someone's dead mother to get what they want."

The demon's eyes glared molten. It stepped closer, soft child's hair stirring restless on its brown shoulders. *This is your last chance to grant me what I have asked, Soolie Beetch. Your attempts to oppose me have failed. This is not your battle to fight. Bring me a young soul.*

Well, since it could read her thoughts, it could suck her cuckhole.

You refuse to cooperate. I must make arrangements without you.

"You should have done that in the beginning and saved us both the trouble."

The little girl's face loomed close to hers, wide golden pools fringed in long black reedy lashes, soft dewy rose petal lips.

Many monsters are made with the souls of dead men, Soolie Beetch. If you wish to stay free of their number, you would be advised to stay alive.

The tender little girl face distorted, golden eyes flashed white, rimmed with darkness, hair flying out like static, the mouth jarred, spazzing sharp shards of jagged bloody teeth that filled her vision and consumed everything into blackness.

Cucking skag always did take the last word.

SEVENTEEN

Bernad hadn't left his bed since the incident, though it wasn't really his bed any more than it was really his room. The house was Mam's domain, both he and Pap knew it. Every surface was polished and dust free. No more than two items of décor per surface, no more than three colors featured per room, and everything tidy and complementarily paired. Bernad was the ugliest thing in the house.

"You ever gettin' out of here?" Pap had asked that morning from the doorway.

Bernad had responded by turning to face the wall.

"Welp," Pap had said. "I'm goin' down to the store." And that was that.

Even Mam was out most of the time. Her son's disfigurement had caused quite a stir in the community, and Mam felt compelled to manage it. "For his sake," she said. What did he care? She hadn't really tried to get him out of bed either. "Just remember to cover your face if anyone visits." But no one had. In the end, Mam was the only one who came by regularly, once or twice a day to clean the room and make sure there was food in the cold cellar. Not that he ate much.

He hated eating. The way he couldn't seal his mouth around a spoon or chew a piece of chicken without the greasy juices dribbling out one side. The way the stiffened side of his face resisted when he tried to open his mouth so he couldn't stretch his jaws more than a thumb's width. Every bite was a labor that made him feel like a monster. He hadn't spoken since the incident.

Bernad touched the withered side of his face. It was dry and stiff under his fingers. It didn't hurt. It had never really hurt. In a way, it would have been better if it had. Instead, it was as if the Beetch girl had punched him in the face and for a flash of a moment, he had felt what it was to die. Then he had felt his face crumple up like an earthworm dropped into a flame. He shuddered.

No one had talked about it around him, how he had been hurt, the unnatural horror of it. Or how it had even happened: no one knew. Even the Doc had looked away before stepping back to exchange murmured words with Mam.

Soolie Beetch. He wanted to scream at her, he wanted to make her look at what she had done to him before he broke her face. He wanted to never see her again. He wanted... A pang of shameful regret twinged in his heart like an infected hangnail. He snarled and stuffed it down with resentment and self-pity. His life was ruined.

Why should he get out of bed?

Hobby and Kip hadn't come to visit. Not even to gawk, point, laugh. Not even to throw things at his bedroom window. Not that he would have responded.

Not even Winny would pay attention to him now. He'd had a real shot with her before. Not that he'd wanted anything with her to go anywhere. She was just after him because he was a Pelig and the alternatives were Hobby and Kip, and she was annoying as cuck. He had no respect for her. But he would have liked the chance to see what was under that tight bodice and those swinging skirts. And he could have, too. If he hadn't seen Soolie taking off into the corn field and decided to go for the interesting one.

He'd just wanted her to let him touch her up a little, that was all. It wasn't any more than Winny had given him already. He'd touched plenty of girls by the time he was her age. If she just hadn't overreacted so much. Leaping across the floor like that after he'd been nice to her, and given her things, and shown her his tree. Running away from him as if he had threatened her or tried to hurt her.

And then...

Soolie was a skagging blood witch. He hoped Mam came back with her head on a spike.

Downstairs, the front door opened.

What time was it? It didn't matter. He didn't move and hoped that whoever it was would leave him alone.

"Bernad?" It was Mam's voice. For the first time that day, Bernad actually wished he had gotten out of bed. He rolled over and faced the wall.

The step, step, step of her feet on the stairs. The click, click, click sound of her wedding ring against the banister. Knock, knock, knock, she rapped on his door.

"Bernad, make sure you're decent."

The hinges didn't squeak as she opened the door. In Mergo Pelig's house, they didn't dare.

"I see you didn't eat any of the cobbler I left you for breakfast. Just as well. I don't think I will have time to fix dinner for you this evening. I'm meeting up with some of the other mothers for a little quilting, to help take my mind off things. Tell your father, if he comes home, there are plenty of eggs in the cold box and half a roast chicken."

He felt the mattress shift as she sat down beside him on the bed and smelled her perfume, a light scent of lilac and rosewater. "A little quilting." There might be quilting, there might not be. Either way, she probably wasn't going to be home until tomorrow. He didn't turn to look at her, and he knew she wouldn't ask him to.

"I want you to know, Bernad, the whole town is in agreement that the Beetch family will never be welcome in Hob Glen again, especially not that horrid girl. To think, Rod Cornell giving them his cart and his horses! He says it's because they were such 'good friends,'" Mam made no attempt to disguise the bitter contempt in her voice.

"Because she was such a 'sweet little girl.' And I know Ellena has always been a bit of a fool for her sister's family, but to run off in the night with them! To show such callous disregard for the abominable crimes of that abhorrent little succubus? I will never forgive Ellena for that. That little girl ruined my son's life, and she gets to just ride off in the night? You have no future, and they want to give some demon child a second chance?"

Mam sighed. "Well!" She patted him sharply on the shoulder and stood up again. "I'm thinking of the two of us maybe taking a trip to Ravus. Your father seems to have the shop well in hand, I could use a getaway, and it's been so long since I've seen Gelda. Perhaps we could take you to a few specialists in Ravus and barring that, there are some very talented artisans who could make you a fitted mask so you could at least walk in society. Plus, Gelda says your cousins see a doctor for the constitution of their humors, which could be very helpful for you."

Three steps toward the door.

"I'll see you when I get back, Bernad."

The hinges were silent on her way out.

EIGHTEEN

Soolie woke up. Her bladder felt swollen and anxious, and she was reminded that she hadn't relieved herself since yesterday morning. She was also starving.

She arched her back, stretching against the uneven boards of the cart and sat up carefully, hissing with pain. There had been a lot of pain lately. Either she was much too fragile, or life was being way too rough. She pulled her legs in and shifted forward quietly onto her hands and knees. Everything was stiff. Her joints felt like grinding granite, and her tendons had most certainly shrunk. Ellena was snoring softly into the quilt beside her. If she was quiet, she could slip out without waking her.

"Soolie?"

Soolie winced and turned. Papa leaned forward from where he was sitting behind her, his face in the dark more shadow than flesh.

"Where are you going?"

"I have to pee," Soolie whispered.

"Do you really need to go now?"

Soolie nodded then, just in case he couldn't see, "Yes. I have to go really bad."

"Very well." Papa's dark form unfolded beneath the tarp and

lengthened out towards her. "I'm coming with you."

"Papa, I can pee by myself."

Papa was beside her now, and she felt his heavy hand on her shoulder. "You don't have any freedoms right now, Soolie Beetch. Let's go."

Soolie scrunched her face, her shoulders sagging, then began crawling forward to the back of the cart, Papa close behind her.

"Put on your boots."

"But I *really* have to go."

"Put them on."

Soolie sat back and squeezed her bare foot into the boot, the leather feeling rumpled and clammy against her feet, and tried not to think about the panic in her belly. She tucked the laces over into the top instead of winding around the hooks. Papa lifted the tarpaulin for her. It was just starting to lighten outside, still dark, but not black. She slid her feet over the edge of the cart and hopped down, but instead of the firm familiar ground, her foot landed on an uneven surface, something soft and slick that rolled beneath her, her arms flew out as she fell towards it with a yelping cry.

As she fell, she saw them. Horses.

It was a great pile, a massive heap of slaughtered horses. Bays, chestnuts and sorrels, gray and dappled, their beautiful glossy coats ripped and mangled, eyes bulging, wild and gouged out. There were twisted limbs, and spilling bowels, and heads ripped entirely free from bodies.

Soolie scrambled away on her back in the mud. There must be several dozen, a whole herd, and they had all died a horrible violent death.

"Soolie?!"

Papa dropped out of the cart and rushed to her side.

"Oh, Soolie." Papa's voice was dull with horror.

Soolie looked up into Papa's face, tears of shock creeping out of her eyes. The cold earth was digging into her palms, and wet warmth of her own urine soaked her nightshirt, spreading down her skirts.

Papa knelt beside her and grabbed her by one arm, pulling. His eyes were full of betrayal, anger, but most of all, fear. Any moments before Ravus with fewer worries and occasional smiles had been ripped away like thin skin over a deep old wound. Papa had never trusted the world. Now, he didn't trust her.

"Soolie." He shook her, his eyes wild with fear and intensity. "Who did this? Who did this, Soolie?"

Soolie shook her head. She was sobbing now. Her nightgown was soaking wet, and the heap of slaughtered horses smelled of death and blood.

"SOOLIE. WHO DID THIS?"

"I don't kno … o … ow." She sobbed. "Papa, I don't know!"

"Silas!" Ellena hobbled barefoot over the cold mud, thick and dark with seeping death.

Soolie just kept shaking her head. "Believe me, Papa. Please believe me!"

Papa pulled on her arm, his bearded face right next to hers. "Whatever did this could *kill* you, do you understand? It could kill you. It could kill Ellena. You *have* to tell me, Soolie. You have to tell me NOW."

Soolie shook her head, sobbing and sniveling. Her face was slimy with tears.

"Silas!" Ellena had grabbed him by the other arm, but Silas shook her off.

"Soolie!" He grabbed her by both arms now, sitting on his heels, his face level with hers. "Look at me!" Soolie met her Papa's eyes, unable to stop sobbing. "WHAT IS HAPPENING TO YOU?"

"I don't know!" Soolie choked it out, clinging to the only control she had.

Papa shoved his arms under her, pressing the wet nightgown up against her thighs, lifted her against his chest and moved towards the cart while Ellena stood by, her hand covering her mouth in horror.

"Get back in the cart, Ellena. Get back in the cart now."

IT WAS QUIET in the back of the cart, but for the creak and gravel of the wheels. Soolie changed out of her soiled nightgown, wadding it up and rubbing the wetness away from her legs before pulling on her red dress with the turquoise buttons. It was a little tight, and the fabric pulled around the buttons and pinched under the arms, but her green dress had been ruined in the city. She had caught a glimpse of blackened, burned fabric when Ellena had cut it off of her last night, and since her nightgown was wet, the red wool dress would have to do.

Across the cart, Ellena was cleaning blood and mud from between her toes with a rag. It was too dark to tell if she was crying. Soolie wanted to crawl over and hug Ellena, but she wasn't sure if it would help.

Soolie started rummaging through one of the packing boxes, lifting up a cooking pot, pushing aside the tinder and lighting sticks.

"What are you looking for?"

Soolie glanced back to Ellena, who was shoving the filthy rag under the tarp and over the side of the cart, dropping it on the passing road outside.

"Do we have any food?"

"I don't think so."

Soolie sat back down. She was so very hungry. She was hungry all the time now. Just another thing she could probably blame the demon for. She almost wished they had taken some horse meat for the road. People ate horse.

"It isn't raining," Soolie offered.

"Mmmhmm." Ellena curled her legs up to her chest and wrapped her arms around them.

"We could pull back the tarp."

"Go ahead."

Neither of them moved.

Ellena was probably in shock. Soolie wondered if she was in shock. Maybe she processed shock differently from other people. It wouldn't surprise her to find she had been in shock for weeks.

Something had killed the horses. A new monster. A new terror.

The demon would know what it was, but she didn't expect it to tell her.

Maybe the demon was right. Maybe everyone was going to die horrible deaths.

Maybe the dancer was right, and she should kill herself, but that wasn't a very easy theory to test, and she wasn't willing to be wrong.

She wished she could ask Ellena how she looked different. There weren't any mirrored surfaces, but she could feel that something had changed. It was in the loose feeling in her skin, the ache in her bones. The way Ellena stared at her when she thought Soolie didn't see, and looked away when Soolie glanced back.

It hadn't been very long ago that all she had wanted was a few friends, to see a bit of the world, to experience a life outside of the four walls of their little home.

Now she would never have friends, Papa would never let her leave, and she felt like she was losing her family too. She was a freak. She was dangerous. She didn't know how to stop the monsters. Papa and Ellena couldn't even look at her without pain.

It wasn't much of a life. It seemed every day she had less to lose.

Soolie scooted across the cart, sat next to Ellena, and leaned her head on her aunt's shoulder. Ellena didn't hug her or lean back. Soolie nuzzled just a little.

"Ellena?"

"Hmm?"

"I love you."

"Oh, honey." Ellena wrapped an arm around her. "I love you too."

NINETEEN

There was only one stop for travelers between Ravus and Hob Glen: a large white farm house with rust-streaked shingles known as the Farm House Inn. Abrum and Claudine had built their home large enough to share with their children and their children's families, but their three daughters had all chosen different paths. The oldest fell in love with a ship merchant, the youngest ran away to the big city on the arm of a wealthy married man, and the middle daughter had married a handsome red-headed local boy with whom she had two lovely children and a little farm of their own a few days back east. So, with a large house and no one to share it with, the barn had been transformed into a stable, and the couple had taken to renting out rooms.

It was late, but travelers arrived on the doorstep at all hours. Claudine had just pulled out her mending basket and Abrum sat down for his evening smoke when they heard the hooves and wheels in the front yard. By the time Abrum had the lantern lit, there was a knock at the door.

Abrum padded hastily down the main hallway, one hand holding the lantern high, the other pumping briskly at his side. He reached the front entry, undid the little latch to the peep-door, and swung it in to get a look at the person on the porch.

The man on the other side of the door was too tall, and at first all Abrum could see was a dark woolen coat collar. Then the traveler took two steps back. He was a formidable man, looming and heavy-shouldered in a dark coat and broad-brimmed hat. He had a serious and haggard face scarfed in a grizzled unkempt beard that did nothing to hide the mirthless bent of his mouth and hollowness of his eyes. The innkeeper nudged his spectacles up his nose with one finger and muttered. "Oh, lands."

"We have come to board for the night. Do you have a room?"

Of course they had a room. There were no other boarders this night. Abrum could see a pair of horses and a covered cart in the yard. They were in no position to turn away a paying traveler. The shotgun was above the door.

"Aye, friend. We've room. And a stable for your horses around the house." Abrum said. "One tic."

He shut the peep, lifted the turn bar, and opened the door. The tall man was already headed down the porch steps toward a woman and a girl climbing out of the back of the cart.

"Ellena!" the man called. "You can go in the house and make arrangements. We only need one room."

The woman nodded, and she and the girl moved towards the house.

"Wait," the tall man said, "Soolie comes with me."

There was a moment of hesitation. The young girl stood between the adults, looking back and forth.

"Come on, Soolie." The man held out his hand and reluctantly, the girl took it.

"See you two in a moment," the woman said.

Abrum stepped out onto the porch to hold the door open so she could enter. "Long day of travel?"

"Oh," the woman smiled. She had a wholesome face, cheeks pink with the evening air, and dark frizzy hair, but her smile was estranged from her eyes. "Nothing a hot meal won't cure."

Abrum shut the door behind them.

"That we have. Come into the kitchen, and I'll introduce you to Claudine."

They didn't make it to the kitchen. Down the hallway, Claudine stepped out of the warmly lit kitchen doorway. Nigh forty years ago, Abrum had fallen for a long-haired bosomy country maid, two traits Claudine had kept into her elder years. She wore her gray hair plaited in a trailing braid down her back, and her loose black dress hung in a straight plain from her low bosom which now swung vigorously as she rushed towards them, arms outstretched.

"Abrum Cliff!" she chided, putting a guiding arm around Ellena and sweeping her down the hallway. "What are you doing letting this poor dear stand in the hallway? Come with me, love. Are there other members of your party? Two? Well, let's get you in by the fire, and I'll whip up something hot for your bellies!"

Abrum shook his head, muttering in his wife's wake.

The kitchen hearth fire crackled bright and welcoming. Emmit the wire hound lay curled by the hearth, and he raised his large black nose from his paws to glower dolefully from beneath long bushy brows.

"Now, take a seat by that fire," Claudine insisted, helping the woman out of her cloak. The woman smiled again, a polite empty gesture. It was a smile Abrum had seen before beneath bruised and swollen eyes. Claudine had seen it as well. His wife handed the woman's cloak to him, and the two of them exchanged a meaningful gaze. Hopefully, there would be no shouting heard through the walls tonight.

"How many rooms for the night, dear?" Claudine asked.

"Just one, thank you."

"You sure? Wouldn't you like a little space after all the time on the road?"

"One is really quite fine."

Abrum hung the cloak on a hook in the corner. When he turned back, Claudine had already set their guest on a stool by the fire and was placing a mug of hot cider in her hands.

"I'll go see if I can help with the horses," Abrum said.

He also wanted to check on the man and that little girl. What was done on the open road was none of Abrum's business. But any ill treatment of women and children on his land he took personally.

Claudine pointed at him. "Tell them to make quick. I'm putting on corn chowder for supper."

"WHAT HAPPENED TO THE PELIG BOY?"

"Papa, I told you."

"Why did you run away?"

"I don't remember."

"Tell me!"

"I don't know!"

"STOP LYING!"

Abrum stepped between the cart and stable. Only one of the horses had been unhitched. In the stable entry, the tall man was shaking the young girl by the shoulders, shouting into her face.

Abrum cleared his throat.

The girl stared at her shoes, but the man looked up. His eyes were raw and wet with tears that glistened in the lantern light.

"Um," Abrum pushed his spectacles up his nose and jerked a thumb over his shoulder at the house. "The wife's put corn chowder on to heat. Can I help with your bags and horses?"

The tall man took a shuddering breath. "Please," he spoke low, "tell your wife we will be in in a moment. Thank you."

Abrum glanced at the little girl again. There was something about her. At first, he had thought she must be twelve or thirteen years, but the shadows around her face showed lines and wrinkles, a puckering about the lips of someone much older.

"Thank you," the tall man emphasized.

"Of course." Abrum turned to go, then turned back, a finger raised. "Don't be long. My Claudine makes a right devil's deal of a chowder." He winked, nodded.

The tall man waited in silence as he walked away.

As soon as they were in the house, Claudine ushered them across the kitchen and into a dining room. Soolie was grateful to have someone else around. She knew that fear could come across as anger, but she didn't know how to comfort Papa and make him stop yelling and shaking and crying. At least, as long as he didn't know anything, that was all he could do.

The dining room was small. Somewhere else in the house, perhaps across the hallway, would be a larger main dining room with curtained windows, a polished table, and full-backed chairs. This room was cozy and dark. The table was homely, hand hewn from halved logs bolted together, supported by small log legs, and flanked by three stools. Papa walked Soolie to the table, directing her with a firm hand that didn't lift from her shoulder until her knees were tucked obediently under the table. He grabbed another stool and moved it so close that when he sat down their legs brushed. Ellena took the seat at the head of the table.

"Silas," Ellena spoke, "thank you."

Papa nodded.

"Ellena!" Soolie gave a little bounce of enthusiasm. "We're staying at an inn! I've never stayed at an inn before!"

Ellena smiled back weakly, but Soolie hoped sincerely.

Claudine bustled in from the kitchen and set a large basket of steaming rolls in the center of the table with a small butter crock. Her gaze lingered on Soolie briefly, not long enough to be a stare, just long enough for Soolie to know there was something to see. Abrum followed bearing three deep bowls of golden chowder on a serving tray which his wife accepted. She placed one steaming bowl in front of each of them, then picked up the tray and stepped back, nodding satisfied. Soolie inhaled deeply of the rich fragrance of sweet corn, potatoes, and heavy cream. No amount of Papa's worrying was going to keep this bowl of chowder from being the best thing she had ever eaten in her life.

"Dig in, dears!" Claudine said. "It won't get any better being stared at."

Soolie grabbed the pewter soup spoon and scooped up a generous mound, stuffing it in her mouth.

"Oooh ooh! Haww … haw, hot." Soolie removed the spoon from her mouth, still full of steaming chowder.

"Soolie!" Papa chided.

"It just smells so good!" Soolie blew on the spoonful lightly until the shiny hot surface began to dull, then lifted the spoon to her mouth and groaned as the salty, sweet, buttery chowder touched her tongue. She swallowed, feeling the warmth spreading in her belly. She wanted to eat a whole cauldron full.

"So," Abrum crossed behind them and lowered himself into a chair in the corner of the room. "What is a family doing out on the road on a night like this?"

"Abrum!" Claudine objected from the kitchen doorway. "Let the folks eat! There are seconds for everyone," she added, "and I'm heating water for baths. Are you sure I can't interest you in two rooms tonight?"

"Thank you for your hospitality, madam," Papa said, "but one room is fine."

"Lands. Call me Claudine." She brushed a wisp of gray hair off her forehead. "That lout there's Abrum."

Abrum had a pipe in one hand and was lifting a packet of tobacco from his vest pocket with the other. He raised the pipe in salute. "Her favorite lout."

Soolie liked Abrum. His mustache looked like organized dandelion fuzz.

"Claudine," Papa corrected himself. "I'm Silas, this is my daughter Soolie. You've met Ellena."

Soolie waved eagerly, her mouth crammed with chowder and oat roll.

Ellena smiled. "Thank you so much for your hospitality."

"Of course, dears!" Claudine brushed away Ellena's thanks. "Now, are you sure you don't want two rooms? You three are our only boarders tonight. No extra charge."

"Quite sure," Papa said. "One room is fine."

"One room it is, dears."

With a swish of black skirts and a swing of her long gray braid, Claudine swept back into the kitchen, and for a moment, the only sound was the clink of spoons on ceramic.

"So," Abrum paused from tapping tobacco into the bowl of his pipe to repeat his question, "what has you folks on the road?"

Papa rested his spoon on the edge of the bowl. "I'm a shoemaker. We had a few deliveries in Ravus and are now headed back home."

"Shoemaker!" The old man considered, looking off to the side, then pointed with his pipe. "The one from back in Hob Glen?"

Papa nodded.

"Heard of you," Abrum nodded, tamping his pipe. "Heard you make the best shoes east of the city."

"I do," Papa said.

"Did you manage to turn a profit without getting filched by the regent's cuck wags?" Abrum snorted.

"By stars alone."

"Count yourselves among the blessed." Abrum rolled up the packet of tobacco on his leg with a practiced hand and tucked it back in his vest pocket. "First topaz addicts, then the dry wells, mysterious deaths in the Dark Districts. Meanwhile the Regent's guard does cuck all!"

Soolie giggled and looked to see if Ellena had heard the old man's language. Ellena was busy tearing open a roll.

"Is he prating on the Regent?" Claudine appeared in the kitchen doorway, this time carrying a long stemmed lighter, the tip dancing with a little eyelet of flame. "Don't you start, you old coot," she scolded, crossing the room with one hand cupped protectively around the baby flame.

Abrum grunted and winked at Soolie. "Forty years of marriage. Can you believe it?"

Claudine pursed her lips at him, lit the bowl of his pipe, and blew out her flame. "Don't let him run his mouth," she nodded towards Ellena, turning back toward the kitchen. "It isn't good for him."

Abrum grunted and took a contented puff of his pipe while his wife left the room. "Regent's a cuckin skag."

Soolie grinned. This must be what having grandparents was like.

"I was wondering," Papa said, leaning forward seriously, "if you'd had any trouble with livestock killings in the area?"

Abrum raised his eyebrows, letting the smoke filter up through his mustache. "Not unless you've heard something I haven't."

"We came upon a herd of slaughtered horses this morning."

"Did you, now?" Abrum's brow lowered, and he leaned back in his chair. "Can't say I have. Horses you say? A whole herd? Could it have been man done?"

Papa shook his head. "We didn't look close, but I saw no clean weapon marks. It looked savage."

"Must've been mighty savage to slaughter a whole herd," Abrum agreed.

Soolie glanced at Papa. He wasn't going to like this question, but she had to ask. The inn was on the road to Ravus, and they might have heard something.

She blurted, "Do you know what happened to the carnival in Ravus?"

"Soolie!" Papa snapped. "That's enough."

Abrum glanced at Papa with raised eyebrows. "You like carnivals, young miss?"

Soolie bit her lip and agitated the shallow slurry of chowder left in the bottom of her bowl with her spoon.

"Forgive us." Papa placed a hand firmly on Soolie's shoulder. "That may not be the best topic tonight."

"Ah." Abrum nodded.

No one spoke for a minute. Soolie focused on scraping up the last bit of chowder, chasing a single piece of corn up the side of the bowl, onto the lip of her spoon, and sucking it into her mouth.

"It may interest you to know," Abrum said at last, leaning back leisurely, "that they've blamed the carnival massacre on the animals. Might be the two are related, and your young miss is on to something."

Soolie glanced sideways at Papa. His face was tense. His fists rested yellow knuckles up on the table.

Finally, he answered tersely, "How is that?"

"The last traveler that stopped this way said a whole carnival of Southerners was slaughtered by their own animals..." He paused sagely and took another puff, sucking in the smoke and letting it start to leak out through his nostrils before exhaling through his lips in a curling stream. He grunted. "Might be one of those exotic Southern creatures is your horse killer."

"Well," Papa pushed back his stool and stood up. "I think we're done with dinner."

As if on cue, Claudine appeared in the doorway. "Ooh, already? Doesn't anyone want seconds? I have apple crumble for dessert."

"Ooooh!" Soolie shot up her hand.

"It was very good, thank you," Papa said sharply. "But I think we've all had enough."

"None for me, thank you." Ellena handed her empty bowl to Claudine who swung up to take it. "But it really was delicious."

"You sure, dear?" Claudine glanced down at Soolie, who studied the tablecloth.

Papa reached in front of her, picked up her empty bowl, tucked it under his still full of chowder, and handed both to Claudine. "I think it's about time for us to wash up and turn in."

"I have one bath all ready to pour." Claudine rested the bowls against her chest, chowder from the edges smudging off on the black cloth of her bosoms. "If the ladies would come with me?" She eyed Papa sternly. "You can sit back down. I'll come back and get you in a moment."

"Oohh," Ellena groaned, pushing back her stool and stretching. "A bath sounds *wonderful.*"

"Well, come on then!" Claudine tipped her head, heading for the kitchen door.

Papa stepped back from Soolie's stool. "Don't take long."

Soolie yelped and bounced up, running after Claudine.

As ELLENA FOLLOWED, Silas reached out and touched her arm. "Talk to her."

Ellena squeezed his hand. "I'll do my best."

The women left.

Silas sunk slowly back onto the stool, leaning forward heavily, arms resting on the table. From his chair in the corner, the innkeeper sucked and puffed at his pipe, one eyebrow raised, watching through hazy billows.

SOOLIE FOLLOWED CLAUDINE into the kitchen. The older woman set the bowls down on a counter and reached up to a top cupboard, bringing down a cardinal red tin as Ellena walked in behind them.

Claudine winked. "If your papa doesn't want dessert, he doesn't have to have any."

She unscrewed the top, reached in, and pulled out a crisp slab of golden hazelnut brittle. Soolie gasped. Candy was a rare treat. The older woman handed it to her and placed a finger to her lips. "Shhhh."

"Oooh, thank you!" Soolie turned the hard candy in her hands. It was opaque with frothy tiny bubbles and smelled like caramelized sugar and toasted nuts.

"I usually save it for special occasions," Claudine said, tightening the lid back on. "My grandmother taught me that recipe. Did you want any, dear?"

"No, thank you." Ellena shook her head. "But that's very kind."

Soolie took a bite. The brittle was crisp and didn't stick to her teeth. It broke and crushed in her mouth, sweet and toasty. She rolled her eyes. "Ohh, Ellena, it's sooooo good! You *have* to taste it!"

"Well, all right." Ellena leaned in as Soolie offered the brittle, lifting to her mouth for her to take a bite.

"Mmmm!" Ellena covered her mouth with her fingers. "Ohh, that is! No, not another bite."

Claudine set the tin back up on the shelf, then turned back, her hands folded. "I do have to ask, dears."

Soolie and Ellena looked at her expectantly, both of them still crunching brittle.

"Do you ladies need any help?" the innkeeper asked, her words kindly meaningful. "Anyone to talk to?"

Ellena's eyes widened with understanding. "Oh, we are quite all right. Nothing is the matter."

"Now, dears." Claudine tsk'ed and wagged a finger. "I raised three girls. I'm not that easy to false-trail."

"Oh, it's just that," Soolie swallowed, "we're all really shaken by those dead horses we saw this morning." She gestured at the dining room with the last of her brittle. "Especially Papa. Papa cares a lot about animals."

"I see," Claudine said.

Soolie grinned and took another bite of brittle. She'd figured the old woman had been listening in.

"Well," Claudine sighed, "if there's anything else, you can always tell me. I've heard it all." She spread her arms. "Now, come on. You two look like a warm bath could do you a land of good."

DOG CIRCLED THE HOUSE ONCE. Two doors, two stories, five humans, one pet. He could break in now while they were awake, feed on the ones he didn't need, and face the girl with the sunlight soul.

Had she found his offering this morning? Was she pleased? Did she understand? Would she accept him? Was she worth his fealty?

He whined nervously and pawed at the neck of his shirt with his claws. Better to be cautious. Too much was at stake. He wriggled backward into the thick of a bramble bush, thorns scratching at his exposed skin, and crouched down, watching the house. It was dark and late. The humans would lay down for the night soon.

Dog shuddered and began grooming himself, raking filth out from beneath his long curved nails against a corner fang and spatting the gunk out into the earth between his feet. Tonight he would meet the one that gathered the spirits of the dead and possessed the body of the living. Tonight would determine his future.

THE INN HAD A REAL PORCELAIN TUB with curved iron feet like upside down morning lilies. Ellena lowered herself into the water, feeling the warmth cocoon her travel-weary flesh.

"Ooh." She leaned back against the slick smooth edge of the tub. Getting into the tub had been easy. Getting out might be impossible.

Ellena looked over at her niece. "Aren't you going to get in?"

Soolie stood by the pile of her clothes, studying herself in an oval mirror that hung on the wall above the hand basin. She pulled at the skin around her eyes with her fingers, massaged her cheeks, and yanked at the flesh under her chin.

"I look funny."

Ellena picked the yellow hunk of homemade soap from the metal dish on the floor and dipped it in the water. It was true. "You get it from your father," she teased.

Soolie twisted around, studying her rear end critically in the mirror and lifting it with her fingers. "No I don't." She sighed. "Papa's not a freak."

Ellena swiped the soap across her arms and shoulders, leaving behind a slick film. "Your father is his own kind of freak."

Soolie put her nose to the mirror, pulling back her hair and studying the roots of her widow's peak.

"Come on," Ellena patted the rim of the tub. "Get in the water, silly duck."

Soolie scowled and stuck her tongue out at the mirror before turning her back on it and heading for the tub.

"Have you remembered anything yet?" Ellena asked, soaping the hair under her arms.

"Nope."

Soolie stuck one foot in carefully on the opposite side, then stepped in with the other. Ellena moved a leg so Soolie could slide in. The tub was hard and smooth, their skin was warm and slick. Soolie settled into the rising water and poked at Ellena's thigh with her toes, wiggling them, and giggled.

"We could never fit two people into our washtubs at home!"

"We can barely fit two people into this one."

Ellena rubbed the soap on her hands and lathered her face. She cupped water into her palms and splashed it against her closed eyes, spreading it back into her unruly hair, damping it down against her scalp. She blinked her eyes open, water dripping from her lashes. She had to keep trying. Not just for Soolie. For Silas' sake.

"Do you have any idea why you don't remember?"

"Not really." Soolie dunked her head forward into the water between her knees, splashing it up to soak all her hair. She raised her head, water streaming down across her face. "We should get a tub!"

"What's the last thing you remember before we found you in the city square?" Ellena pressed.

Soolie sighed and flipped the dripping hair out of her face. "Can't we not talk about it for a little bit, pleeease?"

Ellena wished she could let it go. She didn't like asking questions or pressing her niece. Soolie got enough of that from her father. But this was serious. She closed her eyes and focused her thoughts. "The problem is that your father and I love you. We want to take care of you and keep you safe, and there's obviously something you aren't telling us."

Soolie looked down at the soap residue floating lazily between their bent knees. "I know." She gnawed on her lip. "If there's anything you and Papa can do, I promise I'll let you know."

"How would you know if we can help if you aren't telling us?"

Soolie looked her aunt in the eyes. "There are some things being an adult won't fix, and I need to make some decisions on my own." She shrugged. "I'm sorry, Ellena. I'm sorry for Papa too. I promise I'll do my best to make everything okay again."

It was a thought out response. A reasoned one. Soolie was keeping a secret, and she wasn't going to let it go lightly.

"Well," Ellena smiled and shrugged, "I can't make you tell me anything. But you shouldn't shut me or your father out of this, whatever is going on. We *can* help you. And I'm always here to listen. Aunts can handle things papas can't. It's what we're here for."

Soolie smiled and rubbed soap into her hair. "Thanks. Say, did you see the innkeeper's wife's boobs? They're bigger than Mrs. Svenson's!"

"They are pretty big," Ellena said.

THE INNKEEPER'S WIFE led Silas to an iron washtub full of tepid water. Silas could tell the older woman didn't like him, but he wasn't in any mood to care. He washed up quickly, changed back into his pants and linen nightshirt, and made his way to the room prepared for them.

It was a small bedroom, and the bed took up most of the floor space. Claudine had set a candle on the window sill and laid out bedding, blankets, and a pillow on the floor to the left of the bed, and their luggage on the right.

Soolie and Ellena weren't there yet, of course. They would be a while, knowing them. Hopefully, Ellena was learning something from Soolie. He hated how his daughter was more comfortable opening up to her aunt, but in this case, maybe it would help. He certainly hadn't been getting anywhere. Maybe Ellena would have better luck.

He made sure the bedding on the floor was arranged, then set on the edge of the bed to wait.

It had been a long day. A long ride stewing in his thoughts, in the terror of the morning, in the panic and horror of Soolie's betrayal, transformation, and silence.

If only Tara was here. She would know what to do. She could always understand and communicate with Soolie when their daughter's ways were lost on him. But Tara was gone.

Instead, he had Ellena.

Silas thought of Ellena wrapping her arms around him as he was shaking, his fear flooding his brain, turning his lungs to empty cellars, trapped and airless. He thought of her warm comforting body, her soft hair, her stubbornness. She never listened to him. He didn't want her help, he never wanted her help, but somehow her help was always there.

Silas was still sitting on the edge of the bed when the door opened and Soolie burst in fresh from her bath dressed in the large red flannel nightshirt.

"Papa!" His daughter ran to him, bounced up on the bed, and threw her arms around his neck, her damp hair pressed against the shoulder of his linen shirt. "Thank you!" she gasped, squeezing him tight. "Thank you so much! The inn is wonderful. They have a real white bathtub!"

Ellena stood in the doorway, her damp hair twisted to the side in a loose nighttime braid, her face fresh, pink, and clean in the dim light of the candle. "Silas, a moment?"

"Stay right here, baby girl." Silas patted Soolie's shoulder and kissed the top of her head.

Soolie bounced across the covers and flopped back, her head on a feather pillow. "This is paradise!"

Silas followed Ellena out of the room, and she closed the door quietly behind them.

As soon as the door closed, Soolie screamed silent air. She screamed with every tendon, every muscle, a hissing roar. She dug her hands into the quilts, clutching and wrenching; she arched her back and bowed her neck. She punched the pillows and bit down hard on the sleeve of her nightgown, straining and pulling until her teeth felt crooked and her head hurt. She screamed against her helplessness and uncertainty, against the world falling apart, against Papa's oppressive fear and the little girl who didn't have a care, who bounced, and giggled, and ate her soup too fast, who she was beginning to hate. Alone in the room, Soolie raged a silent storm.

And then she stopped.

She wasn't ready to stop. She gasped, falling back onto the bed, a single tear of distilled frustration oozing from her eye that no one would see. She breathed, stilled her body, relaxed her limbs and face, and prepared herself for Papa and Ellena's return. But inside, the storm raged on.

As soon as the door was closed, Silas impulsively reached for Ellena, pulling her in, hugging her close, her damp hair smelling fresh, clean, and womanly. She stiffened with surprise, but then her body thawed, and he felt her hands against his back as she moved into his arms.

When at last they had held each other for just a little too long, he released his hold, and they separated to elbow length.

"Did you learn anything?"

Ellena shook her head. "No, I'm so sorry. She won't talk to me."

Silas creased his brow. His head hurt.

"But, Silas?"

He looked down into her brown eyes and saw her brow, too, was lined with worry.

"I think whatever happened to Soolie is still happening." Ellena hesitated. "I don't think it's over."

It was his greatest fear, but he believed it. His daughter was in horrible danger, and he had to protect her at all costs.

"Silas," Ellena's hands squeezed his forearms, her face earnest, "you *are* right to keep a close eye on her."

They were words he had never thought to hear from Ellena. Words, in a kinder world, he never would have.

"In fact, I don't think we can watch her too closely."

"I may need your help."

"I'm always here."

Her hand slid down into his, and he held it tight as he turned the door latch and stepped back into the room.

Soolie was spread out, her limbs taking up the whole bed, fake snoring loudly.

"Soolie." Silas released Ellena's hand and poked his daughter in the instep of her bare foot. "Make room for your aunt."

Soolie squealed and rolled over. "No poking!"

Silas pulled back the covers so Ellena and Soolie could crawl under. He walked to one side of the bed, smoothing the quilt and kissing Soolie on the forehead.

"Good night, baby girl."

"Good night, Papa."

Silas stepped back around to the other side of the bed, over the bedding on the floor, and cupped his hand behind the little bobbing candle flame before glancing back at the two in the bed, blankets pulled up to their chins. Soolie already had her eyes closed, pretending to be asleep. Ellena looked up at him with large dark eyes that danced with the little candle flame. She mouthed the words. *I'm here.* He blew out the candle.

GETTING INTO THE HOUSE had been easy. Before turning in, the old man had let his hound out to drop waste. Once the animal had sniffed out his trail, it had only taken Dog a moment to silence it with a sharp twist of the neck, to dump the body in the brush, and dart in through the back door while the man shouted pointlessly into the shadows. Twenty minutes later, the old man had given up on finding the beast until morning, and Dog was hidden in a dark corner under the stair waiting for the people to lay down for the night.

Now, at last, the house was asleep.

Dog slunk down the unlit hallway, his mouth gaping, sucking in the scents of the house, stale tobacco, old grease, wood smoke, and sweet herbs. He could smell years of residue in the wood and carpet left by the animal that lay disposed outside. He paused by a door, listening to the snoring of the old man and woman, frail flesh. Young blood tasted better. He could always come back.

The stairs were narrow and creaky. Dog spread his weight on hands and feet, pressing into the wall-most edge of the stair, curling his toes to keep his nails from clicking against the wood as he crawled up to the second floor.

This floor had many doors, and all but one opened to cold empty rooms. All but the door three down on the left. He could sense her.

He approached slowly, edging along the wall where the wooden boards were more secure and less prone to protest.

He stood before the door. A simple bedroom door.

He breathed. The smell of man and woman, freshly soaped flesh, young and tender life, the seething ember of a strange presence throbbing in the dark.

Dog placed his ear gently to the wood, listening. Three heartbeats, three sleep-slowed breaths.

He placed one hand to the door latch, hesitating, stifling down a nervous whine. What if she disappointed him? What if she didn't accept him? What if this being was no more than flotsam, refuse, trash of the dead world? What if she was not to be served after all? He sneered at the painful thought. An idiot, a fool to hope, to dream he could find a place and be redeemed.

He had to know.

Dog pushed on the latch, turning it slowly as the hour hand of a clock creeping towards a tolling knell, and eased open the door.

Immediately he flinched back, one hand before his face, grimacing.

She sat upright in the bed. The woman lay beside her, curled over asleep. The man lay on the floor, his breathing the shallow halting of fitful fragile slumber. And the girl sat upright in the bed, looking at him with eyes glaring white and pure as judgement.

I sensed you in the city. You walk in the daylight while the rest of your kind walks in the dark. A hound without his pack. The one who kills the horses. Creature of the Dead Man, why do you follow me?

She spoke into his mind, voice hissing, searing like a glowing brand tossed in the water bucket. A voice of power.

Dog folded his hands before his forehead, cowering in the doorway. His words tumbled out of his mouth.

"Dog is shamed. Dog is lost. Dog is alone. Dog has no master."

The blazing eyes judged him.

The Dead Man has discarded you. How have you shamed yourself?

Dog whined. He could not lie to her. He must be punished. He must be judged. He needed to pay the price for his betrayal. He needed to be commanded, to have a place again.

"Dog ran. Master replaced Dog, and Dog ran."

A deserter.

The eyes slanted down, cold and burning. Dog dropped to his knees, writhing in hateful loathing. He wanted her to punish him. He needed it. If she asked him to flay his skin from his body he would do it. He would do anything.

Beside the bed, the sleeping man stirred.

Did he not send his weapons for you?

Dog's claws raked across his scalp, his eyes welling with thick cold tears.

"Dog survived."

And you come to me?

The breathing beside the bed stopped and started; the man turned.

Dog keened, desperate and low. "Dog has no master. Dog is shamed. Dog is alone. Dog is shamed."

I knew your master before he was. If I were to command you, it would be to greatness.

Dog's still heart lurched within him, and he looked up through the grimy thick of his sorrow.

How will you prove yourself? You have failed your previous master. How will you earn your servitude?

"Command me!" Dog begged, bowing low, groveling before the bed. "Any task you give me, I will obey."

TOMORROW NIGHT, the fierce voice razored through his mind. *BRING ME A YOUNG SOUL LIVING. BRING ME A YOUNG SOUL TOMORROW NIGHT!*

"I will obey!"

The man beside the bed shouted himself from his sleep, sitting up abruptly, fist raised, accosting nothing. In the bed, the girl and the woman lay in peace. The room was dark, the door was shut.

TWENTY

Bernad pulled on his other boot. He was getting out of this house. Pap hadn't even come home from the store last night, and Mam was still out attending some meeting, or social, or a courtesy drop in ... whatever she had told him, he hadn't been listening. It was all cuck slough. She was probably sacking with some lonely farmer, maybe a widower, someone with a house safe from prying eyes somewhere outside the town limits

They both disgusted him. He had to get out of this house. He needed a drink, and Mam didn't allow liquor in the house. Maybe after a good dram-up, he'd actually get a decent night's sleep.

He hadn't slept much. There was nothing to do but sleep, and instead, he lay awake listening to the stir of people in the street below his window, grinding his teeth at the sound of crickets and nightwings. Trying not to think about his face. Trying not to think about Beetch.

Cuck this skagging room. He had a full jug of moon piss stashed at his tree. Enough to get full sauced four times over.

He heard the front door open. One of the skag sacks was home. Pap would go straight to the cold cellar. Mam would come upstairs. He hoped it was Pap.

"Bernad?" Clink, clink, clink: the sound of her ring on the railing.

Bernad hopped to his bedroom window, still tying the laces of his boot. He yanked up on the window, but it didn't budge. Of course. It was latched shut. He turned the latch, slammed open the window, and his bedroom door opened.

"Oh, Bernad, thank goodness you're dressed. We need to pack and leave immediately."

He almost crawled out the window anyway. But he would have to turn around to hang down from the sill so he could drop, and all the while she would be yelling at him. He turned around.

Mam startled at his face and puckered up her mouth and nose as if tasting something vile. "Oh, lands, we have *got* to find you something to cover that up."

Mergo Pelig was a lovely woman in a cream dress embroidered with small bud roses and a scalloped collar. She kept her eyebrows neatly threaded, always added a touch of rouge to her cheeks before she let anyone see her in the morning, and her soft copper hair was coiled in an attractive elegant bun. She prided herself on being the only woman in Hob Glen who wore gloves in all seasons.

Bernad stared sullenly at her with his one good eye, but she was looking about the room, her eyes lingering with distaste on the unmade bed. "I came to tell you we are leaving for Ravus immediately. I simply cannot abide this town a moment longer."

He wanted to ask 'why' and 'what about Pap,' but he didn't want to struggle with words in front of her. She stepped over to his bed and began to pull smooth the bed sheet.

"After all, that horrid Beetch family is likely to return. Though you can rest assured, I have seen to it that, should they attempt to settle back into Hob Glen, they will be persuasively encouraged to take themselves elsewhere." Mam tucked the sheet corners neatly and began arranging the woven bedspread. "I hesitate to even speak of such things," Mam continued, "and it is almost too distasteful to even suggest. But, considering your history with the Beetch girl, perhaps it would be best for us to avoid providing her the opportunity to seek you out." Mam tugged the bedspread so it hung even with the floor and folded the top edge over into a neat border. "Considering the circumstances, your father and I are agreed." She fluffed the pillow and placed it carefully at the head of the bed, then stepped back to survey her handiwork. "We will leave this morning."

That was why they were leaving. Mam had talked to Pap. Maybe Pap had even talked back. The result was: Mam was going to stay with her sister and she intended to take him with her.

Satisfied, Mam turned back to face him where he stood by the window. "So," she said briskly, "are you capable of packing your own trunk, or should I do that for you as well?"

Bernad didn't move. Mam didn't really want him in her sister's house. She would be even more ashamed of him there than she was here. Mam probably just needed a carriage driver.

"Well, don't dally." Mam smoothed her skirt with a practiced sweep of her hand, still not looking directly at him. "And when you're done with your things, do hitch up the carriage. Oh, and perhaps it's best if you don't leave the house without a hood."

The skag. He took a step toward her, menacing. To her credit, she held her footing, her eyes upon the buttons of his jacket.

"Well, that's one blessing," she said, her eyebrows raised. "Your misfortune has certainly lessened your verbal abuse."

He sneered and pushed past her to the door.

"Bernad, *where* are you going?"

There was no hood to his jacket, and he didn't stop to collect a hat. Bernad ran down the stairs, across the entryway, pushed through the front door and out to Main Street. The cold air bit the flesh side of his face and was nothing but deadness on the other. He started running up the street. Let her get some farmhand to drive her to Ravus, or better yet, that cucker she was sacking. Tight puckered skag.

He cut between the houses and headed for the trees.

TWENTY-ONE

A dark figure stood at the foot of Soolie's bed. The smell of cold fetid flesh soiled the air. There was whimpering and weeping. And then the demon's voice. *'Tomorrow night.'*

Soolie'd had a lot of bad dreams since the demon had come. Vivid, brutal, violent dreams. Dreams with threats, cruelty, and intent. This dream was surreal and distant, barely recollected as if, had she not grasped after it, it might have been forgotten forever.

Was it a trick to frighten her? Or was it truly just a dream? Soolie couldn't remember the last time anything had been just a dream.

How is that young soul coming? She thought. Should I kill myself by knife or by lockweed? But the Demon was silent.

They left the inn early in the morning. Abrum helped Papa with the horses, and Claudine filled their bread basket with hot golden-topped biscuits that dripped with fresh melted butter. Papa tipped his hat, Soolie and Ellena said their 'thank yous,' the innkeepers wished them a safe trip, and Papa hefted himself up into the driver's seat with Ellena on one side and Soolie snugged in-between. With a light flick of the reins, the horses were turned back toward the Eastern Road. The innkeepers watched. Only Soolie waved goodbye.

"If we don't stop," Papa said, "we can be home by evening."

Ellena placed an arm around Soolie. "We're almost home."
Soolie smiled.
She wondered how much of a home it would really be.

THEY ROLLED INTO TOWN around supper time. First they passed the Barn on the right, its little peaked roof cutting a tiny triangle in the edge of the sky. Then the cart wheels knocked up off the dirt and onto the uneven cobbles. They rolled by Miss Pont's schoolhouse on the left, empty and waiting for tomorrow's students, then the Pelig's house with its clean blue walls, white trim, and tidy gray roof. Soolie stretched her neck looking for any sign of life, but the windows were dark.

Other houses were lit up, windows golden with flickering fire and lantern light that spilled onto the cobbles, contouring every stone and making the shadows dance around the horse's hooves. Dark shapes disrupted the window lights as wives, husbands, and children got up from their dinners to peek out at the street and catch a glimpse at whoever was riding past. As the cart rolled by the Svenson's house, Soolie waved because she knew someone would be watching. Soon everyone would know. The Beetches had returned to Hob Glen.

THE HORSES WAITED outside Ellena's bakery. Silas rubbed his thumbs against the reins. Just around the bend of the street was home. He could envision every house, stone, every tree, tuft of grass that lay between here and their front door. Home. Home was a safe place. Home was healing. Home was where people held on to one another. Home was the walls, the floor, the roof he had built with blood, back, and labor to keep his wife and baby daughter safe and sheltered. Home.

"All right." Ellena closed the bakery door behind her and turned the key. "I grabbed what I need."

Soolie pressed against his side to make room as Ellena handed a bundle up and pushed her way back onto the driver's bench. Silas flicked the reins, and the cart rumbled forward. Ellena's bundle clinked as she took it back from Soolie.

"You look lost in thought," Ellena teased.

"Hmm?" Soolie shrugged. "Oh. Nothing."

Silas glanced down at his daughter. Every time he saw those aged wrinkles on his baby girl's face, he wanted to break.

"Tell Ellena what you were thinking, Soolie."

Soolie grinned and blew a frog's kiss. "Really, it's nothing. Just airing out my brain, I guess."

"Well," Ellena said, "would you like to know what I grabbed?"

"Okay."

"A change of clothes, of course, and," Ellena winked at Soolie, "maybe a few items I've been saving for a special occasion."

Soolie clapped her hands. "Cordial fruit and popcorn?"

"And a little pear brandy for the adults."

"Ooh, I want some!"

Silas strained his eyes against the evening gloom, hungry for that first glimpse, for that familiar bend in the road, that familiar shadow.

And there it was.

The four little gray walls, the dark peaked roof. A small house. A modest house. The house where he had first known his beautiful wife. Where his daughter had been born. Where his wife had breathed her last. The house where he belonged. Where his family belonged. It had hurt him so much to be away.

Silas felt a lump rise in his throat even as a knot melted in his chest. They were home. Now, at least, one of the last moon's many wrongs had been righted.

As soon as the cart wheels stopped, Silas swung out of the driver's bench, made his way around behind the cart, and stood before the dark wood door. He stepped up onto the front step, placed the key in the hole, and turned it reverently, feeling the bolt click back. He pushed the door open.

The house was dark, stale, and cold. He walked into the middle of the floor and stood looking over at his work bench, his and Tara's bed, the ladder to the loft, the dead fireplace, the little curtained window, everything still and silent as if the house had lain down to wait in slumber for them to return.

"Oof!" Soolie tromped in the door and dropped a big wad of bedding on the floor.

Ellena stepped around with a box of cookware in her arms, her bakery bundle balanced on top, and set them on his work table.

Silas sighed a breath that traveled from the top of his head down to his toes, washing away the dinge of the last several days.

"Do you really have to return the horses tonight?" Ellena asked. "Can't the Cornells wait until morning?"

"Yeah, Papa, don't go!" Soolie ran up and threw her arms around his waist.

Silas patted his daughter's head, avoiding the edge of her hairline where the chestnut gold turned birch white. "And leave the horses standing out in the street? That wouldn't be right to the horses or to the neighbors who let us use them."

"Awww." Soolie flopped her arms down and trudged back to the cart. He watched her go.

Ellena stepped towards him slowly, running a hand over her frizzy hair, unruly sprigs bouncing wickedly back. She smiled up at him, her dark eyes crinkling at the corners and shining bright in the pale evening light that slipped through the curtains. She stood so close and warm, he thought he could feel her breath on the underside of his neck.

"We'll have a fire and a hot cup of tea ready for you when you get back."

Silas put a firm holding hand on her shoulder and glanced toward the door. "Keep an eye on Soolie. Lock the doors and don't answer for anyone but me." He stepped around her.

No matter what had or had not happened on the road, they were home now. It was time for things to go back to normal.

They unloaded the cart quickly. He could feel Ellena's eyes on him. He kept his head down and his eyes on Soolie.

"DID YOU HEAR THAT?"

Rod set the last clean dish back in the corner hutch carefully and listened. He glanced at his wife resting in the wicker rocker, a loose knit cream shawl around her shoulders, the tiny plump rosy head of baby Ema cradled against her bare breast, soft pink baby lips wet with mama's milk making contented sucking snuffling noises.

"There." Milin placed a protective hand around their baby and looked towards the window. "Rod, I think someone is at the stable."

Rod shut the glass latticed door to the corner hutch. He had heard it too. "Don't worry."

Rod reached up on top of the hutch and took down the pistol. It was a double-barrel, nearly new, a smooth shiny-stocked gun that had only ever been fired at stumps and over the head of one misplaced coyote. Rod didn't care for guns. They were so loud.

He wrapped his fingers surely around the double-barrel and turned back to his wife and baby.

"I'll check it out, and I'll be right back. It's probably a possum or a mud rat."

"Do you think...?" Milin let the question trail off tremulously. He knew what she meant.

Since baby Ema had been born, all the women of Hob Glen had been through their door. They came to ooh and ahh over every coo and burp, to marvel at the little fingers, ears, and nose, to share advice and stories, and of course, ultimately, to gossip about one thing: the schoolhouse horror, when the Beetch family might come back to town, and what the citizens of Hob Glen would do about it when they did.

Mrs. Pelig and Mrs. Svenson were the worst of all. Rod wished he could have kept them away from his wife, but both women intimidated him something dreadful. Mergo with her arched brows and critical eye, Pawla with her busting bosom and rapid tongue: they were the switch and the dog that drove Hob Glen, and Rod didn't dare step from the herd. So the women had come and sat with Milin. They had sipped their tea and nibbled their biscuits. They had prattled and whispered loudly behind their hands. And when they left, poor Milin had called for him, nervous and crying, needing him to comfort her and make promises he didn't know if he could keep.

But, for her, he would try.

Rod squared his shoulders, hefted his gun, and put his hand on the door latch. "If it is," he said, trying to sound brave, "I will tell them they are no longer welcome as our neighbors, and we do not wish to see or speak with them. Any more."

"Do be careful."

He opened the door decisively, the pistol gripped confidently in his hands, nodded to his wife, stepped through, shut it behind him, and shuddered.

It was dark. It was cold. He was in his stocking feet, and out from the stable shone the dim light of a lantern.

Rod clicked open the barrels. They were loaded, smooth shell butts looking up like coins for the eyes of the dead. He clicked back one hammer, rested his finger against the hard metal curve of one trigger, and stepped off the front step. He couldn't see the ground. He hated not being able to see where he was placing his feet. Rod reached out, testing the path carefully, feeling with the toes of his sock before cautiously trusting the earth.

From the stable he could hear the chuffing of hay. Someone was feeding the horses.

Rod edged along the stable, keeping close to the wall. As he reached the corner, he pressed against the side, holding the pistol near to his chest, and peeked slowly around toward the lantern-lit doorway.

"Come on out, Rod. I know it's you."

Rod froze. It was the voice of his neighbor, Silas Beetch. He raised the gun cautiously, turned, and sidestepped into the light.

"Hi, Rod."

Silas patted Merigold's side and leaned the hay fork against the wall.

"Hello, Silas." Rod held the gun cautiously on his neighbor.

Rod and Silas Beetch had always gotten along. Silas was not an especially friendly or outgoing man. He tended to keep to himself, and Rod knew if there had been just a little more road between their two houses, they might have gone all these years without sharing more than a passing nod. But Silas Beetch was a good honest neighbor. When Rod needed to fill his woodshed, Silas was there, ax in hand. When Rod needed to repair his roof, there was Silas, rain or sun, little Soolie at his side carrying a bucket of roofing nails. Rod never needed to ask, and whenever he expressed his thanks, Silas would say, "We're neighbors." And that was that.

Silas had been that neighbor for nearly twenty years.

"Thank you for the use of your horses and cart. I trust you'll find they've been well cared for." Silas eyed the gun. Rod flinched and lowered his arm.

"You shouldn't have come back, Silas."

Silas nodded slowly. "Well. My home is here. And I had your horses."

"I…" Rod shifted the pistol, the trigger slick against his finger. "I have a daughter now, Silas. You understand."

"I understand."

Rod could see now that past the grown-out beard and the weary lines in his neighbor's face, there was a wretched darkness in Silas's eyes. An anguish and a following curse. Rod felt certain everything he had heard about Silas' daughter was true, and her father knew it.

"Congratulations to you both." Silas stepped towards the door, and Rod brisked back out of the way. "If you will excuse me, I must get back to my daughter."

"Silas," Rod stopped him.

He had to make sure his neighbor knew he wasn't welcome, that he shouldn't come by. But how could he just say it? It wasn't something Silas deserved to hear.

"It's only gotten worse since you left. The whole town is set against you." He whisked the words out. "Mergo Pelig. Pawla Svenson. You know they have the town's ear. With those two teamed up to a purpose, Soolie will never be welcome in Hob Glen."

Silas lifted his lantern off the wall hook. "Give my best to your wife, Rod. And you can tell her Soolie and I have given up gardening."

Rod hesitated at his front door. He balanced on one foot, peeling off his dirty socks one at a time. With the pistol in one hand and soiled socks in the other, Rod nudged the latch with his arm and pushed the door open.

Milin still rested in the rocker. Her dress was rebuttoned, and baby Ema lay sleeping in her arms, nested in loose knit fleece, little face a contented rumple of pink eyelids, nose, lips, and chin. Milin made a soft shushing sound, and Rod tiptoed in on his bare feet, carefully nudging the door closed behind him.

"Well?"

Rod slow stepped across the creaking pine wood floor, stretched up, and replaced the pistol on top of the hutch where it didn't have to be seen. "Silas says they won't come around any more."

"Was … Soolie with him?"

Rod shook his head.

"Oh, Rod." Milin's eyes dewed. "In our own town. Across our road."

"I know." He stood holding his dirty socks.

"Promise me," she whispered, "whatever happens, you'll stay out of it. You won't get involved. No matter what the town does. Promise me, Rod."

"I promise."

This one, he knew he could keep.

TWENTY-TWO

Soolie couldn't sleep. Dread plagued her, clinging to her innards like cold lard. The memory of the dream had not faded. Rather, it seemed to have grown in her mind, playing over and over, each time stronger and more vivid than the last. The shadow of a dark figure at the foot of the bed. The cloying stench of dead rot. Like a butcher shop that hadn't changed the sawdust on its floor, letting it grow sodden and fetid with drippings. Like an immotile feculence that crawled up in her nostrils and soaked into her brain. Like the stench of dread itself. Like a heap of rotting slaughtered horses. And the demon's voice ringing above it all. '*Tomorrow night.*'

That was now. Now was tomorrow night. She lay in the dark staring at the wall and listening to Ellena snore, feeling Papa's waking eyes watching from the rocker in the middle of the room, unable to shake the feeling that something horrible was about to happen and she didn't know how to stop it.

'*Tomorrow night.*'

They had gone to bed early. Despite the treats, no one had been in a festive mood. There had been no games, no stories, no singing. In fact, they'd hardly even spoken.

From the moment Papa had gotten back from returning the

Cornells' horses, his eyes had been on her. Every time Soolie glanced in Papa's direction, he was looking back. Over a mug of tea, as he fed the fire, even while he trimmed his beard, Papa was watching.

Meanwhile, Ellena had sat by the fire refilling her mug with pear brandy. Soolie had tried a sip and found that it tasted sweet and burned pleasantly in her belly, but left a flavor of overripe fruit on her tongue that she didn't care for. Papa had poured a drop in his tea, but Ellena finished the bottle. Aunt Ellena always did snore more when she'd had something to drink. At least one of them was sleeping.

'Tomorrow night.'

"Kill yourself."

What if something horrible *did* happen, and she didn't do anything to stop it? What if she didn't do anything to stop it, and then it was too late? Maybe the demon *had* made 'arrangements' without her. What sort of arrangements could it make?

She felt sick. She wished she could turn herself inside out and scrub her insides with soapy boiling water.

She had to do something. She couldn't just lie here. She had to do something.

Ellena snorted in her sleep. Papa watched from his rocking chair. Soolie stared at the wall and didn't move.

HE HAD NEVER SEEN a town before. It was so much less than the city. So few people, like a stationary herd, stalled up in little box houses waiting to be opened.

Dog hadn't eaten in three days.

There had been so much to see, taste, smell, to want. There had been the new master. He had been distracted. He was afraid of failing, by weakness or by mistake. He needed to know: was this white-eyed girl the thing of masters? Was he fooling himself? Perhaps there could be only one Master, the one he had betrayed.

'Bring me a young soul.'

In the house before him, the humans had finally stilled their stirrings. The girl with the white eyes waited for him. He was Dog. He would obey.

TWENTY-THREE

Someone was trying to wake her, and Ellena didn't wake easily.

"Ellena!" The whisper was urgent in her ear. Strong hands held her shoulders. "Ellena!"

Her eyes shot open, and she struggled to sit up, confused and groggy, floundering against the blankets and the hands that held her.

"What is it? What's happened?"

"Shhhhh."

His finger was against her lips, and she was aware of the foul tang of old alcohol in her mouth.

She blinked dazedly as he helped her out of bed, pulling back the blankets, one arm around her thinly night-gowned shoulders.

"Silas?"

He moved her across the bare floorboards. The house was dark. The fire had gone out. Soolie lay sleeping in the far recesses under the loft.

"Is something wrong?"

He set her in the rocker and leaned in, gripping the arms of the chair, hulking over, shoulders hunching, the muscles on his forearms standing out. His darkly overcast eyes were fixed on her with a bold unwavering gleam, and the white linen of his shirt slung towards her lap, neckline gaping down so she could see past the hollow of his throat to the little curls of hair that crept down the cleft of his breastbone into darkness.

"Why," he demanded, "is it so difficult to love you?"

She blinked groggily. Her eyes felt sore and crusty. The dark cavern beneath his shirt heaved with fervent breath, and the rocker creaked back under his weight. She was waking up quickly.

The question hung between them long enough for her to hear it. It was a question that should have surprised her, but it was a question she knew all too well. Any other, and her sleep addled brain might have struggled. But these were words she knew by rote. She cleared her throat. Slowly, her voice thick and coarse with sleep, she answered him as she had come to answer herself.

"I used to think it was because you thought I didn't need you. Then I thought I was too outspoken or too emotional. Then I thought maybe you just couldn't stand to be loved too easily or too much. And now…" She swallowed. He was so close. And she was only now realizing that she really truly was awake. "I'm waiting for you to tell me."

"I don't know." His voice shook.

"Maybe," she whispered, "there is no reason."

His eyes drifted from her face, and his rough fingers touched the lace shoulder edge of her nightgown, his hand descending gently, his palm warm and heavy through the lace, his thumb tracing the curve of her collar bone.

Her breath stopped.

"I tried not to see you." His eyes shifted feverishly along the neckline of her nightgown. "I tried to not think about you. To ignore you," he winced, "but you kept snoring."

She swallowed, forgetting her brandy-soured breath, lips parting, stomach clenching. "My snoring is very difficult to ignore."

The rough tips of his fingers traced down the edge of her neckline. "Impossible," he whispered.

His touch on her skin scraped raw at her ready heart. Tomorrow she would be sure to doubt the memory. But now, floating on an island of wakefulness in a nighttime sea, it was the day with all its troubles, worries, and conventions that seemed impossibly far away.

She reached up and placed her fingertips on the pulse of his neck, her hand cupping the edge of his jaw, his freshly trimmed beard bristling against her palm. His eyes raised.

He cupped his hand tightly on hers, the glisten of tears welling below the dark recess of his brow. "Aren't you afraid?"

She almost couldn't breathe enough to speak. "I have never doubted my heart. It is one of my greatest flaws."

His hand closed around her wrist, and he heaved her from the chair. In a moment she was pressed up against him, swallowed up into the broadness of his chest and shoulders, his strong hands pulling her in, her hips pressing so hard against his it almost hurt.

His face was close, his hand cradling her head, his arm against her spine supporting her as she arched back. His nose touched hers, his mustache pricked her lip, and he inhaled her.

She had wanted this for so long, for so long she hated to say it, but it was the middle of the night, and she had to ask. She whispered it, lips brushing his.

"Are you sure?"

He kissed her.

His mouth fused with hers hungrily, pulling, demanding.

She wrapped her arms around his neck and pushed back, sucking his tongue into her mouth. His hands were on her hips, and he swung her around. She felt the rails of the ladder against her back and stepped up onto the second rung, leveling herself with him, pulling, inhaling, devouring desperately, her hands gripping the cloth of his shirt, afraid to turn around, afraid to let him go, afraid any moment one of them would wake up and be gone.

His lips moved from her mouth, kissing across her cheek, his hot breath, soft lips, the coarse brush of his beard harsh on the curve of her neck. Now his hands were at her hips, rotating her around. She released her arms from around his neck and grabbed an upper rung, step by agonizing step, turning herself away from him, lingering over her shoulder. His lips teased the tender flesh behind her ear, and she felt oddly unsure of her ability to climb.

As she faced the ladder, once more he wrapped his arms around her, one hand smoothing over her hip bone and down toward her inner thigh, the other fiddling at the buttons of her nightgown. She reached under his grasp to help, undoing the little looped pearls as his hand hovered above hers, one by one until the neckline opened to her breastbone. His hand slid beneath, under the cotton lace of her nightgown, rough against her skin, fingers sliding under to lift her breast, cupping it secure in his warm calloused hand as the soft prickle of his mouth brushed against the curve of her ear.

He whispered.

His hips pressed her, and she felt him rise against her upper thigh. She gripped the rungs of the ladder and started to climb.

SOOLIE LIFTED THE OIL CLOTH and ducked under.

"Oh. Hey."

Bernad screamed.

TWENTY-FOUR

Soolie ducked, and a half-empty liquor jug smashed against the tree root by her head, wet glass falling into the straw, the smell of raw whisky filling the little shelter.

"Ge' way! Ge' way!"

Bernad's wild shriekings had started to take form. He crouched in the far corner of the bedding, bent against the root ceiling, his head touching the oil cloth, one arm over his face, the other searching blindly around his ankles for a second weapon that wasn't there.

Quietly, Soolie put up her hands to show she meant no harm and bent to pick up the pieces of broken glass, cradling a large base piece in her palm, bits of hay and dirt sticking to the wet shards as she stacked smaller chunks and slivers on top.

When the hysterical cries finally ebbed, she glanced up to see Bernad looking wildly back from behind one arm raised in front of his face. His feet shifted, wavering toward the shipman's chest tucked in the corner.

"You have a weapon in there?"

He panted madly at her and tried to push further into the tree root at his back.

"Is it a knife or a gun?"

He shifted his weight and hissed.

The broken edges made grating sounds as she stacked another sharp-edged shard in her hand.

She set the little stack carefully to the side of the doorway, then started searching the floor for stray pieces. "If it'll make you feel better, go ahead and get it."

He froze, cornered, poised. At a drop, he lunged for the shipman's chest, scrabbling at the lid and flinging it up, pulling out a bone-handled hunting knife, still leather-sheathed, and pointing it at her, arm outstretched, his face exposed.

Soolie stacked a few last little chunks of glass and sat down in the hay, looking across at him. It was the first time she'd seen his face since the incident. She noted that the shriveled eye was still attached, laying in the hollow of his socket like an old grape on the pedicel. His skin was so tight and dark on one side, all dried out and mummified as if half his face had died in a cellar and hadn't been found for forty years. It made it difficult to read his expressions. She closed one eye, trying to block the dead half of his face, then stopped, worried that might look like she was mocking him. The fleshy side looked flushed with panic, maybe a little angry, and winded.

He yanked the sheath off the knife, dropping it on the floor, reextending the blade.

"I don't want to hurt you." She started undoing the laces of her boots. "You can sit down if you like. I'll stay over here."

Bernad started edging back towards the bed, the knife point shaking. "Why yuu he-a?" His words came out warped and slow.

"Well," Soolie yanked on one boot impatiently until it freed her bare foot. "My aunt 'n Pap started sacking each other in the loft, and I needed somewhere to go and figure out what to do."

Bernad stepped back up on the bed, half crouching, brandishing the knife in her direction.

She chucked the second boot at its pair in the doorway. "I know it's not ideal for you."

He spat at her, spittle spraying unevenly, drooling out of the corner of his mouth and down his chin.

"Believe it or not, there aren't many places for me to go in Hob Glen right now." Soolie scooted against the wall, crossed her legs, and flipped the edges of her cloak over onto her lap.

"I'll keep my distance. I'm not going to hurt you."

She hoped that was true.

They watched each other. Slowly, Bernad sunk to the cot, legs bent protectively in front of him. It was almost the same position they had been in the last time they had both been here, except this time he was the one pulling away from her.

"Witch thkag," he snarled.

Soolie took a deep breath and nodded. "I suppose so."

"You mewted my face," he whimpered.

"You told lies about me," Soolie countered.

His leathern skull face seemed to leer back, motionless and grotesque.

"Sorry," she said. He had a point.

She almost felt bad for him. She did feel bad. He was disfigured, monstrous. He had deserved a punch to the face, but not this. To be a freak and a pariah. No one deserved that. Neither of them did.

She twisted the edge of her cloak in her fingers.

"Wha the cuck 'th wrong wi' yuu?" he demanded.

She smiled. "An ancient death spirit, apparently, whatever that means."

He flinched, the knife point wavering.

"Remember the carnival woman you were tormenting?" Soolie picked hay off the wool of her cloak. "She passed it to me."

It was such a relief to say it. It was such an absurd thing to say. He glowered at her from around his knees.

"Skagged up, right?"

"I don't gi' a thkag."

"I know." She leaned her head back. "The thing is, I feel like something horrible is about to happen." She looked back at him. "I think it's waiting for something. Something really bad…"

"Wha are yu cuckin' tellin' me thith?"

His voice was alien, charged with rage and fear. Soolie remembered the way he used to play with his hair, smirk, and laugh. She couldn't imagine him ever doing those things again.

"'Cause you don't care about me, I guess. I can tell you anything." She pulled her legs in and wrapped her arms around them, resting her chin on her knees. "Was there anything you wanted to say?"

"Cuck off."

"Yeah, in a tic." She sighed. "It's just that this woman from the Southern Lands Carnival told me I needed to kill myself. Which seems a *little* extreme. How could I even consider that? Killing myself? It's wrong, right? Cowardly, selfish? Ugh," she groaned. "Permanent. I don't know if that's something I can do…" Soolie turned and flopped back into the dirt, knees bent, arms out, looking up at the dark olive gray of the oil cloth roof. Her thoughts swarmed out like ladybeetles from a jar. "But what if that's the only way to stop it? It's hurt people, killed people. And it's inside of me. Meanwhile, handling my pap and aunt is getting more and more difficult, and I don't know what it's going to do next. What if killing myself is the only way to stop it? I don't know."

She waited for another thought to buzz out, but there was nothing else. That was it. That was everything. Everything she'd been holding in for the last several days. In her head, it had been a million bellicose words, but once she had let them out, it had taken so few to say.

Now there was silence.

She closed her eyes and lay in the dirt, feeling her belly swell up and down with breath. Letting gravity strain stillness through her bones. It was so quiet in the base of the tree. There was no wind, no rain. Even the crickets were silent.

"Yu are the firtht pewson I've thpoken to."

She turned her head towards him. "Since the… That?"

He nodded.

"What about your folks?"

"Naw." The hand that held the knife, rested on the bedding beside his feet. "Mam won' even look a' me. Pap'th neva 'round. They'a cuttin' theets. Mam's goin' to Ravus. Pap's thtayin' here."

"Oh," she said. "Who'll you go with?"

"They're both jits."

Soolie propped herself up on her elbow. His tone was bitter and hollow. It didn't matter where he went. There was nothing for him here, there was nothing for him in Ravus. And there was nothing she nor anyone else could do to help him.

His one good eye looked at her. "Yu thould do it."

"Do what?"

"Kiw yoursewf."

"Of course you say that."

He shrugged. "Yu thkagged my life. Yu tuwned me into a monsther. If yu don't gank you'self, you'll cuck up thomeone else. Yu a' not worth that. Kiw youself."

Soolie grew somber. "Would you if you were me?'

He sneered. "Cuck, no. Thkag 'em. But yu thould."

She lay back in the hay and laced her fingers over her stomach. She hadn't really expected him to give her an answer, but she knew he had answered her honestly. Perhaps that was why she had asked.

"Well, thank you for your thoughts."

"Yu can't squat here."

"I know. I'll leave in the morning."

"Don't come back."

"Bernad." Soolie closed her eyes. She wondered if there was any reality in which they might ever have been friends. "If anything happens, don't try to use the knife unless you have to. If you can, just run."

SILAS HADN'T LAIN with a woman in over thirteen years.

The first time with Tara had been on their wedding night. She had bled, and he had cried. He had been afraid to touch her, and she had insisted. Not for pleasure, his or hers, but because more than anything, Tara had wanted a child.

He had knelt on his knees beside the bed where she lay naked, her frail white body fraught with purple and yellow bruises, fresh wounds and raw scars bound in years of thread-thin pink ripples that, if pressed, still dewed blood. He had bowed his head to the covers and pleaded with her to not ask him to hurt her.

She had placed a delicate hand on his head. "You will not deny me this, Silas Beetch. It is my greatest wish, and you will grant it to me. Would you wound my heart as well? Would you kill my love?"

Seven times he had plead, seven times he had been inside her. Seven times she had bled, and many many times he had wept, none more so than when her belly began to grow round with child, and he feared to have taken her very life.

They were never intimate in that way again. For eight years he never even touched her womanhood, not until, weakened by the failure of her frame and in the last moons of her life, Tara had needed him to bathe her, to dress her, to clean her wounds, and every time she had needed to relieve herself, and every evening before she closed her eyes to sleep, he had knelt before her and, with gentle care, cleaned the birthing wound which had never healed. It was the closest he ever felt to his wife.

But Ellena.

Ellena was like an ocean. Pushing, pulling, promising, demanding. One moment a gentle lapping wave, the next a powerful undertow, one minute leading, the next following, answering his every move. Ellena *wanted him*.

He lasted with her as long as he was able, which was all too brief. After he was quickly spent, Ellena had curled up in the crook of his shoulder nuzzling at his neck, brazenly caring to her own needs. So he had kissed the damp curls on her forehead, closed his eyes, and lay in the dark of the loft listening to her breath.

And for the first time in all his years, in the lulling soft seething retreat of that broken wave, with no blood and no tears, Silas fell asleep.

SILAS WOKE CHOKING, his lungs burning. The air was unbreathable, boiling heavy with smoke and heat. There was a roar like a great bear, snapping teeth, popping bones, and a heated breath that shook the walls of the house, creaking the beams.

The house was on fire.

Silas jumped out of bed in the dark. The floor was hot beneath the bare soles of his feet. He grabbed Ellena, lifted her up, then yanked the blanket off the bed, throwing it over her shoulders and pulling her toward the wall.

The air singed his bare skin. He tried not to breathe.

He felt across the slanted roof of the loft frantically, feeling for the hatch. Finally, his fingers found the coarse braid of the rope, and he unwound it violently, pushing the hatch up with such force that it swung full limit on its hinges, slamming against the roof above. He dragged Ellena beneath, bended, wrapping his arms around her legs, and hoisted her up onto the roof.

"Jump!" he shouted, took one gulp of the night air, then dove back into the billowing furnace.

"Silaaas!"

Every tortured breath scalded his lungs. He ripped the top sheet off of Soolie's bed and threw it over his head. He had to get downstairs. He had to get to Soolie.

On his hands and knees, Silas moved forward, feeling for the edge of the loft. By luck, he found it. The edge of the ladder.

Below, the bear raged, roaring hot foul breath.

Silas spun, the sheet over his head, and clamored down the rungs. They held strong. The fire had been lit from the outside and had not yet reached the center of the house.

Silas dropped to the floor on his hands and knees. His heart and lungs were screaming. An angry sunset glowed from the edges of the room.

"Soolie! Soolie!"

He coughed, feeling along the floorboards. Maybe she had made her way out. The bed was right behind the ladder. He had to make sure it was empty. He needed to be sure.

He waved his hands before him, advancing on the hopeful shadow of the bed. His hand touched the familiar dimpled fabric of Tara's quilt, and he scrambled up onto the mattress, spreading his arms in circles like a swimmer.

"Soolie?"

He coughed, choking. She wasn't here. She must have made it out.

Above, the roof beams creaked. He rolled off the bed, dropping the sheet and grabbing Tara's quilt, taking it with him. The door was just across the room. He scrambled low across the boards, dragging the quilt. His head clipped sharply against a corner, bright fuzz blooming behind his eyes. He had run into his workbench.

There was a sudden thunderous crash from above, and Silas ducked and rolled under the table, the quilt over his face, as part of the roof collapsed into the loft, breaking the boards above and avalanching to the floor, rubble and burning wood smashing around him.

He scrambled out the other side of the table, his vision blackened by smoke and dust, the floor cluttered with sharp foreign shapes.

"Silas!"

Ellena's cry came from the dark, beyond the roar of the fire, and he followed it.

"Silas!"

He couldn't breathe. The air was getting hotter.

The familiar boards of the door met his fingers, and he fumbled over his head for the metal turn of the lock. It bit his fingers as he grasped it and turned, then heaved his shoulder into the door. The door blew forcefully out, and he spilled headfirst over the step and onto the cobbles of the street.

"Silas!"

Ellena grabbed him, dragging him across the hard stones away from the little house, away from the hungry red tongues that lapped up the sides and the billowing dark smoke that blocked the stars.

Ellena was rolling him on the cobbles, beating out sparks and cinders, then sitting him up and throwing her arms around him as he coughed and gasped, retching at the air.

"You scared me to death, you jit!" She sobbed into his neck. "I saw part of the roof collapse, and I thought. I just… Oh, you selfish skag."

He pushed her back, wheezing painfully.

"Don't try to speak." Her frantic fingers patted at his face. "Just breathe. Just breathe."

He shook his head, trying to force words.

"Are you okay? Anything broken? Does anything hurt?"

"Soolie?" he croaked.

Ellena sat back, the quilt around her shoulders falling open to her lap. "She must have gotten out."

He wheezed. "Have you seen her?"

Ellena shook her head.

Silas's chest heaved, and he mustered himself, leaning forward and bracing himself on his knees, standing slowly in the light of the growing flames that flickered up from the wound in the roof, his bare naked skin marred with ash and burns, blood and bashed wounds he hadn't yet begun to feel, standing before the home he had built, fourteen years of memories and hope turning to rubble before his eyes, and he turned away.

His daughter was missing. That was all that mattered. He gripped Tara's quilt in his fist and, bare to the night, began walking up the street, Ellena shuffling behind him, her blanket wrapped around her.

"Do you think they'll help us?"

"They don't have a choice."

THE FRONT DOOR was off its hinges. The hanging pegs lay on the ground. Silas stepped over into the doorway.

"Rod?" he shouted. "Milin?"

The downstairs was dark and silent.

Silas had been in his neighbor's house before. He had helped maneuver the corner hutch Rod purchased for his and Milin's fifth anniversary. When Rod cracked his leg felling trees, Silas had carried his neighbor inside before running to get the Doc, and whenever Rod was away in the city, it was Silas that Milin called to usher a night sparrow out of her kitchen or dredge a drowned river vole from the well. Silas had been in his neighbor's house; he just didn't make a habit of it.

"Stay close," he murmured to Ellena, tossing Tara's blanket on top of a shawl-draped chair.

The Cornells kept a tidy home, and everything in the front room looked to be in its place. Halfway across the floor, Silas saw the bedroom door gaping silent and open. Maybe the Cornells weren't home. Perhaps Rod had known about Silas' home being lit on fire and, instead of warning his neighbor, had taken Milin and the baby and gotten out of Hob Glen.

The bedroom was dark, the curtains drawn. Silas stepped onto the braided bedroom rug and edged around the bed with his back to the wall. Beside him, Ellena clung close, whimpering softly.

Silas reached his hand along the wall and across the soft hanging folds of the window curtains, grasped the curtain high near the rod, and pulled them back, pale moonlight shuttering into the room, illuminating the double bed and little wood-barred crib that rested between it and the wall. Something was tangled in the bed covers.

Ellena screamed and hid her face against his bare arm.

There, on the rug at their feet, laying in a pallid patch of moonlight, a shrunken death mask looked up at them with hollow coal eyes and exposed teeth like long corn. Only the hair was recognizable: frail frizz drifting from the scalp and chin. It was Rod Cornell.

Ellena whimpered and clung after Silas as he moved around the body toward the bed. The toss-turned sheets were black with blood, a crow claw hand extended from the pink sleeve of a nightgown, stiff bloodless fingers reaching towards the little bedside crib.

It was empty. The crib was empty.

He had to find Soolie. That thought was the only blaze mark in the black forest that was rapidly closing in on his mind. Find Soolie. Find his daughter.

"Wait in the other room."

Ellena shook her head, clinging to his arm, hiccuping, sobbing.

"GO."

Flinching, she went.

Silas stepped over Rod's body and around the bed to the white oak dresser. He pulled out the bottom drawer, tossing clothes, wools, and knits onto the floor, then the next drawer, upending it onto the rug, then the next. Finally, he turned out the top drawer, full of socks and silkens, onto the bed beside the body of Milin Cornell. It wasn't in the dresser.

In the main room, Ellena stood in the middle of the floor huddling in her blanket, sobbing in hysterical shock. Silas went straight to the corner hutch. He pulled out the middle drawer, tossing it on the floor, napkins and napkin rings spilling out onto the boards. Then, he reached up and felt around on top of the hutch out of view, his fingers grazing the cold barrels of a gun and, behind it, a sharp-cornered box.

He grabbed the box and pulled it down. A heavy rectangle of dark maple with brass bound corners and, when he lifted the lid, tidy ranks of shiny brass cylinders. Shells.

Silas shoved the box at Ellena.

"Hold these."

There was no telling what monsters were out in the night. His daughter needed him to be ready. He grabbed the cream shawl off the rocker, knotted it around his waist, then went back to the cabinet, reached up, and pulled down the gun. The same double-barrelled pistol he had seen Rod carrying earlier that day. The fool Rod had stored the gun cocked, and he hadn't even made it out of the bedroom. Silas depressed the trigger, controlling the hammer with his thumb, uncocked the weapon, and checked the barrels. They were loaded. He snapped the gun straight and pulled back both hammers.

He crossed to the open doorway and turned, looking back at Ellena standing alone, eyes and nose puffy, soggy with grief, clutching the rounds box like a burial gift in her hands.

"I'm going to find my daughter."
Nothing else mattered.

The fire roared white-yellow light that dripped molten from the broken roof and flared up in spitting spumes, luminating the underside of the roiling smoke that melted into the black overhead of night. In his arms, the young soul screamed in short bursts, its underdeveloped lungs pumping nasal grating squalls through its gummy toothless mouth.

The new master was gone.

All three humans had been here only a short time before, and now they were gone.

He shouldn't have taken so much time. He shouldn't have stopped to feed. He had brought the young soul, and the master was gone. He couldn't do anything right. Dog was a failure. Dog was *punka*.

Still the baby human screamed.

Dog covered its face, pressing his blood-sticky palm over the howling mouth, long hooked nails curving around the squishy little head, resisting the urge to crush and silence it with one clench of his fist. The new master wanted the young soul alive.

He had to find her.

TWENTY-FIVE

The Beetch girl lay curled asleep in the middle of the floor between him and the doorway. Bernad stayed awake, the wool blanket wrapped around his shoulders, holding the hilt of the hunting knife with both hands like a candle to keep back the shadows. He had only turned away once, and that was to refill the oil in the lantern that hung near his head. The last thing he needed was to be draped into darkness with the blood demon, Beetch.

Cucking skag.

To think he had felt like a hostage at Mam's house.

From the floor, she stirred.

Bernad sucked in his breath, adjusting his weary grip on the knife, his heart hopping over coals as Beetch's gray cloak bowed, her head lifting slowly from the floor, tangled chestnut hair hanging down, tinseled with dirt and hay.

She sat upright, kneeling, just facing away from him, silent, face obscured. He waited. Was she wake-stumbling? Was it still Beetch?

A cold draft stirred the lantern flame, shaking her shadow upon the wall.

Her head turned slowly toward him. His fingers ached around the knife hilt, knuckles tightly viced, fingernails pressed to white.

His breath clashed cymbals in his ears. Her eyes looked on him and they were white as bleached bones. Demon.

Silently, she turned away and faced the entry. The knife slipped through his trembling fingers.

Bernad pressed against the roots and earth at his back, shaking under the blanket, hiding behind his bent knees, not even daring to pick up the knife that lay at his feet.

Outside in the night woods, something moved. A step, the snap of a twig, a heavy breath outside the tent. Bernad covered his mouth, trying not to cry out.

The oil cloth at the entrance lifted, then dropped. It lifted again, hesitating, the being outside just out of view. An anguished keening howl cut the night air, and Bernad bit down on the flesh of his hand to hold back his screams.

The creature outside the entrance stepped down, one foot at a time, howling like a deathwaker, carrying with it the scent of dead flesh and spilled blood. A figure in filthy rags collapsed into the opening of the tent, prostrating itself before Beetch, arms outstretched.

"Failed!" it cried. "Dog has failed! The soul was to be alive, and Dog has failed!" It howled and grovelled before her. There was no sound from Beetch, but the monster whined, "Yes, master. Master is mercy. Dog will obey."

Maybe if he was silent and didn't move, they would not harm him.

The air in the small shelter turned electric like a dry summer storm. The hair on Bernad's neck and head bristled, and his nostrils filled with a scent like something hot and burning. Slowly, as if every movement was agonizing effort and pain, Beetch stood to her feet and turned.

Bernad closed his good eye tight and tucked his head against his knees.

"Boy."

He couldn't look.

"Look at me."

He looked up.

She stood, hair wild and hay-struck, cloak askew, eyes cold and burning white. At her feet, the monster knelt in the hay, its skin sallow and stretched taut across its stubbled skull. Its eyes were twin nocturnal beasts, and its wild features were drenched and smeared with deep gut cordial red as if it had been weeping and vomiting blood. Blood. The creature's face was dripping with blood. And before the monster, lying in its outstretched grasp, was something bundled in a soft blue blanket smeared in mud red. From the folds of the blanket showed a tiny little fist curled like a conch shell, delicate, pink, and still.

Bernad's stomach lurched, assaulting his throat.

"Tell me," Beetch intoned, "where do I find children."

A high whimper escaped Bernad's lips.

"Speak."

At her feet, the monster's lips split, baring sharp yellow canine teeth.

Bernad tried to speak, his words coming out an airy squeak. "Shchoohouthe," he managed.

"I need a child eight to ten years." Her voice was barely a whisper. Her features never moved. "I need it tonight. Tell me."

The monster balanced back on its heels, slowly rising from a crouch. It flexed long bony fingers set with thick black nails.

"H ... H..." Two sets of eyes watched him: eyes like lightning and eyes like wounds. "Hobby's."

Hobby had a younger sister. Salla. She was simple for her age, and Hobby guarded her jealously. She was Hobby's only virtue. She was nine years.

"Where?"

"Boun houthe," he garbled. "Nea' Bawn."

"What barn?"

"Harvetht fethtival. Off the road. Boun houthe. Boken porch. Yun' gil."

"Years?"

"Nine," he blurted, then squeaking. "Don kiw me! Pease don' kiw me!"

Beetch looked to the monster, then turned for the door. She moved slowly, head drooping, limbs dragging. The monster growled at him and followed. Both stepped out into the night, and Bernad was alone.

Bernad's stomach heaved, and he doubled over, dropping to his hands and knees and vomiting over the side of the bed. The whisky bile ripped at his throat. It surged up into his sinuses and dripped out his nose, burning his eyes. He stayed there, hunched over the edge of the bed, mouth open, dripping bile with every breath. His stomach heaved again, vile green acid splattering off his stiffened lips. He moaned.

When at last he turned his head toward the door, there was nothing between him and escape but a little blood-stained bundle in the middle of the floor.

Bernad stuck the hunting knife into his belt, grabbed the lantern and scrambled, trying not to look at the bundle, not wanting to see, grabbing his boots and bursting out into the night.

Cucking skag this town.

For the first time, Mam was right. He had to get out of Hob Glen.

Dog followed behind the girl. They stepped out from the trees into the moonlight, pale beams cutting the field with dark knifing shadows and making the new frost on the grass blades shine like thick silver dust. The new master struggled, laboring. She was hardly moving now. She swayed slowly into each step, feet flipping as she dragged them forward shushing through the grass, her head lolling, slumping lower and lower, as if at any moment she might curl over sideways into the ground. He stood and watched her. It worried him.

This master was weak.

Had he sunk so low as to serve a weak master? Was this what he had come to deserve? When he had mistakenly snuffed out the young soul she had required, a true master would have punished him, chastised and lessoned him in pain. A true master commanded with terror, power, and wrath.

This master had said, *The vessel was too young.*

There had been no consequences.

Dog didn't even know if he could respect a master who did not punish failure, who did not demand respect.

Perhaps this was the fate he had earned. Dog the failure with his failure master.

It was nearing early morning now. Not long before the humans would begin to wake.

The girl swayed forward again, but this time her feet didn't move to catch her. Her legs went loose, and she fell, arms flopping as she piled into the ground. She lay twisted in the dirt, one shoulder wavering slowly, the only sign of any attempt to raise herself.

Dog did not offer to help. He stood a pace away. A true Master would command him. A true Master never let his lessors see him struggle.

Stand before me. The voice spoke into his mind.

Dog obeyed, trying not to let his anger show. The leader was the strength of the pack. The Master must be greater than all he commanded. Dog didn't deserve to redeem himself. And with a master this weak, he would never have the chance. Hopes he hadn't dared acknowledge cracked and bled out his eyes in cold rivulets of fury.

You do not understand now. Her face was hidden beneath her arm so he could not see her eyes, but he could hear her voice growing dim. *But you will. Lift this vessel and carry me to the young soul. Bring me … to the young soul, and … you will see … and you … will know … it is I … who commands…*

The voice faded into the stillness of the night.

Dog looked down at the body of the girl crumpled at his feet.

This was his chance to leave. To turn his back on this weakness and start anew. Turn haunches. Run away. Abandon another master.

He could not.

Dog could not fail again. Dog was created to serve. Let another master fail Dog, before Dog failed another master.

He knelt before the body of the living girl and turned her over. The white eyes were closed. He placed one arm around her back, slid the other under her knees, and stood with her in his arms. Her head rested on his bony shoulder, long hair spilling over down his back. She was almost as large as he was, but Dog was strong.

He stood in the moonlight holding her. There was no final command to send him off.

Dog obeyed.

SILAS STRODE DOWN the dark of Main Street, naked but for the cream shawl about his waist, burned, bruised, and bloodied, the pistol hanging in one hand.

"HOB GLEN!"

He passed Ellena's bakery on the left, then the Svenson's on the right. Behind him, Ellena stumbled to keep up, holding the blanket around her shoulders and the box of ammunition in her hands.

As the old oak tree of the town square came into view, Silas raised his arm to the sky and pulled the first trigger. The shot was an anvil on a steel drum, jarring down his arm and into his shoulder.

"WHERE IS MY DAUGHTER!"

He strode past the general store, past the house of old Mr. Ander. In the street-side windows, candles and lantern lights came to life, bobbing about in the hidden rooms.

At last he stood before the tall house with the spotlessly painted pale sky sides, the clean white trim, and the meticulous white pebble path to the painted gray door.

"SOOLIE!" He roared at the vacant windows.

Ellena caught up beside him, shifting the quilt about her shoulders, the shells roll-clattering in the box as she turned around, anxiously watching the first lantern come up the street.

"Silas," she hissed, "what are we doing?"

Silas aimed over the roof, bracing the gun with both hands against the kick, and pulled the second trigger, the crack of the shot slamming against his ears.

"WHERE IS MY DAUGHTER!"

Silas snapped the barrels open, shucking the shells onto the street, and reached back to Ellena.

Her hand touched his wrist. Her eyes were large and fearful. "Maybe we…"

He ripped the box of shells from her hand, smacked down it on the stones between his feet, flipped the lid, grabbed two new shells, and stood back up.

Someone in this town knew where his daughter was, and they were about to tell him. The town was gathering.

"Silas Beetch! What do you mean pulling these people out of their given rest this time of night? Good lands, have you left your senses! Why, there's not a stitch of decent clothing on the two of you."

Silas looked up to see Pawla Svenson elbowing her way toward him. The robust housewife was wrapped in a large pink cotton robe, a ruffled night cap sealing the top of her head like a jam jar. Behind her, a dozen familiar faces now gathered, holding high lanterns that gleamed off hastily grabbed weapons: axe blade, pitching fork, and gun barrel.

He thumbed both shells into the barrels of Rod's gun.

"Good lands, where did you get that gun? How DARE you fire it within town limits." Pawla looked him up and down in aggressive disgust. "In the mid of night, no less. What could you possibly think you're…"

Silas snapped the gun into position and cracked both hammers back with one heavy hand. "WHERE IS SHE?"

Pawla whooped, her pudgy fingers splayed tight to her bosoms. "Oh, lands preserve us, he's threatening me. Oh, lands!"

Silas spun back to the Pelig house and aimed for a second story window. He pulled one trigger, the shot ringing in his ears and echoing in smashed glass.

"MY DAUGHTER!"

The crowd stirred, verging on violence.

"Silas!" Torrance Baldrick stepped forward, his hands raised, a tusk-handled revolver cradled against his thumb. "We don't want anyone to get hurt here tonight."

"Then maybe you should have considered that before setting my house on fire. WHERE is my daughter?"

"I also have a daughter," Torrance said, "and I understand your concern. Perhaps if you put down the gun, we could help you find her."

Silas aimed the pistol at Torrance Baldrick's head. "How about I get my daughter back first."

Pawla Svenson gasped and reeled in a near faint. Torrance's brow grew heavy, his grip tightening on the revolver.

"I'm warning you, Beetch."

"Silas," Ellena pleaded beside him.

"Silas Beetch." The new voice was smooth and cool as butter cream. "If you would please compose yourself. Dear Ellena looks practically petrified."

Every person on the night street stopped and looked toward the front step of the house. There, in a long silken pale yellow nightgown, her hair in a smooth auburn braid, her hands clasped calmly in front of her, stood Mergo Pelig.

Silas lowered the gun. "My daughter is missing."

"I assure you," she spread her hands, "none of us have her in our possession. If we see her, you will be the first to know."

He growled through his teeth. "Help me find her."

"Silas," Mergo tipped her head sadly. "It's the middle of the night, and these good people need their rest. I'm sure your daughter is in good health. After all, this would not be the first time she has run away."

Ellena hurriedly clung to Silas' gun arm, his muscles tightening.

"Where," his jaw clenched, "is your son?"

Mergo arched a single eyebrow. "In his bedroom recovering. You may recall he was grievously injured."

"Let me speak to him!"

"I think not. He has been traumatized enough and he needs to recover. It would be better to let these good folk return to their beds. Perhaps in the morning, when everyone is in a better mind and no one in an unfortunate state of undress…"

"I HAVE KEPT PEOPLE FROM THEIR BEDS?" Silas roared, shoving Ellena off. "My DAUGHTER is missing! My house is on fire!"

"Is it?" Mergo clasped her hands. "How truly unfortunate. *Goodnight*, Silas."

Mergo Pelig turned toward her front door, and Silas swung up his gun arm. Behind him, Torrence Baldrick shouted, aiming the revolver over one arm as Ellena threw herself between them screaming. "NO!"

"I see you. Come out!"

Silas wasn't aiming the weapon at Mergo. Instead, he levelled the gun at the dark corner of the house.

Mergo paused, her hand on the door latch. From the lake of shadows, something moved. It emerged slowly into the light, an unlit lantern swinging from one hand, face hidden behind his jacket collar. It was Bernad Pelig.

"You," Silas growled, gun at the ready.

"One move, Beetch," Torrence said, shifting his stance to aim around Ellena. "One move, and I blow a hole in the back of your head. Just give me reason."

"Get in the house, Bernad." Mergo held open the front door, her voice brittle.

The boy shrunk away from the crowd, moving for the door.

"Where is my daughter!" The gun in Silas' hand started to shake. "Where is Soolie?"

Bernad hesitated at the step, his good eye peering over his collar.

"How *dare* you speak to him." Mergo's words were cut tin at the edges. "Bernad, get in the house."

"You've seen her, please!" Silas shouted. "Bernad!"

"Hobby'th," the boy's voice slurred out from under his arm. "She'th at Hobby'th."

Bernad ducked his head and ran past his mother into the safety of the house.

Silas panted, bare chest heaving, mouth open, eyes lost in the air before them.

Hobby's? Hobby Mokrum? What could the Mokrums want with his daughter?

"Silas," Ellena was beside him hissing urgently. "We need to warn them. We need to tell them about the Cornells."

Mergo stood poised in her doorway, her head raised, neck long and white. "My family is going to bed. As should you all. I expect this will all be over in the morning."

The townsfolk murmured her words, nodded, and turned away from the wild man who stood naked but for the shawl around his waist, away from the woman beside him huddling in a blanket, away from the girl who wasn't there, and back towards their homes.

"Wait!" Ellena shouted at the retreating faces. "Rod and Mill…"

Silas grabbed her harshly, spinning her around, the hard pistol heavy on top of her shoulder. "No."

"We *have* to tell them!" She struggled weakly. "Silas! Everyone is in danger! They can help us."

"They won't." He held her tight, looking harshly into her wet brown eyes. "They would *hunt* her."

He hadn't seen much of Bernad's face, but he had seen enough. It was shrunken, it was lifeless. It was like the bodies on Rod and Milin Cornell. Whatever was going on had to do with his daughter, and he couldn't trust anyone else. Taking care of Soolie was his job.

He gripped Ellena at the bare base of her neck and pushed down. "Pick up the box."

A single sob escaped her lips, but she cut it short and obeyed, scooping up the rattling box as the last of the lantern lights were lost down the streets and swallowed by houses.

She was shaken. She was terrified. He could see it. He was hurting her, frightening her, but he was helpless to stop, incapable to comfort. The moment he slowed, the moment he paused, the moment he stopped to breathe, he would fall apart. Velocity was the only thing keeping him ahead of the whirling obliterating scythes of anguish and terror that cut at the back of his mind, gaining. He had to press forward. Soolie needed him.

"Come on."

He pushed her ahead of him, gripping the gun in his other hand, driving them forward down the dark street.

SHE COULD SMELL IT. That cloying cold rotten sickness. It lay in her nostrils and slid down her throat. It was clammy and wet against her forehead and cheek. The smell from her nightmare. The smell of the creature standing at the foot of the bed.

Soolie tried to wake up, but something pushed her back down.

Sleep, baby girl. Everything is okay. Sleep.

Papa's voice. It was warm and soothing, calm and strong. She could feel herself being carried in his arms, strong arms that wrapped around her...

But these arms felt small and thin. Papa's gate was long and rolling, gentle and reassuring. The stride was short and jolting, jerking her up and down. The hands clutched at her shoulders in sharp-edged points like spider's claws. The chest was cold and bony. The smell.

NO! She struggled within her body, her flesh a heavy immovable weight. Open your eyes!

It's okay, baby girl. Don't struggle. I've got you.

IT WASN'T PAPA.

A flash of white eyes appeared in the dark: blazing, angry white eyes.

STAY ASLEEP, SOOLIE BEETCH.

NO! She raged and strained against the stillness, against the poison, the spider's web that wrapped her in darkness. WAKE UP!

DOG STOOD IN A SCRAGGLY STAND of naked trees, the girl hefted in his arms. This had to be the house. He had passed two houses already. A gray one, a white one, but this was the first brown one. It was a small single-story house. There was no yard, only brush and brambles. The front deck sagged like a bad mattress, and the house was flaking paint like an old sunburn. His tongue dripped over his pointed front teeth as he tasted the night air. There were guard animals here. And people. He could smell two adults, an old man, a young man, and a little girl. This was the house.

In his arms, the girl twitched, then spasmed. She moaned.

Dog stepped forward, twigs and fallen leaves cricking and snapping under his toes. From the direction of the house came a volley of deep jowly barks. One set, then two overlapping each other. The guard animals had caught his scent.

"Nnnn!" The girl's chest bowed away from his arms, and her eyes snapped open, rolling back in their sockets. She started bucking. Dog held her body tight, but her head snapped about, hair whipping over her face, and beneath it, the eyes seemed to skitter light and dark.

Something was barrelling towards them low to the ground, slavering teeth gnashing, small eyes set in a thick broad skull.

Dog set the thrashing girl down in the leaves and crouched at the ready as the guard beast crashed into him teeth-first. Dog brought his hands in on the creature's head, catching the small cropped triangle ears between thumb and finger on either side, the beast's jaws gnashing between his wrists as he pulled, carrying its momentum into a full swing and slamming the creature spine-first into the trunk of a tree.

Dog turned back, ready for the second animal, and it was already there, smaller than the first, with a long rat snout and sharp teeth closing in on his exposed calf. Dog kicked up his heel, clipping the creature in the chin, its teeth glancing harmlessly off his skin as it flopped to the dirt, wallowing to get up, front and back legs warring with the leaves. Dog dove his thumb sharp into the side of its neck, gripping the back with his fingers and twisting, cracking its spine.

"Brufis? Lockjaw?"

The humans were awake. He pulled his thumb free of the dead animal's flesh.

In the dirt, the girl master convulsed, her limbs and spine jerking like a pennant in a gale. Dog felt thick black shame gorge his heart. Failure Dog with his failure master.

"Where are those skaggin' mutts?"

"Kol? You're waking the kids."

Dog lowered his head, his lip rippling up in a snarl. So be it. He would bring her her young soul. Let this service be his penance. Dog was created to obey.

He bolted from the trees, digging into the rough cold ground with his hind feet, heels never touching, sprinting in a free fall. The back door was open. A loaf-chested man stood shirtless in the doorway, fiddling with a dark lantern, a long rifle leaning against the jamb beside him.

"Shuddup! There's something out here. Brufis! Lockjaw!"

Dog cleared the back steps in a leap, leading with a heel punch high on the man's thick chest. They slammed back into a hallway, hitting the floor hard, the lantern flying from the man's hands and smashing against the wall as Dog brought his fist straight down into the man's face, crushing his nose, upper teeth, and palate. The man screeched.

In the hallway ahead, a woman in a man's tunic turned to run. Dog caught her by the back of the shirt, his nails tearing through the cloth as he jerked her back and sunk his teeth into the front of her throat, ripping up, blood and flesh spraying into his face as he dropped her to the floor, convulsing, vocal chords shredded, unable to scream. He wasn't here to feed.

He could smell the little one.

Dog busted into a small room with a little hay tick bed. Small toys of tin and carved wood sat in a row on the windowsill. The bedding was upturned and rumpled. It still smelled warm. He crouched by the bed, looked under, and a set of terrified blue eyes looked silently back. Dog grabbed the front of the nightgown with one hand, lifting the edge of the bed frame with the other, and hauled the little one out. Her straight oat brown hair hung in thin strands to her knees. She made warbly whimpering sounds, her eyes rolling back and forth like marbles.

"Oy, you, bluggar skag!" A nasally voice screamed from the doorway.

Dog looked back. A boy, big and stocky with a fuzzy face and snub nose, stood with the rifle in his hands.

"NO cucker touches MY sister!"

Dog yanked the girl in front of him as a shield, her back to her brother, her mouth hanging open in an absent cry.

The boy shouted, his face red and scrunched up, "Le' her go, you limp wag!"

Dog reached back to the windowsill, grabbed the little red and white striped tin top, and flung it sharp across the room. It lodged point-first in the boy's throat, and he dropped the rifle, staggering back into the hallway. Dog hooked his nails in the front of the girl's nightshirt, slung her over his shoulder, stepped over the dying boy, and headed for the door.

SILAS WAITED IMPATIENTLY, angrily, as Ellena hobbled barefoot over the sharp rocks of the road. She was slowing him down. Why wasn't she going faster? Didn't she understand the urgency? Didn't she understand he couldn't just leave her behind?

"I'm ... sorry," she panted.

"Just move faster."

The Mokrum's house was somewhere up ahead.

Soolie. She had to be all right. There was no reality where she was not all right. This was his fault. He had gotten distracted. How could he have let himself get distracted? Ellena. Ellena had distracted him, and now she was slowing him down. And he was letting her.

They had to move faster.

He heard the sound of barking.

Silas broke into a run, leaving the packed dirt of the road and heading for the trees, arms pumping, heart heaving, gun in his fist.

He heard one dog. No, two. No, just one.

He vaulted over a fallen log and plowed through a patch of saplings, twigs lashing his bare skin. A sharp stick punctured his tender instep, and he pushed on.

The barking had ceased. It had been up here somewhere; he had heard it. The sound of a struggle caught his ear. Something rustled in the brush, fighting, wrestling. He gripped the pistol with both hands. He hadn't reloaded the gun. He only had one shot.

There: writhing on the ground beneath a tree. Was it an animal? Two?

He saw the little human feet, the muddied white underdrawers, the red cloth all snarled up in leaves and struggle.

"SOOLIE!"

He ran to her, dropping to his knees, gun forgotten on the ground, and wrapped her up in his arms. Her head slammed forward, forehead bashing him in the mouth, splitting his lip. She clawed at him like a cat in a washtub, her nails scratching his chest, her knee driving down between his legs, crushing the tender parts beneath the shawl. Still, he held her. He wasn't letting her go again. Not ever again.

"I'm here, baby girl. I've got you. You're safe now. I've got you."

"Oh, Soolie!" Ellena hurried up, standing over them. "Was she just like this?"

Soolie wasn't fighting as hard. She quivered in his arms. This was all his fault.

"I'm here, baby girl. Ellena's here too."

"We're right here, Soolie. You're going to be all right."

Her eyes snapped open and they were marble white. They locked on his, her teeth bared, and a screeching growl forced between his little girl's lips.

"GGGHHHHHYYYOU WILL BRING DESTRUCTION." The voice was a shredding shriek, a sound that arched her back and vomited up from her belly. Her small frame went taut as cutting wire, then the white eyes fluttered, and she slumped still in his arms.

At his shoulder, Ellena clasped her hands over her mouth and sobbed through her fingers.

A monster had a hold of his little girl. This was it: the thing she hadn't been able tell him. It was inside of her, and he had to save her. He was her Papa.

Soolie's eyes began to open. They lifted, looking up at him dark and clear as fresh tea. Perhaps she could hear him now. She must be terrified. She needed him to comfort her. She needed him to be strong, to tell her everything was going to be okay.

"Baby girl." He touched her face to show her he wasn't afraid. "I want you to know that whatever has happened, I'm here. You're safe. I won't let anything hurt you. It's not going to win." He kissed her gently on the forehead, just below the graying widow's peak. "I'm here. I'm your Papa. I will always be here. Everything is going to be all right."

She whimpered, struggling.

"Shhh," he hushed, "don't try to move."

"Silas," Ellena's voice was tight. "I think we should get out of here."

Soolie groaned, straining, and he helped her sit up, supporting her across the shoulders.

"Silas, there are two dead dogs over there."

Soolie was trying to say something. He leaned over to catch the syllables fleeting from her lips.

"I think," Ellena was saying, "I think they were just killed. I think we should leave. Silas?"

Soolie's lips moved. "Papa."

It was her voice, his baby girl in his arms, calling him Papa. It didn't matter what had happened. It didn't matter what she'd done. He would protect her. He would keep her safe.

"Yes, baby girl. I'm here."

244

She was on the ground. She was spasming. Grimy leaves, grit, and pine needles abraded her face, bashing roughly at her arms and legs. The cold dirt and air were on her thighs and lower back. Her skirts were wadded and twisted up around her waist. The demon was fighting her.

You must not stop me, Soolie Beetch.

Her muscles turned to razor-edged cords that bound up, biting into her flesh. Her hands and feet were cramped-up claws.

"SOOLIE!"

Papa.

Strong arms lifted her, the skin was warm, the flesh was muscled and thick. He smelled like smoke, but it was him. It was really Papa.

She spasmed against his chest.

"I'm here, baby girl. Ellena's here too."

"We're right here, Soolie. You're going to be all right."

Soolie pulled on her strength, focusing every drop of tenacity and rage, siphoning it down into a single piece of diamond-edged will: This is MY body. These are MY people. I will NOT let you hurt them.

"Ghhhhaaaaaa!" The scream pried her jaws open.

YOU WILL BRING DESTRUCTION.

Soolie opened her eyes.

Papa looked down at her. His face was smudged with black and gray, dampness crusted in his left brow, and his upper lip was newly split, swelling wet and red. His eyes were rage gone cold, dark and still and deadly. He wasn't wearing a shirt, and lying in the dirt beside him was a gun. Above them, Ellena hovered, her hair an undone festoon. She was wrapped in a blanket. Soolie's blanket.

Soolie's body stopped convulsing.

Papa kissed her on the forehead.

"Baby girl." He touched the side of her face, and the severity of his eyes softened. "I want you to know that whatever has happened, I'm here. You're safe. I won't let anything hurt you. It's not going to win. I'm here. I'm your Papa. I will always be here. Everything is going to be all right."

But something was wrong. Something was coming.

Soolie felt it before she saw it. A sense, as if the demon within her was readying itself in anticipation. She struggled to sit.

"Shhh, don't try to move."

She shook her head, pushing herself upright. Beyond Papa, something stirred. Something was moving in the dark. Coming up the hill, striding toward them, teeth bared, its face spattered in death, and beside it, being hauled by the arm … a small girl.

'Tomorrow night.'

The young soul. The demon was getting its young soul.

She couldn't let that happen.

"Papa," Soolie whispered.

"Yes, baby girl. I'm here."

Soolie's hand found the smooth stock of the gun.

"I'm sorry."

She lifted the gun, one hand bracing the butt, the other gripping her thumb against the twin crescent triggers. The muzzle touched her chest, and she squeezed.

"I'M SORRY."

He pulled back and looked down just in time to see the smooth dark gray of the barrel against the little turquoise buttons of her dress, then the gun went off.

He felt the shot pound through her body, entering her chest and spraying out her back, blood and tissue exploding across the cold ground beside him, a violent sneeze that blew back into his face, across his mouth and eyes. The gun was in the lap of her dress. A dark wound like a bitten plum tore her open. Her small face was so white.

He sat, holding her in his arms. His baby girl. His little baby girl.

"No, baby girl, no."

His big shaky fingers touched her delicate cheek. His rough

thumb swiped away strange foreign tears that splattered on her face like rain.

"No, baby girl."

He swiped back the hair, cupping the little forehead in his hands. He kissed her, again and again and again. His lips were wet, and when he looked, her forehead was smeared with red. He had gotten red on her face. He rubbed it away with the palm of his hand. His hands were too big. She was so little in his big hands.

Somewhere someone was howling. Somewhere someone was dying.

"It's all right baby girl, it's all right."

Her brown eyes looked beyond him. Still, empty. Unanswerable.

"It's all right. It's all right."

Something screamed. A bloody sound that rent the dark. At first he thought it came from himself, from inside, that it was the sound of his heart being torn to pieces, but the cry was growing closer.

In a daze, he tucked her head against his chest and looked up as a black shape flung up between the trees, bounding towards them. It devoured the distance in a moment and was upon Ellena where she stood shrieking, grabbing her hair and wrenching her head sideways, her whole body bowing, the blanket falling from her shoulders as she contorted, naked in a clawed grip, black hooked nails buried in her hair and digging sharp points into the bare skin of her belly.

It looked at him.

Dark sanguinary eyes met his over the tortured bend of Ellena's neck. They blinked, moted and spilled thickly over, dripping down the taut skin of its gore-spattered face. It was weeping tears of blood.

Silas stroked the silky hair of the little head that lay against his chest.

"I failed her," he told it.

In the monster's grip, Ellena bent painfully, wildly quavering. "Silas, help me."

"Failed," the monster said.

Silas cradled Soolie in his arms, looking down into her still white face, the empty eyes.

"Silas?"

He looked up. Ellena was in pain. She needed him. She didn't understand. He had already failed.

"Failed," the monster told him.

It bared two rows of sharp yellow teeth and, without looking away, bloody eyes locked on his, every moment on his, it sunk them slowly into Ellena's exposed neck.

Blood spurted out around its mouth, running down, spattering darkly down her bare breasts and belly.

Silas watched helplessly, his daughter in his arms, unable to take his eyes away as it pulled at Ellena's neck, straining at her flesh, and as it did, draining the very life from her. Ellena's rosy face, mouth agape in a silent scream, eyes bulging in horror, shrunk before his eyes. The skin turned dark and gray and crumpled, her arms withered, her breasts and belly dried up and stuck to her ribs, her mouth shriveled, and her eyes wadded up in their sockets.

The monster dropped Ellena's withered corpse on the ground and stood over it, blood dripping from its face, so much blood.

"Kill me," Silas begged.

It looked at him. There was no pity, no rage in its black eyes. Instead, he saw a horrible stillness. It looked on him as if it knew. As if, in that moment, the man and the monster shared an immeasurable loss. Of hope, of self, of all the world. As if it partook fully in the draught of his condemnation without sparing him one lessening drop, both knowing the cup to be infinite.

Wordless, the creature turned away from him and walked between the trees and into the dark.

Silas watched it disappear. He looked over to the brass bound box lying upturned in the leaves just out of reach, the lid open, tubes scattered like spilled wind chimes.

Perhaps this was the better way.

Gently, he lifted the gun from his daughter's still fingers. Grasping it in one hand, he pulled himself away from her, dragging heavily across the ground, earth scraping at his elbows and belly. Ellena's lifeless mummified face gaped at him like a dried apple carving as he picked up one smooth metal shell, released the barrel, and dropped it into the chamber with fumbling fingers.

His death was the only thing he could not regret.

He clicked the barrel straight and lifted it to his mouth.

The gun was wrenched from his hand. The monster stood over him, its face contorted, fangs bared.

"Failure," it snarled, bloody spittle flying. "You don't get to die."

The handle of the gun cracked down on Silas' head, and his vision exploded into darkness.

TWENTY-SIX

The morning light touched the highest tops of the trees and sank slowly, darkness draining away like black water in an unstoppered barrel. The new rays crept through the little window littered with toys, over the wooden man with the oak-nut hat, over the black button eyes of the gingham sparrow and the bright red paint on the bone-bead snake. It rolled out like a pale patch quilt across the boy lying in the doorway with the handle of a tin top sticking out of his throat, and tucked him in for a dreamless sleep.

As the front door opened slowly, cold sun swept the swinging shadow from the sunken porch and lit the way for the little girl with the oat-brown hair and the deaf old man who squeezed her hand as she helped him across the uneven boards and down the warped old steps to the path that lead to the road.

The rays sunk slowest through the trees, waking the shadows where they had lain down in the dark, to move and stretch, crawling over the shrunken body, more earth than woman, skin like wood, black hair like moss. Shadows stirred on the man that lay unconscious in the dirt, a filthy cream shawl tied at his hip, the fringe stuck with leaves and twigs. They touched the daughter's blood that spattered his face and chest, and touched his own blood oozing into his hair from the gouge at the top of his skull.

The shadows collected in the open brown eyes of a young girl's upturned gaze and lay still.

Dog pulled his arm back and slung the pistol over the tops of the trees, the weapon arcing into the darkly waking sky like a lonely winter bird.

The night was over. The master was dead. Dog was lost.

Perhaps it was not he who had failed the master, but this master who had failed him. He did not know.

It did not matter. He would continue to be, because he had no choice.

Dog turned away from the bodies. Perhaps he would go to the port towns and stow away on a ship to the isles or beyond. To somewhere the Master and the pack would never find him. Somewhere he could go mad with age alone. He began to walk.

Dog. Did you think I was done with you?

The voice cut through his mind like a hot blade. He stopped.

Turn. Your master has come.

Dog turned.

Under the dead girl's skin, a light began to bloom: pure, unfolding, bright and merciless. It filled the meaty hole in her chest, knitting up her flesh, her hair and clothing curling and burning away like paper, her skin glowing like a forger's metal. The body began to rise from the ground, suspended in air as in water. It rotated, turning toward him, and exploded in a ball of white fire.

Dog was thrown forcefully to the ground. He lay on his back, looking up at the new star, a small white piece of the morning sun itself, and in the center, the body of a girl, and within the body of the girl, not one, but two spirits twisting as air currents into a storm. They turned about one another, one ancient and incomplete, the other young but bright, the precorporeal and the child.

The spirits touched, and where they touched, they began to fuse together, searing bright rifts sealing shut, until he could not tell where one ended and the other began. Until the two souls burned as one, and they melted back into the body of the girl, rippling fire soaking into her flesh and bone, filling to the tips of her fingers and the ends of her toes until she swallowed up the sun.

As the naked body began to sink back to the earth, Dog scurried forward, head bowed, arms outstretched. As her weight came down into his arms, he felt her heat like molten stone. Where the glowing pale skin touched, his began to blister bubble, tearing and sliding loose, the raw meat smearing, charring black, plum, and cherry like a summer cobbler, cooking against the molten marble of her perfect white flesh.

The skin of his shoulder stuck to her smooth hairless white scalp, the brass buttons of his jacket melted and ran through his belly like wax. But he did not let go. He would not let his Mistress touch the ground.

He had seen her, and she was ancient. She was human, and she was death. She was now, and she was all times. She was beauty and pain, power and agony.

Dog held her close, the flesh on his wrists and fingers melting near the bone, and welcomed the pain with all the joy his lifeless heart could bear.

She was his Mistress. And he was no longer lost. She had found him.

TWENTY-SEVEN

Three days after the Master created him, Horse challenged his pack leader and won. It hadn't been a fair fight. The leader was older, slower, and his brain had begun to fail, turning to goopy gray pudding. So Horse had ground the old pack leader's flesh and bones into the floor of the tunnels and assumed command. Four different times a new hound or pup had challenged him, and four times Horse had swung his hammer and crushed their bones. No one challenged him anymore. Instead, they watched, the whole pack watched, waiting for the first tremor, waiting for him to show that first sign of weakness.

They all had expirations, the Master's pack. Their bodies could heal, and their souls could not be cut loose, but sooner or later, they began to heal wrong. Sooner or later, they began to lose themselves.

It started with the twitches. A lazing eye, a slur-hanging mouth. Few ever reached the madness. At the first sign of decay, the pack would set on one of their own and tear them to pieces.

Horse believed it was why the Master had never taken flesh. Flesh always betrayed with time. The Master wanted to be immortal. Horse wanted nothing less for himself.

Horse was the smartest of the pack. Ambitious, ruthless, calculated, and savage. He was large, too, his body built from the Southern Lands mountain men so he stood a full head taller than most, with a long equine face and teeth too large for his lips to cover. Many a hound and pup, hesitating or distracted, had lost a torn bloody ear to those teeth. He commanded the most respect and inspired the most fear, which was why the Master had chosen him to lead a pack out of the city.

It was a hazard mission. The Master was sending him with thirty-four hounds, large for a pack. Most had never been outside of the city, and those that had, had never left sight of its walls. The open space and new smells would make them skittish, the large numbers would make them unruly, and feedings would be scarce. There weren't as many souls outside of Ravus. The Master said their trip was three nights out, which meant three nights of travelling on tight bellies, killing what they could find, and three nights returning on empty ones. And the Master wouldn't even say what they were looking for.

'A disturbance,' the Master called it. 'An anomaly.' Which only meant the Master didn't want him to know. It was the first time Horse had seen the Master agitated, and Horse took note.

Horse took note of everything. He didn't fight for any Master, he fought for himself. Horse was a survivor. And his cheek had begun to twitch.

A CHILD DOESN'T KNOW when it comes into the world if it's not wanted. A ghost always knows.

Ellena sat up, confused, bewildered. For most of her grown years, she had woken up alone. But this time, not even the world was there to greet her. She saw the trees and the earth beneath her, the house far off down the hill, the collapsed form of Silas Beetch, and the strange withered body beside her, and it all seemed flat and gray and distant like an old tintype.

Ellena supposed she must be dead.

She remembered the monster's eyes, all bloody like a calf's pearls fresh from the cutting. She remembered the cold bony hands with their grimy black claws pressing into her bare skin, forcing her head to the side, the feeling of it behind her, wet, sticky, and cold pressed up against her bare back. She remembered the empty faraway look in Silas' eyes as he cradled Soolie's body in his arms, as she begged him to help her, as he watched while the sharp-toothed mouth closed on her neck and her life emptied like grain from a ripped sack.

So, she was dead then. And this withered body on the ground was her body.

It was a disappointing body. It didn't look anything like her.

Soolie was gone. The ground where she should have been was scorched and blackened like a boiling pot set on a tablecloth.

But Silas was still here.

Ellena crawled towards him, across an earth she couldn't feel. His eyes were open, his face spattered and trickled with blood. For a moment, she was sure he was dead, but then the hairy white of his belly swelled in and out ever so slightly. He was alive.

She forgave him instantly. And felt completely alone.

"Oh, Silas."

She placed a hand against his bespattered bearded cheek and felt his edges ever so faintly. Too faint to caress his flesh, too faint to hold his body, but she felt his soul, cold and black, as if he had fallen into a winter lake and hung there, trapped beneath the ice, no longer struggling, still.

There was no grief in him. No thought and no mourning. There was only a singular insoluble hatred for all things, for existence itself.

He was waiting to die.

She cried for him, for her, and found that it meant nothing. The tears came from nowhere and returned to nowhere as they left her face, empty as heat lakes on hot sand.

So she lay down and poured herself into his skin, one soul beside another, touching, never mixing, oil and water in a jar, and she felt the depths of his hopelessness, the absolute of his darkness, and she prayed that he could feel her as she felt him. She closed her eyes, and sank beneath the winter ice, and waited with him.

They left the city at first dark and didn't stop. Horse was pushing the pack hard. He ran them on the road, not bothering to take to the hills or cut through the trees. Any travelers they met were feed. They ripped the bodies, flung the bones, and went back to running. Hounds who strayed to the side or lagged behind felt the gnash of Horse's teeth or the rake of his claws. So when Horse suddenly veered to the right and slowed, the pack followed.

Horse approached the mound of mangled flesh. Even in the autumn, the corpses had begun to bloat, bellies bursting, flesh and intestines like tangled earthworms melting into one another writhing with cold maggots that crawled and hatched from every open wound and orifice, bare bones frayed and scored by the beaks and teeth of scavengers. Someone had slaughtered an entire herd of horses.

The pack watched as Horse circled the heap of dead beasts and paused. He reached out, hooking a nail in a matted patch of black wool, and pulled until a single body peeled away. It tumbled down the mound of flesh, coming to rest at his feet, wine-turned skin gone shiny with bloat, splitting loose from an upturned human skull, its meaty skeleton wrapped in the soiled clothes of the Regent's guard. Horse's nostrils flared as he sniffed loudly. He sneered as he caught the scent, baring his long thick teeth, and the watching pack snarled with him.

So the outcast Dog had fled the city, and now the pack was on his trail.

"The puppy coward doesn't know how to cover his tracks."

Thirty-four hounds flexed clawed hands and bared savage slavering teeth.

Horse gripped his maul near the head, raised it toward the sky.

"NO ONE ESCAPES THE PACK!"

They chorused and yapped eager whoops and howls, clamoring after their leader as he lead the charge back to the road.

TWENTY-EIGHT

Soolie was not dead. Soolie was not Soolie. Soolie was the Soul Hunter, and this was the Soul Hunter's memory.

SHE WAS TRAPPED in a ring of blood that slithered and moved, winding over itself in convoluted patterns, glistening writhing symbols that formed and melted in and out of one another in an unsolvable prison. It was ancient craft, as ancient as she. Craft that should have been lost to time, the only craft with the power to hold her, and the Man had awakened it. Even so, it could only hold her for a moment. The strength that keened within her, her bright merciless heart, was a piece of the Eternal Realm, and nothing, not even the blood weave, could restrain her for long.

"Aha! Aha!"

The Man laughed a wild laugh, clammy fear slaking off his skin as he cavorted brokenly outside the ring, his twisted spine and odd-bent limbs flailing like a poorly-made marionette.

"I have done it! I have caught you! I have caught the great Soul

Hunter!"

He looked on her feverishly with large jelly disk eyes that stuck to his forehead and cheekbones, darting black pupils in a sclera of undercooked white that she knew were not his own, but the eyes of another that had been peeled and affixed: twin lenses through which to see the world of the dead, and in the black mirrors of those darting pupils, Soolie saw her form reflected back, rippling and burning white.

How many times had she visited this dank room buried in the earth, this den rank with the stench of flesh, old and newly spilled, mildewed skins scrawled with ancient runes rolled and piled like so much wood beneath shelves cluttered with pots and leaking vessels, implements and tools of bone, sinew, and hair. There was no iron, no glass in this den, nothing but flesh and earth. Even the torches burned sticky black with human tallow, and beneath their brothy gloom lay the ones whose pain had summoned her.

They were both pinned to the Man's slab: one small, a boy no more than two years, empty and still. The other, a man, large-meated and thick-boned, shaking in the straps, eyes terror-wide. A large knot had been forced between his teeth to stifle the fretful whines that lingered from too much screaming. It was just as it always was, but this time the flesh of the animated body was firm, not pocked and riddled with festering rot and sudden decay. This time the small boy's soul looked out through the large man's eyes almost as if he were still alive.

The Man hobbled eagerly back to the slab. "You see, I have succeeded! At last! I have revived dead flesh with a living soul! You see, you see!" He clapped his hands on the foreheads of the two bodies, and the larger let out a panicked whine. "I have learned. I have discovered. I have mastered! Old souls are too brittle. They break. But the souls of the young are supple. Ha ha! Yes." He bent by the man's face and stroked the stubbled bronze cheek. "No more living rot. No more decaying flesh. I have unlocked eternity. And soon," the jelly eyes turned to her, "I will master all the souls of men. I will take new flesh and know eternal life."

262

Soolie could feel the blood weave growing sluggish and dull around her, its ability to contain her weakening. Soon she would be free to release the soul of the small boy from the flesh that held him and send him on to rest just as she had so many souls so many times before. Then she would depart. She would not touch the Man. The living were not her concern. Soon enough he would die, as all men did, and be forgotten.

The Man sneered and the seal around his lenses cracked upon his cheek, leaking clear ooze inked with blood. "There is only one thing left that would stop me."

He lurched across the room to a scaffolding she had not yet heeded. It stood no more than the Man's height: a convoluted hive of rune-carved bone fused and intricately fitted as if it had been plied and knotted, merged and melted, molded like wax. Soolie listened and sensed the wail of soul cries trapped in the marrow of the machine. It was ancient craft, but it also showed the touch of the Man's alchemations. It was ancient and it was new, an abomination. She did not know its function, but she sensed its wrongness. She needed to be free of the blood weave. She needed to be free now.

She struggled, throwing her strength against the bonds, white fire pulsing and throbbing, but the ties were not yet weak enough to break. The Man placed himself behind the contraption and buried his arms inside the tortured coils of bone.

"I have slain death with my own hand!" His voice was hysteria. "I will know eternal life! And death will die!"

A sudden crack and something shot from the belly of the hive. It was flesh and it was body, it shrieked and it throbbed, it was tangled blood and weeping, with long sharp bones that hit her and pierced her being. She was spirit, but it tore into her like a living thing, burrowing into her core, pulling itself in and seizing her strength in talon-jaws, wrapping around and tearing it from her.

Soolie felt her strength depart. She was aware that this was the moment before she became lost, the obliteration of herself, the ruination of her being. She knew what the Man had done in removing her strength, and she didn't yet know how to feel regret.

The world is lost.
The room was consumed in light.

Soolie was adrift in a void beyond darkness. Emptiness, weak beyond weakness, existing only because she could not cease to exist. Unable to be, unable to cease being, she was tossed in tides of nothingness and time until she landed upon a cinder, bright and glowing, small and frail, but it warmed her. And that cinder was the soul of a child.

It could not heal her. It could not fill the void left by the strength that the Dead Man had stolen, but it brought her back from the nothingness, and she began to be again.

TWENTY-NINE

Soolie opened her eyes. A curved veranda overlooked distant twin mountains dusted in evening gold, fixed in settings of lush emerald green jungle that, drawing near, gave way to a city of stone as white as salt. Overhead arched a white stone roof and, below, smooth tiles swirled in flowing mosaics. She was sitting on a wide bench upholstered in velvety purple cushions before a table bearing a platter of strange fruits, sticky red berries, prickly green apples, and globes like plums with skins like river lizards. There were nuts the color of coal, white meat coconut pieces, and thin translucent wafers that glistened with a honey-colored glaze. A silky sky-blue tunic ruffled softly against her skin, and deep coral colored pants billowed around her ankles.

The last thing she remembered was dying. Pulling the trigger. Watching Papa's blood-spattered face sink into a field of blackness. But she also had other memories, the Hunter's memories: of a dark room full of flesh and bone and writhing blood. Of a corpse with the soul of a little boy. Of a Man with a twisted body and jelly eyes. "And death will die."

Now she was here. In the sort of place her daydreams were made of. If only it were real.

When we met, I showed you a memory of your past and angered you.

The Hunter appeared sitting across from her, wide eyes and rippling ebony hair, the same caramel skin in the loose pale yellow shift. Soolie remembered what it felt like to be behind those eyes, calm, empty but for a singular purpose. She understood it now. She didn't want to.

Now I have shared a memory of my past, of when I was made broken. I ask that you accept this as an offering of peace that we may start anew.

"The Dead Man wasn't dead."

He is now.

A light breeze toyed with its glossy child's hair, carrying with it a smell like sandalwood and the loose melody of wind pipes. *This is an environment one of my first vessels enjoyed very much. I thought you might find it preferable to 'the blankness.'* It gestured toward the laden table with a small hand. *You may eat if you would enjoy it.*

Why was she here? With it? The thing she hated. A fat green beetle was crawling across her pant leg. She let it walk up on the tip of her finger, and it buzzed off into the air and out the veranda. Her head was full of questions she didn't want to know the answers to. Perhaps she already knew them.

"I thought I killed myself."

Yes, it said solemnly. *You forced me to make a very difficult choice. And now we must both bear the consequences of our decisions.*

Must we? Well, skag you, Soolie didn't feel like it.

Didn't this jit chaos ever end?

She looked out at the azure sky, the sun glinting off the white railing, warm and inviting and false. Life had been nothing but consequences lately. Difficult decisions and consequences, struggle and pain. The Hunter had chosen to invade her life and destroy it. It could live with the consequences. Soolie'd already made her decision; she'd decided to be dead.

It tilted its head, wide golden orbs observing. *You no longer think of me as 'demon.' You think of me as 'the Hunter.'*

Soolie didn't look at it. She didn't want to understand. She wanted to still think of it as a 'demon,' but she couldn't. She wanted to be angry, but she wasn't.

I am not evil, Soolie Beetch. I am necessity. Ikma na Sitari, *created by the Ancient Ones to return lost souls to the Eternal Realm.*

"Well, you're doing a skagged up job of that."

It nodded. *This is true. Which is why you must aid me.*

Soolie shrugged, picked up a wafer, and turned it over in her fingers. It felt brittle, like a piece of thin ice, or the hope of a life she had left behind.

I could not stay with your body once your soul had left it. Your soul would have gone where I cannot follow, and I would have become lost again, perhaps for a long time. So I have brought you back.

In the absence of my strength, your soul stands in the gap. Your body anchors us to this world, and your soul binds us and lessens my incapacity. I am still weak, and there is much risk, but I am not as weak as I was. We are united, you and I, Soolie Beetch. We cannot be undone.

Soolie remembered the wide terrified eyes of the little boy looking out through the eyes of a man. What had the Hunter told her? "*Many monsters are made with the souls of dead men.*" She crushed the wafer in her fingers, grinding sticky granules between her fingertips, pieces fluttering to the tiles at her feet.

"So that's why you wanted a young soul? To lessen your weakness? To reanimate a dead body for you to walk around in?" She already knew it was true.

I would have chosen another, but you left me no alternative.

She looked at it. "You're as cucking rot as he is."

It blinked, and something resembling offense tinged its eyes. She could have imagined it, or it might have been artifice, but Soolie couldn't help wondering if, after hundreds of years of human vessels, the Hunter had itself begun to change.

We are nothing alike. The Dead Man toils towards destruction. More and more souls are becoming trapped in the realm of the living, and they are draining the life from the world. In time, the dead will overtake the living, and all will be cast into darkness.

It would have been better for me to have taken a submissive soul, but what has been done cannot be undone. Opposed, our strength is nothing, but together we will take back my strength from the Dead Man and bring rest to the lost. You must side with me to defeat this enemy, Soolie Beetch, or all will be destroyed.

It folded little brown hands on the table top.

Soolie stood up and stretched, hooking her fingers over her head and bending back like a bow. She shook out her hair, walked out to the railing overlooking the city, and breathed deep of the warm fragrant air. Below, woven mats and sun screens dotted the rooftops. In between, tall trees with leaves the size of hammocks cast welcome shade. A bird of marigold and bright turquoise glided past the balcony almost close enough to touch.

Soolie leaned on the railing. "You are counting on me loving the world more than I hate you."

Yes, it said.

"I can understand and still hate you."

But can you hate the world, Soolie Beetch?

A world that was never as beautiful as dreams? Perhaps.

I have also found us a weapon, it said. *One of the Dead Man's creations. He calls himself 'Dog.'*

Soolie was aware as it appeared behind her. She turned. The monster stood in the middle of the veranda, ghastly and grotesque, leering vacantly with empty dark eyes. It didn't move, only an image, an illusion that looked real like everything else. So this was the creature at the foot of the bed, the monster coming up the hill with the little girl. The one who killed the horses.

"Why are you showing me this?"

From beyond the creature, the Hunter watched her. *Does his image bother you?*

Soolie grimaced. It was naked, and the warm evening light did nothing to help the sickly pallor of its skin. She was not familiar with the male form except from what she had seen in the beasts of the home and field. But though the creature before her stood on his hind legs and had many of the parts of a man, he was most certainly not a man. Everything about him bothered her.

"No," she shrugged and stepped away from the railing. "It's just skagging ugly."

She was surprised to see he was barely taller than she was. His arms hung too long, thin sallow skin clung tightly to corded sinew and thick purple veins that snaked down across the backs of overly large hands ending in wickedly hooked black nails. His waist was small like hers, but his legs had thick powerful haunches with long leathery padded feet and sharp nailed toes. His chest was heavily muscled, yet narrow and sunken like a young boy's with a sharp collarbone and slender but powerful neck … and then his face.

Under a skull stubble of crow-black hair, his face was gaunt and sallow, more skull than flesh, as if his skin had not grown there, but been stretched and pinned taut, a canvas for violence. His pale lips bulged over wickedly pointed yellow canines. The eyes were almost black, the irises blended darkly into the pupil, round and wide like a night hawk's caught in lantern light. A killer.

The Dead Man, his maker, rejected him. He is now ours. Soolie looked into the vacant animal eyes and snorted. She didn't want him.

I believe it will obey.

"More than you can expect from me."

The Hunter's eyes glittered, hair stirring, its little girl face fixed like fired clay. *I have come to you on your terms, Soolie Beetch. I have treated you as an equal.*

"If you'd done that in the first place, we might not be in this muck."

I have done so now.

"You're fighting your enemy with his own weapons."

He stole my strength from me. If I must, I will fight him with his.

"Doesn't sound like you stand a cucking chance."

I am the only chance.

Soolie turned away to step out again to the veranda. It was so very beautiful, so peaceful, so exotic and unknown. So unlike the waking world.

Papa couldn't save her. Ellena couldn't save her. No one could save her now.

She traced the edge of the railing with her fingertip. The stone was smooth and cleanly cornered.

The Hunter was beside her, looking out, inky curls glowing glossy in the light, golden eyes peeking over the top of the railing. A real child would have popped on tiptoe, hands on the railing, but the Hunter stood flat-footed and still, arms at its sides, a little inhuman statue. Soolie doubted it could even appreciate beauty. She doubted it knew what loneliness even felt like.

I will give you some time to say goodbye to what you have known. Do not take too long.

"Do they think I'm dead?"

Yes.

Perhaps that was for the best.

"Can I wake up?"

Yes.

"Then I would like to now."

As you wish.

"Take care of the horses and bring in the bags," Mam said, stepping out of the carriage. "Oh, and whatever you do, keep your hood on."

Before she could step entirely free, Bernad flicked the reins, urging the horses forward so his mother stumbled and cried out as he pulled away from the front door of the Farm House Inn.

"Bernad! Behave yourself!"

The Peligs didn't own a wagon. Mam said she was a lady, and ladies rode in carriages. But much to Mam's consternation, even though the Peligs were well off by the standards of Hob Glen, Pap never made enough money with the store to hire help. So when the Pelig family took to the road, Pap usually drove. Bernad would have been glad to, but Pap insisted, grateful for any excuse to get away.

Bernad pulled the carriage up outside the stables and swung out of the driver's perch. He groaned, stretched, and massaged his backside with his hands, sore from hours of sitting and bouncing along the road. Mam said she had no intention of showing up at her sister's doorstep looking like a vagabond. She needed a bath, a bed, and a hot breakfast. So, equipped with a purse of savings clasped in her gloved hand, she had directed Bernad to the Farm House Inn where she was presently acquiring two rooms for the night. Bernad was grateful for the room and board, if just to shut Mam up. They would have to bed down in the carriage tomorrow night, and he wouldn't be surprised if she made him sleep with the horses. Then again, he might prefer it.

Bernad stroked Maple's soft nose and scratched her behind the ear. Ivory nickered, and both horses stretched their necks out, snuffling for his pocket. He fished out two pieces of dried pear, one for each of them; they'd never forgive him if he wasn't fair. He put a piece in each hand and smiled as they softly lipped the treats out of his palms.

"Yu don't care if I hide ma fathe, do yu?"

He patted Ivory's flank as he came around to take the lines. He was already beginning to speak more clearly, adapting to forming words without the use of half his face, minimizing his impediment. He tucked the reins under his arm and began undoing the buckles of Ivory's harness.

Not that he would have much use for jawing in his life to come. He couldn't get tied, no woman would want him now. He couldn't become a man of stature or business, what man of weight and shine would trust a cuck fool without a face? He knew that, before the incident, Mam had been hagging Pap with the idea of sending him to a gentleman's academy to be trained in the ways of the upper class, to gain respect and connections. There was no fear of that now.

Maybe he was meant to be a coachman. That or a man outside the law. After all, the only way he was going to get any wet leg from a woman now was if he paid her. He was going to need a lot of shine.

Once Maple and Ivory were out of their collars and traces and safely stalled in the stable, Bernad began to wipe them down, starting with Maple. Her powerful flanks twitched from the long day's ride as he rubbed away the sweat and dirt of the day with a towel, checking her chestnut hide for any sore spots or marks.

"Hey, there." An older man's voice sounded from the stable

doorway. "Your mother sent me out here to help you bring in the luggage."

Bernad didn't turn, ducking his head low inside his hood.

"You want me to just untie it from your roof and haul it in?" The man walked closer and stood on the outside of the stall looking in, peering at Bernad over round wire spectacles. "You are 'Badard,' aren't you? She said look for a young mister with a hood on, and that seems to be you, but you haven't said anything. Under the circumstances, I'm kind of wishing you would."

Bernad patted Maple reassuringly on the back and moved around her to wipe down her other side. "Bernad," he said. "My name'th Bernad."

"Oh." The man scratched at the thinning white fluff of his hair. "My faulty. I'm a right cheesecloth for names."

"I care for the horses firtht," Bernad said.

"So you should. So you should. Look. My name's Abrum, the missus is Claudine. She's the boss." The old man winked at him. "Though your mam is giving her a right run for her coin. Look, I'll care for those bags, and you look to your animals. There'll be a hot meal for you in the house when you're ready."

Bernad nodded, and the man tipped a hand to him and walked away.

It was peaceful in the stable. The soft snorting and shifting of the horses, their rich smell mixing with the smell of hay and hide. He liked being alone. He was going to miss being able to escape and hide out at his tree. Even though the Beetch girl … he felt nauseated at the memory. Cuckin' Beetch.

He couldn't think about it. Any of it. Any of them. Sometimes disasters struck. Monsters attacked. And the people who survived were the ones who ran the fastest. It was all best forgotten. Pap would be okay. Pap knew how to keep his head down, and if Bernad never saw him again, nothing lost. There was nothing for Bernad back in Hob Glen. He wasn't going back.

He wondered what his Aunt and Uncle were like. He knew he had three cousins. The oldest was a boy about his age. The other two were girls, and the youngest had just been just a baby last time he saw them. That had been almost five years ago. He remembered their house being big, but still feeling too small, as if someone had crowded two houses into the space of one. He remembered being bored. And that the oldest sister had a little toy fox sewn out of rabbit fur with glass eyes, and he and her brother had stolen it from her and played catch with it until she cried. He wasn't even sure he remembered their names.

He wiped down Maple, brushed out her coat and mane, then moved on to Ivory. When he finished, he still didn't feel ready to go back into the house and be stared at by strange people, even if it would embarrass Mam. There would be plenty of time for that. He sat down in the hay in the corner of Ivory's stall and sighed. He leaned back and, breathing the familiar comforting musk of the stable, he closed his eyes.

"WHAT ARE YOU *DOING?* Sleeping out here like an uncivilized island slave?"

He must have nodded off. Bernad squinted his one good eye against the bright lantern light. Mam pursed her lips disapprovingly.

"I did not pay good money for two rooms for you to bed with the horses. Our hosts have expressed *concern* for you, Bernad. What do you expect me to tell them? Oh, yes, my son *prefers* the stable to the company of his own mother? My son is an animal?"

Bernad raised his hand at her in a rude gesture.

"Get to your feet and get in that house."

"Cuckin' skag," he muttered.

A week ago she would have slapped him for that, but he was too far away, and she wasn't going to touch him if she could avoid it, especially not on the face.

She raised her chin proudly, holding her lantern aloft. "Then I will stand right here until you regain your senses."

Ivory snorted and twitched her tail. Her ears lay back, and she shuffled restlessly in the stall.

"Look what you've done," Mam said. "You've disturbed the horses."

Maple whinnied nervously in the other stall and tossed her mane. From the back of the stable, the other horses stirred. Suddenly, Ivory threw her head, front legs hopping off the ground, back legs bucking close to Bernad's shins. He scrambled to his feet in the hay, pressing into the corner. The horses started screaming.

"Bernad!" Mam shouted, holding up the lantern, "Get out of that stall! Now!"

Ivory's hooves were flashing, her tail whipping behind her. Her ears lay plastered to her skull, teeth bared aggressively. There was no safe way to get past.

"Bernad!"

Ivory reared up, and Bernad darted forward, the horse's tail lashing his neck as he dove for the stall gate, fumbled with the latch and pushed through, shutting it behind him just in time.

There was something terrifying the horses.

Mam ran towards the barn door, but Bernad caught his mother's hand, jerking her back.

"No!"

"We must…"

"No!"

He yanked her toward him, and she tried to wrench away, but he wrapped one hand behind her neck, pulled her close, and hissed in her ear.

"Something out-thide!"

Mam's eyes went wide with fear. Bernad grabbed the lantern from her trembling hand, put it out, and dragged her towards an empty stall. He may not have much of a future, but he'd be cuckholed if, after everything he'd been through, he died in a stable with his *mam*.

Bernad scurried into the dark corner of the stall, crouching down with his back against the wall, pulling Mam down next to him. She was whimpering like a crawler, and he hissed to shut her up.

On the other side of the wall, he could hear a myriad of strange sounds and voices. Voices howling in wild chorus like drunken men playing a pack of rabid hounds. There was the crack of a gunshot, braying, then a human scream that sent an icy blade of fear into his gut, a wild shriek of undiluted terror.

She's followed me, he thought. That skagging bitch, she's brought that monster to finish me off.

Mam was shaking, her eyes clenched shut. She had a grip on his arm, the tightest she had ever held him. Then Bernad realized something was with them in the stable.

He hadn't heard it enter over the high guttural panic of the horses and the sound of his own fear rushing in his ears. It must have come in the side door. Mam would have left it open. He wrapped one arm around her, grabbing her fierce, willing her still and holding his breath.

The creature yowled.

Another snarled from the doorway. "We run! Move!"

He could hear the first sniffing, snuffling near their stall. A throaty growl. Had it caught their scent?

"NOW!"

The roar was followed by a scuffle, a snarl and a yelping squall. The creatures scrambled out of the stable. From the direction of the yard came a chorus of primal cries that rallied and sounded in tumult, then loosed into the night, growing faint, retreating to the edge of hearing, and were gone.

And they were left alone with the panicked horses.

It must have been a full hour before the animals stopped screaming and bucking. Yet another hour before there was silence. Bernad waited. Mam had long since remembered herself, released his arm, and pushed away to sit beside him, her back to the stable wall, hugging herself and shivering. When at last he heard the creaking of crickets, Bernad rose slowly to his feet.

"Where are you going?" Mam whispered.

He ignored her and began creeping forward in the dark.

"Oh!" She gave a distressed whisper, getting up to follow behind him. "You can't just leave. You're just like your father."

He should have let her run outside.

He moved toward the draft and found the open door, pale moonlight shining through, and stepped into the doorway.

It was a cold clear autumn night. The trees were black chimney brushes against the spangled sky, and the stars winked as a night sparrow darted between them. The white farm house looked almost blue.

Bernad crept forward away from the stable and across the yard. Mam had started whimpering again.

There on the front porch of the inn lay a human-sized heap, and on the step, something glinted in the moonlight. As Bernad stepped onto the front path, he saw that the glint more clearly. It was a pair of false teeth. The heap on the porch was wrapped in a blue flannel nightgown, spilling a loose curtain of gray hair.

Bernad turned back and sprinted toward the stables.

"Wait!" Mam cried as he sped past her.

He didn't answer. He didn't care if there might be survivors. He didn't care if their belongings were in the house. He didn't care if it was the middle of the night.

"Bernad! What about our things? Bernad, I command you as your mother!"

She had better catch up, or Mam was on her own.

THIRTY

Soolie groaned and sat up, twigs and pine needles sticking to her skin and leaving cross-hatch marks on her arms and legs. The sky above was the deep blue of Mama's dress curtains, stretching out achingly wide, and beside her, the rocky earth collapsed into a steep cutaway cliff revealing rolling dun and fawn hills, farm houses and tiny ant-sized horses and cows separated by the wiry lines of cattle fences. Beyond that, on the brown snake of road, the little clutch of houses like eggs in a basket: Hob Glen.

Cold wind buffeted her bare skin, whisking around her chest and legs and over her skull, burning her ears. She reached up and touched her scalp where her hair should have been, and it was smooth as a baby pig's back. She was naked, and her hair was gone. She ran her hands over her skull, then down the back of her neck and around under her chin. The looseness in her skin had disappeared. Her neck and eyes, cheeks and belly were all taut, young and smooth.

Someone had set her here by the edge of the bluff. They had laid her on a mat of woven evergreen. But the needles had all turned orange and fallen off. How long had she been lying here?

A day and a half, the Hunter said. *The one called Dog brought you here. He is waiting behind you.*

Soolie tensed and turned slowly.

He was almost invisible crouched several lengths away, halfway to the tree line, still as a stone. As soon as she looked at him, he bared sharp yellow teeth nervously and began worming over the rocky dirt towards her, head near the ground, eyes looking up from below stubbly eyebrows, the ridges of his spine and ribs showing sharp under the tight yellow skin of his back.

She grimaced, and he flinched back like a whipped puppy.

He is showing submission.

He was disgusting.

The monster whined, groveling at the earth, bare behind in the air, long black nails scratching against the gritty rock. He started inching his way forward again.

Soolie sneered, and again he flinched and stopped, shoulders hunched, clawed hands curling up, eyes darted back and forth guiltily, then back up, pleading. Waiting.

Rather than feeling threatened or afraid, Soolie found herself simply revolted.

At last, he spoke. "Mistress?"

His voice was human, which was worse.

"Mistress?"

"No."

Soolie stood slowly. The only part of the monster that moved were his eyes. She stood to her full height and stretched, arms up above her head, the cold air nipping at her legs, chest, belly, and about her bare neck and head.

He whined up at her. "Dog didn't know where to take Mistress. Dog wanted to give gifts, but Dog didn't know what Mistress might want."

She put her hands on her hips and flexed her chest, then twisted her back. Her body felt exhilaratingly strong. She felt like running, leaping, but looking down at the monster groveling at her feet, she didn't feel like being chased.

"I don't want you. Go away."

He flinched. Crimson began to seep into the creases around his eyes, thickening in the corners near his nose.

"Dog cannot go away. Dog has nowhere to go. Dog follows the Mistress."

Soolie turned and walked along the bluff, heading back toward town. "This mistress doesn't want you."

She picked her way over the bluff, around the rock outcroppings and down the steep hill through the trees. All the way, she could sense it behind her. The snap of a twig, the swish of a branch, a pebble that knocked loose and tumbled down the hill into brush.

Why the cuck was it so set on following her?

It was created to serve, the Hunter said. *It means you no harm.*

Are you just going to chime in all the time now? Soolie thought.

It is important that we learn to act as one. I am endeavoring to show consideration for your past humanity in the hopes that it will ease your transition.

Soolie laughed bitterly. I wouldn't think you were much for hoping.

I am not.

SOOLIE STOOD JUST OUTSIDE HOB GLEN looking across the field at the blackened burned-out husk that had been her home for thirteen years. Behind her, the monster stalled, panting quietly at a distance.

So this was why Papa had smelled like smoke.

She turned toward the bakery.

SOOLIE SCAMPERED STEALTHILY around Ellena's dead garden plot. The last thing she needed was to be spotted now. She just needed to know that Papa and Ellena were all right. And then … she didn't know what then.

She paused at the back door, listening.

"Mistress?"

"Shh!"

The monster skulked in the shadow of the bakery wall.

"The house is empty, Mistress."

Soolie scowled, and he withered. She would have figured that out. Then where were they?

She pushed on the back door, and it didn't move. The front door was probably locked too. She sighed, turned, and leaned back against the rough wood of the door, tilting her head up and closing her eyes. She had to think.

What was she even doing? She didn't have a plan. She was teasing trouble by even being here. When she found Papa and Ellena, what then? She might be tempted to say 'hello' or run in for a hug. To assure them she wasn't dead, that everything was okay.

She was, and everything wasn't.

Maybe the best thing she could do was go far far away and keep these monsters away from everyone else.

On the other side of the door, the jamb lifted.

Soolie stepped back as the door swung in. Dog cowered beside it and bowed out of the way.

"How did you get in?" she snapped.

"Upper window, Mistress."

Soolie resisted the urge to kick him in his filthy face.

The back kitchen was cold. The large clay oven hadn't been used in half a moon, and the metal top was fuzzy with dust. Ellena's grandfather had made that oven. Ellena said it was the foundation of the bakery's success.

Soolie snagged a towel off the hook beside the oven and tossed it in a tin pail. She hefted the pail by its wooden handle and ducked past Dog, back out behind the bakery and around to the water pump, set the pail on the ground to the side, and began working the lever with both hands. Ellena had taught her to never put the pail under the spout until you'd cleared out the pipes first.

Dog watched uncertainly from the door. "May I help, Mistress?"

Up and down, up and down. The old pump squealed and groaned in protest.

"Cuck off," Soolie muttered, working the pump with renewed vigor. A gurgle sounded at the base of the pipe, and the spout belched and spat a splatter of old gunky water out onto the ground.

Soolie kept pumping until the pipe arced a stream clear like glass. She slid the pail under the water and went back to the handle.

What is it that you are hoping to accomplish, Soolie Beetch? Perhaps I can help. The Hunter almost sounded sincere.

The bucket was splashing over; the rag floated near the tin lip like a rumpled dumpling. Soolie went to the bucket, her feet squishing in the gritty, muddy earth, and swished the towel, slopping water over the sides. She lifted the saturated cloth before her face and mopped it over her forehead, eyes, and nose, the frigid water drizzling down her bare belly and legs. She rinsed the towel, dredging it back and forth in the bucket, then pulled it over the top of her head, water running over her skull and across her shoulders and back in frigid rivulets.

Disease is no longer a threat to us, it said. *Cleanliness is unnecessary.*

Maybe dying and being laid out naked by a naked monster made her feel like she just needed a wash.

A ritual. I understand.

Soolie doubted it.

She wadded the rag up in a fist and scrubbed at her arms, legs, and crevices until the water was low in the bucket and her skin was ruddy and mostly free from grime. It was certainly easier to get clean without a head full of long tangly hair.

She dumped out the bucket, slopped the towel in the bottom, lifted the handle, and walked back to the kitchen, ignoring the black eyes of the monster that followed her.

Now that you have completed your ritual, perhaps it would be a good time to discuss our next...

Plug it, Soolie thought back.

When you have finished, it said.

She set the bucket by the door and walked through to the front room.

The front of the bakery smelled empty and stale. The bread racks and counter were bare. The three familiar paintings hung quiet on the wall. Soolie walked past them and tiptoed up the stairs.

The living quarters above the bakery was a single room. Before Papa had come to Hob Glen, Ellena and Mama had shared the upstairs with their grandparents. Ellena's grandmother had sectioned off one side of the room with curtains so the girls could have their own space. (Ellena told Soolie the curtains didn't provide much privacy, and that she and Mama used to get scolded regularly for talking and giggling when they were supposed to be asleep.) Since Papa and Mama had married and Soolie's great-grandparents had died, Ellena had pulled down the curtains and made the space her own, though the furnishings were all still inherited.

A four post bed was on one side of the room with a lovely oak carved vanity dresser and matching wardrobe that touched the ceiling. On the other side of the room was a floral love-seat across from Grandad's red armchair, and in the middle of the room sat a full size table Grandad had made from floorboards and the legs of an old chicken chopping table. Granddad had sanded the table smooth and varnished it so the top was a honey gold, though the legs were a mismatched dark walnut. Six simple chairs were arranged around the table. Just enough for Grandad, Grandma, their two daughters, and two guests. Papa said Soolie had gotten to meet Grandad and Grandma before they died, but she was only a baby and didn't remember.

Soolie headed straight for the wardrobe. In the top drawer she found a sleeveless lavender cotton shift that looked old and about her size. She threw it on. It was loose and a little large, but it would do.

"Mistress." The monster stood by the stair, shoulders hunched. He looked more naked and filthy indoors.

Soolie pulled a short hooded cloak of heavy black wool from inside the wardrobe. She didn't feel like she needed the warmth, but she swung it over her shoulders and clasped the hook at her neck.

"Should Dog clothe himself, Mistress?"

She wasn't going to have any shoes. Well, the dead didn't need shoes.

"Mistress?"

"Cuck if I care."

"Yes, Mistress."

Dog pulled the white cotton shirt over his head. It settled loosely over his shoulders and soiled around the collar where it had dragged over his skin. The Mistress had washed herself. Should he have washed himself?

Already she had gone back down the stairs. She said she didn't want him. Dog didn't understand.

She had found him. He had watched her being born, experienced the raw beauty of her birth, the fusing of her spirit, the coming of her being. He understood she was two in one: two spirits in one body. He did not understand why this was, or how it had come to be. That wasn't his place, he didn't need to. It was enough to know that she was and to love her for it. His Mistress. She was not the same as the Master. She was a she. A Mistress. The Master was his past, his failure. She was his hope and his future.

Mistress.

And she didn't want him.

He reached into the back of the bottom drawer and found a loose weave pair of drawstring pants. Loose was good. His haunches were large. Even with the loose fit, his rump and thighs strained at the rustic cloth which piled too long at his feet. He tied off the string at his belly, then balancing on one foot, grabbed the pant leg in two places and ripped the bottom several inches off and tossed it to the floor. Then he did the same to the other side.

The clothes smelled old, human, and like the oak dresser they had been stored in. Clothes were not something he needed. But they made him look more human in the city. The Mistress wore them.

He would prove his worth to her. He had to.

He padded down the stair and slowed. She stood with her back to him, looking at one of three paintings that hung on the wall: a purple child's painting of a moon and a hill. He crouched at the stairs, waiting.

"The two who were with me, do you remember them?"

"Yes, Mistress."

She turned and faced him, her sharp brown eyes judging coldly. "Did you harm them?"

He whined, wrapping his hands about his skull, hiding behind his forearms.

"DID YOU HARM THEM?"

"Dog didn't know Mistress was coming back! Dog thought Mistress was gone!"

"I am *not* your Mistress," she snapped. Her eyes flashed white. "What did you DO?"

He howled in anguish. "Please, Mistress! Dog didn't know!"

NEVER BEFORE IN ALL OF SOOLIE'S THIRTEEN YEARS had a house burned in Hob Glen. Now there were two.

Soolie looked down the hill at the smoke rising from the crumbling frame of the Mokrum's house like tea brewing into a clear gray sky. It seemed unattended. The fire had grown old and been left to burn itself out. She didn't have to ask to know there were bodies burning in those walls. Dead casualties of a dead war.

These bodies are but a few, the Hunter said. *The Dead Man would end the world at the cost of all.*

The Dead Man began with 'but a few,' Soolie thought back. Maybe it's time you learned the value of a human life, *demon.*

Soolie squinted at the stand of trees where she had last seen Papa and Ellena. She couldn't see clearly through. She had tried to find out exactly what had happened, but 'Dog' had started groveling and wailing so loudly, she'd had to tell him to shut the cuck up before he brought the whole town to their door.

Suck it. Let the skagging murder-monster follow her. She wanted him in reach when she figured out how to remove his head.

What if Papa and Ellena were dead?

Soolie took a moment to consider it. She felt prepared.

Since she was a little girl watching Mama grow more and more frail and weak, she had tried to ready herself for the day when she would be alone in the world. Soolie had always hoped she would handle it in a way that would make Mama proud.

If Papa and Ellena couldn't be alive and well, at least they wouldn't be suffering.

The monster would suffer. Dog would pay for every tear and every drop of blood. She would make sure of it.

"Stay here."

"Yes, Mistress."

The ground beneath her feet was hard, cold, and pebbly. The near-winter air sliced up underneath the black cape and through her summer shift. It should have been painful and chilled her quivering to the belly, but it didn't.

The grove of trees was all shades of brown. Mottled gray-brown, orange, and dark earth. The first thing she saw through the trees was a singed splotch of black like a fire lizard had wandered by and passed fumes.

Then she saw the bodies.

One desiccated, shriveled, and dark. The other collapsed nearby, bare-skinned, a shawl rag barely covering its parts. Papa.

She didn't run to him.

First she went to the shrunken corpse and knelt. There were no clothes. Just the dirty wad of her own blanket behind it and the wild muss of fluffy black hair damped down and riddled with stray fallen leaves. She touched the weathered leather of its face, fingering the sunken curve beneath the cheekbone. It reminded her of Bernad's face. The thin skin of the neck was ripped and torn. She could count the ribs.

"Soolie?"

Soolie froze. The voice was far away and wasted thin, but she knew it as well as she knew the identity of the body in front of her, as well as she knew, impossibly, that both belonged to the same person. She stood and turned.

Ellena looked just like she had the night of the Harvest Festival. Her hair brushed and swept back with a crisp white ribbon, her red and black dress clean and starched. The only difference was that her body was like her voice. Thin and flat like rice paper.

"C ... can you see me?" Ellena's voice was high and quavery.

Soolie nodded.

Ellena stepped forward hesitantly. *"Is it ... is it really you?"*

"It's me."

The shine of tears filled Ellena's distant eyes and traced down her pink cheeks. *"Are you sure?"*

"I'm sure."

She scrunched her lips and wrung her hands. *"You seem ... different. And I saw you. You died."*

It was such a silly thing for a ghost to say. Soolie opened her mouth, then just shrugged. She had thought she was prepared for Ellena's death. She wasn't prepared for this.

"What happened? What's happened to you?" Ellena shook her head frantically. *"You were on the ground in a fit. And your eyes, and that horrible voice..."* Ellena swallowed a spasm, forcing out the words, *"And ... you shot yourself. You shot yourself! And Silas was looking up at me with those empty hopeless eyes, and this monster ripped out my throat."* The words were almost a thin wail now. *"I could feel it killing me. I could feel it. I knew I was dying, and he just sat there holding you with those horrible eyes and watched me die. He just..."*

Ellena kneeled weakly, her hands flopping onto her lap, and started sobbing.

Soolie looked down at the ghost. Should she kneel too? Should she say something? She had seen spirits in Ravus. She had known they were possible. She had seen monsters and spirits, visions and death. But to see Ellena like this ... it was wrong.

Alive, Ellena had been so lovely, so strong. Now, she was a pale reflection of herself, sitting in the dead leaves weeping, shaking. So helpless, so emotional. Like a crawler not getting her own way. As if Soolie could do anything to help her. This was worse than death. It would have been far better if Ellena had just died.

"And I'm still here." Ellena looked up, eyes full of anguish. *"Why am I still here? Why?"*

Soolie twisted the corner of her cape around her fingers. "I'm sorry."

"I can't spend death alone too, Soolie, I just can't."

Soolie wished she could say, 'you won't.' But that wasn't a promise she could make, and she was almost irritated at Ellena for saying these things, for being here, for suffering so much. This wasn't a problem Soolie was supposed to face. People died. Eventually, everyone died. They didn't hang on suffering helplessly afterwards asking for help and comfort that no one could give.

She is stranded, the Hunter said. *The light that should have opened her way was drained by Dog to feed his hunger. This is what the creatures of the Dead Man do.*

"I'm sorry," Soolie said again.

Ellena just cried.

Once it was clear the weeping wasn't going to stop, Soolie began edging around the ghost gingerly, awkwardly, then turning away to kneel beside her father.

He was pale. His eyes were open, but they didn't see. His face was still spattered with brown crusts of old blood, and when she placed a hand on his arm, his skin was cold. Was he dead? She held a finger under his nose and thought she felt the slightest of breath. She stared into Papa's brown eyes, waved her hand in front of them, but they didn't waver. Finally, though, they blinked.

He was alive. Papa was alive, and probably suffering from dehydration and cold sickness. She had to get him back to the bakery.

"Hold on, Papa."

She grabbed him by the wrists and pulled. His heavy body turned over on itself, dragging on the ground. She put his arms over her shoulders and tried to heave him on to her back, but he was too heavy and too long.

"What are you doing?" Ellena was on her feet.

"I have to get him inside." Soolie let go of his arms, lowering him to the ground and stepping away to look for a branch to make a sledge. "He's dying."

"No, Soolie, don't!" In a spasm of light, Ellena was standing arms outstretched between Soolie and her father. *"You need to let him be."*

Soolie scowled. "If I don't do something, he'll *die.*"

"He wants *to die!"*

Soolie gaped.

"You don't understand." Ellena edged back towards Papa. *"I've felt what he feels. I know. He doesn't want to live. He wants to die."*

"Well, he doesn't get to," Soolie snapped.

"It's what he wants!"

Soolie set her jaw, feeling the anger grow, welcoming it. Anger was an easy emotion. Anger made her feel strong. Soolie knew how to be angry.

"No," she delivered the words like iron blows. "It's what *you* want. You think if he dies, you'll be together. You're wrong. If he dies, he'll go be with my mother. Because when he could have had either of you, he chose her."

The color bleached from Ellena's ghostly face. *"You're not Soolie."*

"And you're dead."

Soolie spun on her heel and marched up to the treeline. Halfway up the hill, the monster sat cross-legged, waiting. As soon as she came into view, he scrambled to his feet, poised.

"Dog!" Soolie snapped. She didn't want to use him, but she had no choice.

He hurtled down the hill, scrambling to a halt in front of her. He clasped his hands before his forehead. "Mistress."

She walked back through the trees, the monster keeping pace one step back at her side.

"The man in the trees, can you lift him?"

"Yes, Mistress."

"I am ordering you to carry him for me."

"NO!" Ellena stood in their way, arms outstretched, barring their path. *"I won't let it touch him!"*

As Dog stepped forward, Ellena shrunk back, her arms pulling in. *"You can't. Please, don't do this. Please…"*

Dog swung one arm and batted her out of his way easily as sweeping a spider from a doorway. She was there one moment, and the next violently gone, reappearing in a streak ten lengths away, a ghost at the mercy of the dead.

Dog knelt before Papa, lifting one arm and hauling Papa's long heavy body over his shoulders. He stood, Papa's arms and legs slinging down to his knees on either side.

"Ready, Mistress."

"Please!" Ellena blinked back, standing at Soolie's side, shying fearfully away from the monster, her hands folded, begging. *"Whatever you are, you can't. If there is any shred of Soolie left in you, don't do this."*

Soolie looked into her aunt's faded eyes. "The aunt I know would never ask me to let my father die. I'm going to save my Papa's life. Don't get in my way."

SOOLIE TOOK THE LONG WAY HOME, up through the trees north of Hob Glen and cutting quickly down behind the bakery to avoid being seen. She ran in the lead, Dog keeping pace. Close behind them Ellena followed, quietly keening.

At the bakery, Soolie rushed to start a fire, striking the lighting sticks until the tips skittered with flame and touching them to the soft fuzz of tinder, coaxing it to life. As soon as the kitchen stove started to heat, she propped Papa beside it against the cooking cupboards, ran upstairs, ripped the blankets off of Ellena's bed, and took the stairs two at a time on her way down.

In the kitchen, Ellena hid in the corner, shying out of the way, watching the monster pace back and forth.

"Can Dog help, Mistress?

"Sit down. Shut up."

"Yes, Mistress."

"Just stop this, please!" Ellena begged. *"If you are Soolie, think about what you're doing. You're with a monster. You're not yourself."*

"You too," Soolie pointed at her aunt's ghost. "Not a sound."

The ghost obeyed.

Today they were all monsters.

Soolie knelt and tucked the fluffy pink and blue floral blankets around Papa, the lace ruffle sticking out from around his neck like a fop collar. His face was filthy. His lips were cracked and crusty as if coated in a thin layer of dried paste. He needed to be washed. He needed to eat something. He needed water.

Soolie ran out back to the pump, filled a pot, and set it on the stove. Then she filled the tin bucket with water, hauled it in, and sloshed the water swirling into the bottom of Ellena's washtub. She would boil the water from the pot, dump it into the cold water in the tub, and then stick Papa's feet in the warm bath.

The water in the pot was just starting to warm, and she scooped it up with the blue clay mug and knelt by Papa, tilting it to his mouth. The water spilled off his thin dry lips, burbled through his beard and down his chest.

"Come on, Papa," Soolie muttered. She clasped his head and looked into his brown eyes, vacant and empty like wooden bowls.

"Papa, it's me, Soolie." She bit her lip and tried to sound like the little girl he loved. "It's me, your baby girl. And I neeeed you to drink. For me, Papa. Pleeease, Papa. You have to drink."

She pried open his jaws with her fingers, then tipped the mug to his lips again. The water spilled through his teeth as from an open water skin. Not a drop went down his throat.

Soolie screamed and slammed the mug down on the counter top. Behind her, Dog whined.

"He doesn't want you to save him," Ellena whispered quietly.

Soolie snarled. "He doesn't KNOW what he wants."

You're angry.

What else is cucking new.

She rummaged loudly through the cupboards, scattering kitchen spoons and clattering bowls across the floor until, at last, she found the leather funnel. She refilled the mug and tilted Papa's head back, trying to keep his throat straight, and forcing the funnel between his teeth. Holding his head firm against her chest with one arm, Soolie poured part of a mug of water in the funnel. She had once seen Papa do something like this with Rod Cornell to help a baby goat that wouldn't take milk.

Papa made choking noises, water splashed, but she thought some of it went in. She repeated the process a few times, not too often. She didn't want him to get sick and vomit it back up.

Soolie set the funnel down next to the water pitcher. If possible, Papa looked even worse. His eyes looked like someone had used their thumbs to push them further into his skull. His skin wrinkled and sagged beneath his dripping beard.

Soolie gritted her teeth and muttered, "Is there anything you can do?"

The Hunter responded, *I don't know.*

Soolie growled, "What do you mean you don't know?"

I have never bonded to a vessel before. I do not know what we are capable of.

Great. Soolie got the towel from the tin bucket and rinsed it thoroughly in the hot water on the stove. She lifted it steaming from the pot and wrung it out, hissing through her teeth as the hot water splashed between her fingers. Then she crossed to where Papa sat on the floor, propped against the cupboards, and kneeled by his side. She folded the towel around her fingers and began washing the blood and dirt from Papa's face. First from his brow, then pulling at the loose skin around his eyes. She moved her fingers to a clean piece of the cloth, then swabbed his cheeks, chin, and scrubbed his beard, peeling back the ruffle of the blanket to work her way down and around his neck.

Once his face was mostly clean, she tossed the dirty wet towel across the kitchen floor, cupped one hand behind Papa's head, and leaned in until her lips were right by his ear. She whispered, "You do *not* get to die."

Soolie poured the steaming pot water into the washtub with the cold and tested it with her finger. Together, the temperature was unpleasantly warm, but not so hot as to scald. She hauled the tub, scraping it heavily across the floorboards, and then swung Papa's legs over the edge one at a time, the rim of the tub coming right up under his knees, his feet stuck in the hot water.

Soolie stepped back, her hands on her hips, and looked down at him, his feet in the tub, his body flopped against the cupboards like a husk doll wrapped in pink and blue floral quilts.

From the corner, Ellena detached and flung herself to him, wrapping her arms around Papa's neck like a frail scarf, sobbing into his shoulder.

Lost souls can be unstable, the Hunter observed.

"No spak," Soolie groaned, massaging her bare head with the fingers of one hand. "And don't think just because you're stuck with me, we're on terms."

Understood.

What she didn't understand was why Papa had given up. How could he just decide to die? Why wasn't he fighting for her? She was still here, and he was disappearing.

To make matters worse, Soolie had lit a fire, which meant that, if they hadn't figured it before, there was no doubt now that all of Hob Glen knew someone was in the bakery, and Soolie didn't imagine they would be well received by the townsfolk. They needed to leave Hob Glen, but they had no shelter, no horses or cart, no money, little food. If they stayed, the people of Hob Glen might show up on the doorstep with torches. If they left, Papa might die tonight.

"Mistress?" Dog spoke hesitantly from his place crouching by the door.

"No, you can't help."

"Yes, Mistress."

That settled it, they were staying.

Soolie marched out of the kitchen, through the front room, spun the latch on the front door, threw it open, and stepped out into the street. Evening was coming. Down the street towards the square, townsfolk huddled watching the bakery, watching her. Soolie couldn't imagine the spectacle she must make, the bald demon girl. 'Yes,' she thought. 'I'm still here.'

"PEOPLE OF HOB GLEN!" Soolie flung open her arms and yelled. "WE'LL BE GONE BEFORE DAYBREAK IF YOU JUST LEAVE US THE CUCK ALONE!"

She turned, stepped back into the bakery, and slammed the door. Who knows, with any luck, maybe that had bought them a little time.

ELLENA HAD LOVED SOOLIE. She always had. But Soolie had been Tara's dream. And Silas had been Ellena's.

For fifteen years, she had loved him. She had loved him from the moment she had looked up from her game of straws with Tara and seen him striding across the backyard beside Grandad. She had loved him when had she helped him court her sister's favor. She had loved him when she told him how to propose the one way that would make Tara say 'yes.'

Other men had courted her over the years. Merchants and farmers, young and old, but it never went far. Sooner or later, Soolie would get an ear infection, need help with her arithmetic, new undergarments, or start her blood, and he would need her, and she would be there. Because the hope of Silas was always more powerful than the promise of anyone else.

Which was why he had to come to her now.

She had waited for him for so long. That had to be why she was here, why she was a ghost. For him. She had loved him in life, and now she loved him in death, and he would come to her. He had to. Death had made everything so simple. That hope was now all she had.

She lay her head against his chest and listened to the faint thumping of his heart. By the door, the monster watched her with black eyes. Ellena tried not to look at it, looking only on Silas.

She curled up in his lap and nestled against the curve of his neck. How she missed his warmth, his smell. Like the wood and leather he worked with, like him. Even the touch of his skin was vague: a hard stream of air, a soft lake surface, a feather's weight from slipping through. But there were some things she could feel now that she hadn't been able to feel before.

"I'm here."

She slid into him, laying down against his bones. It was here, within his flesh, that she felt him most strongly. The absolute of his hopelessness. The depth of his need for an end.

"You're not alone."

And when that end came, she would be here for him. Just like she had been for all these years.

"WHAT are you DOING?"

Ellena startled out of Silas' body, looking up at where Soolie stood in the kitchen doorway, her brown eyes flickering white in her pale hairless face. The monster snarled and flexed his claws.

Ellena flinched back, retreating to the kitchen corner, her arms up tight to her chest. *"I'm comforting him."*

"You CUCKING stay AWAY from him!" Soolie knelt by Silas, feeling under his jaw with two fingers for a pulse. When she found it, she closed her eyes, pushing air fiercely through her nose.

"If I EVER see you do that again." She looked up at Ellena, eyes snapping open, mouth in a bitter hard line. "You will *never* come *near* him again. Do you understand me?"

Ellena nodded. There was something about Soolie that burned, that consumed. Something that called, demanded, terrified her. Something that was not, and never had been, human.

"Dog," Soolie jabbed at the monster with her finger, "take the man upstairs and lay him on the bed."

"Yes, Mistress!" The creature sprung to its feet and scrabbled across the kitchen to Silas' side.

"Carefully!"

"Yes, Mistress."

The monster knelt beside the washtub and scooped Silas up like an oversized infant. Silas' head lolled back, his long feet dripped water from the toes, the blankets heaped up to the monster's nose as it edged sideways into the front room.

Soolie glared at Ellena, jaw jutting, eyes tight. Her voice hissed like a kettle boiling over. "*You do not get to have him.*"

Ellena hugged herself and didn't move as Soolie turned and followed the monster out of the room.

Ellena clasped a hand to her mouth and let out a small sound. It wasn't Soolie. That couldn't be Soolie. The little girl she knew was bright and dramatic, full of wit and joy. Quick to laugh, quick to fling her arms around the ones she loved. This wasn't the Soolie Ellena knew. This was cold and vicious, hateful and unkind. This wasn't even a little girl. This was a devil.

But no matter what happened, Ellena wasn't going anywhere. She wouldn't leave him. She slipped toward the front room door.

For the last day and a half she had waited with Silas, absorbing his pain, feeling the shallow swell of his breath, listening to the somber rhythm of his heart slowing in the nighttime freeze. For the last day and a half he had been growing weaker. She wouldn't let him die alone. She would be there for him. She would wait for him. She knew she wouldn't have to wait for long.

THE THICK GRASS HIDE of the bog had been cut-turned, hunks of turf scattered haphazardly about disturbed black muddy wallows. As the sun sank behind the distant trees, the wallows began to stir. Wet earthed hands clawed their way to the air. Muddy roped grasses slopped sideways and dripped down necks and shoulders, becoming hair. Clawed fingers scraped icy slop from cheeks and noses. The bog filth split, revealing black eyes like slimy wet toad's eggs.

With a heavy shlopping sound, Horse pulled his hammer free from the mire and trudged up out of the slough onto solid ground. The cold mud had protected them from the burning light of day. Now that the sun was behind the hills, they would run. It wasn't far now.

He turned back to his pack, watching the hounds drag themselves up from the wallow, and spat out a wad of black mud that had slugged in through lips too thin to close. His long gray tongue flicked around the outside of his teeth, swathing at the coat of grit and grime. Beneath the mud on his face, his left cheek jerked like a rat on a string, and he snarled, gnawing it still, and spat again.

"PACK!" he roared.

Thirty-four sets of eyes looked to him, thirty-four sets of claws flexed, thirty-four sets of teeth bared.

"NOW, WE RUN! TONIGHT, WE FEED!"

THIRTY-ONE

Soolie sat beside the bed in one of the dining chairs. She had smoothed out the covers and tucked Papa in, snugged the pillow up under his head and brushed back his hair. It had been years since she'd seen Papa lying in bed. He always crawled in after she was in her loft and got up early to light the fire. In the last moon, since the carnival woman, he hadn't slept in a bed at all. Now he was the one asleep in the bed, and she was the one sitting up in the chair all night.

The blankets were too frilly and floral. His face was so slack, sunken, and grizzled. He looked old. Like a homeless gutternaper they had dragged in from the cold. He looked like he was dying.

Mama always said you could smell death on a person right before they died.

You could ask Dog.

He wasn't dying. She wasn't going to ask.

To her left, the monster sat cross-legged against the wall, his chin propped on his fist. If she didn't turn her head, out of the corner of her eye, he looked almost like a human boy. But one glance in his direction, and there were the black nails, the animal eyes, the yellow pointed teeth.

On the other side of the room, waiting behind Granddad's chair, Ellena hovered, quiet now, waiting.

They were all waiting.

Papa hadn't eaten anything. Soolie had tried. But when she had spooned soft oatmeal gruel into his mouth, he had choked and stopped breathing. She had fished down his throat with her fingers, swiping out the thick warm goo, and rolled him onto his belly with his head off the side of the bed. Somehow he had started to breathe, wet rattling frail breaths. She hadn't dared try again.

She didn't know what to do. She didn't know how to save him. She couldn't even send for Doc Wilkins. No one would help them.

Why are you trying to save this man's life?

Soolie gripped Papa's hand in hers. His big strong hands had grown soft and clammy like loose cuts of meat.

I wish to understand. The Hunter appeared, sitting on the foot of the bed, little smooth brown ankles hanging straight, feet not quite touching the floor.

Soolie scowled. Was she dreaming?

No. It tilted its head. *I thought a visual representation might be useful.*

"Unless you have something useful to say, I don't want to talk to you."

I don't understand why you choose to do things you don't want to do. You don't want to be caring for this man. You don't even want to be near him.

"You don't know what I want."

This man wishes to die, and you resent trying to save him. You would have accepted his death, but you fight his dying. Why?

"What do you care?"

It blinked. *You have seen the Dead Man and witnessed his abominations. Yet you waste time fighting a futile fight for an insignificant life. It may be useful for me to understand.*

Soolie's grip tightened on Papa's hand. From his seat against the wall, Dog watched as she spoke to the image in her head. Behind her, she knew, Ellena was watching as well, watching as she turned into a monster, waiting for her to fail to save him. Waiting for Papa to die.

"He's my Papa."

Why is that significant?

Soolie clenched her jaw. It meant he wasn't allowed to give up. Mama never gave up. She lived as long as she could, and she taught Soolie how to be brave. Even when her body betrayed her, even when she was sick and dying, Mama was there, Mama was strong for them.

I understand now. The Hunter nodded. *Your relationship is a contract. You would rather see him suffer than see him betray it.*

Soolie sneered. "You don't understand at all."

I do. The little girl faded into the air. *Some laws are more important than kindness. I understand this very well.*

IT WAS THE SECOND NIGHT on the road. Horse had been pushing the pack mercilessly, and they were making good speed. They had to. The pack was giddy and skittish with the new smells and open spaces, and the hunger made them unreliable. There weren't enough souls along this road for a pack of this size, and Horse knew every day without sufficient feeding was a liability. The Master had sent them three nights out, but with the long autumn dark and Horse pushing them, the pack had traveled that span in two.

It was still early when Horse caught the scent of the town, far off, warm and throbbing, the taste of life seeping through the night air. A stir raked through the hungry pack, and they picked up pace, careening through the dark like a frenzy of viper fish tasting blood in the water, Horse at the lead, arms pumping in rhythm, unhindered by the five-stone hammer in his fist.

He didn't have to herd the pack now; they were all behind him, ready for the kill. There was no need for stealth. They raced at full speed, some sprinting on legs alone, those with longer arms leaning forward and pulling at the ground, loping with all four limbs. Their mouths lolled open, drinking in the smells, saliva lathering at the corners of their mouths, night filling their eyes with blackness. They ran as one beast with one mind.

Horse saw it distant in the dark: the black cut-out corners of houses. It was a small village, but it would be enough. They would bathe in blood and drink their fill tonight. The hound beside him whined querulously, nosing at the air, and Horse bared his teeth to their full length, lips curled back against his gums in warning. Then he scented it too.

Horse sucked it in over his yellow fence picket teeth and growled, grinning with voracious appetite. It was faint but unmistakable. The scent of the outcast, Dog, the banished one. Finally. The pack running behind him began to yelp and whine. Horse barked, snapping his teeth to keep them in line.

He didn't know what they had been sent for, but tonight he was going to rip the flesh from that puppy's little bones and follow it up by drinking a small village dry.

He did not use words often with the pack, but when he did, they listened.

"Follow and obey! Then we feed!"

The pack loosed a keening cry, their human voices churning with rapacious animal lust, bearing down on the small vulnerable sleeping village.

It had only been hours, but Soolie felt like she'd been sitting up with Papa for moons, and she knew he was only getting worse. She no longer held his hand. Every once in a while, she leaned forward in the chair to check if he was still alive while the monster and the ghost watched her.

She wanted to roar. She wanted to smash every vase and glass jar in the kitchen downstairs. She wanted to upend the sheet racks and put a cooking pot through the display case, to crack the chairs to pieces against the table, turn over the wardrobe, and take a kitchen knife to Grandpa's arm chair. She wanted to punch each painting out of its frame and rip the canvas to ragged strips with her bare fingers. She wanted to see a third house burn.

Instead, she sat. She sat and did nothing. And she knew that by doing nothing, she, too, was waiting for him to die.

Suddenly, Dog stirred. He rolled up into a crouch, staring sharply toward the far corner of the room. Pointed yellow teeth bared. He breathed open mouthed and snarled through his nose.

"Mistress."

Soolie didn't respond.

So, the people of Hob Glen couldn't wait until morning. Let them storm the house. Soolie almost hoped they would attack. She wanted an excuse.

"Mistress."

Dog whined. He was on his feet now.

He senses something.

Soolie didn't care.

I do not think it is human.

"Mistress." He looked at her, fanged mouth gaping. She could smell the cold malodor of his breath. "I sense the pack."

Soolie felt her body tense, and the Hunter's voice was like snakes dropped into flame. *The Dead Man has sent his weapons. We must leave now.*

Soolie tucked her chin down. She wasn't leaving.

Her veins tightened beneath her skin, and lightening skittered over her vision.

THIS IS URGENT, SOOLIE BEECH. I HAVE BEEN PATIENT. WE CAN WAIT NO LONGER.

The words cut. Soolie felt her body move against her, bending forward and standing to its feet.

WE ARE NOT STRONG ENOUGH TO FACE THE PACK. WE MUST RUN.

It was moving her body without her consent. Soolie snarled.

Cuck you!

She spun and tried to slam her forehead down into the seat of the chair, but at the last moment, her hands snapped forward and latched onto the heavy carved wood to catch her. Soolie threw herself backward, the chair sailing over her head and cracking against the side of the bed. She landed hard on her back, but her head tucked forward to avoid bouncing off the floorboards.

THE PACK WILL RIP US APART.

Her body rolled over onto its hands and knees, and Soolie lurched forward, grabbing hold of the edge of the quilt, hauling herself toward the bed, reaching to grab hold of the solid oak leg, but her feet moved her backward, dragging the flowered quilt slowly off Papa and over the tossed chair.

"NO!" Soolie screamed, and her own voice answered her back. *"HE IS DEAD."*

Soolie threw her weight forward, and her leg tried to catch her, but she twisted in the air, slamming into the floor, the quilt wrapped over her.

"Not yet he isn't! *IT IS TIME TO DO WHAT YOU DO NOT WANT TO DO, SOOLIE BEETCH!"*

She thrashed, tangled in the quilt, limbs pulling at and against her will.

"Mistress?" Dog howled.

STOP! The Hunter spoke in her head.

YOU FIRST!

Soolie sat up suddenly and flailed the quilt off of her, throwing it to the side. The monster stood over her, looking down, panicked, whining, cringing like a beaten child. In the corner, Ellena was pale, frightened, and silent.

Soolie snarled. "WHAT?"

Dog cowered, hands gripped before his forehead. "The pack is coming, Mistress. The pack is here."

Soolie pounded her fists into the floor and screamed. "THEN STOP IT!"

The monster's clawed hands lowered a little, and his eyes sought hers out. "Mistress would have Dog fight the pack?"

"Isn't that what you cucking want? To be ordered about like a whip skag?" Her vision had gone bleached and pale. "What are you cucking good for, you sniveling spak peck cucking corpse? GO!"

He seemed to grow small, his hands curled up, his feet turned inward. He looked at her over his shoulder. "Dog senses some three dozen hounds, Mistress. Mistress wishes Dog to face these hounds?"

Soolie sneered. She wanted him gone. She wanted him torn limb from limb. "Am I your Mistress, or are you useless?"

You are asking him to destroy himself, the Hunter said.

Soolie felt nothing but rage.

Dog straightened himself. His hands came down to his sides, his feet faced forward, his head raised. He stood before her.

"Mistress knows she is sending Dog to a fight he is unlikely to win. Dog has one request." He spoke quietly, almost with dignity. There was no keening or howling. The words were thick over his pointed teeth, but his voice was the closest to human it had ever been. "If Dog survives this fight, Mistress will let Dog serve her. She will command Dog, and she will be his Mistress."

"Fine," Soolie said.

"Mistress promises," he insisted.

"I promise," she spat.

He touched clasped hands to his forehead and bowed. "Then Dog will go and fight for Mistress."

The monster turned, crouched, leapt for the stairs, and was gone.

He could have been useful in the future, the Hunter chided. *He will most certainly fail, and we will still have to face this enemy.*

Soolie pushed herself up, walked over to the table where the lantern sat, lifted it, and walked to the head of the bed. She held the lantern up, leaned over, and pried open one of Papa's eyes. As the light hit the pupil, it shrunk like a touched seaflower.

Maybe, she thought back, he'll get lucky and survive.

THIRTY-TWO

The pack was drawing near. Dog could smell Horse at their lead. He had never trusted Horse, had always doubted the hound's loyalty to the Master, had always watched the pack leader, anticipating the day Horse would turn traitor and he would have to put Horse down. But now Dog was the traitor, and Horse was on the hunt.

There would be no running tonight. It was time for Dog to fight.

He stood in a cobbled round at the center of the small town beneath a bare white oak that split overhead like a skag's legs. There was no hiding tonight.

The pack would have caught his scent. Horse's hammer was thirsting for his blood. Dog didn't stand a great chance in this fight. He was faster and stronger, but vastly outnumbered. And he was fighting for a Mistress who didn't even want him.

Dog crouched and closed his eyes, his shoulders sinking low, his long black nails curling near his bare ankles. In the houses, living souls slept like couped birds for the culling. In the stones beneath his feet, he could feel the tremor of the pack's coming. Eager yelping howls filled the cold dark night.

They were here.

He opened his eyes as the ragged black forms boiled into the clearing, Horse in the lead, large teeth pale lit by the moonlight, the iron maul in his fist swinging, the pack beside and behind: all hounds, no pups or runts, all large, all strong. Dog sprung forward, charging for Horse.

The leader's black bead eyes met his, and Horse cackled, swinging his hammer up, and slowing back, the hounds closing in before him. Horse was throwing the pack between them.

These hounds were all big, and Dog was small.

Dog ducked, tucking in, spinning around the first hound and kicking out low, connecting with the side of its thick knobbly knee. The knee cracked sideways like a dry tree branch, and the hound screeched, flying forward into the stones.

The pack was upon him.

Dog drove his hand up, claws extended into a belly, tearing through rotting cotton, plunging his hand into the slick cold entrails. He slashed across a face, nails ripping at eyes and cutting lips and cheeks to skirt fringe, kicking out with his foot, clipping a heavy saliva-slick chin, then flipping up onto his hands, catching a sinuous neck between his ankles and twisting sharp, bringing the long hound down onto the stones. He stamped his heel back as he stood, crushing the hound's neck, blood and flesh bursting out like meat from an overstuffed sausage skin. Sharp claws raked at his back, and he whipped around, snatching the wrist in his talons, twisting and ripping, bones snapping, tendons splitting, the hound's thick hand tearing free from the wrist and flinging over Dog's shoulder. Dog drove the heel of his other hand up into the nose, driving the bone back into its brain like a peg and crushing the bridge between eyes gushing blood.

Sharp teeth clamped down on his shoulder, shredding tendon and muscle as he tore away, snarling. The street stones were slick with blood. The fallen hounds, broken and shredded, writhed and snapped their teeth underfoot. Sharp claws cut into Dog's haunches. He snapped a neck and dove his nails into eyes like cold jelly eggs. Teeth ripped at his ankle and he stomped down, his heel crushing through the sharp-toothed open mouth and into the back of the throat, crunching the monster's head, its fangs ripping deep black gouges in his foot as he pulled it free.

"Hello, puppy." The words were wet and close. Dog spun his head as the large thick teeth bit down on his ear, the bottom half ripping and tearing from his skull in a spume of blood.

Horse grinned and spat out the torn piece of ear, blood spittling from his mouth and down his long chin. Dog roared and drove his claws for Horse's throat, but something held him back; hounds latched upon his arms, grabbing hold and dragging him from the slaughter, hauling him backward as Horse advanced, leering, the heavy maul swinging in his fist. Dog screamed, hounds anchoring his limbs. And Horse reached for the leather belt about his waist, his long claws clicking as they closed on metal, and he drew a iron ship spike the length of a longdag, the length of Dog's forearm.

Dog felt the oak trunk hard against his spine.

Horse raised the long spike and pulled his lips back from teeth wet with Dog's blood. "I relish this."

Dog bucked and struggled, skull and shoulder blades battering against the hard wood at his back. Horse swung the iron hammer once and drove the spike through Dog's chest, spine, and deep into the oak.

Dog gnashed the air with his teeth, pulling with his lungs to roar and feeling the ripping collapse in his chest, his own blood burbling up in the back of his throat and over his tongue. He tried to push his ribs away from the trunk, up the spike, straining toward Horse's leering grimace. Horse swung the hammer again, pounding the spike deeper through his chest and deeper into the tree.

Horse nodded, and the hounds released Dog's arms and legs, scrabbling back, forming a black-eyed wall.

Dog snarled, blood and spittle flicking from his teeth, kicking with his heels against the smooth curved rooted base of the tree, long nailed fingers scrabbling at the broad rectangular head of the ship's spike. He was pinned to the tree like a jungle moth on a collector's board.

Horse's tongue flicked out over his teeth. "Dog, the Master's pet. The runaway." Horse cackled. "Do you know what I'm going to do now, puppy?" Horse waved the hammer in front of Dog's face. "I'm going to pound your bones to paste."

The pack roared, snarling, yelping, screaming. Horse hefted back the hammer, long-lengthed arms extended, both large hands about the handle, and swung, powering the blunt iron head into Dog's thigh, the bone crushing like dry reeds, flush pulping and mashing into the cloth of his pants, his lower leg jerking, clawed foot twisting, and Horse swung again. The other leg mangled.

Mistress. I have failed.

The pack was a constant ocean roar. Again Horse swung, crushing first one of Dog's arms, and then the other, all four limbs hanging misshapen and broken, twisted like wet rags, useless. The pain was the blood in his veins and eyes, but his brain did not haze.

He would stay alert for all of it. He had been one of the Master's pack.

Horse leaned close, his teeth clicked in front of Dog's nose, the hammer thunked heavy, resting into the tree beside Dog's shredded ear.

"There's just one thing I have to know." Horse's voice was both nasal and low. "What made the coward puppy turn and fight?"

Dog coughed a spray of cold blood across the larger creature's eyes. Horse cackled.

"Has puppy found a new master? You always were too weak to follow your own command." Horse dragged the edge of the hammer scraping by Dog's head and hissed in his other ear. "I will find your new god and feed you its heart in the name of the one you failed."

Horse stepped back, raised his arms, and bellowed. "WE OBEY! AND THEN WE FEED!"

The pack roared and thrashed a violent storm about the tree. Dog wheezed, trying to draw speech through the spike in his chest.

Horse raised a hand, and the pack stilled. "A word, puppy?"

Dog fought with the air; it cracked in his chest, tearing at its path. He bared his teeth, and the words came out a bloody cough. "Your hand," Dog forced the snarled words. "IS SHAKING."

The pack froze. Every pair of black eyes were on Horse's raised hand.

Horse shrieked a screeching roar and slashed Dog's face, thick nails splitting his eye and nose, ribboning his cheek.

"HORSE DOES NOT SHAKE!"

But it was too late. Every black eye had seen it. Horse was going wrong. Horse's reign was ending.

"I am the STRONGEST OF THE PACK!" Horse howled at the sky, his bloody hammer held high. "I will DESTROY THE ONE YOU SERVE!"

Mistress.

Dog could barely see through his one good eye, blood smeared over his face, his body was all brokenness and pain. He hung from the tree, helpless, a waking shattered corpse.

Mistress.

A weak failure Dog serving a Mistress who did not even want him. Who fought and warred with her own self. Who did not even know her own strength,

She could not see herself the way he had seen her. She had not watched herself being born.

He believed in her.

And it was why she needed him.

It was why she still might save him.

Mistress.

THIRTY-THREE

Soolie could hear the distant whoops and howls, wild like drunken youth, ragged and raw with rage and pain.

Can they smell us?

They don't have to. They can follow Dog's trail.

She gripped the handle of the kitchen knife tightly and watched the stair.

Are they here because of you?

Yes.

Will they find us?

Yes.

As soon as the monster had left, Ellena had rushed to sit at Papa's side. She crooned, stroking his waxy cheek with her shadow fingers. *"It's all right. I'm here. It's all right. You're not alone."*

Soolie didn't look at them.

He will not join her. The golden-eyed Hunter stood beside her, looking the same way, watching the stair. *He is dying a human death. He will pass into the next realm as is right.*

He is not going to die.

The distant howling voices roared in bloody chorus. Dog had failed.

I have been fighting for long before your soul existed, the Hunter said. *To survive, to reclaim my function, to keep this realm from an end.* It looked up at her. *Now, it would seem, after all this time, you, Soolie Beetch, have undone me. It is the end of all things. And yet you cannot accept this one man's death.*

When he dies, Soolie thought, he'll die fighting.

The yelping howls were coming closer.

You should say goodbye.

Soolie would not.

You feel so much for these two. Very much. Its eyes were still on her, and if she had looked back, she might have read something near sorrow in its gaze. *The realm seals its end tonight, Soolie Beetch. If I felt the way you feel, I would have a need to say goodbye.*

Something snarled outside. Scrambling and stamping circled the house. Ellena went silent. Soolie gripped the knife. She had bolted all the doors. There was no pulse in her ears. She didn't breathe.

There was a scraping sound from the side of the house.

The window.

Soolie spun, knife raised as the glass exploded into the room. A monstrous gray fist rested a blunt iron sledgehammer on the length of the windowsill. Another long thick-knuckled hand with black gunked nails reached in, crushing glass beneath its palm, and heaving in a long head with beetles for eyes and bed-slats for teeth. The hammer thudded heavily on the floor as hulking bony shoulders heaved up, barely squeezing through the double window.

Soolie charged, swinging the knife for its leering yellow face, but the creature moved impossibly fast, pulling itself through the window like a wizard's trick, large body unfolding, one hand lifting the massive sledge, the other striking viper-like, clamping on her wrist, the thick point-nailed fingers digging sharp between the bones, the kitchen knife clattering to the floor.

Soolie kicked out, trying to bite its hand, but it stood full height, hauling her up at arm's length until her toes barely touched the floor. She could feel the muscles of its grip twitching and spasming, sharp nails digging, gouging, splitting her skin. It was taller than any man she had ever seen. Its head was bent against the sloped ceiling, and it leered down at her, the familiar stench of rotten blood and putrid meat hanging from its clothes and drifting over its large teeth like dank fog.

There was a splitting crack downstairs of a betraying door. Yelps and howls and scrabbling nails on wood, clamoring on the stairs. There were more of the creatures behind her.

"It's you," the monster sneered, its voice grating low. "The puppy's god is a dead girl with a knife."

It seized her by the throat and moved, hauling her across the room in great strides as she clung with both hands to the cold fist that gripped her neck, twitching, tightening. Ragged creatures with black eyes and jagged teeth scurried out of the way.

"Bring the other two."

It ducked down the stairs, hauling her after, her bare legs and feet flailing, battering down every step. Above her, Ellena screamed.

"NO ONE FEEDS UNTIL I SAY SO!"

There were monsters in the streets. A heavy body in a pink cotton robe flopped on the stones like an over-stuffed cushion. The creature standing over it hissed, baring bloody jagged teeth as Soolie was dragged by, the large beast's spasming grip crushing her windpipe so she should have blacked, but she continued to see.

She screamed, but she couldn't scream. She kicked, but her bare heels only bashed cobbles. She dug her fingers into its cold vice hand, but it was like trying to wring pain from a stone.

Yelping, howling cries sawed in her ears. The monster threw her, and she hit the stones, sliding in a sludge of cold slick that soaked into her tunic, sticky wet over her arms and legs. Beside her, something moved, and she scrambled back as a clawed hand scratched at her calf. An eyeless crushed face turned toward her, disemboweled bodies drug broken limbs, parts stirred in the thick of a death stew.

The clawed hand grasped at the air like an overturned crab, nothing but torn flesh beyond its wrist.

"I WILL SHOW YOU WEAKNESS!"

The large creature roared, lifting its hammer high. From around the town square came the response. Barking, growling, grasping hands and long sharp nails. They were tall and lanky, short and compact, legs like tree trunks and arms like willow stalks trailing rotting rags and shredded clothes, chests like hay bales and emaciated bellies like runt pigs. They had skin pale as cheese and dark as beetroot, hair wild and long, bare scalps and bunched shoulders. They snarled savagely, snapping eager teeth.

Soolie looked behind her to the white oak and saw him hanging from the trunk like a clotted pelt, face split, slashed and bloody, limbs bent at tortured angles. The head jerked, and a gargling sound came from a blood-filled mouth. Dog.

The large monster strode forward, stepping over a jerking headless body, and Soolie rose to her feet, the cold bloody material of her shift sticking to her hips and legs. There was no hope in running.

It was upon her in a moment, hand gripping the front of her shift, nails slashing, cutting into her small breasts. It slammed her up against the oak tree, holding her up beside Dog's mangled body like a pair of tools hanging on Papa's wall.

It roared. "DO YOU CARE FOR HIM? DO YOU CARE FOR THE DOG?"

Beside her, Dog's slashed meat face gargled, lolling towards her.

Soolie snarled back, "I don't give a cuck about him!"

It lifted the heavy sledge under her chin, the bloody iron head as large as her own, and growled. "He is nothing."

"NOTHING." Soolie clenched her nails into her palms.

"HE SACRIFICED HIMSELF FOR NOTHING!" It swung the hammer cracking into the oak between their heads, crushing the wood, white splinters flying, scratching her face, embedding in the red pulp of Dog's cheek.

The monster hauled her away from the tree and gripped her by the neck, a heavy cold hand that could have encircled her waist weighing down on her shoulders. It turned to face the swarm of creatures, holding her for every night-black eye to see.

Ellena was there, captive in a bony grip, struggling to get away, her translucent gingham held tight in solid black claws. On the street beside her, Papa, dressed in Granddad's nightshirt, slung face down onto the cold bloody street like a hunt's kill.

"THIS IS THE ONE WE WERE SENT TO FIND!"

The creatures snarled, jagged teeth, broken and thin, wide and long, uneven and pointed, gleaming in the moonlight.

It shook her. "WHAT ARE YOU?"

Soolie gasped a pained wheeze. "Skag if I know."

"WHAT," it roared, rotten phlegm spittling the back of her neck and bare head, "ARE YOU?"

"Soolie ... Beetch."

The large fingers curved, thick sharp nails punctured the skin of her neck. It squeezed. "WHAT ARE YOU?"

Soolie's eyes met Ellena's across the sea of blood and stirring death. Her ghostly eyes were wide terror, her body pale, distant and thin. She was helpless and afraid.

Soolie choked hoarsely, but her words were twisted off by the monster's grip. The claws released, a thin trickle of blood running down into her collar.

Soolie rasped. "*Ikma na Sitari*, the Soul Hunter."

Ellena's eyes held her gaze.

It's going to be all right, Soolie thought at her. *Everything is going to be all right.*

The creature roared, "WHY DOES THE MASTER CARE ABOUT YOU?"

"I killed him." It might be true.

I won't let them hurt you.

"KILLED HIM!" The monster raised its hammer and shook it at the sky. "THE MASTER WAS KILLED! THE MASTER HAS WEAKNESS!"

The creatures shrunk back, whispering and growling, black eyes blinking, claws ready.

"YOU ARE NOTHING TO HIM! I HAVE LED YOU! I HAVE BEEN YOUR STRENGTH!"

The monsters stirred, snarling, watching

"I WILL KILL THE FALSE GODS!" it screamed, its grip tightening on her neck, the hammer swinging above her head. "I WILL DESTROY THE MASTERS!"

The monster spun and slammed her back against the oak tree. She felt the base of her spine and skull crack in a torrent of pain. The world should have exploded into a festival-cannon of stars, but everything was clear. The monster roared, shoving her body further up the trunk until her eyes were level with its long sickly potato face.

"SOOLIE!"

Ellena was calling for her. Ellena was calling her name.

The monster's face leered up close to hers, pebble eyes gleamed cold as it bared long flat yellow teeth in a sadist's grimace. Its face was so close that when it spoke, she could feel its breath in her mouth. "After I drink your bones, I will make the man and woman suffer until there is nothing human left."

Soolie remembered the Hunter's words: *Many monsters are made with the souls of dead men, Soolie Beetch.*

The slug-like tongue slithered slowly over its teeth and curled across her cheek, snaking cold and wet over her face, flicking between her open lips, smelling and tasting like rotten meat.

"And to think. We came all that way for this."

Soolie screamed and bucked, slamming forward, her forehead connecting with the monster's forehead, and she felt the soul inside of him. It wasn't bright and it didn't shine. It was sodden, black and stagnant. She pulled. She grabbed hold of it with every ounce of her being and wrenched it toward her, willing it to leave this monster's body, but it was like trying to pull a vein of pitch from a winter tree, thick and sickly. It didn't move. She pulled with every measure of her will, her tenacity, her heart, but her head slammed back into the tree trunk with a splitting crunch.

It cackled, teeth flashing, eyes wild. "FOOL! YOU CAN'T TAKE LIFE FROM THE DEAD!"

Soolie gasped, but her words were cut off. The monster's hand jerked and tightened, squeezing, crushing. She felt the bones in her neck buckle and snap, her windpipe collapsing, her vision finally blackening as her spine was severed, but she could still feel every little thing, the shards of bone rubbing against each other, jutting into the skin of her neck, her legs quivering against the oak trunk.

In the blackness, the Hunter appeared before her, its golden eyes a dim bronze, its hair hanging lank against the grayish yellow of its tunic, its small brown hands hanging clasped before it.

Inside her betraying flesh, Soolie was a voiceless scream.

She felt the monster's grip change, its talons biting deep into her neck, stabbing her flesh. It was going to rip her head off. The world was slowing down.

You should have said goodbye, Soolie Beetch.

That monster has a human soul!

The soul is human, but we are not strong enough to take it.

I thought that was what you were for!

It looked at her with flat eyes, its head tilted down. *Its soul is anchored to its flesh. We are weak, our light is dim, and I am without my strength.*

There was nothing but blackness and immeasurable wrongness and pain. The monster's claws met in her throat. Ellena was out there. Papa was out there. They were in the hands of monsters.

YOU'RE QUITTING.

The Hunter began to fade. *Even if we had the strength of a hundred spirits, I cannot open the realms. I am broken and beyond my purpose.*

Humans are BORN broken! Soolie raged in the darkness. That's why we can NEVER QUIT! *IT'S THE ONLY STRENGTH WE HAVE!*

The Hunter's eyes blinked. It looked at her. The golden orbs warmed, brightened, and began to stir with flame.

The monster's nails were pulling upward, separating her spine, ripping her flesh.

The Hunter's eyes torched white.

The realms will open for the departure of the living.

Soolie understood. Cuck you, demon.

We may fail.

It didn't matter.

They will all have to die.

Then they die.

The Hunter stood before her, eyes blazing, hair wild, its shape burning away into a figure of pure white. It met her and was her, something ancient and unknown; space dropped away in an infinite free fall, and it spoke into the void with her own soul.

THEN WE FIGHT.

The world opened up, new senses coming alive, and she felt the souls of Hob Glen like a shining galaxy of a hundred golden stars tied together with bright filaments and tracers, threads that all lead shimmering back to her. She felt the grass and the trees, the small rodents, the pets and the stable animals. But most of all, she felt the people … the mothers, the fathers, the infants, and the old ones, each a glorious molten pot, waiting to be tipped, waiting for her to draw them in: their light was power, their souls were paths to the Eternal Realm. She grasped the threads and she pulled.

The stars streaked in, light spilling out into dazzling golden rivers that rushed into her waiting void, filling her up with heat and fire, aligning her spine and healing her bruises. The human souls spun up into a desert storm of golden tinder sparks, flying up into the blankness, impossible to keep, not meant to stay. Reality began to split.

She opened her eyes.

She was on the ground, collapsed against the foot of the tree. The monster stood over her, haloed in a tornado of Hob Glen's souls, spinning up into the glimmering void of another realm. Its tiny black eyes reflected the light of a burning sun. It roared, large-toothed maw gaping wide, swinging the hammer down full speed with both arms at her upturned face.

Soolie raised one hand and caught it at the thick wood handle, right below the heavy iron head. Her hand glowed white hot, and she stood slowly, lifting the maul as the monster screamed, his long waxen muscled arms shaking, trying to force her back down, trying to crush her beneath the weight, but still she stood.

"I DON'T WANT YOUR LIFE." Her voice was an unhallowed howl that warred about their heads and rattled the bare oak branches. *"I AM TAKING YOUR SOUL."*

She shoved her hand against his chest and felt it there. Thick, sludge black. The human soul. She pulled, and it tore from the body to which it had been bound, bound to every beam and wall and mortar and room of this monster's flesh. She ripped the soul free, and with it, the flesh began to unravel, spilling out of its chest, ribs dissolving, splashing at her feet like boiling jam, dissolving up to his neck and through his throat, his face caving in to the back of his head, large butter teeth melting from a fluid jaw. He split apart, legs collapsing, arms falling, hands dripping thickly down the handle of the hammer, flesh splattering formless to the ground. As the last ink-black drop of his soul tore shrieking free, Soolie released it, and it was sucked away, flung up into the golden maelstrom of souls. Then the storm sucked itself into the void, swallowed up, and was gone.

On the ground, the monsters broke into hysteria, scrambling over each other in a mad frenzy to get away.

Soolie lowered the maul, setting it head-first on the cobbles, and tipped the handle away so it swung down, smacking loosely onto the stones.

The life of a hundred souls swarmed inside her like a hoard of angry bees.

"Soolie!" Across the square, Ellena knelt at Silas' side. *"Come quick."*

As the monsters fled into the night, Soolie stepped through the bloody mash, liquefied flesh squishing up between her toes, parts convulsing in the muck about her feet, and she moved straight to the stones where Papa lay.

She knelt at his shoulders and gently turned him over, shifted him, lifting his head up on her blood-soaked lap and stroking his hair back from his forehead.

She could smell it. Through the flesh and blood and rot in the air, she could smell him dying. Like the scent of near snow. His soul was coming loose. Any moment now, it would begin to drift and slip away into another realm.

"I could hear you..." Ellena looked down a moment, struggling. She smiled shakily. *"You sounded just like him."*

Soolie didn't respond.

They sat, kneeling in the dark cold street, the night silent now but for the stirring of the sticky slur and the gargled wheezing of the corpse on the tree. The ghost and the dead girl looked down on the slack face of the dying man.

Soolie stroked Papa's head. The light of a hundred flames swarmed within her, the captured fire of a multitude of souls. But Papa was a lantern going out, the last flake ember on a wick winking away.

She was nothing like him.

"I know I haven't," Ellena's brow was creased, *"been a very good aunt lately."*

Soolie stopped her, reaching out and touching her aunt's pale hand. Ellena gasped, hastily clasping Soolie's hand in her own, lifting and brushing Soolie's fingers against her cheek. Her aunt was light and wispy, but Soolie could feel her. Ellena's eyes filled glimmering wet.

"The only touch I've felt..."

The words trailed unfinished, but Soolie understood. The monsters weren't alive. The only touch Ellena had felt since her death was the touch of the dead.

Soolie reached around Papa's head and pulled his left arm up, bringing his hand onto his chest. She reached with her right. "Give me your hand."

She took her aunt's hand in hers, lacing her flesh fingers with Ellena's hollow papery ones, and lowered Ellena's hand to where Papa's rested on his chest. She slid Ellena's smaller hand into Papa's larger one, the two hands overlapping until she was holding both laced together in one grasp.

Ellena smiled sadly. *"Thank you,"* she whispered.

"Ellena?" Soolie said it slowly. The word felt foreign on her tongue. *"Yes, love?"*

"I'm sorry that you died." It was almost what she meant: I'm sorry you're still here.

"Me too." Ellena sniffed, tears glazing her cheeks. *"And I'm sorry. This is all just a little bit much. Oh, lands."* She wiped the tears with her free hand and looked at them shining on her fingers. *"They're not even real, you know."* She held up her hand for Soolie to see, and the wet of tears melted away, soaked up by the air. *"Everything is right horrible, isn't it?"* she nodded at the carnage. *"All this awful grossness, and you all demonized, and I just keep wishing I could cry a decent tear."* She shook her head. *"I can't think about it all. I'm really not strong enough."*

Soolie couldn't hear Papa breathing. His chest was still. His eyes were closed.

"He looks awful."

He did. It was time. Soolie could feel Papa's soul letting go.

"Ellena?"

Her aunt looked away from Papa's face, her eyes full of bewildered tears. *"Yes, love?"*

"I still can't let him die."

The life glow in her body throbbed, golden light pent up, pulsing, the people of Hob Glen. Their souls were gone, but she could feel them all: Mrs. and Mr. Svenson, old Mr. Hobbin, Doc Wilkins, and Miss Pont, the students: Kip, Winny, and the other children, more faces and lives than she could separate to count, a living torrent inside of her. She gripped Ellena and Papa's hands, holding Papa's head tight in her lap, and let the light go, surging out of her and into him until his soul burned bright with the verve of a hundred fold.

YOU DO NOT GET TO DIE.

SILAS' MIND WAS ENTOMBED in a deep black tar of despair. He didn't want to live. He wanted to sink down into the numbing heavy blackness that obscured all thought, that smothered his senses, that promised silence.

Then the tar lit on fire.

Something grabbed hold and pulled, ripping him to the surface, merciless, relentless, undeniable as the push of birth, it commanded. *YOU DO NOT GET TO DIE.*

His mind began to come awake, and with it, his agony.

His despair grew, ravenous as a sea beast, black tentacles rending his heart like an ill-fated vessel starless in malignant seas. He cried out for mercy, but the grave closed its mouth and would not answer him.

He knew the impossibly unknowable. The undreamable nightmare. The reality that could never be, but was.

His sweet little girl was dead.

That fragile baby girl he had first held against his chest, fresh and wet from her mother's body, had died in the same arms that welcomed her into the world and swore to keep her safe. That same beautiful girl who held his hand at her mother's burial and refused to cry, saying, "I already said goodbye," had turned his gun—the gun he had taken to protect her—against herself and ended her own life. Her eyes had grown dark, her face had grown pale, her precious blood had spilled out between his fingers.

He had murdered her. He had failed her. Her blood stained his hands.

Air invaded his throat, stabbing his lungs. Raw fire, a heatless blaze, charged his bones, awakened his flesh. His eyes snapped open, and he was alive in a world without her.

IT WAS DARK AND COLD. It smelled sickeningly of blood and death. His head was cradled in a lap, and a pale face looked down.

It was a young face, mostly. With creamy skin and a little pointed chin, but no brows marked her countenance, no lashes fringed her sharp brown eyes. Her skull was smooth as ice-glazed snow, and her eyes were nearly as cold.

She cupped his head in small supple fingers and slid away, laying his skull on the cold hard stone ground and standing up. Her skirt was muck-black in the moonlight as if she had waded in a mire or sat in the middle of the butcher's bleeding floor.

"Don't worry about the bodies," she said. "They will burn off in the sun."

Her voice was smooth. He knew that voice. Drifting in gentle laughter across a summer-gilded back yard. Softly whispered words on the bank by Malswood Pond, a fragile slender hand in his. A promise in a ruffled blue dress in the town square under the white oak tree: "Until death come between."

He tried to raise himself, but his muscles were fragile jelly. His head buzzed. His body buzzed. He was painfully, unbearably alive.

He rolled himself toward her, the pale girl in the wet dress, walking away from him. The stones at her feet seemed to melt and roil like the undergods' pit. And there was the tree. The white oak. Its bare branches split above from an old storm, and hanging from its trunk, something black and bleeding.

She went to it, reaching up, grasping and pulling. A long metal spike fell from her fingers, clanging and rolling on the stones. The black heap fell, slumping against her with a strangled sound, and the girl lifted it in her arms, heaving it up, black, dripping and ragged, strangely flopping limbs lolling out as she turned and spoke to him again.

"Everyone is dead. But everything you need is in the houses ... so..."

She bounced the ragged sodden body on her knee, grappling for a better purchase, standing on one foot and re-hoisting it in her arms.

Without the hair, it was difficult to tell. It could have been Tara, but the skin, smeared with black and blood, was perfect, no wounds or scars. Tara's hazel eyes were distant at times, whimsical, placid, wistfully sorrowful more for him than for her. These eyes were carved mahogany. The sort of eyes that spelled cruelty for the ones who loved them.

"Take care of yourself," she said. "I have to go."

He formed her name on soundless lips, "Soolie?"

"And I'm never coming back."

Familiar words. Her mother's words in her mother's voice.

"Wait!" It was an urgent whisper. He couldn't force his limbs to take movement, his voice to make sound. He was full of fire, but his body was still so weak.

She turned away, walking around what he now saw was not the moving of stones, but the stirring of a pool of monstrous wet death that had begun to smoke in the light of the cracking sun. He tried to pull himself towards her, to stand, but his arms shook and folded beneath him, his thighs were wobbly aspic. She walked barefooted away in the haze, the body held in her arms as if it were no more than a weight of straw.

He screamed her name and found his voice, a raw desperate cry. "SOOLIE!"

She paused, turned. For a moment, he thought she would come back.

"Ellena is with you."

They were her last words. She never said goodbye.

THIRTY-FOUR

Dog woke on the bluff. The wind scoured down from the open space of sky, rushing out over the expanse of land below. Clouds like wadded wool were coming in heavy-laden from the west. It would snow soon.

He ran his clawed hands over the taut skin of his arms. His flesh was sound. His bones were straight and new. She had healed him. He had felt her strength flooding his brokenness as she carried him. She had made him whole again.

The Mistress had defeated Horse as he knew she would. And she had saved him. The Mistress had carried him in her arms and saved him.

And she was here.

He scrambled up, kneeling prostrate, supplicating hands clasped against his brow.

She sat, cross-legged and bare, white as bone, sharp eyes watching him. She was so beautiful, so perfect, he wanted to weep.

"Mistress."

"You will obey me."

It was not a question. It was a command.

"Yes, Mistress."

"For always."

"Always, Mistress."

"Seek out the ones who escaped and kill them in the sun. Then come back to me."

He leapt to his feet and bowed. "Yes, Mistress."

She had commanded. He was hers.

IT TOOK FIVE DAYS to hunt the remnants of the pack. It would have taken only three, but on the second day snow began to fall, covering their scent and tracks. Still, it was only a small delay. He found some of them alone, hiding from the sun beneath the earth. Others had run north in groups and found shelter in the caves. He found a few on the road back to Ravus, and still others scrapping for inhabitants in the hills. He hunted down each and all, broke their bodies, and scattered their bones in high places to be cleansed by the light of day.

Then he turned back to her.

THIRTY-FIVE

The little farmhouse nestled at the base of the snow-covered hills like a carved toy against pillows. The wire fencing around the hen hutch was crocheted in white, and every roof was tucked in with a feathery comforter. From the farmhouse stone chimney, a gray scarf wound overhead toward the field-blue sky, and under foot, strands of footsteps left a tangled triangle between the front door, the hen house, and the barn.

Dog scuffed through the footprints, collapsing their fluffy edges over on top of his gray bare feet. There was no porch to the front door, only a few small steps. He stood on the narrow top step, his clawed fingers on the cold brass handle.

Should he knock? Would it be open?

He pressed the handle, heard the slide-click of the moving latch, and pushed in slowly. A glossy aroma of sugary spiced apples and butter greeted him as he stepped into the warmth of the house. And her. He could always smell her.

Snow that had dusted and caked in his clothes and hair shifted loose and pattered on the floorboards as he closed the door behind him. He stepped carefully through a small dark parlour toward the warm honey firelight flickering from the next room. He could hear the creak and clatter of movement. He could hear her.

Self-conscious now, he pulled on the bloody rags of his clothing. He should have found new clothes. He should have scrubbed himself in the snow. The Mistress bathed. The Mistress put on clean clothes. He was shameful, unclean.

"Come in," a voice called from the next room. Her voice.

Dog hunched his shoulders and stepped through the glowing doorway into a small well-lit kitchen. To the left rested a simple dining table with four wooden chairs, and before him, the curtains were pulled back from the little window, pale natural light drifting over a chopping table laden with steaming towel-draped platters. Herbs hung from the ceiling, and against the wall the fireplace crackled brazenly, buffing the bright copper pans and kettles on the shelf above.

And his Mistress.

She stood with her back to him. She was dressed in an oversized dark green cable-knotted sweater and men's britches. Around her bare ankles, a caramel and cream striped cat curled and twined, looking up expectantly with green almond eyes as she stirred a large copper pot that hung over the fire.

Dog dropped to his knees and hunched, his hands clasped, his teeth bared in submission.

She didn't look at him. She walked to a corner of the room with the cat briskly pawing behind, small eager scratchy cries escaping through tiny white fangs as Mistress set a plate laden with corn cakes, boiled sugary spiced apples, and little rivers of melted butter on the floor. The cat stuck its face in, licking and gnashed its fangs into the hot food, its tail curling up at the tip.

Mistress crossed to the chopping table. She peeled a towel off a broad wooden platter mounded with golden scorch-marked corn cakes.

"Have you ended them?"

She didn't look up. The bare skin of her scalp gleamed white and clean in the winter window light.

"Yes, Mistress."

"All of them?"

"Yes, Mistress."

She took the platter to the fire and ladled steaming heaps of glistening spice-flecked apples over the top of the cakes.

"Take this."

He scrambled forward to receive the platter from her hands. Her brown eyes saw him and said nothing. He stood in the middle of the floor, clutching the rim of the platter to his bloody snow-stiff chest, the heat from the bowl soaking into his warmthless fingers, his black claws curling over the smooth-sanded edge, sweet spiced steam wafting over his face.

"Did any survive?"

"No, Mistress."

She uncovered a large bowl heaped high with the corn cakes, carried it over to the fire and upended it, splattering, into the large pot. She then set the bowl down, wrapped the metal pot handle in towels and heaved it off the hook, holding it away from her, bracing her elbow against her hip as she waddled stiffly for the door.

The cat's head popped up from its food and turned, alert. It curled a tongue around a whiskered mouth and padded quickly after her. Dog followed into the parlor where Mistress set the pot on the floor to open the front door, then re-hefted it and stepped barefoot out into the brightly lit white of the front yard, the cat bounding in her footprints, shaking its head and flicking its ears as the frozen dust puffed up over its nose.

"Take the platter to the hen house," Mistress said, hauling the pot towards the barn.

Dog followed the tracks in the snow to the wire fencing gate, held the platter with one hand, turned the hook latch and pushed in, the bottom of the gate dragging against the snow, the top leaning inward. He scraped through and followed the trodden snow to the wooden coop door that stood tall and straight next to the little hen hole. He lifted the simple wooden bar and leaned into the door with his shoulder.

The inside of the hutch was narrow and chill, the floor blond with a thick mesh of hay, the left wall rowed in wooden boxes. Round nestled bodies of rust, cotton, and iris feathers sprouted gawky heads that blinked and muttered as he set the steaming platter in the middle of the floor and backed out, closing the wooden door behind him.

Across the yard, the cat's tail whisked in through the open door of the barn.

Dog squeezed back through the wire fencing gate and pushed it closed, turning the hook latch.

He had only just returned to Mistress, and already she was commanding him. He didn't need to understand her, he didn't need to be valued *by* her, he told himself. He only needed to be valuable *to* her.

He had traveled many miles for her over the last few days, but he bounded across the yard, shuffing snow off his shins to get to the barn door, eager just to lay eyes upon her again. He crossed the doorway from snow to dirt and fell reverently to his knees inside the barn.

Mistress was scraping hot cakes and apples into a trough for two waiting roan mares. On the other side of the barn, a highlands milking cow lowed and rattled its stub horns against the wood planks of its stall.

"I know, I know. I'm coming," Mistress scolded. "It's still hot. Careful you don't burn your tongue."

Dog raised his eyes. It was a humble barn, unremarkable but for the back wall where someone had brushed a collection of spiky round patterns in thin white paint. The earthen floor below had been disturbed, and against the base of the wall rested several human items. Dog could smell that the paint was fresh.

The cow bellowed brassily, nosing the air and stamping its feet as Mistress lowered the heavy pot over into its stall and set it on the ground. There was a clank as the animal shoved its head into the pot, her horns scraping against the metal curve as she eagerly lapped up the food scraps.

Mistress stood and faced him. She was so perfect. Even in the bulky dark green sweater and men's pants, he could remember the way she looked on the bluff standing naked in the light of the sun. Smooth and white as albumen. She had achieved for herself the one thing the Master had never dared: flesh. And she was more than flesh, she was power and she was flawless.

"When did you last feed?"

He bowed again, nose dipping near the ground. "Yesterday evening, Mistress."

"When you kill, you make ghosts."

"Yes, Mistress."

"I am going to rid the earth of the lost souls. You are not to make any ever again."

He bobbed. "Yes, Mistress." He wondered if the Master was a 'lost soul.' He wondered if his new Mistress intended to fight the Master. He wondered if he would have to face the Master's new creature again, the one he thought of as 'Wolf.' Perhaps it was best not to wonder.

She nodded, "That is all," and turned back towards the far wall of the barn.

Dog scrambled up, unsure. The handle of the kitchen pot rattled as the highland cow turned it in the dirt, scrounging for the last bits of apple cooked to the bottom.

"Mistress?"

She hauled a sealed metal tin and a little folding ladder out from a back stall. "Yes?"

Dog hesitated. It wasn't something he had done before. "May I wash myself, Mistress?"

"There's a creek behind the house. Soap and pail are in the pantry."

He bowed again. "Thank you, Mistress."

Mistress spread the ladder's legs and set it against the back wall. She knelt and began prying up the lid of the tin can with a flat knife. From the corner, the cat watched with disinterested cut green eyes. The Mistress seemed to favor it. Such a useless creature was not worthy. Dog, and Dog alone, belonged at the Mistress' side.

The cat stretched a hind leg behind its neck and began stroking the fur down with its tongue. Dog bowed his way out the door.

SOOLIE DIPPED THE BRUSH in the whitewash at the bottom of the can, scraped the fringe over the lip to remove any excess, and swept the paint in a soft curving swirl between the stars. It wasn't nearly as beautiful as she wanted it to be. It was meant to be a gloriously radiating sun cupped in the cool embrace of the crescent moon, overshadowing the two smaller stars, all four floating in the swirling motes and currents of a night sky. Instead it was blobby, wavy and thick. It was the same problem she'd had painting the moon in the oblong picture that hung in Ellena's bakery. She understood now that she'd been asking the wrong questions about that painting. There weren't three in the picture, there were four, and Mama had been the moon. But it was too late now. Her aunt's niece and her mother's daughter were both dead, and Soolie was painting this sky for someone else. Dral, Neya, Token, and Trill. She'd gotten their names from the mother's journal.

Soolie had found the farm her first day alone a few miles outside of Hob Glen. The father had been in the barn. The mother in the kitchen. The two children in their bedroom, still under the covers, already dead. Soolie wasn't sure why the children had died first. Their bodies shrunken up, their souls gone. Perhaps they had been among the number of the whirling torrent in the town square. Perhaps they *hadn't* lain shrunken under the sheets, wheezing out their last breaths as their parents lay nearby, too weak and damaged to reach them. She'd asked the Hunter, and the Hunter said it didn't know.

The parents had suffered. Their bodies half-dessicated, most of their life gone, their souls barely clinging on, their breath crackling through shriveled lungs, lips prunish, eyes waxy and clouded. If they had been only half of a mile closer, Soolie thought, they would have died—tragically—but cleanly. At least they wouldn't have suffered, lying there helpless, thinking about their children.

She had carried Dral and Neya back to their bedroom, tucked them into the blankets side by side, placed Neya's flesh-clung bony hand in his, sat beside, and waited for them to die.

The cat's name was Poko, which was Island for 'fat baby,' and it liked her immediately, hopping up into her lap and following her about the farm. After the parents passed, it sat and watched her dig their grave in the barn, deep enough that she needed the ladder to get in and out. She laid the family side by side by side and shoveled the cold winter-hardened earth in to cover them up again.

The journal had been in the nightstand. Neya wrote about all the details of their farm life. Soolie learned that the axe had been Drol's father's, and the boots were a two year-old pair he'd had resoled by the gentleman who made them: a man in Hob Glen who charged reasonable prices and made the best shoes this side of the city. The staff was Token's. He'd found the wood by the creek and carved it himself. Neya made the bunny for her daughter Trill, who called it "Pink Nose" and couldn't fall asleep without it. It had been in her gray claw arms when Soolie found her.

We will have to leave soon, the Hunter said. *He will need to feed again. If he starves, the hunger will make him unstable.*

Soolie stood tiptoe on the top of the ladder and brushed a paint streak that whisked over the top of the moon.

She had known her time at the farm was short. That he would find her, track her down, and then she would have to leave. Still, she hadn't been able to stop hoping that he might have come to an end at the claws of some wayward monster, or an angry mob, or the Dead Man himself, or that he had simply lost her trail in the snow and turned away. Every morning she had woken up thinking, 'Just not today,' and now it was today. Dog had found her, and they would leave tomorrow.

There was no reason to stay. This wasn't her home, and these weren't her dead. She would be sorry, though, to abandon the animals. Perhaps if she loaded their troughs and blanketed the horses—the highland was protected by its shaggy winter coat—someone would find them before they succumbed to the cold. She hoped so. She had rather enjoyed having pets for this little while. Soolie looked down to the corner where Poko usually sat licking himself while she was painting, but he wasn't there. Most likely he was off tormenting the chickens again, the little beast.

She swept the brush around the inside edge of the can to lick up any last drops of white and, as a final touch, dotted at the rough boards with the corner of the brush to make a trail of little constellation spots fading up towards the roof.

DOG HADN'T BOTHERED to haul water into the kitchen to heat over the hearth. He stood knee-deep in the burbling creek that swirled around crusty ice-frilled banks and glass-globed rocks, attacking his sallow flesh with a soapy brush, scouring at his chest and loins, raking it over his eyes, and scrubbing under his lips until his teeth were rabid with foam. The soap that had started as a large lavender and chamomile hunk was now no more than the inner leaf of an onion. He'd been scrubbing himself for over an hour.

Soolie stood under the black limbs of a whipwillow and watched as Dog reached across to the bank for the bucket, scooped the pail into the rushing water of the creek, and lifted it over his head. His underarms were almost blue, and his nipples were dark tobacco thumbprints in the rubbery tallow of his harshly carved soap-slick chest. She could see where his chest muscles hooked into his sternum and his belly sunk in as if his navel had been sutured to his spine.

He dumped the water over his skull. It sluiced over the ridge of his back, running over his haunches, carrying soap suds into the burbling black of the creek. Then he scooped the pail into the current and did it again, and again, and again. He didn't even bother to close his eyes. The water dripped from his nose and ears, running through hair which had grown out like black mold. Her own scalp was still as smooth and bare as the day she died.

"Don't forget your ears, and get all the gunk out from under your nails."

"Yes, Mistress."

Soolie thought of those hands in women's hair, those talons splitting open bellies and stabbing eyes. But he didn't just kill people. He killed monsters too. And Soolie was going to kill all the monsters.

He scraped at his waxen ears with his fingers, the sharp black claws raking the dark holes. He scowled, digging and scraping, flicking gunk off his nails. At last, satisfied, he stuck one of his long filth-black nails into his mouth and raked it along his sharp canines, digging out the rotten sludge that stuck under his claws and spitting it out into the creek as a tiny red rivulet of blood trickled out of his ear and down his neck.

He swished his hand in the water, inspected it, and began gnawing at his nails again.

The Hunter appeared at Soolie's side, her small golden feet making no mark in the snow, her yellow shift and glossy coiled black hair casting no shadow in the midday sun.

It is good that we saved him.

Soolie spoke silently so the monster wouldn't hear. He may be useful. He isn't 'good.'

Dog moved on to his other hand, scraping and gnawing, a determined snarl on his face.

These were the creatures that the 'Dead Man' made. Soul feeders. Thirsty monsters with no conscience. Killers.

Soolie had killed people. Many people. Drawn the life from their flesh and ripped out their souls. Untold families lay unburied and unmourned with no one left to remember their names, because of her. She was covered in the blood of their slaughter, and no amount of scrubbing could wash that stain away. She couldn't bring back the dead.

But she could end them.

And she would. No matter what it took. Every ghost, every spirit, every monster and pack. She would end them all, and she would do so without touching a single living life. Never again would she bring such death. She would protect the living. She would end the dead. Though she had been made a monster, she would not become one. She would never be like him.

At last Dog turned toward her, baring pointed yellow teeth, holding up his gray clawed fingers for her inspection. He was repulsive, but his flesh was clean.

"Get back to the house and find yourself some clothes."

He braced his feet on the slick creek stones, water curling around his knees, and bowed, hands clasped, fingers knitted together like curving ribs, head bent until she could see the top knob of his spine.

"Dog obeys Mistress. Dog serves at Mistress' side for always."

It was a devotion. And a reminder. She had made a promise.

"Then obey."

He gave a giddy yelp and sloshed eagerly for the bank, gathering up the brush and pail and bounding bare and dripping through the snow for the front door.

The girl and the Hunter watched him go. The Hunter twisted the bright gold edge of her tunic around her little brown fingers.

There may come a time when we will have to end him.

Soolie smiled.

She was counting on it.

Acknowledgements

Jack, whose devotion to her art never fails to remind me that I am not alone. My father and mother, for their love of reading and their love of me. Besstie for listening. Todd for his insight and commiseration. Proofreading goddesses Callie and Kelley, for knowing the difference between British and American spellings. Hadas, for her feedback, proofreading, and incredible encouragement. Andrew, who is not only the best Jewish Fairy Godmother a gal could ask for, but without whom this book would still be sitting unfinished in a drawer somewhere. And Robert, who has never denied me my obsession, but rather provided encouragement, endless hugs, and tried to get me out of the house once in a while: I love you always.

Gypsie Raleigh grew up off-grid in the Mount Hood wilderness area of Oregon where she used books and endless expanses of solitary time to create her own friends. She now lives in Portland, OR with her Husbert and knows many wonderful real-life people. When not writing her next novel, Gypsie can be found performing as a sing-er-songwriter and improvisational comedienne.

Contact her at gypsie@sooliebeetch.com.

www.ingramcontent.com/pod-product-compliance
Lightning Source LLC
Chambersburg PA
CBHW051328250626
47155CB00007B/2504

9 780997 198300